Also by Robert French

Passion of Shadows

The Diary of Nellie Mill

Josephine Littletree

Lynch

Sigurdsen

Robert French

Sigurdsen

© 2020 Robert L. French

First Edition

978-1-9990223-2-7
978-1-9990223-4-1 (KDP MOBI)
978-1-9990223-3-4 (EPUB)

Cover design by Caligraphics.net
Formatting by Polgarus Studio

Wikimedia Commons, File: Maskesten, Moesgård.jpg, Gardar Rurak (CC BY-SA 4.0) unmodified
Wikimedia Commons, File: Forest Moonlight (193503497).jpeg, Clarise Samuels (CC-BY-SA-3.0) unmodified
Wikimedia Commons, File: The Group of Cult Statues in the Temple of Despoina at Lykosoura. 190-180 B.C.jpg, George E. Koronaios (CC-BY-SA-4.0) modified

Questions, comments, contact: afterwords@shaw.ca

Table of Contents

From the Sigurdsen Notebooks
Undated

I, Sigurdsen, above the crouching hegemonies of power, a cloudship tinted by sunset for a bon voyage to the stars, floating towards some lizard hand out there or glories of effulgent light, I, cumulus, accumulate the glimmering traces of the invisible.

It's a start, isn't it? as a cashier once said to my handful of coins. A redheaded lass, buxom for her height, an emerald glance that wouldn't let me leave the checkout. Handing me change. Change my life. Touch of fingers in my palm tender to my clasp. She called security. I told the ex-cop I was a prof with writer's cramp.

I do not need help. No ologists or iatrists to twist my tristes. I need company. It's the single man's right to look. I thought I found the woman of women once in that land of shebe. Inflicting the genital wound, the gentle remind her. Good exercise in forgetting everything else. Marriage, or political strategy. Power struggle with a daily coup/coo. Cuckoo. Nightly truce. Tearing off the white flag of her underwear. Armistice of arms. What's wrong? What's wrong with you? Analyzing the obvious. Who won't give in. Pretends. There's a mirror called conformity. Look into it. I wouldn't. One glance and you're stiff. A pause here for moronic laughter. Appropriate farewell, my wife. A joke on both of us.

Humanity is dust on a windowsill, blind to the light. But I, with cosmic eyes, see the glint and glitter, put a hand through the glass, splinters fractured sharp as fish hooks streaking my wrist with blood. How much of your life can you write with eight pints? Keep to the important stuff. Which is? Love and all like things. What about the reason for everything and a reason for anything? That's for/what philos soffers. To make thinking respectable. They've got to have something to do. What about your sky entitists? The universe in a handbag, collapsible or a terrorist bomb. Let's not be little. They've done some good stuff. All these elec troctities? The nuke clear falling out from overreactors? Smeltdowns, tox sick waste? There's your comp uters surfing for drugstore sales and saying hi to someone in Bhutan. Then we're headed for world peace. Don't be sour castic. All this means something. Because we did it? You didn't. You know what I mean, and that's the end of this cloak we, hm.

Everyone has a reason for being here: those rambunctious to sanctimonious ends, those defenders of virtue's anonymous pleadings, those whelps of the unknown, those determiners of the determined, making sense from what they can see, including all scienterrific things and such respectables, and inner splurgings, blood spouts above the eight-lane sclerosis and heartslump expiry date and forms of meaninglessnesses to fill in for jobholders to keep the universe on schedule, monumomentum of incidental dreams meaning no matter to anything.

I look at my life now and again. See how it's going. I'm careful not to interfere. And since I'm too busy being busy being, it's a good bargain. My life goes its way, I go mine. A casual glance every so often. There's nothing I can do about it, anyway. Lives have a way of living themselves. Interfering doesn't do any good. The truth is, your life isn't yours. It belongs to a lot of other people. So why bother doing anything about what you can't control? I'm only I apart from those who insist on intruding. That's when I'm living. Which is a different thing. What you do when nobody is looking. Not easy, because most people don't live, they hang around in other people's lives. Having nothing to do with my life, I leave to others whatever they can find in it. I will bear no responsibility and take no blame for their prejudices against my sole true self. I do not exist. I live.

The world spins stiff-necked ponies on a merry-go-round up and down as they go around to a tinkle-tune melody, eyes childwide to go on or get off. What's the loss either way? Nothing but chance, my timeworn travellers. Enough of this chatburst solo. Press the button, I'm off.

Professor Peter Sigurdsen
Department of English,
Mackerness Hall, Prairie University
April 30, 20—

Dear Professor Sigurdsen:

I regret that *Contemporaneous Literature* is unable to use your article, "Haircut Theory of Mental Illness in the Literary Mind: One Snip Leads to Another." It does not meet our needs at the moment or reflect the general tenor of the magazine. Among a number of suggestions by our staff about where your article should go, I would mention Marg and Phil Dowd's monthly, *Self-Help Psychology in Everyday Life* (if they are still publishing) and *Aberrant Psychology and Self-Analysis: a Clinical Approach*, an occasional annual published in Heidelberg, Germany, by ex-American Harry Feinlein. Good luck.

Yours,

B. Coutts, ed.

July 19

Dear Professor Sigurdsen:

CL is unable to use your articles, "The Fictional Female A-mused-d: Schizoid Dreamgirl or Obsessive Fantasy?" and "Undiscovered Literary Genius: Paranoid Delusion as Wish Fulfilment."

Yours,

B. Coutts, ed.

August 26

Dear Professor Sigurdsen:

Re: your letter of August 2. *CL* did not agree to publish your article, "Persecution Mania in the Great Literary Minds." We returned it to you along

with a rejection slip. Please check your submission records and files.
B. Coutts

September 29

Do yourself a favour. Don't send any more articles. We won't publish them. And stop trying to contact us with phone calls, letters and email. We won't answer you.
B. Coutts

Prairie Herald-Times
May 16

Bats Solution to Mosquitoes?

At the regular Wednesday night meeting of the city council, a spectator called for bats to be imported to fight mosquitoes. Wearing a long sticklike nose attached to a pair of large glasses and a pair of wings made from plastic wrap stretched over a wire frame, he stood up in the gallery and announced himself as Mr. Mosquito. After some laughter, Mayor Andy Kowalchuk suspended council business and asked Mr. Mosquito to identify himself. The winged spectator turned out to be Professor Peter Sigurdsen of Prairie University, who said the city authorities were wasting a lot of money every spring spraying pesticide along the banks of the river and the sloughs on the outskirts. It would be cheaper to bring in a colony of bats to eat the pests. Councilwoman Samantha Sadowski asked if Prairie City was too far north for bats to survive the winter. The professor said the bats could be kept in cages in a warehouse over the winter months and fed flies bred for this purpose. Councilman Ted E. Chaluka said the professor had "bats in his belfry." Councilman Corey Schildkraut asked why Sigurdsen would want to kill off his own kind. The professor said it was a death wish arising from remorse over all the bloodsucking and the resulting spread of disease. He would happily commit suicide in the cause of public health. Making a droning noise, he flapped his wings and left. The Mayor said the council would take the suggestion under advisement. The mosquito infestation has been worse than usual this year. It will be a problem well into the fall, according to experts. A warm winter and late and insufficient spraying are said to have caused the problem. Asked about bats being used to control mosquitoes, they said they never heard of such a thing.

Prairie Herald-Times
May 20

Doctor Condemns Prairie City Climate

The climate in Prairie City and the surrounding area is unfit for human habitation, Dr. Simon Weissberg of Prairie University Jubilee Hospital said in a speech Monday night to a meeting of psychiatrists here for a convention. He said it is too cold and dry this far north to be healthy, and the perennial mosquito infestations spread diseases. The lack of rain and warm weather mean that only lichens, stunted trees, weeds and clouds of flying insects can survive. Where plants find it hard to grow, so do human beings. They both need moisture and warmth, not refrigeration, and there's too little of either. Physical deprivation means mental trouble, such as chronic depression and other neurotic and psychotic disorders. Long winter months, short summers, and no spring or fall put an extra strain on the nervous system and prolonged exposure almost guarantees mental trouble. Over the long term the results of living in a climate like this could be congenital mental illness, including psychic aberrations. "In my four years at the university hospital, I have seen many cases among students and staff of neurosis and psychosis I would directly attribute to the climate. I'm convinced that large groups of settled people were never meant to live under these adverse conditions, because it isn't a climate, it's punishment." Dr. Weissberg will be leaving at the end of this academic year. He will assume new duties at a post in Florida.

1227 59th Street
Belvedere District, Prairie City
May 27

"I won't do it, Peter. I've told you that before. Take off those stupid ears. And don't mope around me. I'm getting ready for bed."

. . . .

"You can use the bathroom now. What's the matter with you? Why haven't you changed? Give me those ears. I'm throwing them away. Don't ever ask again. You're a complete ass. You don't have to dress like one. Go ahead and sulk. Sit on the floor all night."

June 28

"You got another pair. What did I say last time? Don't you ever listen? And don't tell me about your goddesses again."

. . . .

"This is it. Can't even sleep. Waking me up braying like an idiot. Take them off. Do it right now. Now. And the tail. The mask. That other thing, too. You're not sleeping in here tonight."

July 16

"Take the book away. I've told you, I'm not interested in mythology. You keep this up, I'm leaving you. How much do you expect me to take?"

August 3

"Hm? What? Ow—ow. Get off me. Said—get off. You bastard. You hurt me with that thing. I told you what I'd do. You're sick, Peter. I'm leaving you."

August 31

Dear Professor Sigurdsen:
Please be advised that your wife, Daphne Spratt Sigurdsen, who filed for divorce on August 7, wishes no further contact with you. She has made this

clear on several occasions. If you persist in contacting her by phone or email or attempting to see her, she will go to court and obtain a restraining order. This is your final warning.

Sincerely yours,

Hillary Kravitz

Attorney at law (BA, LLB)

Fifth in the 1997 graduating class at PULS.

Winner of the Polk Prize.

From the Sigurdsen Notebooks
Honeymoon and marriage poems

When we
gazing out
over the harbour
the colour
of old puke

and you said
to go inside
I tripping
on my neolites
fell headlong

into the
glass partition
splintering into
sunset spokes
of my love

and the gulls lining
the seawall
grinned over
their plump
satisfaction.

Marital Muse
To Daphne

In the bowels of lost prominence
where we shall lie together
pondering the far shores of forever
there will be terpsichorean
coeval supernal adumbrations.

We could survive them,
and hoariest of horrors,
the loss of desperation.

Leave the scrollwork of your hair,
my tiny angel,
and lapse with me on the breasted foam,
bee bride all buzz,
I licking the nectar between your legs.
How domestic my honey.

Be done, have some cold cuts
and grossome hair like bristles on pigskin,
flap your coatwings.
I love brisket but can I risk it?
We were close enough to kill each other.

Is there room for footnotes?
Only the best authorities
according to Mith Ology,
including Her Greekness
and that Roman broad.

It's all covered by the price of fame,
feesome beast she is, flamehot,
eager with her tongue.

The least wind will lift your reputation,
whereas it was cold this morning
without sleep when the car wouldn't start
in the snow and breathghosts giving up
already with their curses.

The specialty of the day?
A classroom full of snot
and what litter occurs
from preaching gosh spells of poortry.

Testa Ment

Everyone's here.
She prone and decidedly naked,
entered rearward,
those postilioned white flanks
and soaring posteriori

to be considered
by Publius Gregorovich
von Plotkin,
he of Reekie Dick's
clan of Highland recognitions,
those tartan peaks
of the Circassian Caucasus—
Europe's united, anyway—

belly folds for curtains
over the pubic tufts
of her genteel
as she lying pushed

and considering herself
the future of those fortunate millions
of intestate testicles will be hers—

split like a soft melon
unto her descendants—whit.
He's coming sputtering sputum
and the lower halfing lust's little bit
of squibbly in her.

Hooray. We can all go home.
She'll burgeon and the babe held aloft
for us to see cheeks' fat privileges.

And Publius well served
can go back to little
Miss Tress the schoolmarm
with a jammer you
couldn't get slick spit into.
There's a happy gasper
on her ladylikes,
the slimsilk bulges,
the tittie crescent mouthfuls.

Or maybe some sweaty barmaid
in a cavernous tavern
who pisses beer in front of him
and squeezes her goatbeard armpits
with fat vaccinated flesh
and farts to famous pop tunes,
eats hard candy and jujubes,
couldn't tell you which philosopher
liked piccalilli.

But that's ignorance, isn't it,
not bumcrack's nepenthes
or Lethe, and if she will—
well, here's a consumer—
and on that mattress of a billion
caressings they madly crawl
with a cockroach towards dawn.

How

could

you

be

so

soft

and

take

me

in

like

that?

To you, my once and legal wife

Forthwith all heretofore aforesaid
iniquities will be considered
exculpatory if you'll only
slowly take off your panties
so I can see what I love.

Student guide to undergraduate courses, fall semester
Prairie University

p. 5
English 200, section E, Professor Sigurdsen
Expects footnotes and bibliography to follow the department style manual
exactly. Stops lecturing and talks to himself. Says he ponders irrevocably,
whatever that means. Been known to chant and dance in front of classes. The
bright side if you're a babe: wear a tight sweater, short skirt or a blouse with
a couple of buttons undone and you're guaranteed an A.

p. 7
English 425, Modern Novel, Professor Sigurdsen
Ditto comments on his English 200. And be prepared to listen to diatribes
you won't understand. Has to be reminded the class is over. If students leave,
he doesn't notice. Too busy listening to himself.

Professor Reid Abercrombie
Chairman, English Department
Mackerness Hall, Prairie University
September 29

Dear Professor Abercrombie:
We have received complaints from several women in Professor Sigurdsen's
classes that he used suggestive language, bordering on the obscene, in speaking
with them. Also that he invited them to participate with him in moonlight
ceremonies of a strangely bestial nature. We ask you to speak with Professor
Sigurdsen. If he continues in this manner, the Coalition for Women's Safety
on Campus will go public with the complaints and approach the Dean of Arts
and President.
Yours sincerely,
Penelope Boozer

Acting Coordinator
BA (PU), graduate student, Women's Studies
Writing thesis on women inventors.

English 200, section E
Room 104, Arts Building
September 30, 10:15 a.m.

"You finish your essay?"

"Yeah. Have a look."

"Your footnotes. You got op. cit. here. Should be loc. cit. Should be a period and a comma after this ibid. You've got an ibid. and no page number. You use ibid. if the citation comes from the same book or article as the preceding citation. Loc. cit. means it's the same page. Op. cit. is for when another reference comes in between."

"Why can't we put the author's name and the title and the date of publication the first time, then short form afterwards?"

"We have to follow the style manual. Look, this is wrong. You've got here it's the fifth volume of the second, revised edition, but you used all Arabic numerals and didn't abbreviate correctly. It should be lower case Roman numeral five for volume and Arabic two for edition. And you have to put 'nd' after two and a period after 'rev' as well as 'ed,' and a comma between 'ed' and place of publication, followed by a colon between that and the publisher, then a comma separating the date."

"I can't change it now. Today is the deadline."

"Look at your bibliography. You got everything listed alphabetically, but you're supposed to use periods, not commas, after name and title. And the second line of each entry has got to be indented four spaces. Sigurdsen always goes over the marker's marking. Anything wrong with your footnotes or bibliography, you get a failing grade."

"I'll get an extension."

"He doesn't give them. Why don't you leave before he gets here? Fix everything. Drop it off at his office later. Write a note saying your sister's bringing it because you're sick. Put some perfume on the note. He's weird."

"Lucky we're not grad students. Friend of mine has a brother doing an MA. There's a bibliography course they take. Run by this old fart, Stanley Biddle. They've got to memorize four hundred items. Or they don't pass. They all signed a petition last year so they wouldn't have to memorize everything. Department ignored it."

English 425
Room 110, Arts Building
October 2, 3:24 p.m.

"You got your notes from last class?"

"You missed a lot. Here."

"'Music of the spheres and human anatomy. Rotundities in orbit. The earth mother. The moon goddess. The Milky Way. The narrative gut and the Middle Ages: Great Chain of Being. Author—reader, monarch—peasant, the plot thickens. Imagination as urge produces stool. Dross of creation: storyline.' We supposed to know this?"

"Guess so."

"There wasn't much at 3:30, so I had to take this. Was the only free time on my schedule."

"Same here."

Graduate seminar in "The Problem of Technique in the Modern Novel"
Room 202, Mackerness Hall
October 5, 1:16 p.m.

"Come up with anything for your term paper?"

"No. Not due till March."

"I'm thinking of constipation and writer's block: lack of fibre in the creative urge."

"Be glad he's not your supervisor. Remember Poniatowski."

"I wasn't here then."

"He was Sigurdsen's last doctoral candidate. Had a nervous breakdown. Some of us went to see him in the university hospital. He was reading a book upside down. Smiled a lot. Went to China after he got out. He's teaching kindergarten."

"What happened?"

"He got a scholarship but didn't write his thesis on campus. Went out to the coast. Sigurdsen was pissed. When Poniatowski mailed his chapters, Sigurdsen wrote crazy remarks all over them. Poniatowski showed me. When he came back. 'I didn't think I'd be correcting freshman grammar in a doctoral thesis.' This was for a typo. Sigurdsen said that one quote was wrong. Poniatowski proved his author wrote it. Know what Sigurdsen wrote? 'If he said this, he's stupid.' He rejected every revision of every chapter for three years. I looked at the thesis. Seemed all right to me. Poniatowski disappeared. We found out he was in the hospital."

"Couldn't he go see somebody? Have his work looked at?"

"Nobody helps you. The department head isn't going to second-guess a tenured professor. They all know each other. They have to get along. Committee members can make things tough for a while if they want. But they'll back off. But if your supervisor gives you trouble, you are finished. Committee members won't question his judgement because they wouldn't want theirs questioned. And the ones out for tenure are busy kissing ass. Picking your supervisor is everything."

Faculty Club lounge
October 10

"Sigurdsen's at it again. Wore a toga to class. Singing or chanting something. Dancing."

"Vine leaves in his hair?"

"Classically Sigurdsen. Remember last year? Set fire to a pile of laurel boughs and junk mail in the quad. Did some kind of dance, chanted about the mysteries of the muses. Grass caught fire and the sprinklers had to be turned on."

"Took his degrees here, didn't he?"

"First successful doctoral candidate. Worked under old McGinty. Something about literary talent genetically transmitted down through the ages. From ancients to moderns."

"McGinty was Reid's predecessor, wasn't he?"

"He was out of it by then. Ideal supervisor for Sigurdsen. Talked to his dead wife. Pissing his pants, wore diapers. Drooled."

"Early retirement?"

"Professor emeritus. After he delivered the inaugural McGinty lectures."

Official notice
P. Sigurdsen, English Department
September 25

Campus Security has received complaints that you are violating the parking regulations behind Mackerness Hall. According to the complainants, you have been parking in stall nos. 39-40 and 42-45, as well as across these stalls. Your allotted stall in the parking lot is no. 41. Continued violation will result in your parking privileges being revoked.
W. Beedey
Officer in charge
Diploma, Northgate HS, Graduate, Police Academy
Transferred from PCPD ("nervous exhaustion").

Conference with academic administrator
Office of Reid Abercrombie
September 12

"Let's cover what I've missed since I left in April. Who's this guy Dawtrey recommended as visiting professor?"

"Hugh Ashenden-Boyce. Comes with good credentials. Degrees from Oxford and Cambridge. Published three volumes of poetry in his twenties. Teaches somewhere over there."

"What did we give him?"

"A seminar. And an upper division course. Dave Krieghammer is on sabbatical. Ashenden-Boyce is doing his Dickens seminar and 395, Nineteenth Century."

"What's he like?"

"Met him only once. When he first got here, a couple of weeks ago. Likes his brown ale. What he calls the 'local lager' doesn't impress him much. Plans to take the seminar beering."

"He'll only be here for a few months. Who's our writer-in-residence?"

"Marlene Stumpf. Poet. No academic background. Local writer. Katie Krips recommended her. Says she's outspoken. Unorthodox."

"Hm. Temporary, like the other one."

English 355, Shakespeare
Professor Dolan Mulcahey
Room 206, Arts Building
September 22, 9:31 a.m.

So far I've talked about the Elizabethan theatre. Performance practice. Theatre companies. Before I go into Shakespeare's tragedies in detail, I want to give an overview. I'll begin with *Antony and Cleopatra*, which I'm including with the tragedies.

Is Antony in love with Cleopatra? Is he after a good fuck? Looking for an ally, does he get in too deep? Does he lose everything for love, or is she a good fuck? Is there some fatal element in their relationship—ambition or envy? Caesar had fucked her. Antony's arranged marriage to Octavius' sister, probably frigid, and the loss at Actium to Octavius' forces are part of the general fuckup. The naval battle is coitus interruptus—notice the sperm imagery of opposing fleets—but Cleopatra is the one to pull out. Their suicide, by sword and asp, is symbolic. He fucks himself and she, with the feared fuck symbol of the snake, administers the poisonous fuck.

Is Hamlet afraid of a good fuck? What is his real attitude towards "country pleasures"? The key to the play is what I call Hamlet's "fuck-fear." Consider the situation: Oedipal overtones, Claudius having done him the favour of killing his father. Look at Hamlet's attitude towards the "fair Ophelia." "Get thee to a nunnery, go." No sexual threat to him there. There's a suggestion in the swordplay with her brother that Hamlet would like to substitute Laertes for her. The poisoned sword points symbolize Laertes' rejection of homosexual advances. There's the relationship with Horatio—it's probably platonic—who calls Hamlet a "sweet prince." His farewell to Horatio ("If thou didst ever hold me in thine heart, Absent thee from felicity a while") conveys more than anything he says to Ophelia. By killing her father, Polonius, Hamlet drives her insane, her suicide by drowning indicating a back-to-the-womb escape. Her ravings about flowers suggest transference and objectification of sexual frustration in a mock deflowering. Hamlet certainly hasn't fucked her. The tragedy is that her prince is gay and must keep vacillating about revenging his father's murder because of guilt about getting access to his mother, a taboo he can only respect through the classic redirection of sexual feelings to men. The ghost of his father is an obvious case of objectified guilt, and that others see it too is an example of mass hysteria. There's a hint, reinforced by Gertrude's quick remarrying, that the father was a ghost in more ways than one and as useless in bed as his son. "To be or not to be, that is the question." Will he come out of the closet? Or will he keep playing with himself and with any woman who gets too close? The play is about a woman who is fucked up by a man who can't.

Why does Lear turn against Cordelia the way he does? We're dealing with the results of incest, of a father who's fucked his daughters. Two of them get revenge by flattering him until they have the necessary power to destroy him. The third daughter, Cordelia, is incapable of saying anything when he asks for praise. She's so traumatized by sexual abuse that she can hardly speak. He subconsciously knows this, which is why he treats her so badly. Her conduct is an uncomfortable reminder. How can we account for the viciousness of Goneril and Regan except as revenging a great wrong? And when they reduce his retinue and he protests ("O reason not the need"), it is an indirect plea for forgiveness. At the end, carrying Cordelia's dead body, Lear realizes he can't right the wrong ("Never, never, never, never, never"), grief making him acknowledge his guilt. The effect is so strong he dies. It's a love death, father collapsing on top of daughter in one final symbolic fuck.

Why is Othello so prone to jealousy? Because he feels inadequate as a lover. At the end he admits his mistake ("You must speak of one who loved not wisely but too well"), his way of saying he didn't pay enough attention to technique and too much to fucking as many times as he could. He's sorry because he'll never have the chance to show Desdemona he could've been a better lover. Iago is obviously jealous, hates Othello for fucking a beautiful woman. He succeeds because Othello has an inferiority complex about his sexual prowess. Which is why he fucks so much. Convinced Cassio has cuckolded him because he hasn't satisfied Desdemona, he smothers her in bed. It's a symbolic masturbation using her pillow and substituting Desdemona's covered mouth for her vagina. We can only believe that Othello is symbolically blocking Desdemona's vagina so she can never fuck again. In his jealous rage her lying mouth and her lying in bed with the other man have become the same thing. There is some suggestion that he believes she may have had oral sex with the other man, which probably accounts for his smothering instead of strangling her. "Down, strumpet," has the connotation of forcing her to swallow another lover's imaginary ejaculate in a re-enactment of the supposed fellatio. As the instigator now of what he hasn't done with her, and because it's another man's fuck, he becomes a self-hating voyeur punishing both himself and her.

In committing regicide, MacBeth upsets the natural order of things. He has symbolically killed the father, but where is the mother? She is mother nature and the witches speak for her. Their prophecies promising so much are really a curse on MacBeth for what he's done. And a curse on his wife and accomplice. Lady MacBeth is a frustrated woman. She's got to push her husband to commit the murder. She wants to be "unsexed" so she can do what he is avoiding. Wants to be a man. Tough, unyielding and pitiless, would dash out her babies' brains to get what she wants. What kind of woman is this? A frustrated lesbian who's had to fuck a man to get what she wants. But she's not happy. Power becomes her way of compensating for not being one of the weird sisters. Duncan's blood stains her but not with guilt. It's her own curse of menstrual blood, which she cannot and yet desperately wants to be rid of ("Out, out, damned spot"). She's been spotting and bleeding most of her life, stained by the natural law that puts a king over her, symbolically keeping her under him. So she has him murdered, and yet there's more blood than ever. To get rid of it, Lady MacBeth would have to destroy herself because the blood in her veins is the blood seeping from her vagina. Her vagina that means she must be fucked in a man's world. Insanity is her recognition of this, the woman's role she doesn't want. She would rather have joined the weird sisters in stirring the cauldron and flinging curses at men. Self-destruction is her only alternative and takes her husband down, too. Better a witch than a bitch who can't ever clean herself. No one has to stick this butch to remind her she's a born bleeder.

Current research: *A Midsummer Night's Dream*
The dirty little men of folklore: Puck among the leprechauns.
Comic anal eroticism: Bottom and the hole in the wall.

Poetry reading
Professor Dawtrey Bowness
Terence Binyon Theatre, Prairie University
October 3, 8:30 p.m.

Before I go on, let's admit that they all masturbated. The philosophers, the great thinkers. They were all masturbators. All your great men. Painters. Composers. Poets. Dramatists. Sculptors. Architects. They all masturbated. All the scientists. Astronomers. Mathematicians. They all did. They were masturbators. Every one of them.

Published work: *A Geometry of Muscles,* Beach Press, 1998 (chapbook).

Faculty Club lounge
October 6

"Dawtrey's at it again. His masturbation revelation. One of my students attended his reading. She's new here."
"He gets all the. . . . That crowd. At his readings. Not that I'm. . . ."
"Of course not. Like Mulcahey."
"Didn't Mulcahey get his degrees from Catholic universities? Not that I'm. . . ."
"A personal thing."

Meeting of junior staff members comprising a department committee set up to organize course in contemporary poetry
Seminar room, Mackerness Hall
October 8

"Have you got the list?"
"Where did you get the names?"

"I talked with Jonathan Scavell and Janice Blastow. They said they were the best. It's not really my field. They teach creative writing."

"You're doing modern poetry."

"This is different."

"What about poets outside of the local area? We're supposed to include the best poets writing in English. That's our directive. As I understand it."

"Some of these are outside. I had to check again with Creative Writing."

"Have you seen this, Sheila?"

"John showed it to me before you arrived."

"Marianne?"

"I saw it too, Michael."

"I'm looking at their publications. Sitonit Press. Tonguebite Press. Chapbook publishers, I'm guessing. I haven't heard of the magazines: *Wind Chaff, Loco Motive.* Must be very small. Reading tours up north. Don't know if that's helpful."

"Whose idea was this?"

"Dawtrey's, Marianne."

"Did he make any suggestions?"

"He's leaving everything up to us."

"Are there any texts, critical works?"

"Nothing, Sheila."

"How are we supposed to put together a syllabus, compile a bibliography?"

"It's not my field, and I don't read contemporary poetry. He's the department poet."

"What do we do?"

"We could report back that there isn't enough data yet to set things up. It's tentatively scheduled to begin next fall, anyway. The whole idea may be dropped. If that doesn't happen, we could suggest supplementing the modern poetry course with a different contemporary poet or two each year. It won't matter which."

Between My Lips (the autobiography of Marlene Stumpf, in progress)

This is supposed to be a bit of auto for the shitheads in the department. But it's not what I sent. Even La Marlene must compromise. They would like to announce a poetess coming to deliver her significant insights—some timeworn hag who's been exotically fucked in several tropical and Middle Eastern locations on hot desert nights and now rents an empty loft downtown in the cold north and collects prizes for her trendy shit as she slowly goes whammo. Isn't it about time these holy cunts were dropped into the rancid romantics bin? But enough. About me. I knew I was girlie bound at ten, when I grabbed a curly cutie behind the school one afternoon and gave her a hug. Spontaneous love. The purest of virginal passion. I didn't reach for anything. Pressed her duffel coat to mine. It was late September cool, the kind that tingles on your legs if you're forced to wear a skirt as I was that day. Which gets me to my mother. Pie-faced Mom, who baked pies all the time. Wouldn't know if pastry flour was drizzling over her head. Didn't know my little brother at twelve was trying to screw his fourteen-year-old sister. Jumped me from behind in the basement. Good thing I was big-boned and tough gristle. A shot to his groin and a bloody nose cured him. But my father sneaking peeks at me in the bathroom was tougher. Had to lock myself in. The bedroom was a problem. Moved my dresser in front of the door. But I knew good old Dad was going to jump me soon. He'd groped me at Christmas, one of those drunken gimmeakiss hand dives male relatives are good at. Aftershave stink and five o'clock shadow scraping your cheek off while he's finding where the gobbler goes. Square male fingers grabbing at your tenderness as they assure themselves of the obvious. Sometimes I wish I could get all the dumb moms and shove them up the Amazon, where a tribe of nakeds would teach them the gummy truth. But they'd still have that dumb doll look. I was ripe enough for the old master. Pear tits and perky nipples, no udder hangover jobs, and ass curves you could drool over in frayed cutoffs pale as my summersky eyes. My hair was tawny blonde and cut short despite my mother's preference for long. "Don't you want the boys admiring you, Marlene?" On my only date so far I'd had to tell Marvin Gluemouth I was having my period. "Yeah?" "Yeah. Wanna see the blood?" "Ugh, no." Tried to get himself off against me in the car, smothering me with oil of musk ox deodorant and getting a hand down between my ass cheeks. I bit his lip and told him I had herpes. He got mad, wanted to fuck me no matter what smelly sewage was leaking out. My brother had given me practice. So while Marvin Hammerhips was pulling down his pants I gave him an elbow in the mouth. He was boxcar seventeen and not twelve and started pounding on me. This is war, I thought, and kneed his flabcock and doodlebags. I crawled out of the car with one good arm. He tried to run me over, drove up onto the sidewalk. I stepped aside and he crashed through the plate glass window of a dress shop. Deirdre's Delights. Glass and mannequins everywhere. Plastic tits on the windshield. Seamless cunts under his tires. I went home and took a bath to wash the man smell off after locking the door.

I was almost sixteen. Time to get out or get ambushed by a beerbrain suffering from daughter itch. Didn't want to end up one of those hookers trying to fuck their father off their mind. And wind up sliced into choice cuts by some freak with a mother complex. I knew that if Dad tried to plop onto me, I'd be the one using the knife. Why go through that? All I left with was a suitcase, the little round kind girls are supposed to love, a gift from an aunt who thought girls should be petite. She weighed two hundred pounds. I took a bus out of Smalltown to Anywhere and ended up in Bigcity Someplace. It's always colder when you get to a new place if you're by yourself. I stepped off, shivering. Professional girlnappers were standing by in cool duds, ready with pickup lines and chocolate bars. I walked past them and went into the depot diner. I sat at the counter, unsteady on a wobbly stool. A worn-out waitress, cobweb hair and spidery fingers, came over. "What'll it be, honey?" I had fifteen dollars saved from birthdays. I ordered a chocolate milkshake and a hamburger. Eating slowly to stall for time, I wondered what to do. I remembered the sign I'd seen in the diner window. Waitress wanted. When she passed by again I asked and she said to see the boss, pointed to a swinging door behind the counter. After finishing I went around and pushed the door open. The boss, a short bald guy who sweated a lot, had a mustache that covered his mouth. He couldn't speak much English and I found out afterwards would usually say only "How much?" "Too much," "No," or "Sure." I lied about my age and experience. Said I was registered with the unemployment office. He didn't believe me but I was tall and filled-out, so I was hired. The place was only closed from midnight till six in the morning. I worked six till two, Saturday through Wednesday. The boss was the cook except on weekends, when his younger brother took over. His brother was skinny and had bad nerves, kept of bottle of apricot brandy in the kitchen. When he felt good he would sing. They were an Armenian family and lived together with their wives and the brother's son in a house the boss owned. They didn't pay much attention to me except to say, "Big girl—how you get so big?" The first week was bad, sore feet and bumping into things. I dropped a couple of dishes and made out the wrong change a few times. After that I got used to everything. Most of the customers were quiet, especially the early ones, but some of the lunchtime crowd thought they got a piece of ass along with their burgers. "Wanna go for a ride?" "Are those for real?" "What time d'ya get off?" And worst of all, "What have ya got that's hot today?" I had to pretend my little clit and tight hole were throbbing for action. Couldn't let them know I thought they were smegma crud. One asswipe waited outside and revved his engine as I walked by. Got out and followed me. I ignored him and he gave up with, "You must be a fuckin' lesbo, huh?" The one time his toxic sludge of a brain guessed right.

My first sexual experience. That's the usual lingo. As if sex comes in parentheses, instead of sticky cotton candy. I was renting an attic room. Another girl had the other attic room our bloodengorged landlord was renting. She was a university student. Education. Sometimes we'd talk around the communal hot plate. And right away I liked her lots. Slim curves, soft face, long sandy hair and big eyes. Those littlebit calf muscles. Sweater and skirt, pastels. Fuzzy socks, white sneakers. Oh, cute. I used to dream about her panties. I'd get wet at work and have to lean against the wall. They thought I was sick. Once I bumped into her. By accident. I was too nervous around her to do it deliberately. She smiled, so shy. The something that's love told me she liked it, so the next night I bumped into her and she smiled again. Next night I gave her a hug, a slight one. Remember, I was a virgin. I waited for a tingling tortured few days. One evening we were frying wieners and eggs in a symbolic sacrifice and I embraced her most fulsomely, as they put it in old books. We kissed softly, she holding the spatula as I held her. We let the wieners curl and shrivel. The eggs looked like yellow rubber balls. We knew nothing until our landlord hollered up the stairs about the blue smoke. We broke apart and joked about burning everything. I suggested going out for a pizza. Over a large salami and pepperoni we talked and didn't listen to ourselves, thinking about something else. When we got back I led her into my bedroom and undressed her, my fingers shaking, and I could see hers trembling. Her panties were soft milkwhite cotton, and when I pulled them down I saw the thatch of light curls around the slit of her cunt. I put her on my bed and undressed so quickly I forgot to take off my socks. I fell onto her and squeezed and she cried out. We started kissing and crying. I put my leg inside of hers. She shifted over onto her side and we rubbed against each other till we came, smothering each other's screams with our mouths. I turned and put my hands under her ass and parted her with my lips. I tongued her clit, teasing till she lifted to me and held my head with her thighs. I could feel her hands squeezing my ass harder and harder as she came. I moved over and gripped her head with my thighs and I could feel her tongue inside me licking, the wet tip probing my creases. I came and she came, straining and jerking. I lapped up the sweet wetness between her lips, my chin nuzzling her clit. I felt her go slack and her legs fall away. And I didn't stop. I wanted her smell, lilies and a trace of the sea. I collapsed on top of her, panting between her legs. I turned around and pulled the bed sheet over our wet bodies. She aware again, we kissed in feathery touches. "I love you," I said, falling asleep holding her and kissing her tearwet mouth.

My first love affair. Everything. We used to watch each other on the toilet and wipe each other afterwards. We would lie like babies, have our blood stoppers fitted and changed. We nursed the beloved through colds and flu. We dressed and undressed and made up the beloved. We held hands in public. We had sex under water, in a tent, on an inflatable raft and in a birchbark canoe. Nobody existed but us. There wasn't anything except what we did. The landlord, in his thirties with mosquito wings for a mustache and muddy eyes that felt you up, tried to make me. High-class pass when he took the rent, nuggets on fingers holding onto mine, look of drooplip smartass. "Let's see what we can do about your rent, baby." I iceberged him and he went back to counting money for his family, who ran a string of houses with rented rooms. He was supposed to be studying architecture. The only architecture I ever saw him study was female. I thought he'd stay in his rathole. But mother nature can be a bitch. I had to help fill in for a few nights after one of the other waitresses quit. During breaks I slept in the back on a cot and went home at midnight. On the fifth day, a slow Sunday, the boss's brother told me to take off early that night and get some rest. "New girl starts tomorrow." It was too quiet in the house. The kind of quiet that means something's happening but you can't hear because you're not supposed to. The stairs to the attic were old and creaked loudly when you climbed them fast. I was so tired I climbed slowly. I heard them, the landlord grunting and her soft answering moans. That female pleasure between torture and paradise. The bottom fell out of me and crashed into the basement four floors below among the rats. I wanted to turn around and run away. But I kept climbing. The attic stank of mansweat and there was a whiff of the perfume I'd given for her birthday a month ago. They were naked on her bed, he behind on his knees and ramming his stub in deep thrusts into her raised ass. When I walked in they heard the strutting sound of my knee-high leather boots. He wanted to keep going but she didn't, instead turned and stared at me. I couldn't read that look. It wasn't like anything I'd ever seen, as if I walked in on a stranger. I still had that feeling in my gut for her. I had to go through the whole thing, like doing something even though it's useless.

"Bitch."

She, the injured innocent, now safely in the kingdom of man.

"You took advantage of me, I was lonely."

"Lonely? I wiped your pisser."

He got off the bed, his fat boy's finger dangling.

"She told me everything, you fucking lesbo."

I ignored him. He was dog shit.

"You said you loved me."

"I did not. Never."

She was right. I was the one who smothered those cleavages with devotion. She never used the word. I did. He moved towards me, stinking of male hormones, groin hair sprouting, his macho membership shrinking into the darkness like a worm but his voice full of sneer. Landlord making with the respectable. Spokesfink for the born righteous.

"You gotta nerve. Get the fuck out of here or I'll kick your ass out."

Closer, then close enough. I jabbed his shin with the toe of my boot. He swore, lunged at me. I was tired and upset, didn't aim carefully. Probably would have missed if I had. Luck goes to the easy. A perfect kick got his hangdog and dewflaps. He screamed and clutched. Master was out of business. She'd have to wait. She was down on the floor murmuring loverwords to him dearly. I packed and left, slept on the cot at work until I found another place.

For three years I picked older women. But there were drawbacks. Too much like my aunties. "Want some cocoa, dear?" Warm blankets, hot toddies, liniment and television ("Let's see what's on"). I wasn't ready for the old folks' home. What saved me from bifocals and embroidering? The hog. I was working at a roadside café. Bikers hung out there. I'd go and look at their bikes. Ask questions. Got a couple of rides. That did it for me. Had to get one. I bought a small used bike for a few hundred. Drove it to work. Bought my first leather outfit. No more sewing circle. A gang called the Broadways stopped by the café sometimes. That's how I met Mike. He was looking at my bike once when I got off work. We started to talk. He invited me to a Sunday picnic. It was in a park. Dozens of bikers there. Some nice-looking chicks but all hetero and taken and I've never muscled in on anyone else's action, hetero, gay or bi. Cases of beer and bowls of potato salad and cold cuts and chips were set out on green wooden trestle tables. And there were kids. It looked like a church social except for the leather, studs, chains, boots and helmets. And they accepted me right away in my black skintight outfit, though my pisspot bike didn't rate. A bike's a bike, though. They weren't going to sneer at a young chick whose heart was with them. I made some friends. Later on Mike and I sat on the grass and drank beer. I had to take a piss. There were some bushes nearby. I was pulling my pants back up when I saw him coming in after me. I finished zipping and buttoning and faced him. The truth and fast. He had muscles he'd never seen.

"Forget it. I'm wired for chicks."

"I don't believe you."

"I'd be dead meat."

"Could force you. Might lose my balls. You look tough. We'd find out how tough."

He was talking too much to be thinking of doing anything. But I had to get him out of it nicely.

"I never had a choice, same as you. If I could go for a guy, you'd be the one."

He got close, rubbed the back of his hand against my cheek. I liked him and meant what I said. But the mother of us all said no. He took his hand away and pointed, grinning.

"If I ever see you with a guy. . . ."

Mike's been a good friend ever since and helped me when I needed it.

I was twenty-two now and had been writing seriously for a couple of years. Before that it was dear diary, what's pubbed in po mags and wins prizes. Written in her own menstrual blood, Pop goes the weasel. Her passion for: fill in the relative kind. Witchfaces who'd have scared their mothers into a miscarriage if they'd seen them before birth and have the nerve to put their mugshots on a dust jacket. Romance junkies embracing their own farts. Cleverererer bitches who want you to sniff their so-literary trail of droppings. Right up to their assholes. Those who knit poems, those who tickle themselves with a pen. Symbol and metaphor grads who mimic the profs mimicking life, mirrors in a funhouse. All the lukewarm brains, the miracle of whose indrawn breath will always escape them.

So who am I? La Marlene, a rider who takes off on words sometimes. The trip is everything. Because where you're going is already gone. This poem from my last collection explains.

On the hog,
flight of sister bee
a line across curvature
coastal green, prairie yellow,
east towards morning glory, pale trumpet
over dewskin lakes,
west towards sunflower drooping in Aztec gold,
pollen drizzle into the purple nectar of the Pacific,
a throb between hips, leaning into speed
at the moment of birthlight,
in the sliding twilight,
into the never, butting the wind
black-leather blonde biker bitch,
steelsilver, aluminum grey,
spinning roulette of spokes, cubetread tires,
hydrocarbon of orthodoxy, piston and clutch,
plug and brake breaking the ballistics of falling
into a future without apologies.
Standing naked, toes into tide,
sea air licking crotch sweat
before I wade over my depth
into the green embrace
and release, four spokes rolling over,
drifting wheel wrapped in rubber whips of kelp,
festooned with sea ribbons,
a footed mermaid bride of the anemones
till I surface gasping into the skylight bloom,
shiver out arms folded
and see her on a blanket,
red and black awning-striped bikini,
a forlorn princess femme
I kneel before, she staring
at my cunt bulge embossed with salty curls

as I undo the sporadic language of the flesh,
cream tits and coral nipples,
tan lines a vee to a quiver seam.
Pull her into beach scrub
and get her down, a thumb up her wincing ass
prying her open, fingers spreading the fruit apart,
peeled raw and lapped and lip nuzzle
my snake in every fold squirming
clitstiff shudders, clitsuck tugging tenderhard,
she murmuring mercies
and open, drawn back and ready
and I can enter wholetongue to hipbuck,
holding her down, thumb ramming
her cries into a red horizon,
legs ripped and cunt engorged, asshole thumblocked
she spasms, sphincters sea creatures mouthing Os,
screaming straight up at throatstretch
and arms semaphoring, her thighs
locked onto my head.
I throw myself onto her, knees into armpitshave,
forcing her down hysterical,
I'm too strong and go back between her
tonguedeep, chin at her clit,
thumb hooking hard and everything goes slack
and the crazy laugh of a fucked-out woman
dribbling giggles, eyes blank,
every crease licked and sucked
and the smell of sunhot skin beachsalty
and getting our clits together
I grip her to me and shove till I come
all budding from the stung rose
at the base of my spine
as I crykiss her babbling mouth.

Back on the hog
into a night of sunburst thoughts.
Who was she? Somebody's lover once. Mine.
She'll forget everything except the mortgage,
get a lift back to suburbia
and wash away the sand fleas, for ouches ointment.
She won't walk right for days.
Apply excuses liberally. Plenty of bed rest.
Dream an amazon rising out of the surf,
cobra-tongued goddess with high tits,
peeling a bit on the shoulders, smelling of seaweed
and come, ass clenchings like fists,
cords of thigh muscle
but smoothsoft and supple and scent
of a tall flower after she's scrubbed.
Expect less of a goddess?
Like mad love she will insist.
Sandspitting tires and the last of her
lust bentover cheeks sleek
as midnight planets eclipsing.
This has a where?
A skin of memory,
slicksilk corrugations, tonguerasped wavelines,
plungings, knowing her asscurves anywhere and
up to armfuzz a goldred meadow.
She's the nameless one out there beyond me
among meteors flaring a second in luminous curves
before I think I've seen them
as I race through the others heading home.
When I've stopped I'll dream.
Naked and riding the witchbitch bike,
embracing her from behind under the ribcage,
the skinwrapped bones,

my wrists locked, swallowing her flung hairwhips,
sniffing the scorch of tread,
not wanting her to turn, not wanting to see her,
hearing the whining scream, guessing the skull,
eyeless glance relentless
as we head off into stardrift
and knowing what I've always known, girl and woman
alone, traveller on an empty road.
Mother, you betray us all without pity.

"Biker Bitch," from *Ruts in the Mud*, Clitoris Press, 20—.

Seminar in Prairie Literature
Katie Krips' house, Belvedere
October 6, 7:00 p.m.

"I think we're all here. Tonight it's my pleasure to introduce Marlene Stumpf, a prairie writer with a distinctive point of view. I first met her four years ago at the Pink Club. She gave a reading from her first book, *On My Own Bike*. Since then Marlene's published *Ruts in the Mud*, which last year won the poetry award of the Northern Prairie Writers Guild. She's outspoken, as you'll hear. I won't keep you in suspense any longer. Marlene Stumpf."

"Hi. These introductions are like taking a long shit. There's some in the bowl but you know there's more coming. You sit and wait, staring at the wall. A good little girl. What I call poetry isn't what po biz people think it is. None of that stanza shit. Or showing how smart you are by quoting classical crap. That's like fucking statues. No wifie confesssions or dear diary bore. That's listening to some chick who thinks she has the right to dump her fuckups on you and call it art. I don't do girl in from the farm getting fucked against the desk by her boss, or your homely lonely middle-aged small-town spinster trying to get laid. I don't do praise the pioneers, especially my great-grandmother, or play identity crisis, gimme a grant to write the immortal prairie poem, and include a travel allowance. I don't do hearing her voice behind my back while I'm getting a coffee during the break and realizing I've always been a lesbian. I don't do feminist, oh they're sucking the blood out of my veins, my sisters. They've snipped my nipples and rammed a technocock of male arrogance and space-age metals up my cunt to fuck me to death. I don't do word acrobat stick a finger up my ass, empty the dictionary onto the page, swallow my snot and call it postmodern. I don't brother-sister with gays who halfway through their boring peekaboo say, 'Your cock's too big for me' or 'I could suck you off forever.' I don't do the world's a shithole, the world's an awesome place, or lying in a hammock watching the sun set and thinking, oh, this is life. I don't think telling you my lover farts or picks her nose is being real. I don't belong to any new latest counter-revolutionary protest groupthink, or writers' groups of fossil farts reading poems about their grandkids, and housewives working ten years on a novel about ancient Crete or some other makefakehistorycake, or attend conferences full of failed geniuses, or enter contests run by cliqueshits who know a poem when it kisses their ass. I don't know what the fuck 'language arts' means, or any of that other sucktalk. I don't do readings to stand up in front of a bunch of sucks and play I'm a great writer. Then gasp ooh-ahs when they get up and read and giggle-goo at their puns. I don't have some publishing whizzo who'll push my stuff and get an asslicker of an artsgradlitcrit in the local paper to say some great writer would've cut off both arms to write metaphors as good as mine, and prints one that's so bad it's a joke.

"The best makes your clit tingle. Makes you feel you're going to shit. You get warm in the holes. Feel your belly's going to explode. Po biz shits don't want truth. They want words to play with and a bit of titillation. I know a few big words but I don't show them off. When my pants split, they fall out. Tell it plain and tell it true. Anything else makes me puke. The word 'poetry' makes me think of ladies drinking tea and guys wearing silk scarves and corduroy. As if the rest of us can't feel exalted—another one—by something that happens to us. The real trick is making people feel what you feel, as if they're one person and everybody at the same time. That's hard, and sometimes I think I've never done it. Other times I think, yeah, my stuff is not bad. Nothing between you and me, even a sheet. Don't think, caress my ass. Poetry isn't thinking, it's fucking the world, diving off a mountaintop, naked in the ocean, tromping on the hog until it flies, loving everything you can't name. Don't lie to yourself and your heart will tell you. And if it doesn't, you're already dead."

Main office, Creative Writing Department
October 29, 2:15 p.m.

"I want to see Scavell."

"Do you have an appointment?"

"I don't need one."

"You can't walk in. I'm sorry, Professor Scavell, I couldn't stop her."

"That's all right, Candace. Who are you?"

"Marlene Stumpf, writer-in-residence. Why haven't you answered?"

"I haven't any idea what you're talking about. Perhaps you should leave."

"Don't give me that politeass bullshit. I phoned. I emailed. You ignored me."

"I think I remember now. You suggested you speak with the creative writing classes about your work. We're a different department. Nothing to do with English."

"Why didn't you tell me that?"

"Not answering is an answer, Ms Stumpf."

"No wonder dickthongs like you end up in crate lit. Bunch of write-offs collecting pay cheques. Letting notalent dreamsniffers think you'll teach them what you can't do yourself. I wanted to let them know what writing is about. The piss and shit. They've got me talking to Prairie Lit grad students over there. That's like talking to gopher holes. Thought I'd have more of a chance to reach somebody here."

"I'm sorry but we have a staff of qualified instructors with a history of publishing in reputable journals and with established publishing houses."

"There's nothing wrong with Clitoris Press."

"Our schedule of classes is filled for this session, and because of financial constraints we can make no provision for impromptu teaching. Much as we would like to accommodate the occasional unusual request."

"Don't give me lit biz. Did I ask for money? I'm already being paid. I wanted ears, that's all. You make a good Brit version of Abercrummy."

"I have a class to teach."

"Get yours and hold onto it like a limp prick, Scumsell."

"I don't think I have to apologize. I'm listed in reputable directories of English poets."

"You're dead. A book on a shelf where nobody goes."

"I have no interest in continuing this conversation. Excuse me."

"You were excused before I was born. I've wiped better shit off my boots."

Telephone call
October 29, 4:53 p.m.

"She was quite abusive, Reid. I explained the department's financial situation and that once the schedule is set I can't simply bring in an additional instructor."

"No, of course not."

"None of us have heard of her. How was she chosen, if you don't mind my asking?"

"Katie Krips, our Prairie Literature specialist, recommended her. From what I've heard so far, I think it was a mistake."

"I shouldn't like a repetition of this."

"I'll speak with her tomorrow."

Office of Dawtrey Bowness, Mackerness Hall
October 30

"All right, Dawtrey Boneupyourass, prick wiper. You've been spying for Abercrombie. You heard me complaining to Katie. You told him I went to see Scavell. Abercrombie called me in this afternoon and gave me some shit about academic protocol."

"Scavell would tell him, dear."

"Why?"

"Well, you can't go around telling people off without repercussions. He was bound to complain. What did you expect? Congratulations?"

"I told the shit off to his face. He deserved it."

"I don't know what he deserved. There are rules."

"Holes you guys hide in."

"Call them what you like, that's life here. Reid won't do anything unless you give him a better excuse."

"Like what?"

"It's called a moral lapse. Take a survivor's advice, pin up your skirts."

"I can't live that way."

"Then you're not long for PU."

"Fuck it and Abercrombie too."

"It'll be the other way around. Go in peace."

"You're like the rest. Title on a door. Jerking off, calling it research. You're bookends with whiskers, prof props. Lit biz posers, store dummies. Lecture notes and a dry sherry. Dead words from dead minds."

"I'm a published poet, dearie."

"Your stuff's nothing but decorator fucks. Profile of a queer. Showing your best side. The department femme."

"I think you should go."

"Tell Abercrummy all you want. My crotch is my business."

"Belvedere Elegy," first draft
From Marlene Stumpf's workbook
November 9, December 14

You were there when I flung the hog against the side of Mackerness Hall. Letting it rest, crotchwarmed, hugged. Watching cutie, tight jeans, ribbed white turtleneck, pink sneakers, face tinted with September light. You weren't fooling anybody, honey. That so innocent look. Giving me that I wear no makeup gaze of purity, lambskin. Oh honey, yes, already. And thinking of you splayed under my tongue and heaving nipple-swollen breasts wobbling with their tiny goosebumps. So we played the conversation game, you admiring me shyly in my skintight leather outfit, top torpedo-breasted. Is that your bike? Yeah. Take you for a ride. Sure. Got to see somebody. Be here at four. Later you huddled sweetly against my back and the wind embracing us. And when I peeled off your sweat socks on the futon and pulled down your stonewashed on blonde-downy legs and eased the bikini panties off your pink plums to the golden horde and the nub of clit switch folded in the tender place and my witch tongue curled wickedly like a panting bitch's dipping to the slit to find it, tipping it up and listening to you moan softly, bucking gently to me, my lips open to a mouth and sucking your soft cactus, lapping the guava wetly. And you groaning loudly now fucking my face, thighs clamped. One thing left to do, my spit finger splitting your ass cheeks and finding your tiny hole tightened to me and worming it open and you wild at me screaming as I hooked and pulled and my snake tongue deeper into your cunt jabbing soft lips apart sphincter slack to let me into you. You scream-crazy trying to buck me off and your wetness drenching us. A hand to your hair I pull back your head, my cunt rasping yours, ass finger out now and I made you suck it. And I came my sponge baby so tearwet, muscle-fucking you limp, and bit you blind, belly nips and deep into your ass wobbles my red-marked horseshoe brand. Sweat, blood, spit and come. We lay in it. We had our first love fuck. Made you sore for a week, sweet puss. So who needs a dildo?

Domestic arrangements. I hang my pants and you fold yours, love pussy. There's a drawer for you and it's marked hers, pretty one. There've been others, so if you wanna hang with this bike-thighed mamma, better play softie. I love them good but when they get bitchy they go, with my boot in their ass. Settle in and do your homework. Mamma will take you travelling. We'll tour and I'll show you off, plum pudding, belly button. Come over here, see if you're wet where it's naughty. Not the futon, the bedspread. We'll lie like a mirrored woman. Breasts against breasts, cunt to cunt. Arms out, fingers locked together, legs split, toes touching we'll kiss till our lips ache.

Till we can smell the fuck.

Hog slaughter in the parking lot. That asswipe Sigurdsen backed up blind shit and toppled me and sweetie. Love bud uninjured but my knee whacked. Prickurdsen yelled. I went over and hammered him two black ones, flattened his nose and was going to kick his balls over Mackerness Hall when the cops grabbed me. Prickurdsen holding his nose, spouting blood. Cops said he wasn't supposed to park there any more. No problem when hushmouth Abercrummy's covering your ass. All of a sudden I'm a stuck pig. Like he never heard of Sappho. Yeah. I'll bet he thinks Santa Claus and the missus don't fuck. Or she doesn't get the elves to backdoor her over the workbench when fatbelly's soused. Lineup at the North Pole. So PU's pulling out, the jerkoffs. Got to go or they'll use a morals clause in my contract. Seducing a virgin and living with her openly a bad example.

Injuries. Not only my knee but my shoulder and a couple of ribs. And sweet puss left yesterday. Bitch found some librarian cheekpecker who wears a dress and drinks tea. Worst thing is I miss her. Thought I was beyond that. Told her I'd take her with me. She could sign up at some other university. Anything's better than this shithouse. When will I learn young stuff is unreliable. Fickle fuckle. Fuzz wuzz. The hog is fixed. I'm packed. I'll end this dribble. This chick is heading out. But fast. Will deep pink stain my so-oh memory? Yeah, it's the clitsucker supreme, and way up inside, the longest tongue. I don't boohoo, I keep my shit to myself and move on. It's the road and wind in my blouse—yeah, I got one—and curls top and crotch tight and my thighs riding into wherever.

Faculty Club lounge
November 12

"What is Ada MacWhinnie, seventy-five?"

"Probably. Doesn't want to retire. Reid keeps her on the staff. Department dinosaur, like Stanley Biddle. She teaches the first semester of the eighteenth century undergrad course. He does the second. Long grey crew cut, always knocking ashes out of his pipe. Does the grad studies bibliography course. Made it a torture test for the memory. Been here longer than Mackerness Hall. MA from somewhere."

"What about Ada?"

"MLitt, Edinburgh. She won the 1971 Sir Walter Scott Auld Reekie Award for tragic immobility in a studio pose with Highland backdrop. Sigurdsen came up with that at a party at the Abercrombies. She doesn't know, of course. Story I got is that Reid went to all her tea parties when he joined the department. She'd been giving them since the Seventies but he helped make them a tradition and she boosted him up the ladder. You've attended them. Ada in her tartan tam and skirt reciting border ballads. Buttered scones with marmalade, oatmeal cookies, the wee dram and bagpipe music."

"I remember at the last one Alison Janeway recited something from 'The Battle of Maldon.' I thought Ada was going to clobber her with a bottle of Highland malt or go after her with a claymore."

"One of those cookies would've done the job. Big as cowpats. Like biting into asphalt. Best thing is to soak them in the wee dram. Kills the taste."

"Ever see anybody so sexless?"

"Janeway? Yeah."

Mailbox, Reid Abercrombie
Main office, English Department
November 16

Professor Abercrombie:
I thought I was entitled to an occasional diversionary trip through your vast wasteland. I don't enjoy being lectured, as I was last Friday in your office, on the subject of my duties here. I do the damn seminar and the undergraduate course as well. Where I go and what I do are my business. You can have the stipend back and I'll leave the campus. I thought that on the Great Plains one only "rode herd", if that's the expression, on cattle. I know you've put a spy in my Dickens seminar to inform on me when I cancel or reschedule a meeting. Are informants an accepted part of academic life in this institution?
Hugh Ashenden-Boyce
MA (Cantab), DPhil (Oxon)
Tripeus, Top Wangler, Newgate Prize ("The Fields of Youth")

Graduate seminar, Dickens
Room 306, Mackerness Hall
November 17, 3:31 p.m.

"Somebody in this seminar went to the main office and complained about my cancelling the last meeting. I was called in by the chairman and told off. I've half a mind to leave. They can keep their damn money."

"Why are you looking at me, Professor?"

"I happen to be glancing your way, Ms Pankratz, that's all. And since I am, I would ask you to cover them up from now on."

"What do you mean?"

"Your tits are showing."

"They're not tits, they're breasts."

"I'm fully aware of what they are. Being a feminist activist or active feminist or whatever you are, you'll probably want to sue me for using vulgar language."

"All I want is to be addressed and described as a woman. I'm here to study, not display my body"

"You're showing it off. And you're wasting your time."

"I'm sorry."

"Don't be."

Faculty Club lounge
November 24

"Our visiting professor is leaving. He brought his seminar over here last Wednesday and they were beering pretty good. All of a sudden he got up and leaned across the table and grabbed one of the seminar members and started to kiss him. Knocked over glasses and a pitcher of beer. Another member, a teaching assistant, said he'd fallen in love with a girl in his freshman class. Ashenden-Boyce, quite drunk at this point I understand, said 'I love someone too' and made a blind grab for the student. They fell onto the floor. The guy complained to Reid and the others backed him up. Reid's been looking for an excuse to get rid of him, and he wanted to leave, anyway. Those cancelled classes and unscheduled trips. He was discreet until last week."

"That's sort of a tradition at Oxbridge, isn't it? I mean the beering, and the other. I'm not making a judgement. It's their business."

"Of course. Who's giving the McGinty this year?"

"Somebody from back East. Bellowspore. Ivy League. Got a book out on the modern novel. Something about narrative form as precept and concept, or something."

"Sounds like that guy last year. Wimmer. The hierarchy of grammar, imperative or ideational choice. Something like that. What did it all come down to?"

"Don't really know. Substantives and fragments. The importance of the subjunctive slide into anachronism. Relevance of the dative case. Inflected transponder elements in the historical present."

"Remember, Sigurdsen walked out of the first lecture. Told the guy off.

'Too bad psycholanalytic crit bit the dust. You could've talked about Jack and the Beanstalk as phallic symbolism. Fee fie foe fum, I smell the semen of a wet dream. Or given us an updated version of Goldilocks. The three bears and psychosexual role playing, subject, predicate and object, the leader, the led and who gets her in bed. You're either pigeonholers with Bibles and assorted mythologies or mutated grammarians now. The really dull among you still do close textual reading as if it's a critical technique instead of an indication of literacy. But the works you'll never understand will survive your best efforts to explain them away.'

"I was glad to see him leave. Wimmer was a guest lecturer, didn't deserve that."

"The man is extreme."

The first of the 20— McGinty Lectures
Professor C.S.T.A. Bellowspore
Student Union Building lecture theatre
November 28, 8:00 p.m.

In the Narrative Center

I would like to begin this series of lectures with some definitions. You will hear me refer in these talks to the "I/You" center. This is I believe the core of the modern narrative form, the sense of obliterated identity, the narrator and reader as teller and told about. Ideally, to tell is subjective and to view or record, objective. But we know that these categories are in reality blurred. Fiction writers have come to accept this, so at present there is virtually no distinction. The narrative center has been imploded with the subjective-objective dichotomy. The old grammatical categories persist as pronouns of distinction, "I" as the collector and "You" being collected. However, in the storytelling timeline "I" is no longer collecting "You." They have become the center, an ongoing colloquy between two seemingly opposed forces that in reality are one, seeking to understand what the center means. So who is the narrator? In an epistemological sense "I" is unknowable in the modern novel, which searches a cosmos of isolated stars in an ironic attempt to gain insight that paradoxically is confounded by a double helix of knowing and unknowing mirroring an endless planned creation of which the storyteller is merely the result. This accounts for the instability of its form against the traditional hierarchy of pronouns, "I" being dominant, with its plural, the "royal we," and the rest subservient. In this matrix, order is traditionally enforced in syntactical relationships in which the subject predominates, usually appearing before predicate and object. To counter this order of dominance writers began early in the twentieth century to bring the "You" closer to the "I" through the "You-understood" mechanism, as easy process in first person narration, where all that's necessary is to borrow from the imperative mood ("Get me some, too"). From this it's only a matter of a simpler, more straightforward grammar to bring the reader into an understood relationship ("Nobody ever knows the reason for war"). "You" and "I" are one in a view that is the narrator's as well as the reader's. Such an equality of standpoint is unique to modern fiction, the storyteller having come down from the heights to share beliefs and a world all readers know. With third person the novelist simply relinquishes omniscience in favor of a direct telling of the facts. Characters become "You" and the reader is made to seek the narrative center there. The novelist is there too, a place of shared disillusionment. Understanding can only be understanding the isolation of modern life. Reader and writer have become the character in a fundamental way, and the story is about them as a single entity. Everything has resolved itself into a single space, an ontological holograph of the contemporary psyche.

I will turn now to that psyche for the other important definition in the series. Novelists only reflect what they see, and what they've seen for a hundred and fifty years is industrial man struggling for his self in a mass society. The fundamental difference between it and the pastoral society preceding it is that self replaced soul. Spiritual considerations aside, and I slight them not except to note their irrelevance to the contemporary mind, soul meant time, the eternal verities, and self means space, by which one acquires an identity through job and education and family and in which one accumulates and uses things to achieve success and create a self-space. I mean by that the significance of a person in contemporary society. I note in passing the irony of implied stasis in a society emphasizing the very time ignored. We defy instead of accommodate time, by organizing it so well, treating it like a commercial commodity. And time is that element around the self-space, isolating it from others and bringing to bear the novelist's attempt to breach the barrier surrounding each of us. Imploding pronoun identities in a grammar of fiction reduce distance and attempt to counteract the essential loneliness of each atom of the mass mind. In a fictional world teleologically prepared, entelechies must be assumed, so a complex of identities can become an overarching mode leading to a simplified view.

With these definitions in mind, I want to move on. . . .

Professor Reid Abercrombie
December 2

Dear Professor Abercrombie:
I have been awarded a doctorate by another university after having failed to get one here under the supervision of Professor Sigurdsen. My thesis ("Textual Superfluities in Old English") will be published in London next year as *Grendel's Revenge.* My question is, doesn't anybody ever come to the aid of a doctoral candidate, or is his/her supervisor immune to criticism and censure? And a related question, isn't a professor's competence to teach in a specific area or familiarity with an author ever examined? My thesis was savaged by an ignorant man. Professor Janeway was on sabbatical when I looked for a supervisor and I had to take pot luck, or should I say the bottom of the barrel. Professor Sigurdsen has little background in Anglo-Saxon. He thinks *Beowulf* is a cartoon without pictures written at a moronic level for savages. That the alliteration is a maddening drone to anybody sensitive to poetry. Bards are only PR men mouthing obvious propaganda for clan chieftains. It's a crime there aren't any women. My list of his ignorance is endless. Will my case be

the last or will others be victims? Supervisors should be competent specialists.
Yours,
John Wren
Curriculum vitae attached
Article in preparation: "Causal Relationship of Clauses in Old English, a New Textual Reading."

Official notice
P. Sigurdsen, English Department
December 18

Your car has been towed to the City Yard, where it has been impounded. Because of your continued violation of parking regulations, your parking privileges have been partially revoked. You are prohibited from parking behind Mackerness Hall. You are now limited to the general and student parking lots. Further violations will result in a complete revoking of your privileges.
W. Beedey
Officer in charge

Dick Meagher On Line, a radio talk show
December 20, 10:00 a.m.

"My guest this morning is Penelope Boozer. She's from the university and is representing the Coalition for Women's Safety on Campus. Her organization is going public with a complaint against a professor. Good morning, Ms Boozer."

"It's 'Booser.' The 'z' is pronounced 's'."

"Sorry about that. Your complaint is that for a couple of months now this professor has been swimming in the university pool every time a certain woman student swims there."

"Yes. He bothers her. Swims too close. He tries to engage her in conversation. And sings."

"In the pool?"

"He wears a life preserver. Or water wings."

"Are they allowed?"

"No. But Professor Sigurdsen seems to be able to break the rules. He has a history of bothering women students. This student is being harassed. We want something done."

"We invited him on the show to air his side of this but he told my producer the moon wasn't right. I mean, come on."

"We think he should be prohibited from swimming in the pool, so this student and others can use it without being embarrassed or harassed."

"Has anybody talked to him?"

"Our organization has sent letters to the chairman of the English Department about this and other matters but nothing has been done. We're given assurances and nothing happens. The complaints are ignored. The student says that she won't return to the pool until something is done."

"We have the chairman of the English Department, Reid Abercrombie, on the line now. Good morning, sir."

"Good morning."

"What's your reaction to this?"

"Professor Sigurdsen's behaviour isn't to everybody's liking. Universities are, I should point out, aggregations of individuals who are measured according to high intellectual standards. Common decency is to be expected, of course. But harmlessly eccentric behaviour is not unknown."

"What's he doing, teaching classes?"

"Yes, and he writes articles for scholarly journals."

"What about the pool business?"

"Strictly speaking, he should be more scrupulous in keeping his distance. I do understand the young woman's difficulty. But he is notoriously unaware of conventional restrictions. And must be reminded."

"From what I've heard off the air, he seems to do what he wants. Doesn't sound too good. Makes you wonder what's going on over there. My listeners are going to be having doubts about what's happening to their hard-earned education tax dollars."

"I can say the situation will be dealt with to everybody's satisfaction. So we can get back to a university's proper business, which is educating students."

"We'll take some calls. You're on the air."

"That professor guy should—beep beep."

"Come on, keep it clean. You're on the air, go ahead."

"Mizz Booz, how'd you like to—beep beep."

"I said, keep it clean. Go ahead, you're on the air."

"Listen, Dick, they're after me. They won't leave me alone. They want me for something. You got to help me."

"Sorry, this is a talk show. Next caller, you're on the air."

"Yes. I fully support the aims of the Coalition for Women's Safety on Campus, and groups like them. I think that professor should be fired. The poor woman shouldn't be hounded like that. That mealymouth you got on there should be thrown into the pool when it's empty. Those guys sure stick together. It takes women to look out for women."

"We'll take another call. You're on the air."

"Hey, Dick, I heard they don't have any clothes on over there when they use the pool. The women too. Everybody swims together. Do you have to be a student to get in?"

"We'll take a break. Stay on the line, callers. We're coming right back. You're listening to Dick Meagher."

Are you bothered by bathroom noises? Is your toilet too close for comfort at parties or when you have dinner guests? Is running the tap a little too obvious? Is turning on the exhaust insufficient? It's designed to get rid of smells. Not sounds. Now Soundawaze has developed a series of soundtracks for problem noises. Easily installed, with adjustable volume within handy reach. Turn it on before the dinner party starts and avoid embarrassment. Choose from Beachplay, Amusement Park, Takeoffs and Landings, parts 1 and 2, Surfsup, Tropical Birdcalls, Locomotive Whistles, or Ducks on a Pond. Perfect for apartment dwellers. Also suitable for condominiums, townhouses and downstairs toilets in two-storey houses. Available at Snowy's Hardware and Northern Mart. We're online @ www.Soundawaze.com.

Editorial, *Prairie Herald-Times*
January 23

Surviving the Great Freeze

The people of Prairie City have survived the Great Freeze. For six weeks the temperature hovered between -40 and -45 °C. Yesterday marked the return of warmer weather. We are assured that this is part of a long-term trend. People here expect hard winters. But this cold spell was unusually severe. Not since the winter of 1903 has the thermometer stayed that low for so long. We responded with good-humoured stoicism to the tougher than normal conditions, keeping our temperature down as well. And there were heroic incidents. Among them the rescue by Professor Peter Sigurdsen of a student from Atherton Hall, the undergraduate women's residence at the university. He happened to be passing by when he noticed smoke coming from the building. He entered despite the dense smoke and carried out wrapped in his coat the unconscious body of a girl from the women's shower on the first floor. The fire was apparently due to a malfunction in the heating system because of the cold. Reports of a man dressed in a parka and earmuffs lurking near the building immediately before the fire were discounted by police and firefighters. Incidents like this made the frigid temperatures easier to live with. The *Herald-Times* is offering free "I Survived the Great Freeze" pin-on badges. They're available now at our offices, by phone or by visiting the *Herald-Times* website.

Prairie Dog
January 24

Anonymous Letter Condemns Sororities

Your campus newspaper has received an anonymous letter declaring sororities to be nothing more than "bawdy houses selling artificial virgins at extravagant prices" and condemning their initiation rites as "barbarically puerile attempts to prepare the pledges for eventual sexual degradation in socially contrived marriages, perpetuating the mistakes of previous generations of likewise genetically engineered families." Calling this a "debasement of classical ideals to the level of an ant colony," the writer says, "In a democracy such aristocratic pretensions, though obviously ludicrous, perpetuate insidious ideas that threaten common standards of civilized behaviour." The writer calls for a boycott of sororities by women students, driving them off campus, expressing the hope the boycott will spread and they will disappear everywhere. "Do we need," he (presumably) says, "gatherings of young women solely for the purpose of shutting out others they consider unworthy? At the time of their greatest beauty and fascination women should gather without regard to social or any other status, in order to celebrate the mystery of cosmic enchantment embodied in them."

Prairie Dog contacted campus sororities for their reaction. Storey Hoaresham of Gamma Theta Psi said "Sororities are open to everyone and perform charity and community services and sisters form lifelong bonds of loyalty and friendship." Missy Alton of Eta Lamda Upsilon said, "This guy is obviously crazy and should be put away." Copies of the open letter, printed in red ink, were posted on the SUB noticeboard, in Mackerness Hall and at several other locations on campus.

Gamma Theta Psi sorority house
January 24

"I bet Sigurdsen wrote it."

"Who's he?"

"He is a maniac. I got him for English 200. He tried to grope me after class. Put his hand right here. I had to move. He invited me to some kind of party. Called it a festival. He said it would free my spirit of earthly dross. Some shit like that. Said I was busy. He wouldn't give up. Went to touch me again. Got long bony fingers. Ugh. Tall and skinny, wears these big glasses. Like a praying mantis ready to grab you. I kept backing away."

"I hate skinny guys."

"He's the skinniest. And the weirdest. The guy's like your total freak. I heard his wife left him. He drives around with a bumper sticker—'Available for a date.'"

"Pardon?"

"Yeah. He's parked a couple of times in the student lot lately. And he leaves his car so it's blocking the exit. It gets towed."

"I had Dolan Mulcahey. For English 200. Once for a whole class he said nothing but 'fuck.' Don't remember anything else. Talking about a play. Shakespeare. He's a little fat guy. Face like a potato."

"I can't stand fat guys."

"He wears corduroy pants and the ass is shiny on them. He has this woven yellow belt and wears shirts with too many stripes. They look like pyjama tops. French cuffs, big stone cufflinks. Walks around in floppy red sandals."

"Oh, excellent."

"Stinks, too. I don't think he washes. Keeps putting on deodorant. I got gassed whenever he came near me."

"Don't guys that stink disgust you?"

"They're the worst."

Amanda Fairmont, senior, pre-law, graduate of Exeter House; Sibey Moritz, junior, pre-med, graduate of St. Hilda's (boarded).

Prairie Dog
January 27

Professor Demands Religious Equality

Describing himself as a devotee of Artemis, Greek goddess of the moon, chastity and the hunt, Professor Peter Sigurdsen has demanded that Prairie University recognize his religion. This is part of a statement he issued to this newspaper. He wants to build on campus a temple to his goddess and have it qualify as a tax-free recognized religious institution. "My religion is an honourable one, Artemis roaming with restless pride among fallible mortal man. As one of those mortals who worship the female principle in its beauty and truth, I see her as its ultimate form and I prostrate myself before her." No administration officials or campus churches have commented on Professor Sigurdsen's demands. Our impromptu survey found students indifferent. None had heard of the classical deity.

From the Sigurdsen Notebooks
Prayer to Artemis
January 30

O thou, look with favour upon my ventures into the realm of female beauty. Thou knowest of my devotion to thy unknowing votaries, gum-chewers unaware of thy mystic powers. I have spurned too obvious Aphrodite for thee, for the silver lawns that carpet thy feet along the silent streets of thy nightly wanderings. And I have seen thee glowing, an orifice in the dark. Also the blood-smeared harvest yolk lying fecund on the horizon. Of the openings and closings in thy mystic monthly cycle I will not speak. There are things female ever beyond my knowing or wish to know.

I too am a nightly wanderer and brave the dogs that bark at and chase me and the police that stop and question me, the muggers that would beat me for my wallet and the gangs that harass me for sport. Like thee I am fleet of foot and race thee down the sky, evading my pursuers, feeling thy spirit is with me as I flee through streets and alleyways to reach a door and bang on it, seeking sanctuary inside. I have thought of protection, a dog, a gun, martial arts, a flamethrower, but I eschew all these and trust in thy help as a final boon. Thou wilt not fail me, thou great and tireless huntress. I have not lain with a woman much lately due to the departure of Daphne, my uncooperative wife, but have not despoiled young virginhood for compensation or revenge, though tempted by temptings painfully beautiful, instead soiling myself with coarse arrogant sluts who rail at my devotion to thee and overcharge. To that chaste ear of thine I must tell of dreams that disturb my sleep, of swollen pudenda like cleft seeds sprouting with stalks of future harvests, and fields of girls' plush bottoms billowing out like mushroom caps from dark loam. To thee I repeat a rhyme that has lately come.

> There's a nymph in my lymph
> and I swear she does there
> what I would if I could
> get to her hidden lure,
> make her purr, speak in slur,
> stir that snatch, fur and thatch,
> if I were not so sure
> Miss Demure is a blur
> of a wife with a knife
> and I feel the fine steel
> cut so thin from within
> blood will bleed when it's peed.

1227 59th Street, Belvedere
February 2, 4:05 p.m.

"I don't like going to that house. He's crazy."

"Don't you want to sell these cookies? He buys more than anybody. We can get rid of everything. Come on."

"What does he do with them all?"

"I don't know. My father's a professor. He says never to go in the house. Get paid and leave."

"Last time he said, 'Ah ha, I see you are selling the golden grains of serious, little girl, a satisfying job.'"

"Don't listen."

"You go. I'll wait here."

"Help me carry the stuff."

"I'll leave it by the door. Wait for you on the sidewalk."

"Hey. Something's burning in the living room."

"Let's go."

"I want to see. It's a fire in a big pot. He's pouring something on it. It's smoky, I can't see. He's singing."

"Let's get out of here. He might put us in the pot."

"That's stupid. You've got to help me sell these cookies."

"I don't think he wants any tonight."

"He saw us. He's coming to the door."

"I'm going."

"Better stay. Or else."

"Else what?"

"I'll tell about all the cookies you ate and said you lost."

"No fair. I'll tell about that time you fed them to your gerbil."

Campus Market, Belvedere
February 2, 6:23 p.m.

1 250 ml jar Secret Valley Passion Fruit/Guava Jam ("Ideal on a cookie. . . .")
2 honeydew melons, Paradise Hills brand
1 doz. Martha Clare's Homestyle Doughnuts with pink icing ("You can
    hardly find the hole in a Martha Clare")
1 475 ml bottle Red Madness BBQ Sauce (5-bell alarm)

Campus Drugs, Belvedere
February 3, 9:01 a.m.

1 package Nardil anti-nausea tablets (12-tablet size)
1 350 ml bottle Glistomin antacid (mint flavour)
1 Pro-Tek lip balm (cherry flavour)
1 25 g tube Formula A with screw-on anal insert "for easy application"

From the Sigurdsen Notebooks
Prayer to Artemis
February 5

O thou, chaste mistress of my soul, hear these troubles of thy faithful one. I tell thee, for thine ear is the cool arbiter of the night's agonies. High among thy mystic stars, be thou receptive to my plea for hope and rest. And send me, if not the flesh, the soft-furrowed dream of it.

I've been standing over the toilet bowl of late yelling at my penis to hurry and pee. I fix my bed endlessly, pulling the sheets around so they are perfectly aligned with each other. In that empty bed my pyjamas are constantly riding up my legs, keeping me awake. And I am plagued by an old problem, the fundament's revenge for too much cheese and too little fibre in the diet. After a bowel movement my posterior feels as though it's been scraped raw and bloody with sandpaper. The bowl looks splashed with slaughtered guts. Afterwards, walking is painful. For sleepless nights I have sought relief in alcohol, choosing Australian wines, Riverbed Sec Boojerong champagne, and vintage port, Quinta da Mulligan Bodega Smasheroo. Even the latter had little effect, though an employee at the liquor store assured me one bottle would knock out a herd of camels. Each night is only a few hours of slurred, half-heard snores and a headache.

The source of this unrest is the unacknowledged killer of man, loneliness. Bought women bring only a respite of crude claspings and cruder language. Stretched pudenda, cynical lips. I, worshipper of women, of their fragrant smells and silken recesses, of the enticing earlobe and the slippery inner thigh, of flubadub nipples, roseate areolae, of soft belly fuzz thickening down to the pouched cleft furrowing below all the skin's stretched treasures, I seem doomed never to know again anything but store bought bargainer's flesh. The young beauties walk past into another's arms.

I am constantly bedevilled by uneasy thoughts. Pardon my profaning of thy chaste ear and thy starry dominions, but it's confess or go mad. Life chews us whole, digests our dreams and shits us out as little turds down the anonymous drain into the running sewer of eternity. I'm in the boa constrictor's gut being squeezed. Uncoiling by the millions from the walls the probing tentacles of cilia are sucking up the slop of my disintegration and I'm turning into my own stench of floating sludge, pushed along by peristalsis, snakesqueezed until the anal sphincter snips me off and I plop onto a pile of others. My pounds of bacteria in this life's entrails, a crawling zoo of unseen decay, multiply and die. I congeal to a slimy pod ready for the drop. I watch my putrefaction and can do nothing except slide along the dark tunnel, bulging in that gut until the end's release, a lump like any other.

Dost thou see the depths to which I've sunk, the stinking thing I am? The worse is, I enjoy the fundament's revolting odour from bloody feces passed and abraded veins distending outwards their bunch of bruised and pulpy grapes. I unbuckle and sit, inhaling pork-fried posterior as the rare rear's perfume to a punishment. Awaiting the scouring scrape and drops of blood, I breathe in humanity's personal barbecue, hoping there is enough cream up there to prevent major bleeding. I ponder a way out from a meaningless life's draining of energy. Surely something awaits besides the daily pain and itch of wanting and not getting. A sign from thee would be a balm to one who, sorely in need, worships thee from his lowly seat of professor. Send thy disciple some glowing imprimatur of thine.

Southgate District, Prairie City
February 10, 12:09 p.m.

"You're blocking the light. I can't see to put the key in. There we are. What are you a professor of?"

"English."

"Better watch my grammar. I usually don't meet guys like you at the Igloo."

"My first time. My wife left me."

"Thought so. I'm divorced, too. We didn't get along. I usually don't invite guys up to my place the first night. But you look like the bookworm type, if you don't mind my saying so. Sit down. I'll get us something to drink. I like wine coolers."

"Drinking Australian wines lately: Kangaroo Cabernet, and a late-picked Riesling, Outbacker Walkabout, select vintage, Burntgorge."

"Don't have anything like that. How about Catalina Sunset?"

"All right."

"We can listen to some classic rock while I make the drinks."

"Oxymoron."

"You calling me stupid?"

"It's a literary term. Means an apparent contradiction."

"My mother said my father was dumb as an ox."

"There's nothing classic about that music. Traditionally the word refers to the cultures of ancient Greece and Rome. It implies a certain standard of excellence. It's been debased to promote the products of mass culture. Anything with a half-life longer than a nanosecond. Cars, movies, and the raucous and whining mating calls of pop music. I was exposed to that noise during my youth but fortunately was immune to it."

"Sorry if you don't like it. I don't think everybody has to like the same thing."

"Fortunately."

"You got better taste, huh?"

"Quite different."

"So I'm a moron. And you, you're a smartass."

"Oxymoron."

"That's it. Out you go. I should've known. Asking about my cup size at the club. Shit about goddesses, sacred rights. I never heard of any church having the right to do what you want. You're a mental case."

Janice Blastow's apartment, Belvedere
February 12, 7:45 p.m.

"You know, Peter, right away I thought it was a great idea. A play with no dialogue. Who needs it if the movements are eloquent? As you said, a piece of soundless music. When Jonathan asked for my opinion I said, 'Sounds great.' You should liaison with Creative Writing more often. Our ideas committee is always open to a fresh approach. We're going to stage your play in a couple of weeks."

"The idea came to me. I'd been looking to do something different. Get away from the academic. What are we drinking?"

"Pilgrim's Repose herbal tea. It's got chamomile and hibiscus in it. When you said you wanted to see my work in progress, I thought, yeah, right, he'll give me a different slant. I've never done anything like this before."

"Somebody has. Everything we do is a pale copy of the golden age, the classical world."

"Mine is something new. You'll see. I'll go get it. More tea?"

"No, thanks. I'm getting a bit sleepy."

"Well, we don't want you nodding off on my couch. I'll be right back."

"I haven't been sleeping much. Since my wife left."

"I couldn't hear you from the bedroom. Here we are. My latest opus. And my best. Not quite finished."

"I can't untie the ribbon."

"Let me do it. I keep all new work in this folder from high school."

"Looks like a diary."

"That's the idea. Except the entries are deliberately mixed up so you aren't sure what happened when. That's the way memory works. I've taken it a step further. You don't know what happened to whom."

"Um."

"Don't you see? It doesn't matter. We're all meaningless entities sharing the same desires and fears. I stress the common nature of the experience. The shared anonymity and pain. Identity through crisis. Intensification."

"You use 'lap' and 'cane' a lot."

"I slept with my grandfather."

"Sounds cosy."

"He fucked me."

"Um."

"Since then I've had only older men. Most of them pensioners. Some of those guys can surprise you. What do you think of my poem?"

"I think it should be performed without words."

"Like your play? Great idea. I'll see Jonathan. He'll go for it right away."

"I'd better be going."

"You finished reading?"

"I'm a quick reader. And these ancient bones need rest, Janice girl."

"You're not that old."

"Don't believe your eyes. I keep my age well. Be retiring in a few years. Looking forward to a rest."

"You don't look your age."

"I've got spry genes. I'm energetic."

"Like this pensioner I'm seeing. You'd never guess he was eighty-five."

"Rub a bit of liniment on my rheumatic joints and I'm as good as new."

"Sorry. I've run out of liniment."

Party at Laura and Reid Abercrombie's house
1106 53rd Street, Belevedere
February 15, 8:14 p.m.

"Laura pointed you out to me. Said you were the most interesting man in the department."

"I'm a pale replica, a Don Wan. First department party I've attended in a while."

"This could be your lucky night."

"Didn't I see you arrive with somebody?"

"My husband. We have an open marriage."

"How late are you open?"

"I could take a taxi home."

"One ride after another."

"Are you getting drunk? You've had two glasses of wine since I've been talking to you."

"Don't worry about me. I can dink with the breast of them. A connoisseur of Australian wines, my current appraisals include a Kookaburra Special Reserve vintage claret, in an unbreakable jug for festive occasions. Has an aftertaste of ten thousand years. Also a Canberra Koala Corker Classique, aged two weeks in eucalyptus."

"You'd better stop or you won't be in any condition to drive."

"Nothing to it. I like stick shift. Yank that lever around. Shove it back and forth. Wiggle it around. In and out. Any tread left on you?"

"I'm sorry, I was waving to somebody. I didn't get that."

"Thought you did all the time."

"What are you talking about?"

"Have you ass—ociated with lots of men?"

"I've known many men. So what?"

"You remind me of the piggy bank I used to fill with coins when I was a boy, only your slit is at the bottom. Gives an ironic twist to that threadbare seduction line guys have used on stubborn girls: what are you saving it for?"

"You trying to insult me?"

"Would seem so. Are you a stun fuck? Do you lie there like a bedspread or do you get involved? What are cunts going for these days?"

"They're not going for pricks."

"The body beautiful to every man she meets. Bottoms up. Then the lines come and the sagging starts. Have you been stitched to make it tighter so you can feel something smaller than an elephant? I prefer it to be hygienic and free of all foreign substances for at least twenty-four hours before I get involved."

"You're an insulting bastard. Are you one of them?"

"No. Anatomy pointed the way. I already had one, why would I want another one? But you, as one of the randomly rammed, would be an expert on that."

"What did you say to her, Peter? She's walked out. I'd better go get you a towel. Your jacket is a mess."

"In vino veritas, Laura. Or expect the wine and duck if it's the glass."

"I thought you two would get along."

"I don't like wives on loan, even one-nighters. It all ends at the bottom, but I like a bit of kissing in the moonlight beforehand. Pastoral airs. Hint of the shy shepherdess. Idyllic idiocy."

"When you're in this mood, Peter, no one can talk to you."

"Not a mood, a phase, like the aspects of the moon."

From the Sigurdsen Notebooks
February 16

I, Sigurdsen, renounce all interest in middle-aged women, the neurotics, the bitches, the conventionally deformed, the nutritionally depleted, the hideously resurrected. I reject their bleached hair, tanned hides, their jogging and workouts, their supermarket conversation, their rush hour lives, their dietary fanaticisms. I want nothing to do with light toppings and desserts, guides to better sex, drenchings of perfumes that smell like old whores, romantic music that would deflate the tumescence of a bull moose, social clubs that empty the cemeteries, dances that look like bad comedy routines, small talk that would interest only the slower gastropods, opinions on the state of society and the world best delivered while wearing a wizard's cap. I don't want to hear about wayward kids, superior brats, ex-somethings, psychics, tea leaf readings, astrology, reincarnation, or have to read incestuous poems about fathers. Hereafter over the perennial seasons of my dotage my attention will be lavished in unstinting measure exclusively upon young women, and they will receive in spite of expected derision and indifference from them, all my devotion, and yea, my love.

Heartsnflowers Online Dating @ www.heartsnflowers.com
("Your true love is a heartbeat away.")
February 16

Prof, 40s, dashing, suave, debonair,
lots of je ne sais quoi, savoir faire,
seeks buxom young woman, pref coed,
for more than a place in my bed.
She should look good in skorts and hot pants,
though I have my heart set on romance.
In spring a man's fancy turns to love
if your shape matches the above,
will fill this learned man with delight
in firelight, moonlight, candlelight,
starlight, northernlight, parkedcarlight,
nakedbulblight, publicwashroomlight.
We'll butt heads, talk doggerel,
stroll the beach like a bad commercial.
Nothing about you, belches, a sharp toenail,
gut rumblings, breath liver stale,
blood spoor, foul-smelling flatulence,
fishy places, excretory sediments,
urine distilled in panties for days,

will stop my praise in end-stopped lays.
So write and include a recent photo,
You might win this lovers' lotto.
We'll meet somewhere for coffee and chat.
The rest is chance, my lovely brat.

Café de la Jeune Fille, Belvedere
February 24, 7:10 p.m.

I thought your poem was so romantic. I write poetry, too. About love mostly. My last boyfriend. . . . Well, forget him. He was. . . . There I go. But anyway. I like older men. They're not always after you. So you're really a professor of English. I'd better watch my grammar. I'm taking Fine Arts. I might go into Education, become a teacher. I want to do some travelling before, though. Go to Europe and see all those galleries. The Loof, the Uffizzy, the Ashmoulden, the Hermantage. There's nothing around Prairie. They're all farmers. I've been told I have artistic hands. Shapely fingers. Narrow palms. My kitty scratched me there. See? Right by the nail. What are you doing? Let go of my hand.

Bonnie Jean's Quick Eats, downtown
February 25, 8:39 p.m.

Don't mind me. I like butter. No, thanks. One is enough. Bun, I mean. I'm on a diet. I put on as much as I can. Seven on this one. They never say anything here. I grabbed a bunch of those little containers when we stood in the line. My last lover said I smelled like butter when we made it and I started to climax. You know, when you see coloured lights going on and off. I do. I'm going for more little butters. I've got half a bun left. This is the poem I told you about. I write in pencil. My thoughts come easier. I don't know if you can read my writing in here. Oh, you wear glasses. I thought so. You were blinking so much. It's about when I sold paintings from the back window of my mobile home. A friend painted them. I sold them to my customers. I ran an escort service. The cops came around. I told them I was selling art. They said I had to get a licence. I didn't want to get busted, so I left town. That was in Beaver Falls. I got chased out of Bear Paw, too. I'm a psychic now. Easiest money I ever made. You'd be surprised how many men come to me for advice. It's love or money, those are the two. I'm Dunella. A friend of mine is a publisher. He's going to publish my poetry. When I put it all together for him. I think I'm going to wait a while. I want to have some different experiences. So I can write about more than being a sex worker or a psychic. You going? You haven't read my poems.

1227 59th Street, Belvedere
February 26, 9:15 a.m.

You've reached the Sigurdsen residence. I'm not at liberty to take your call. Don't bother leaving a message unless you're a young woman with an interest in classical religious rites. I'll get back to you when the appropriate time arrives.

. . . .

Your credit card isn't worth shit, Sigurdsen. You still owe me for Honey Burns and Leila Lowe. For the stuff you want you should be paying a lot more. I don't think I can get the donkey again, anyway. You've got two days. Bring cash or a bank draft made out to Sinta Petters. Hey, I know guys that'll make you wish you were a woman.

The Astral Experience
#108, Prairie Centre Mall
February 28

No one wishes to speak with you.
No voices are coming through.
There is interference—can't hear.
Leave your money on the table, dear.

Madame Circe, mystic at large
(Diploma, Occult Studies, Univ. of the Hellenes)

From the Sigurdsen Notebooks
February 28

Mr. Nobody gets nothing.
Love is the art of the possible, sex the art of the probable.
Buying sex is like eating a hamburger. It leaves a lump in your stomach.
Call girls should not be called girls.
Wives are girlfriends with a binding contract.
Time is a habit most married couples need help to break.
What a husband wants a wife may refuse; what a wife may want a husband will abuse.
A beautiful girl is promise unfulfilled; a beautiful woman is a threat to all promises.
Where there is beauty there is woman, unless she has an appointment.
To love a woman is to love the world, the easiest of all heroic acts.
Only a woman knows how much of the truth matters.
A divorced man needs a maid to pick up occasionally.
Mr. Desperate says too much too often, as if it matters.

During sex a man may find himself wondering, what the hell am I doing?

Distrust any woman who doesn't sew but keeps a large pair of scissors permanently in her possession.

From the Sigurdsen Notebooks
March 3

Dr. Disease, specialist in political correctness
Faculty of Medicine, Prairie University
Status: at large

"Ministering to the politically incorrect"

About PC I'm an agnostic with twitches. Currently in my inner office with my secretary. She's a buffin muffin. Has enormous control where it counts, nuff said. Let's move on to our questionableaire.

Have you been well adjusted cranially?

Have you been well adjusted manually?

All saints are now political, correct?—as long as we get to do what we want whenever and with whomever we want ad infinitum. Check, pleas.

Do you love every race creed nationality religion group gender posse gang soirée get-together species (hairy crawlers)?

Are you politically aware? Colours, genders, neuroses, religions, oligarchies, plutocracies, friendly anarchists? Have you succumbed in the voting booth? Many times?

Would you vote for an ugly woman? Accept one as your leader? Would a boob job make any difference?

Does hate speech bother you if it's from a blonde who displays her curves with obvious recklessness?

Do you have internet rape fantasies?

Are there cervical circumspections you've thought about?

Do you think about animals when you're not petting them?

Do you cry over the species you eat?

Do you eat kale? Steamed, chips, raw, fermented, ready-rubbed by garden gnomes?

Are you being briefed by extraterrestrials (e.g. Alpha Centauri)?

Is life an inflatable raft? Are we sinking fast? Slowly? When the water gets to your knees, will you be bailing out?

Is the world coming to an end? Date?

See spots larger than a random mote?

Butterflies terrify?

Are you ever wormy? Do you bleat profusely?

Guilt magnet? Feeling guilty about not feeling guilty enough?

If your answer to any of these questions is "yes," what are you doing in my office?

Poster in the SUB
March 5

Colour Awareness Week: Know Your Subspecies

European: includes the Great Northern White of northwest Europe (on the endangered list due to changes in breeding habits), habitat increasingly being occupied by other subspecies); the eastern European, or Steppe White, and the Mediterranean Littoral White; these subspecies have migrated to North and South America, where they have established hierarchies and largely replaced the local subspecies.

Extinct in the European subspecies: Crested Phalanx (Aegean, Tiber), *Vive l'Empereur* (In-Seine), Lesser and Greater Pithhelmets (Brit. Imperialinsists, et al.), Goosefooted Nurembreed (Preuss, et al.).

African: Saharan, includes the Nile Sandfoot; subSaharan, Ebony spear-the-lions, eco-subsub, spare-the-lions.

Asian: too many to list.

Aboriginal: they survive among us.

We are all subspecies. Know yours. Look up at the stars. The time is coming. P. Sigurdsen, English Department

Prairie Herald-Times
March 7

Universal Condemnation

Campus organizations at Prairie University have called for the dismissal of English Professor Peter Sigurdsen after he posted a notice in the Student Union Building. The notice, also posted at various other locations on campus, proclaims a "Colour Awareness Week" and contains comments on various races. The reaction has been a storm of protest, denouncing the poster as racist, inflammatory, intolerable, and the product of a diseased mind. Penelope Boozer, who represents a women's support group, said the poster "hints at a coming race war." Heidi Schmidt of Students Against Racism said, "racism has no place here and neither has this professor."

Dick Meagher On Line
March 11

"This is Dick Meagher. My guest in the studio this morning is Dr. Deborah Rasminski, spokesperson for the Campus Coalition Against Prejudice. She has a complaint against a professor and she's going public with it. Says she's forced to because the university won't do anything about him. Welcome to the show, Dr."

"Mr. Meagher."

"What is going on over there? This is the same guy we did a show on a few months ago. Then it was sexual harassment. And now it's prejudice. Let's identify the guy."

"Professor Sigurdsen. The authorities will not, as with the other complaint, do anything."

"Again my producer tried to get him on the show but he told her that Artymiss, whoever that is, wasn't in favour of it. Last time the moon wasn't right. I mean, come on. Why do you say he's prejudiced, Dr. Rasminski?"

"He's posted a racist notice on campus. Something about whites being endangered by other races. He writes 'the time is coming.' It seems to be a call to organize. And he's made remarks after class to students about religions and beliefs other than his own. Students came to us and told us what he said. I thought seeing him personally would be better than sending a letter. He never seems to be in his office, so I went to see him after a lecture."

"What happened?"

"He became quite hostile. I identified myself and told him why I was there. I said the coalition wanted to warn him to stop spreading racist ideas or it would be forced into taking serious action. He said he'd been telling 'these priestesses,' as he called them—some students who'd stayed behind—that Western culture is a direct descendant of the classical tradition. Those without cultural and religious links to it can play the instruments but can't write the music. And no campus headline grabbers were going to muzzle him. I told him I didn't think his attitude was very helpful. 'My attitude is my business,' he said. It went on from there until I said we were going to take all the complaints we'd received to the authorities. He sneered at me. 'I wouldn't expect somebody like you to understand.' I asked what he meant and he said, 'Take it from there,' and walked away."

"We've got the chairman of the English Department, Reid Abercrombie, holding on the line. Are you there, sir?"

"Yes, hello. We speak again under trying circumstances."

"This sounds bad, sir."

"If it's true, it's serious. I have to say, though, that a university traditionally is a place where diverse opinions, some of them unpopular, can be heard and tolerated."

"There's a limit, isn't there?"

"Indeed. But we'd do well to remember, in the heat of battle things are often said a little more stridently than necessary and sometimes exaggerated by the memory."

"Are you saying Dr. Rasminski is hearing things?"

"Indeed not. I am merely suggesting she may have become emotional and allowed her feelings to get in the way of her judgement."

"What about the students?"

"Impressionable young women sometimes become excited and exaggerate. We've not heard everything and weren't present on those occasions. The complaints will be looked at carefully, I can promise you that. And if there's a basis to any of them, appropriate measures will be taken. I've talked with Professor Sigurdsen about what he posted and he said that there's been a misunderstanding. He's calling for, as he puts it, 'colour awareness,' not stirring up race prejudice, and says calling attention to our physical, cultural and historical differences is positive. In his words, 'misusing them is wrong, not the differences themselves.' His way of expressing his opinions is unorthodox and can be confusing."

"We talked earlier off the air, and he's no longer swimming in the pool."

"That's right."

"We're going to open the lines for calls. How do you react to what you've heard so far, Dr. Rasminski?"

"I agree about being careful with accusations and that complaints have to be thoroughly investigated. I would add that the investigation should be conducted by an impartial body like the university senate."

"How does that strike you, sir?"

"I agree. Impartiality is crucial, yet I would caution against inadvertently turning an unfortunate situation into a public show. Sometimes there's more heat than light generated that way, which does not help anybody. We should be careful about a completely unnecessary arousing of public emotion."

"That sit right with you, Dr. Rasminski?"

"The inquiry must be truly impartial and unbiased."

"You don't sound convinced."

"The sexual harassment incident took months to clear up and there wasn't even an apology. The man wasn't censured in any way."

"How about that, sir?"

"Professor Sigurdsen has given up his pool privileges. The woman is free to swim any time she wishes. I don't know what more could have been done in this matter. His absenting himself is a de facto apology."

"What should happen, Dr., if in fact these complaints are true?"

"That's up to the body of inquiry. Let's hope it's not a complete whitewash."

"What do you think personally?"

"I think his attitude is outrageous and he should be censured by the university, and if an apology is not forthcoming he should be discharged."

"How about that, sir?"

"In Professor Sigurdsen's account of the altercation he said, 'I wouldn't expect someone with your views to understand.' I should also mention, and remember we haven't established anything yet, that he contends Dr. Rasminski questioned his sanity and his feelings about women students. He repeated what he said were her actual words and they were quite blunt. I don't offer this as exculpatory or even as fact, but simply to remind everybody that there are two sides here."

"You're on the air, caller. Go ahead."

"Hey, Dick, I heard there's this secret high-level organization meeting somewhere in Europe that's getting ready to take over like everything."

"We're talking about prejudice."

"I mean, if it's true maybe it's serious and, you know."

"You're on the air. Go ahead."

"I vus in the Chermin army, Dik."

"Yeah? So?"

"I vus."

"Next caller. Go ahead."

"This professor sounds sick to me. I'm surprised at the university keeping a guy like that and covering up for him. I used to think I missed something by not going. Guess I didn't miss much except a bunch of weirdos."

"You're on the air. Go ahead."

"Yeah, Dick. Could this have anything to do with the water supply? All these pesticides getting into the ground water. I think they affect your brain."

"I think they've affected yours. Next caller."

"Hey, Dick, you find out about the pool? About girls swimming naked there?"

"Next caller, go ahead."

"I vus in the Chermin army, Dik. I vus."

"How did this guy get back on? Marilyn, please check the calls. We'll try another line. We're talking about prejudice. Go ahead."

"I think the guy's got a right to express his opinion. It's after class, on his own time. Since when can't you say what you think in a free country? Who says you've got to like everybody and keep your mouth shut? I'm sick of all these rights groups telling us we've got to watch every word we say. It's going to end up with us being able to say nothing. Always crying about freedom of speech for themselves. Don't want anybody else to have it though, do they?"

"Go ahead, next caller."

"Yes, Dick. I can't believe what that guy said. Free speech doesn't mean bad-mouthing anybody you don't happen to agree with. It's after class but it's still in a classroom in front of students, isn't it? He's supposed to be teaching, not spreading his twisted ideas. And about what he posted. 'Colour awareness,' my ass. 'The time is coming.' Pretty clear to me. I agree with that woman who says he's being protected."

"We'll take one more call before the break. You're on the air."

"How's it going, Dick? Did I hear a guy say something about girls swimming naked?"

"We'll take a break."

Do you have full chest expansion? All true lovers do. Scientists have found that chest expansion is the truest test of being in love. Lovers describe it as giddiness or euphoria. Tests prove it's true, the swelling of millions of air sacs in the lungs to their fullest extent possible and held for longer than a usual breath. Blood is more fully oxygenated as a result, with that I'm-walking-on-a-cloud feeling lovers describe. This is not the same as deep breathing and cannot be achieved in any other way, including exercise of any kind. It comes naturally with love, as all true lovers know. But many fool themselves into believing they are truly in love. And up until scientific studies revealed it, the truth couldn't be seen. Now, thanks to the Dodge-Comfrey Clinic in Minneola, there is a simple home test that shows if you and your partner have full chest expansion. Be in doubt no longer. Know the real state of your love. Scientifically tested. Send today for the easy-to-use kit and also receive at no extra charge the instructional DVD, "How Always to Achieve and Ensure Full Chest Expansion." In ten easy-to-follow procedures. Includes the testimony of many who have achieved this wonderful state. Feel what poets have felt. Only $69.95. Full money-back guarantee if you're not satisfied this is absolutely the best you've ever felt. Order online @ www.feelyourtruelove.com.

Prairie Dog
March 12

Extremist Politics

On Monday evening a student was thrown through a second-storey window in the SUB cafeteria. Blaine Sidcup fell twenty-five feet, landing in snow and suffering various cuts and bruises. He is the prairie leader of Worldwide Anarchism. A group of agricultural students sitting nearby took exception to some remarks Sidcup was making to others at his table. The aggies picked up his chair with him in it and promptly heaved both through the window. Sidcup was treated at the university hospital and later released. Campus police detained the aggies for questioning, releasing them until further notice. According to Aird Mund, an aggie witness, "The guy knocked our society, said it was no good, he's going to start a revolution and change things so nobody owns anything so everybody can take all they want from anybody else whenever." Sidcup, a political science student who transferred here, said he will not prefer charges. "They are the dupes of an entrenched power structure," he said. Officer Beedey of the campus police said the incident would be looked into but wouldn't comment further. Worldwide Anarchism has a total of seven members on the prairies.

Prairie Alumni
March

A Glimpse of the Man Who May Be the Busiest Professor
The upcoming session in September will be Reid Abercrombie's eighth as chairman of Prairie University's English Department. As head of the largest department in the Faculty of Arts, he has used a firm hand to guide it through some challenging times. Coping with fluctuating enrollment at a time of cutbacks in government grants, he has managed with unflagging energy and unfailing good humour. Class size has remained stable and there have not been any drastic cuts in staff. He has solidified his reputation as a pre-eminent Middle English scholar while fulfilling his duties as chairman. In his office last Wednesday afternoon as he was preparing to teach a seminar, he said his dual role as scholar and administrator was a matter of balancing enthusiasms, the desire for harmony among colleagues in their joint pursuit of excellence and great satisfaction from intellectual discourse in the classroom. "They are symbiotic, the pleasure I take in each being greater because of the other." Usually working a twelve-hour day, he has been known to jog around the campus before donning his caps of scholar and administrator. Early arrivals have seen his burly frame clad in green plaid sweat suit and athletic shoes jogging across the academic quadrangle through blustery winds and freezing rain and walking briskly with the added protection of muffler and earmuffs in subzero temperatures. Coming here from Midwestern University sixteen years ago he quickly became one of the most recognizable figures on campus in his tweeds and oxblood brogues. Sporting a plaid scarf and tie, he would invariably have his other trademark, a bent bulldog pipe, clamped firmly between his jaws. The bent bulldog is no more, put aside when he began jogging. Popular with students from the beginning, he used to make a practice of talking with them informally during the noon hour. Like the pipe that's gone as well, a consequence of his assumption of the chairmanship. Too many demands on his time have curtailed or ended such pleasures. This has been difficult for someone so gregarious. But discharging his duties conscientiously left no alternative. One of the more pleasant of these duties was his speech recently at the dedication of

the McGinty Reading Room in the Main Library. Named after his predecessor as chairman, the McGinty Room will house local collections of interest to English and history scholars, including the original manuscripts of Professor McGinty's great-grandmother's cookbooks, journals and letters, among the oldest and rarest manuscripts in the library.

As he was leaving for the seminar our busy professor of Middle English stressed the fundamental reason underlying his untiring dedication. "There has never been a greater need for us to appreciate and enjoy the wisdom and art that are so much a part of great literary works."

Faculty Club lounge
March 12

"Reid's giving that professorship to his old supervisor at Midwestern. The selection committee will be told. Be a surprise. After all the applications and interviews."

"Did you tell Bill?"

"Sent him an email yesterday. Answer was short. He was obviously upset. So were a lot of others. Been talk of taking legal action. Won't go far."

"Bill wanted to come back, didn't he? Grew up north of here."

"Notices will be sent out. Fifteen candidates. All well qualified. That's that."

Professor Ronald Lintot
English Department, Midwestern University
February 24

Dear Ron:
In our recent correspondence you mention you needed a change. Our other Middle English specialist will be leaving at the end of this session. I can offer you a full professorship. Second-year survey and an upper division course,

supplemented with a graduate seminar. Departmental duties would be light, the committee on faculty relations. I'm submitting your name before the selection process goes any further. Send CV immediately. The climate here should help your bronchitis. I hope Ellen is feeling better. The climate here is healthier that way, too. Looking forward to seeing you. It's been almost seventeen years since I trod the quad there. Plenty of good memories. Best wishes to both of you.
Reid

Scarecrow
Midwestern University student newspaper
December 3, 20—

Another Victim of the Creature

Mrs. Ellen Lintot, the wife of English Professor Ronald Lintot, was attacked last evening. Her attacker, the "campus creature," preys on professors and their families. He has written this newspaper about his grievances. A disgruntled undergraduate, he left without a degree. He says he wants to protest a system that treats students as a bunch of sheep and stamps degrees on them. He uses a can of aerosol paint to spray a four-letter word on victims. The paint is blue or black, the university colors. Mrs. Lintot received bruises on her leg, where the "creature" wrote a word for a nearby part of the female anatomy. After being treated at the university hospital, she was released. Professor Lintot says his wife is resting comfortably. Campus police have been under pressure for several months to find the deranged man. Sources close to them say there aren't even any suspects.

Prairie Alumni
April

Appointment

The English Department announces the appointment of Professor Ronald Meritt Lintot, a noted Middle English scholar, to its permanent teaching staff. Professor Lintot, fifty-nine, was a member of the department at Midwestern University for thirty-one years. His wife Ellen accompanies him. An accomplished ceramicist, she will teach extramural classes in the Fine Arts Department beginning this September, when her husband assumes his post. The couple's only child, Mercy, died after her school bus collided with a truck driven by escaped convicts from the maximum-security state prison nearby. She was the only fatality, killed when a convict tried to escape. Wearing a coat he took from a girl on the bus and covering his head with her umbrella, the convict was spotted fleeing the scene. State troopers shot at and wounded him and took him into custody. Tragically, a bullet glanced off a lunchbox and hit Mercy. With Mrs. Lintot's kind permission we reprint "Farewell," a poem from the commemorative volume she wrote on the death of her daughter.

> Mercy you were to us
> And to all who knew you
> On our quiet campus,
> Awakened on that day
> You were taken from us
> To where only the good
> And precious from this rumpus
> Down here go. I'll no
> Longer make a fuss
> About your hair and dress
> Or your father cuss
> About the boys you knew.
> No further loving ruckus

Will you hear from us
Except, Lord, please have Mercy.

From *Mother's Mercy,* Purelove Press, 1989.
A division of Dearlove Enterprises ("Nobody sells love for less").

Midwestern University
March 20, 1994

"Is Professor Lintot in?"

"You're Reid Abercrombie."

"That's right. I'm dropping off a chapter of my thesis."

"Ron had to fly to a conference. Come in. You were here before. A few months ago."

"Professor Lintot invited the members of his seminar for a social evening."

"You were the one who got a little drunk, weren't you?"

"It wasn't a proud moment. Would you mind if I wrote a note to him?"

"Of course not. Come into the living room."

"The scene of my debauchery."

"You fell, that's all. Sit down."

"After grabbing at a lamp and knocking it over on my way to the floor."

"You didn't break it, and if you had I would've thanked you. I've never liked it. You're left-handed. So am I. Would you like a cup of coffee?"

"Thanks, I've finished. I'd better go."

"I'll let you out. Oh, it's started raining."

"My car is across the street,"

"It's pouring. I'll get you an umbrella. It's in the bedroom. I can never find it. Got one he sticks in his coat pocket."

"That's all right, Mrs. Lintot."

"Maybe you should come in and look. It's his big one with the walnut handle. He never uses it. Could be at the back of the closet. I can't quite reach."

"It's not raining hard now."

"He's forgotten he's got the damn thing."

"I'll be going. Thanks for the offer."

Midwestern University
May 22, 1994

"Are you listening to me, Reid? Stop writing. I asked you a question. When are we getting married?"

"When I finish my degree. I'm doing the chapters as fast as possible. Lintot has to approve them. And the other committee members have to agree."

"Other people get married before they finish. Why can't we? I'm teaching. You've got your instructorship."

"Lots of people don't finish their doctorate, they get sidetracked. Bills pile up. Years go by. Babies come along."

"You weren't like this when you were writing the exams. You wanted sex all the time. And chocolate bars. Now you hardly want either."

"I've told you, Laura. The sooner I finish the better it looks when I apply for a job. Lintot will keep me on as an instructor if I can't get anything right away. But Midwestern is a dead end. There's no opening in Middle English. To get an assistant professorship I'll go anywhere except overseas. That's another cul-de-sac."

"Are you sure you want to get married?"

"Don't be dumb. You're going to have to wait a while longer, that's all."

"There isn't anybody else?"

"Would I have time?"

"Thanks for the endorsement."

Faculty Club lounge
March 15

"Dave Krieghammer got his grant."

"What's he doing?"

"An edition of somebody's letters. Some minor Victorian essayist."

"They're all minor with him, aren't they? He did an edition of a girl's poetry."

"She's not well known. Died at seventeen. The poems were discovered in a trunk in Cornwall twenty years ago. Threw herself off a cliff. She'd fallen for a married man, apparently the local vicar."

"Thought it was hereditary insanity."

"The poems are fantastic ravings written in hundreds of concentric circles. In her own blood, some of it menstrual."

"I heard it was urine and soot."

"That would be black. I've seen photos, and the colour looks like burnt sienna."

"Didn't she die around 1840 or so? After more than a hundred and fifty years any substance would fade, be hard to tell without chemical analysis what it was."

"Dave and his wife spent a year in Cornwall—research. They went to London regularly. He knows what to pick. Editions sound good. Gather the stuff. Check it. Write an intro with a brief bio. Summarize the work's publishing history if any, add editorial comments and finish off with some canned criticism. They all count. Got three articles out of his doctoral thesis."

"What was it on?"

"Some minor Victorian novelist. He gets his articles published in the *Journal of Victorian Research,* put out by the Skorenskys, a husband and wife team."

"Never heard of it. What's his stuff like?"

"Competently written. But some very minor thinking. Not like Reid. Nothing but memos. Has one article to his credit, on the Middle English lyric. Published seven years ago when he took over from McGinty. Got the letter of acceptance only days before the department meeting to vote on a new chairman. Walked in with MacWhinnie and Biddle and with that letter. Made McGinty's job of electing him easier. Within a year he got his reward, became professor emeritus and the McGinty was named after him. The other two became fixtures. But it was close."

"What happened?"

"Two candidates and deadlock. Then Sigurdsen rushed in late, surprise of surprises—he never attends departmental or committee meetings—broke the tie, cast the deciding vote."

"Who ran against Reid?"

"John Morell. He was our Shakespeare man. Departed soon after the vote. Skinner replaced him, along with Mulcahey, Skinner doing the Elizabethans in general, and his favourite writer, Phineas Fletcher, and Mulcahey Shakespeare's plays."

"Sounds bitter."

"Morell was 'publish or perish' and wanted hiring, promotion and tenure based strictly on publications. He had published a couple of articles in respectable journals. Nobody else had done anything. Dave was new here, and besides, he's never made the big journals. There were rumours that Morell was going to get rid of anybody without tenure. He wanted no more doctoral candidates until the department's status had risen. He was a disciplinarian. Told off teaching assistants who wore jeans and tie-dyed T-shirts in class. He wanted the chairman to be limited to a four-year term. Reid wanted an unlimited term. The full professors, McGinty, Morell and Reid, had tenure, of course. There were only two associate professors, MacWhinnie and Biddle, and they had tenure as well. As McGinty had declined everything slowed down, including the awarding of tenure. Many people were waiting. McGinty's retirement had been rumoured for months. Reid was running things by that time, thought the chairmanship was his. Then Morell announced his candidacy. Reid set the election for the general department meeting in April. Everybody attended except Dave, doing research in London. On some minor Regency or Victorian novelist. He mailed in his vote. It wasn't for Morell."

"Didn't he respect his scholarship?"

"It was something else. There was a rumour Morell was gay. Spread probably by Reid. And backed up by his stooge, Dawtrey Bowness."

"Was he?"

"Don't know. He was always alone, never attended parties. Nobody knew anything about him except his Ivy League degrees. The other rumour spread along with that was what probably turned Dave against him. Morell supposedly was going to staff the department only with gays. Like a certain California state college English department. Reid knew how to use that."

"Why was he afraid of Morell?"

"The idea of an unlimited term didn't go down well. There were more than a few who would've voted for Morell to stop Reid."

"How much had Sigurdsen heard?"

"The rumours must have penetrated that brain of his for him to show up. It wasn't the usual meeting. This election was going to determine the future of the department. As I mentioned, he turned up late. Reid entered the conference room in Mackerness Hall preceded by Ada and followed by Stanley. He was leading McGinty on a leash. MacWhinnie and Biddle had made themselves joint chair. Ostensibly to help McGinty. Reid carried a folder containing that letter. Routine business was swept aside in a flurry of motions, secondings, carrieds and not carrieds, yeas, nays, all the parliamentary stuff done with fast. Something was tabled and something else referred to a committee for an in-depth study. Nobody was paying much attention to the preliminaries.

"McGinty was seated at one end of the long oak table. Biddle sat next to him, to prompt him when necessary. When everything was out of the way, Biddle handed McGinty a paper. He said he was nominating Reid and read some stuff Reid no doubt had written about himself. Biddle seconded the nomination and made a speech. A couple of Morell's supporters did the same for him. Reid praised McGinty, who was staring out of a window. Reid opened the folder, took out his letter of acceptance, read the whole thing, mumbling when it came to mentioning the name of the journal. Morell followed with a summary of his plans to upgrade the department. McGinty began muttering to himself and Biddle spoke to him.

"At this point Sigurdsen walks in and grabs a chair, pulls it away from the table and sits in it with the back tilted against the wall. He says to McGinty, 'Artemis sends greetings, Professor,' and McGinty thinks he means his dead wife, whose name was Agnes, and starts to cry. Biddle leans over and sticks something that looks like a dog biscuit into McGinty's mouth. Finally there's a show of hands, first for Reid, then Morell. Biddle raises McGinty's hand. He opens Dave's envelope, announces his vote. Pru Sawatzki, the senior secretary, is taking the minutes and records it and announces it's twelve each. But Sigurdsen hasn't voted. Ada asks him why. 'I'm waiting for a sign,' he says. Morell suggests the candidates restate their positions for Sigurdsen's benefit and offers to go first. When Reid speaks he adds something and Sigurdsen asks him to explain. He does and Sigurdsen raises his hand, shouts 'Reid,' gets up and walks out. Over."

"What happened?"

"Ada knew there was a sure way to get his vote, leaned over and whispered to Reid. I'm trying to remember exactly what he said.

"'I should mention in passing, Peter, that I believe a department shouldn't be a homogeneous collection of scholars, so that only one type of person becomes accepted. Such a point of view frustrates the normal intercourse between academic and student bodies. We are not obliged to be peculiarly different ourselves, only to respect differences in others. Our personal preferences must not condemn us. The first step against what you like is another man's preference for what he likes. Keeping abreast of student problems is as important as academic excellence. Male-dominated departments such as ours can easily become guilty of ignoring the individual student, especially the women.'

"Sigurdsen says, 'What's this about frustrating normal intercourse?' Before Morell can jump in Reid says, 'Those who have a natural interest in our coed student body shouldn't be discriminated against.' That gangly arm never reached any higher. Morell left immediately after Sigurdsen. MacWhinnie and Biddle ended the meeting with a motion, quickly seconded, and some imaginary yeas."

"So Reid smeared Morell and played upon the fear he would staff the department with gays. Would he have done that, I mean if he was gay."

"I couldn't see it happening here. This campus and the whole area are conservative. Morell only wanted a four-year term. Even if he was after creating an all-gay department, he'd have known that's almost impossible unless you're in a predominately gay area."

"You obviously voted for Reid. Or you wouldn't be here."

"Yeah, I voted for Reid. I've never liked the 'publish or perish' idea."

"Was it only that?"

"Maybe."

Poster in the SUB
March 18

Get Your Culture Here
Gala music concert and art exhibitionism (donations unwelcome)

Symphoney Concertainty in P (after Mosthardt), for chocolate chunks, peanuts, gnarly currents and two scoops (rocky road) on a food processor, frappé.

Intermezzo: recordings of dog howls while the crowd feasts on chips and jerky (bring your own and some for the performers).

Second part

Twelve tone cereal music gut cleanse, based on a Lutheran hymn or Balkan folk tune, "Why am I doing this to myself?"

Peace will be restored afterwards by a shepherdess in classical dress who will play on a flute satisfactorily sad mountainous airs (bewaires).

The walls will be festooned with Professor Sigurdsen's opusses, *Réalités à la mode noir*, *les Daubs Immortale*. To wit: consanguinities (splatters), pro-linearities (stripes) and modalities (squares) (for sale to the lowest bidder).

Friday, 8:00 p.m., in lecture theatre (come all or come one)

Prairie Dog
March 19

Swordplay in SUB

Last night a packed crowd in the SUB lecture theatre was witness to a swordfight between defenders of modern art and music and Professor Peter Sigurdsen of the English Department, who believes art and music since the early twentieth century has been nothing but trash. The evening began when Professor Sigurdsen and his students, all women, performed "modern music," turning a dozen food processors on and off in various sequences. At the climax of the performance lids were taken off the processors and the contents filled the air with what the professor called "messy stinks." The professor was dressed as an eighteenth-century gentleman in lace shirt, satin jacket and knee pants, silk stockings, buckle shoes, periwig, sash and sword. A man in the audience stood up and identified himself as Magnus Malvern of the Music Department. He said the professor didn't understand modern music or art. They had adapted to reflect a changing world to be relevant. The professor was stuck in the past, like his costume. "We don't wear swords or paint dead birds or go to concerts in carriages and sit in draughty candle-lit assembly rooms." A student stood up and said he was studying art. He asked the professor, "What do you want us to do, keep repeating the past?" Malvern laughed, saying "Maybe we should all go back to wearing wigs."

Professor Sigurdsen stepped to the front of the stage and replied to his critics.

"If music is any sound or sounds thrown together, even you can do it. And if you can steal from the past and get away with calling it yours, you're set. The summits are receding fast and you're on the downgrade. All that's left is convincing yourself you're not a fraud, and that'll be your only real talent. And you, the art student. There's nothing left for you but playing with shapes in a sandbox or taking a shit on a canvas or taking selfies. There's immortality for you."

The professor looked up at the ceiling.

"The unapproachable summits of the classical past are still before us. All

Europe has since profited, spurred by genius, until it vanished. And now we listen, we look and we see and we sicken. The mob at the gates has broken through and taken over: the deaf and dumb, the blind, who try to convince us they can sing and see. We turn away disgusted and they smirk, their last defence we don't understand their work. But we understand what the heart rejects and we know what gives it joy. Time and talent in the balance, and when they're gone nothing can be the same."

Professor Sigurdsen turned and signalled to a student who had operated a food processor earlier. She wore a short white gown with a belt, a crown of ivy and open-toed sandals and was holding a pan flute.

"It's culturally stifling in here. I need some pastoral air. Leave thy woolly flock. Come and beguile this herd of cattle."

She came to the front of the stage and played a simple, ancient-sounding tune. The crowd, which had been loud, quieted down. The professor went to the back and brought up another student and performed a courtly dance with her with lots of fingertip touching and bowing. At this point some in the audience began turning on their own music and started dancing in the aisles between the rising tiers of seats. The professor stopped dancing and shouted over the noise at the audience.

"Quiet. I'm journeying in another world. Peasants are always with us. Swine and kine without end."

This had no effect except on the flute player, who quit because she couldn't be heard now. The art student who had spoken up earlier stepped onto the stage waving one of the professor's paintings, which were on display, at him. Obviously drunk now, he had taken the painting from its place on a wall and trampled it into a compact mass. He waved it like a club at Professor Sigurdsen, who pulled out his sword.

"*En garde.* I'll have at ye."

They duelled until campus security arrived, phoned by somebody in the crowd. Officer Beedey and his partner restored order and took the student's and the professor's names. Last seen, the professor was taking his paintings down and saying he would burn them. Officer Beedey warned him not to do so, but to place them in the proper trash receptacle. The professor replied he was speaking figuratively, and the officer's answer was, "speak any way you want, but don't burn them."

Prairie Dog
March 20

Editorial

The bozos in Creative Writing have done it yet again. English Professor Peter Sigurdsen, resident zany, has come up with a play without dialogue and they are staging it as sound effects. No words are spoken. The sounds of the action are all that's heard on stage. For instance, when there's a party all you will hear are the sounds of bottles being opened and glasses being filled, sofa cushions being sat on and shoes being scuffed on carpets, all clearly amplified by many strategically concealed microphones. So far no bathroom or bedroom scenes. We can hardly wait. You can catch this madness at the Terence Binyon Theatre on Tuesday and Friday evenings at 8. You'd have thought their last public effort, stories and poems from contributions written by the general student population on a roll of paper in a booth set up in front of the Main Library, would have cured them of trying to push the frontiers of art into laughland. The latest idea, carried to its logical conclusion, would put them out of business. But considering the level of ability there, that might not be a bad thing. We suspect a secret hatred of writing among the staff, who can't make a living from their own because no one will read it, and who have to teach people with even less talent than themselves to avoid going on welfare. All they succeed in doing, besides getting a pay cheque for themselves, is deluding would-be Shakespeares into believing writing is a matter of using the right techniques. If this were true, we'd have signed up years ago and elbowed the Bard off his pedestal. We nominate Professor Sigurdsen to replace the chairman of the Creative Writing Department, Jonathan Scavell, who since coming here from England fifteen years ago to set it up has managed to get more people to shut their eyes than Lady Godiva.

Prairie Dog
March 28

Professor Proposes Uniforms for Academics

Professor Peter Sigurdsen of the English Department is proposing that university teachers wear uniforms. In a letter to this paper he calls for each faculty to have its own colours and each department its own garb in those colours. Within departments specializations would have appropriate insignia. Using his faculty and department as examples, he is suggesting scarlet and Lincoln green for Arts, beefeater uniforms for English professors as guardians of literary treasures, and an Elizabethan scholar would have an image of Shakespeare embroidered somewhere on the tunic. He says he's open to other suggestions. He explains that the idea behind his proposal is to identify each subgroup in the university community, so like medieval craft guilds each would have an increased awareness of its self-image as well as have a clearer view of its role. Heraldic emblems would not be out of place. He says "We ought to get away from the drab anonymity of academic life, in which many people and what they do are hidden from public view."

From the Sigurdsen Notebooks
Prayer to Artemis
May 14

O thou, great spirit, thou hast shown me the way. Tonight on my lonely journey across the streets and lawns of Belvedere I received a message in a form I could not fail to understand. Stepping in the murky droppings of some pet dog taken by its owner for a walk, I forsook my usual cursing at such a misfortune and laughed. In his refusal to clean up in a show of civic pride, the owner of the mutt had inadvertently shown me something.

But it took thy light, clouded over with purpose at the time, to tell me. O goddess of the wild, goddess of the moon, thy virgin spirit has led me on a hunt too, to find the reason for these nightly wanderings. As I lifted my befouled shoe to look, thy refulgent orb, piercing through the dark like the stroke of a searchlight, came out from behind a cloud and I could see that my Achilles heel had been hit, but to enlighten rather than slay me. I have become soiled by my profession, which picks over dead matter that should be left to disintegrate into the growing verdure that is literature. The corrected and annotated texts, the critical and variorum editions, the glossaries and appendices, the voracious paper-eating insects called footnotes, are work that does not need doing. All this is part of an industry creating jobs recycling material on the excuse of an idealized correctness, a grammarian's dead touch. Added to such is the dog vomit of articles and books professing to explain what an author's words actually mean, how a novel or poem justifies some theory, psychological, political, metaphysical, linguistic or economic, all to justify the scholar's existence, a pathetic imitation of the scientific method. The only thing ever proven is that proof is inexhaustibly pliable. Their only real myth is the myth of academic excellence and their vaunted independence is only another way of saying tenure. With this comfortable lie I lived for many years, a fanatic lost in ibids., op. cits., loc. cits. and bibliographical eternities, seeking a nonexistent infallibility. No more, and I seek for another path away from Prairie University.

From the Sigurdsen Notebooks
Prayer to Artemis
June 1

O thou, I have seen thy gleaming message and the path away from Prairie University is clear. It was in front of me all the time and I did not see it. I was crossing the quadrangle on the way to my office in Mackerness Hall when I saw thy radiant fullness directly above the Main Library, bathing its granite walls and toothed mock battlements in haunting splendor, a castle on the plains. What has thou in store for me, I thought, and changed course for the library. Hurrying up those broad steps and pushing open the heavy oaken door I felt excited yet restrained, as if some holy purpose were awaiting me.

Even the rude undergraduate who bumped into me as I stood gazing at the polished granite staircase rising from the entrance hall did not disturb the mood. Entranced, I climbed to the second floor. I showed my card to the nymph stationed at the entrance to the stacks (she of fecund promise, bursting cups, peach rump, sweatered, jeaned), who responded with an insouciant stare to my inquiry as to the sufficiency of her thin tight sweater in keeping her warm and stopped chewing the wad of gum behind those poutsoft lips. Artemis awaits, I said, lunging past and colliding with another churlish lout sneering his pimples at me. Into the recesses I went, down flights of stairs and along interminable aisles of bookshelves, stomping past chatterers in carrels and finally reaching the basement. I stood in abandoned silence. No one around, nothing except aisles of bound volumes of old magazines no one read any more, and odds and ends, bibliographical curiosities, donations from professors' widows and wealthy alumni, and in a far corner piled lumber and cans of paint. Standing below street level, under sprinkler nozzles and garish fluorescent tubes, I had reached bottom. Below my feet was concrete and under that the earth. I went over to the windows, high along a wall and covered in wire mesh. The evening sky was indigo and distant and softly lit by thy light, thy benediction to all who travel by night. In that vault I felt hopeless and turned away, then saw a carrel desk on which lay a pen and blank notepad. For me, for me, my true purpose to write, not be a literary parasite. Exhilaration. Acceleration. Up the stairs and out past that maddeningly tangible nymph and into the night air. Sapphire vault of my soul. Starry cape of shouldered heavens. Both arms raised to thee, my deliverer. My life and desires were as one.

Madame Circe
July 10

About your future career
As a creative writer
There's nothing yet, dear.
We'll go into your past
And see if anything is clear.
Look into my eyes,
Relax, back to another year.

Hey man, cool it, the pigs are here, flush these joints. Open the windows and burn some incense, like we're flower children, that'll fool the man. Chant the mantra. That's like far out. Once the fuzz takes off, we'll crash over at the commune. Peace and love and the environment and tie-dyed shirts and down with the establishment. Like don't nuke us, man. That was good shit. Didn't get ripped off. Wanna drop some acid sometime? Trip out? That's real heavy. Like you can walk on the roof of a building and not even know. You see a clock, only it's melting, the hands are limp. Time is like forever, man. Walls move. Flowers keep opening. Colours glow, psychedelic. Too much. Don't do acid if you got anxiety, you freak out. Bummer. Stay cool, flower power. Get your shit together. Keep on toking, man. Do your own thing. Oh, what a downer, it's not the pigs—landlord wants his rent. What day is it?

Hey, daddy-o. Slip me some bread for a pad. Sweet skins to the tune times ten. I got a chick but no wheels. Can you dig it? A drag, real square. She blows it sweet, dig? Wild. Take it from the top. Slow. This phone's the worst. You gotta score a hit? Dig old lady nature in the park? Crazy. I can dig it.

The government announced today the war effort on the home front is exceeding quotas set at the beginning of the year. No sector of the war economy has failed to meet its quota. Though this is cause for congratulations, we should remember that our enemy is far from defeated. Much more will be required before the unconditional surrender of the Axis is a fact. Our soldiers, sailors, airmen and merchant marine deserve the best effort we can provide in supporting their sacrifice for freedom.

When all is said and done, the trouble is the workers at the end of the day don't get their fair share of the profits. The bloated capitalists take everything, leaving them barely enough to live on. Cheap labour fuels the economy, making big profits for factory owners. Workers are thrown onto the scrap heap. The pen prostitutes in the capitalist press pay lip service to the idea of fair wages, but these hired lackeys are merely mouthing platitudes while the unemployed hop freights and ride the rods across the length and breadth of the land. Hobo jungles are everywhere. The despairing are becoming slaves to cheap intoxicants. The desperate are walking miles for a handout. Are we, the labouring classes, going to allow such outrages to our brothers and sisters to continue? It is well past the time that the government recognized it must do something. Or the workers will take matters into their own hands. In a more fortunate part of the world the economy is in the rightful hands of the agricultural and industrial workers. A just share is given to all. When that day comes in our land, capitalism will have become the historical dinosaur prophesied by far-seeing thinkers, its passing lamented only by the selfish.

At the beginning of a new century our young nation can be justly proud of its accomplishments. Our ties with the mother country are still strong and will be for many years. But the pioneering spirit that enabled us to turn a wilderness into a modern state is now forging a new identity. Much remains to be done, especially in the West, where the immense prairies stretch hundreds of miles to the foothills of the Rockies and where already the production of wheat has made this proud nation a major exporter to world markets. The land of the buffalo has become a sea of grain. And although we lament the passing of those vast herds of the noble beast, we give thanks for this agricultural bulwark of the national economy. Here in the East agriculture on a smaller scale helps support a growing industrial and commercial base, and the coastal region harvests the Atlantic. From there to our newly-settled Pacific Coast, rich in fish and timber, the country spans a continent blessed with an abundance of natural resources and a people that can use them to build a remarkably bright future for our children's children. So farewell to the nineteenth century and welcome the twentieth. One gave us much and the other promises more yet. Two coasts, great mountain ranges, countless lakes and the magnificent prairies are a wonderful and awe-inspiring challenge we shall not shirk. May God grant that we be wise and humble in meeting it and never fail to be grateful for His gifts.

Reach for the sky, ya lowdown sidewinder. Say your prayers. Ya tried to bushwhack me, ya polecat. You're durn tootin' I knowed what's what. Dadblame it all, if I warn't a law-abidin' cowpoke I'd fill ya full of lead with my trusty six-shooter and you'd be buzzard vittles. Or maybe we'd have a necktie party. String ya up. Bury ya in boot hill and the coyotes gonna be rustlin' up some grub. Let that there schoolmarm blubber over ya. I got no booklarnin' 'ceptin' the Good Book, so I knows 'nuff to abide by the law. I'm takin' ya in. One false move and it'll be your last. I'll drill ya. You're headed for the hoosegow and you'll be tried fair and square. A tenderfoot, a consarned greenhorn tryin' to drygulch old Sagebrush Swifty, if I ain't a son of no good claim jumper. I've had my say, spoke my piece. So spill your guts, ya varmint, or keep your lip buttoned up. If ya know what's good for ya. My old paint stepped into a prairie dog hole roundin' up strays. Come up lame. Now I got this here muleheaded good for nothing cayuse. I'm a hired hand over at the Bar X, bronco bustin' and steer brandin'. I string wire now too, fencin' the range. Trail drives to the railhead is gettin' well nigh scarce. What them Injuns call the iron horse has 'bout crossed the West. We'll get some chow from the chuck wagon 'fore headin' out on the trail back to town. Giddy-up.

You would not believe, Mary, the desolation of this place. God has a reason for everything and one must be thankful for what is provided, yet what we are to make of this endless flatness I am at a loss to know. There is no timber worthy of use for building, so each family in our little party has erected a rude habitation from piled clods of turf, and in these sod huts smelling of dry earth and roots we try to live. They provide warmth enough now in May, but the winters, we are told, are long and fierce here, and we shall know soon if our crude dwellings will be adequate in sheltering us from oppressive summer heat that will quite suddenly vanish with the first freezing wind. We have planted the seed stored with our provisions and are hoping for a harvest sufficient enough to feed us through the desperate winter. Everything is in God's hands. Flying insects pester us interminably. Several of the children have the croup, but thankfully no one has fallen seriously ill as yet. I send my letter, not knowing when it may reach you. Forgive the hand, dear sister. Our tasks have been so numerous of late my weary fingers bear the marks and strain of the hard and tedious labour this place demands, and there has been little time to make a more than serviceable ink from soot. Dearest Mary, pray for us.

The herd stretched for many miles, a shadow moving across the land, filling valleys as it passed. A thunderous noise of hooves reached us on the hill above. It took many minutes before the beasts passed. No one spoke amongst the party of company men and native guides, everyone's eyes being fixed upon that vast and speeding multitude.

His Majestie's government having granted a charter, pursuant to the purpose of establishing a company of his loyal subjects to follow the trade in furs, the Bristol Maid duly set out mid-June, and with a following wind much of the journey sighted land less than a fortnight later. We anchored in a small cove, the crew much heartened after the long voyage out, and at once I ordered the longboat lowered and a party to search for fresh water and what game was chanced upon, bidding the men be vigilant, as there might be savages in the woods that grew close to shore. I used the glass again to scan the dense cover. What movement there was appeared due to the wind, which I noted had risen within the hour. I must confess my agitation was so great I added somewhat to that sensation of motion, the glass not being entirely steady in my hands, the sight of the boundless woods crowding the very horizon awakening a profound emotion in me. What forebodings I had felt earlier and at that moment I readily put from me, for we are in God's hands. I believe that He will surely grant us good fortune.

Sigurd, the son of Edwaerd and Frieda the Swede, he of the shining helmet and war-chief of the Iron-Geats, left his great mead-hall, pride of his people and best in all lands, left his bed-companion, the young Brestha, daughter of Behemoth and Hirgith, and gathered loyal thanes in that famous folk-hall called Hereweare, for glory he sought. They sat on the mead-benches in ringed mail-shirts, their war-helmets and ash spears and battle-shields around them. Sigurd entered, he of the long bones and sky-tall, his mail-shirt bright and ringing as he walked, his sword battle-hardened and bright-edged, the iron-blade war-sharp. He spoke, the son of Edwaerd, "You battle-brave earls to whom glory in battle was given, stood beside me in the shield-crashes, you know my brave deeds in slaying the ahspestoes-dragon and the night-walking monster that spied on our marriage-maidens. Now I am set for the whale-path until the ring-hoard is full. You then shall know my generosity again. This promise I make to you as your lawful liege-lord." The shouting was loud in acclaim from the mead-benches for the brave-hearted chief, most generous of kings, and there were many cups of beer emptied by him and the thirst-dry thanes to warm-hearted words, this fellowship delaying the departure past dawn. When they gathered at the wooden ship of curved prow, deep-bosomed and well-braced, the seafarers were heartened by the sea-goer, the best of all boats to brave the broad wave-way.

Many weeks passed as the foam-necked sea-boat flew over the swan-path northwards until the coast was unknown, a tall ship she was journeying over the deep water hiding sea-beasts. The party put ashore for food and water, but there were days of sea-waves and nothing more. Then they saw the wave-way locked in ice-bands and felt the wind cold and bitter to them and ice-knives grew from their snot-horns. Little there was to eat then and the thanes looked to their lord. Sigurd was strong in his desire for gold-glory, told them sagely to sharpen their eye-spears for land. That was his great hope, and he would show nothing of fear to those men. Southwards slowly the boat went, and now close to a shore of sea-cliffs and headlands green with small trees, and berries and fresh water there were and fish could be caught. At such a place Sigurd decided to stay some time, moored the sea-goer and built a hut of stones for himself and the earls. Vineland he called the green-land, claimed now by the Geats. But lonely for Brestha, and the gold-glory forgotten, he spoke to the men, he told of winter coming, a need to depart until a future journey would bring them back. Wind-whips and ice-swords hunted them, hurt flesh as the sea-boat travelled the sea-waves home, and the war-chief found his bed-companion gladdened by the return and she spent her days in noble service and worthy worship of her lord. This lay is finished, song of the scop, save that none returned to the snow-land, devourer of men, where the ice-monster seals the heart.

Grkhgheeaaaa. Ugkh.

Nothing is coming through,
Those voices weren't you.
The best thing to do
Now is teach and write, too.
Keep the old with the new,
The false and the true,
Before making your debut
With the better of the two.

Writers' Workshop
Converted loft, former Great Plains Hay and Feed Company building
August 16, 7:05 p.m.

Fees: oral report, $150; written report, $250
    Panel: Gordon Mifflin, creative writing instructor, Prairie College
    (short story, "Pinto Beans," published in *Pitchfork*)
    Pam Mintz, poet and short story writer (*Up in the Hayloft*)
    Craig E. Brinton, English instructor, Prairie College (MA thesis:

"Prairie Archetypes in *Dust*")
Nina Kozenko, novelist (*Slough Woman*)

"Hello, Peter. I'll begin by summarizing the panel's reaction. Your novel, *sentence let the goodbyes go,* is obviously experimental, without chaptering, paragraphing, upper-case letters or punctuation. You describe it in your introduction as dual stream of consciousness taking place in the mind of a virgin student and an English professor as they fall in love. The interplay, as you call it, takes place beginning on page 231. Are the spots of red ink on that page deliberate? The streams run together until the breakup, somewhere between pages 1215 and 1229, it's hard to tell. And there's an additional two hundred pages. By the way, it would've helped if the pages had been numbered. I did the pagination myself, in pencil, if you're worried about that. Helped me keep track of things. The panel agrees the first problem is length. A novel written in a month is going to require editing, anyway. You should realize, if you haven't already, that marketing a novel this size would be a problem. The other area of concern has to be its experimental nature. You should be aware, if it hasn't occurred to you, that readership will be limited, and so will financial returns, if that's an important consideration. Also we have some sympathy for your idea that typos create constructive linguistic ambiguities. But you might consider using the spelling correction function in your word processing program. Some of the language was puzzling. A few examples: 'glubsucks, slickins, peesor, labsunk.' There are lots of places where the reader has to do extra work: 'has sheesh dlug ins snuf den use mus mor phened hero in my arms.' In fact, even with radical editing and rewriting your book would take months, maybe years to understand. We have to ask, is it worth it? We suggest you try again."

"Hi, I'm Pam. I'd add a couple of things to what Gordon has said. I don't know how you did all that in a month. It takes me a year to get a story right. All the nuances. Being a poet, I know the right word is vital. Size doesn't count. Try something smaller. I think of myself as a painter working on miniatures, adding one painstaking brushstroke at a time. Don't throw words around. Language is specific, not spacific. And I for one would like to see some prairie landscape described. Nina? Craig?"

"I'll jump in before Nina. Do I detect sexist rant in here? I mean, behind all the learned stuff and so on. It seems you're praising young women at the expense of older women. One could say your protagonist is a father figure committing incest. I found the love scenes boring, in the few places where I could actually read something not full of typos, tortured syntax and horrible puns. You should examine your writing for content as well as style. May be things lurking in there that you should notice. Serious problems. Nina?"

"I noticed the sexism, too. The way the student worships him is pathetic. It's the writer's sexual fantasy, not a novel. What a strange combination, an attempt at avant-garde style together with a paternalistic relationship. Is there a woman anywhere who wouldn't be insulted by the condescension? The only good thing is almost none of this screed is readable. I gave up after five hundred pages."

"Are you a masochist. I got through half that. Pam told me she managed to read almost seven hundred. Gord is the only one who looked at the whole thing. But he's used to reading aspiring novelists and handing out passing grades. This one is a sentence at hard labour for your eyes. That pun is almost bad enough to be in this book."

Prairie Herald-Times
August 17

Professor Gets in Last Word

Last night at a writers' workshop Professor Peter Sigurdsen of Prairie University attacked a panelist for remarks made about his novel. Craig Brinton, an English instructor at Prairie College, was hit over the head with a loose-leaf copy of the novel and was treated for concussion. He said Sigurdsen overreacted to constructive criticism. "He shouldn't ask for it if he can't take it. No writer has ever reacted to our criticism in this way." Brinton said he will not prefer charges. Workshops are held regularly in the former Great Plains Hay and Feed Company building on Main Street, in the old downtown core.

Conference with academic administrator
Office of Reid Abercrombie
September 12

"Bring me up to date on the visiting professor and writer-in-residence."

"Visiting professor is Colin Trott, red-brick, modern novel."

"He isn't. . . . ?"

"I checked. Nothing. Supposed to share teaching duties with Peter. But considering the way he's been going lately, we're giving Trott his seminar and upper division course. That leaves him with his second-year course."

"Good. Damage control. Peter may be leaving us, so this won't bother him. What about the other?"

"P.S. Smithson, Katie's choice again."

"She's entitled to a mistake. I've heard of him. Describes life in prairie towns years ago. Wrote a novel about the Depression."

"That's him. Very traditional."

"Good."

Faculty Club lounge
September 17

"Sigurdsen's really gone."

"What's it now?"

"He's renouncing grading and exams. Posted a notice in the department office and sent a letter to the campus newspaper. And he's admitting being too hard on masters and doctoral candidates. Says he no longer wants to be one of the crucifiers. Meaning Reynard Skinner and Ruth Braun."

"That guy who slides along the hallways whistling, ass against the wall?"

"It's like Reid's election. You've haven't been here long enough to know. Reynard's present wife, Caroline, came from Africa with her husband, a physicist, enrolled in the doctoral program and picked Reynard as her supervisor. She promptly dumped her husband, got her degree and married

Reynard, who had dumped his first wife. There's a rule, get a Prairie doctorate and you can't work here for five years. Reynard got her hired as soon as she finished and got her a graduate seminar. Other department members with more seniority had been waiting for years. Reid was still acting chairman, doing McGinty's job. He let Reynard get away with all this because he wanted the Skinners' votes, crucial in that upcoming election for the chairmanship. They knew they'd get tenure from Reid and a boot in the ass from Morell."

"So his wife has Skinner by the balls."

"He wasn't much, even before Caroline came along. Would never look you in the eye. Stared up at the ceiling when he talked to you. Wouldn't ask you to sit down when you went to see him in his office. After they got married, she would dress him in safari jackets and polyester leisure suits. Her idea of the fashionable academic. Sigurdsen can't stand them. A few years ago a cartoon was stapled to the noticeboard in the main office. Everybody knew who'd done it. Good likenesses. Especially Reynard's hair. A black plastic helmet with a ducktail. Caroline, half-bald stick, foot-long fingernails. There were written comments. 'Hank of bleached hair, leathery flat-face, cheerio accent enthusing over her favourite characters in the English novel.' Mentions her kids' names. Steerforth and Dorrit. The journal she started here. 'Publish my stuff. And my pals. Neat-o.' Went a bit far."

"When doesn't he? What about Ruth Braun?"

"She's from Midwestern. Came a year before you. Every summer she takes a trip with a platonic male friend, Laura told me. She saw her once in a mall parking lot staring out of her car window. Went over and asked if anything was wrong and Braun said she couldn't decide what to buy her father for his birthday. Laura told me she glares at handholding couples. Said two years ago she flunked everybody in her upper division course. A guy she liked was handholding with a good-looking girl in class. She gave everybody a failing grade on the final exam. Some guessed why and the honours students complained to Reid. Dave remarked the exams. Reid limits her to sophomores now. If Skinner is supervising a masters or doctoral candidate, he'll put Braun on the committee for support. And courtesy of Skinner, she teams up with him on the tenure committee."

"What a doggy face, scrawny body, and those baggy sweaters. Always a cross between those flabby tits."

"Smoker's breath, too, if you're unlucky to be close enough. The undergrad course guide warns students not to get friendly in front of her. The word is, if you get her and Reynard on your thesis committee, you're in for it. He's carrying around that load of guilt like shit in his pants. Takes it out on applicants, making up for his wife. He seems possessed, especially if Braun goads him. They try to sway the other members. It can get ugly and those two seem to love it."

"He's meek at parties. As remote as wallpaper. Talks about how safe air travel is. If he talks at all."

"Happened to see him walking to his seminar. He approached the room as if an executioner was waiting for him."

Oral examination, doctoral, pre-thesis
Room 304, Mackerness Hall
December 8, 3:00 p.m.

Kenneth Draper, doctoral candidate
Professor Reynard Skinner, supervisor
Professor Ruth Braun, committee member
Professor Dolan Mulcahey, committee member
Professor Alex Macclesfield, external examiner, Department of History

Skinner: There were questions about the adequacy of Mr. Draper's answers on the examination papers. The objections came mostly from Professor Braun, but I concurred to a certain extent. I have spoken with Mr. Draper and he has satisfied me he knows more than his answers would lead one to suspect. Consequently, I've decided this committee should meet for the oral part of the examination. Perhaps we should begin by having him outline his thesis proposal, a copy of which each of you has been given.

Draper: I'm interested in Shakespeare's depiction of innocence, especially in the tragedies. How he portrays innocence in female characters and makes them doomed symbols of purity. I'm thinking of Desdemona, Cordelia, Ophelia and also Lady MacDuff. In the romantic tragedy, *Romeo and Juliet,* both lovers can be seen as innocent. But Juliet is more sensitive to, more aware of their predicament ("wherefore art thou Romeo?"), whereas he is motivated by blind eagerness. And Romeo's banishment leads to her death. I see a pattern in the tragedies of male failure or fallibility offset, balanced by female innocence. In *MacBeth* I see delayed innocence in Lady MacBeth's insanity, felt by her husband as a death blow before MacDuff kills him.

Mulcahey: You see anything peculiar in her speeches?

Draper: How do you mean?

Mulcahey: Talks about being unsexed. She pushes the guy all the way. She's the dominant partner. She can't wipe off the blood, the woman's curse of menstruation. I think we have to see lesbian tendencies in her.

Draper: I hadn't thought of that.

Braun: Do you know Latin?

Draper: A little, from school.

Braun: Candidates should have a solid grounding in it before proceeding with any Elizabethan author.

Macclesfield: Didn't a contemporary say Shakespeare had small Latin and less Greek?

Braun: Do you know the Shakespeare bibliography well?

Draper: I've taken Professor Biddle's course.

Braun: Obviously or you wouldn't be here. But your author's bibliography. You should be able to recite the major works offhand. If I asked now?

Draper: Um.

Braun: We'll let that go for the moment. I want to get to your proposal. What exactly do you mean by innocence: simple ignorance, ideal purity, a foil to worldliness or some kind of benign stupidity? Your thesis proposal rests on that word. It should be clearly and carefully defined.

Draper: I think Shakespeare is borrowing from religion. When his tragic figures betray a woman they damn themselves, because women represent their soul.

Braun: Even if I accept that, and I'm not sure I do, your idea is thin when it's applied to Lady MacBeth.

Draper: She goads her husband to murder, like a bad angel or corrupt soul, and then goes insane, and that can be seen as punishment. And that's his punishment for listening to her. The death of Lady MacDuff and the babies is symbolic. It's the death, at least temporarily, of any hope of a successful kingship or succession because the lawful order has been upset by ambition.

Braun: How can Lady MacBeth be a corrupt soul and be innocent?

Draper: Ambition has corrupted her and she helps to corrupt MacBeth. In the king's blood she sees her guilt. Trying to rid herself of it shows her unbalanced mind destroying her ("Out, damned spot!"). She also has a new kind of awareness now ("Yet who would have thought the old man to have had so much blood in him?"). The amount is symbolic. It stands for the consequences and enormity of her crime. She has been made newly aware by insanity. I see this as a kind of innocence. Her ambition gone, she sees things differently. As if a blindfold has been taken away.

Braun: I don't see how going insane could make anybody innocent. I thought your thesis was that women in the tragedies are betrayed.

Draper: She betrays herself, but MacBeth betrays her by not saying no. He's her superior in that society and it's up to him to show good judgement.

Braun: Are you saying he doesn't keep his wife in line?

Draper: Yes.

Braun: That's hardly the same as corrupting her.

Draper: I think Shakespeare's idea is that when authority doesn't function the way it's supposed to, for whatever reason, the person responsible is to blame.

Braun: That makes Lady MacBeth a mere cipher, inherently morally subjugated.

Draper: She's a strong woman who misuses her influence as a wife. So she's betraying the moral order, too.

Braun: We're back to betrayal. Who is betraying whom?

Draper: I think they betray each other by betraying the moral order.

Skinner: Perhaps the thesis proposal could be amended. *MacBeth* could be dropped.

Braun: That would necessitate a redefinition of tragedy. I have a question about your outline. You've written, under Chapter 1, "The Elizabethan conceit and innocence." I'd like you to expand on that, giving me examples.

Draper: Shakespeare uses the extended metaphor to convey complexities of meaning. For example, Ophelia becomes identified in her madness with the flowers she talks about. She is a flower, and like the violets she mentions, has withered from Hamlet's rejection of her. The flowers Ophelia wears to the brook she drowns in are called "coronet weeds." She is mourning the death of love. And grieving over her father's death. Hamlet killing him has brought on her insanity. Cut flowers represent both lost loves. And the garland is the interweaving of those loves, and in trying to hang it on the willow (a weeping willow, conveying the idea of a woman's head hanging down, her loose hair draped in bereavement) she falls into the brook. There's also the significance of each of the flowers, such as rue. It's a symbolic language used to say what she's thinking about her father and Hamlet.

Braun: What's so innocent about a flower?

Draper: Its fresh beauty and its newness. Women, especially young women, have traditionally been compared to flowers to say they're attractive.

Braun: Not the same thing. And we don't really know she's attractive.

Draper: Hamlet calls her the "fair Ophelia."

Braun: That could be poetic licence, alliteration.

Draper: I don't think Ophelia is unattractive.

Braun: Why does she have to be beautiful?

Draper: A plain woman wouldn't get Hamlet's attention. I think that she's at least attractive.

Braun: Your assumption is presumptuous.

Draper: A leading woman in fiction or drama is usually attractive. Even girls in fairy tales, like Cinderella. Jane Eyre is an exception, but her character helps make her appealing. Personality traits can help a plain woman. Who's going to care about an ugly bitchy woman except her parents?

Braun: I think I've heard enough. I have questions on various tropes, in regard to your thesis.

Skinner: Tropes were covered in the written papers, though Mr. Draper's answers weren't entirely satisfactory. He could satisfy you on another occasion, in writing or orally. Perhaps you could arrange it with him. If there are no further questions on the thesis proposal, I will ask Mr. Draper to leave.

. . . .

Skinner: Well?

Braun: His thesis proposal is inadequate. He didn't satisfactorily define innocence, for one thing.

Skinner: Dolan, any thoughts you'd care to share?

Mulcahey: His thesis isn't revolutionary. I've heard some way-out ones. He backs up much of what he says. He's read the plays.

Skinner: Alex?

Macclesfield: He did better than many of the other candidates I've heard. He was a bit rushed, but that's to be expected from the pressure one feels.

Braun: He is obviously not ready to proceed with the thesis. The shortcomings evident on the written papers were evident here. Lack of preparation and thoroughness. More questions would have exposed more shortcomings. He should do the oral again.

Skinner: There were weak points.

Braun: He simply wasn't prepared.

Skinner: This won't happen again.

Braun: He should reconsider his thesis proposal.

Skinner: I was surprised by his lacklustre performance. The written papers again.

Braun: That's when I first began to have doubts about his candidacy. He should consider the intellectual rigors involved in attempting a doctoral thesis and whether he's actually capable.

Skinner: I'm beginning to have serious reservations.

Prairie Dog
October 7

Meeting of Dickens Scholars Disrupted

On Wednesday afternoon an unscheduled event interrupted the third day of an international symposium of Dickens scholars. During the reading of a paper on "The Primal Scene Revisited as Deathbed Mourning" by Professor Ian Mcnuthy of Southwestern A and M, a man dressed as a medical doctor and wearing a surgeon's mask wheeled a girl in front of the lectern in the SUB lecture theatre. Dressed in a white gown with "Little Nell" printed in red on it, she had gold-coloured wings attached to her shoulders. Her head was bandaged, "angel" written in red on the bandage. As the surprised scholars looked on, the man tore off his hospital gown and mask to reveal ragged clothes and another, hideous mask underneath. He hunched over the girl, who screamed, jumped up out of her wheelchair and rushed out of the lecture theatre as the man ran after her while he clutched his mask and dragged the bouncing wheelchair behind him up the stairs. Following the muted reactions of the scholars, Professor Mcnuthy finished reading and answered questions. A late arrival limped in using a cane and wearing dark glasses. The man asked the professor whether Nell was "a case of arrested nymphomania or simply a cock-teaser?" Professor Mcnuthy said he would not use such an unliterary term. He would classify her as "a little sister type who in dying achieved a spiritual orgasm for herself and the author, the deathbed eroticism having a deeper level, a transmuted primal scene of girl-woman transference hidden by the author's love for his sister-in-law, who died young." The questioner said the professor was "confusing aesthetic pedophilia with the Oedipal complex, seeing a mother where there was a girl's hairless pudendum under delectably arrayed bedclothes." Professor Mcnuthy said that "the girl's very youth makes her an acceptable mother substitute, defusing the guilt." Turning to hobble away the questioner said the professor "wouldn't know a nymph if she asked him to feel her up."

At the session today Professor Ved Varma will read his paper, "A Survey of Pagan Archetypes in Dickens' London," and the symposium will conclude on Friday, when Dr. Ursula Duboyne will present a paper, "The Dread of Drood," a chapter from her forthcoming book, *Uncovering Dickens' Demons: Personal Horrors in the Shadows.*

Journal of Victorian Research
Fall, 20—

Victorian Fiction: Stasis and Flux
David Krieghammer, Prairie University

In the lengthy exegesis that is the usual Victorian novel, pathologies are depicted as character traits, sentimental, quirky, humorous or villainous. Obvious cases of psychosis, such as Mr. Rochester's wife, are treated with an almost eighteenth century mixture of horror and voyeurism. That pre-psychoanalytic age had no way to delve into the recesses of human cognition to reach a more profound understanding of psychoses. And compounding this was a rudimentary awareness of nutrition and digestion and an ignorance of the relationship between brain and gut. Novelists could offer only social remedies for problems sourced in the physiological depths. Dickens attacks the poor laws, schools, the court of chancery, slums, industrialism. In the smoky industrial atmosphere of Coketown Josiah Bounderby suddenly drops dead of a stroke in the middle of the street, Smike dies from mistreatment at Dotheboys Hall, whereas lucky Oliver is rescued from the workhouse and Fagin, and Pip is made to see the hollowness of his snobbery through Magwitch. Very convenient morally but not the whole truth. For that we have to examine something else in these and other novels of the time, a sense of unease, of unfinished business close at hand that cannot be accomplished, some nagging affliction going uncured, and a resulting frustration and gloom. Psychological stasis, and the reason physical, the toilet.

Brain and gut are made of the same material, so a problem in one area is felt in the other. The slum and working-class diet of the time was little better than fat and offal, led to rickets, pellagra and scurvy, outright and subclinical. But for an examination of contemporary fiction, the diet of the middle class is far more germane. That diet of fatty meats and viscous gravies, peeled boiled potatoes, and refined white flour and sugar in bread and desserts guaranteed poor digestion and intestinal blockages, and a bowel movement perhaps every four or five days if not longer. Coupled with a lack of exercise and fresh air and sunshine in polluted cities (hint of racism here, too, white bread and white skin both being highly prized), such a diet meant frequent recourse to nerve tonics such as Mrs. Leakey's Restorative Tonic and Dr. Ridley's Evening Elixir, consisting mainly of alcohol and sugar. Some women inevitably became semi-invalids, neurasthenics subsisting on these quack remedies. Many men smoked, adding more pollution to lungs and home and complicating the effects of bowel blockages. Those strained faces in photographs are sadly lacking colonic irrigation. Solemn and serious, they reflect a buildup of waste products, and because hot spices were not widely used in Britain, a natural flux was lacking. Victorians did use laxatives such as castor oil, but they further weakened the digestive system, flushing out beneficial bacteria while not affecting intestinal parasites imbibed from tainted food and unfiltered water. Prevailing standards of hygiene undoubtedly contributed parasites as well, most toilet facilities still being rudimentary. Many in the middle class were always waiting for something to happen. An endless cycle of blockage and purge only enervated the victims. The taboo of the toilet ensured silent suffering, and strain had to seek other outlets.

In Victorian fiction the long slow unwinding of complicated plots, the lengthy paragraphs and dialogues and heavily punctuated sentences all reflect a stasis being slowly and painfully overcome, in contrast to the flux of sudden dramatic force that generally occurs at the end and clears the air. The euphoric effect of sudden relief is felt by the modern reader to be arbitrary and unnatural. Within this context of strain and release there is an attempt to reach equilibrium, to establish a more natural flow of events. This is elusive, the author frequently having to assist good winning out over evil as the reader waits and watches the convolutions of the plot. What did kill Bounderby? His own choleric temperament, as Dickens leads us to believe, or rather a hypertensive and constipating diet of salt beef, saddles of mutton and pork roasts and goose, which led to arteriosclerosis and atherosclerosis, and undoubtedly very high homocysteine levels from the digestion of so much protein. On the fateful day the pollutants in the Coketown air added the final touch, after smoky decades of free radical damage. One dead Benthamite, unmourned except perhaps by parasites looking for another home. Certainly less visible than the various streams of lice that left Thomas à Becket as he lay dead on the flagstones of Canterbury Cathedral,[1] they were probably more harmful in their effect on health, breeding on impacted hard stools clogging and putrefying in the intestines. Such stools had even led to strokes and cardiac arrest. George II died straining on a toilet.[2]

If we look for an emblem, an archetype thrown up by the subconscious to show how far constipation could go, it must be Miss Havisham's wedding feast that never was, a travesty of mouldy cakes and soiled garments. In the dark bowels of her house, drapes closed, she feeds on her own entrails, festering in her shame and imparting her poison to Estella, who in turn infects Pip. When he finds the source of his snobbish expectations is not the jilted woman but the convict Magwitch, and the taint of filthy lucre clings to him as well as his benefactor, he is purged of conceit and of false pride. The purge of fire comes to the bitter woman too late. It kills instead of liberates. Peristalsis proves too much after so many years of congested self-poisoning. When Estella and Pip meet in the burnt ruins of her house, they find they have been released from the bowels of their prison into free air. He has already sought the forgiveness of Joe and Biddy for his previous conduct towards them, and they, living on wholesome country food and out in the windy air of the marshes have no stasis to overcome. They lead simple regular lives. But the lawyer Jaggers, constantly washing his hands, goes on ministering to a society immured in filth, the product of a diet lacking the raw stuff of life and the fibre of hope to carry it through, and which must subsist on fantasies of

---

[1] Edmund de Loussier, "The Blisful Martir's Ende," *Chronicles, BM MSS, 153-5.*
[2] John Badham, Lord Exeter, "His Royal Majesty Passes," ch. xv of *The Full and Glorious Reign of George II,* London, 1772, pp. 159-62.

freedom. A combination legal proctologist and peddler of fake remedies, he probes into the social depths, making a career out of misery. Nothing moves easily down there, and even the lives of the privileged suffer from a common need.

If Miss Havisham is an archetype of self-destructive Victorian constipation, Heathcliff surely is one of psychopathic behaviour resulting from intestinal blockages. His monomania about the dead Cathy and his lengthy revenge upon the next generation are almost unreal, and critics have speculated widely on the origins of the dark boy Mr. Earnshaw brings home from Liverpool.[3] The answer to his complexion and behaviour actually lies in diet. When he is brought to Thrushcross Grange he is a starving street urchin whose racial origins are probably Celtic and more specifically Irish, and his natural pigmentation has been further darkened by malnutrition and subclinical jaundice. He eats better but the milk and meat and white flour and refined sugar ensure he will have nutritional deficiencies and stasis. A lack of fresh vegetables and fruit would aggravate his inherently moody temperament[4] and lead to an abnormal behavioural pattern.[5] What began as incipient paranoia, fed by Heathcliff's diet and outsider status at the grange, ensured his love would become obsessive after Cathy's death and finally monomania.[6] Loving a dead woman is easy for him because he's dead inside and the only flux that can free him is death. Even revenge proves unsatisfactory and he yearns for the end. In a repudiation of the poisons that have clogged and corroded his bowels he starves himself, hoping to bring about reunification in a gutless world. Though the vengeance he planned and

---

[3] See Sadhu Mukherjee, "The East Indian Origins of Sahib Heathcliff," *Anglo-Indian Review*, vol. 22 (Feb., 1993), pp. 83-89; and Steve Zanetti, "The Case for Heathcliff as an Extraterrestrial," *Journal of Cosmological Studies*, vol. 1 (1998), pp. 18-26.
[4] Dr. Gebhard Aschoff, "Phytosomes and Mood Disorders," *Current Psychoanalysis*, vol. 2 (January, 2015), pp. 60-81.
[5] Michael Manners, "The Role of Anthocyanins in Sociopathic Behaviour," *Creative Sociology Review*, vol. 1, new series, (May, 2010), pp. 106-17.
[6] Friedrich Münch, *Paranoia, Its Origins and Diagnosis,* Heidelberg, 1901, 1986 trans. of 2nd rev. ed., pp. 10-25; Max Lichtenfels, *Leib und Drang,* Potsdam, 1975, pp. 29-43.

executed eventually bears different fruit, he has chosen far different nourishment.

So the middle class was not alone in choosing a bad diet. In the countryside many of the lesser gentry took to eating white bread and refined sugar as a mark of class. The wholesome rural diet had had its defiers, including the squire laid up with a painful foot because of gout from uric acid in wine and meat. He was becoming rare, but so were coarse peasant bread and other healthy fibre-rich foods. The ploughman's lunch of wholegrain bread, cheese and onion lost out to sugary jams and white loaves. Cookbooks such as *Ye Olde Potte, Its Usse* (1614), *Atte the Merrie Hearthe* (1679), and *Moll's Favourites, being a true account of diverse savourie dishes served at the tables of Fashionable Householdes* (1725), had fallen out of favour, replaced by *Mrs. Terwilliger's Complete Cookery* (1847) and *The Housewife's Kitchen Guide* (1889).[7] Recipes using denatured ingredients replaced traditional favourites using whole-food ones. Tea and coffee made even greater inroads than in the eighteenth century, adding their dehydrating and acidic effects to the general malaise. We should not be surprised at the flighty women, town and country, we encounter in Victorian novels. Dora Spenlow and Rosamund Vincy show symptoms of sucrose and caffeine addiction. Constipation has been complicated by pancreatic distress and natural equilibrium upset by frenetic highs and lows. Giddy selfish behaviour of impaired constitutions leads to nothing except misery for the men who love these women. If we limit our understanding of postulated character traits to genetic inheritance or to social conditioning, these and other works in which such characters appear are seen as simple exercises in artistic imagination, not examples of a matrix of accumulated behaviours. Surely diet is part of the matrix, and bad diet and behaviour related, though presented to the reader after having passed through the author's imagination. Behavioural defects related to alcoholism abound in stories, the relationship obvious and accepted, and so should the more subtle effects of food on a character's disposition towards others and view of life.

Because the toilet taboo put a lid on any discussion of bowel problems, it

---

[7] Gertrude Parmenter, *A History of English Cookbooks*, Tynehead, 2008.

was through the unconscious that novelists sought ways of expressing discomfort. Dickens found an outlet in what have been called his "grotesque" characters, those oddities of his imagination presented like creatures in dreams or nightmares. They are, in fact, the counterpart of his ideal characters, in particular his heroines, like Agnes Wickfield and Esther Summerson, bodiless creatures who lack intestines as well as personality and represent a standard of behaviour impossible even for Victorians. It is his grotesques who provide fitful glimpses into a subconscious tortured by repressed sexual desires and anal eroticism.[8] For if the gut is crammed with the poisons of improper nutrition, it is also a place of forbidden desires.[9] In his contortions of humility Uriah Heep winds himself around Agnes Wickfield like a snake, insinuating himself into her pure being, the more attractive for being so spotless. Moral dirt transmuted into a writhing excuse for his origins at the lower end of society, he is a snake of constipated feces attempting to enter and so violate the sanctity of an impossibly clean embodiment of the more public virtues of the middle class. He is exposed finally by another grotesque, Mr. Micawber, whose anal fantasies revolve around his philosophy of money and so is no threat to the threatened heroine. But a shared subconscious desire enables him to understand the villain and foil him. Dora Spenlow conveniently dies, a victim of constipation and debilitation, and David Copperfield can be remarried to someone untouched by the nutritional deficiencies of the Victorian diet. His characters names reveal Dickens' unconscious intentions. Uriah Heep urinates on his own pile of feces, an act of self-loathing and

---

[8] See Milton Abrams' pioneering work, *The Hidden Dickens: Comic and Serious Grotesques,* New York, 1957; also Barry Mikowski, "Anal Eroticism, Victorian Style," *Journal of Victorian Research,* vol. 2 (April, 2012), pp. 39-45; Lynette Pontillo, "Little Nell in Bed," *Victorian Themes,* vol. 1 (October, 2013), pp. 70-79; Kelsey Leutsen, "Why I Like Reading Dickens with My Breakfast Bran Flakes," *Prairie Elementary Teachers Monthly,* vol. 11 (Feb., 2016), pp. 52-54 (prize winning grade six essay); Pamela "Peachy Cheeks" Borukhovich, "In Taking Off a G String Don't Forget the Second Hole," *Strippers Bulletin,* No. 28 (Sept., 2018), pp. 9-12.

[9] The classic works in this field are Heinrich Schickendantz, *General Theory of Erotic Impulses, Manifestations and Outlets,* Jena, 1995 trans. of rev. 1923 ed.; and Wilhelm Stahnke, *Auf die Stürm unter Alles,* Berlin, 1929.

perversely proud exhibitionism. Mr. Macawber is a crow, a somewhat comical scavenger threatening no one. Spenlow has spent her childish life of little value, a victim of too many teas. Wickfield is an unfleshed candle, an idealized personification of a string of entrails free of dirt and therefore of reality. There can be no fire, no germination in that barren place. Nothing will grow in Wickfield, who, like an unconsciously ironic answer to a society poisoning itself through bad eating habits, can offer purity only as unreality, and like a mirror image her perverse attraction as an anally ideal lust fantasy.

Stasis meant solidity to the Victorians and they accepted it as part of their serious view of life. It became a moral statement, part of the spirit of the time, constipation being punishment for having bowels and having to evacuate them. Unrelieved irregularity meant slow poisoning, and many became bedridden or eccentric. In creating harmless eccentrics and malevolent villains, novelists were actually describing the effects of bowel poisoning.[10] Another drama was taking place under their noses.[11] There was the long wait and then the foul smell of hard stools that had festered inside for a week or longer, and the bleeding of swollen painful veins protruding from the anus like a bunch of hard rubber berries. Induced flux brought its own discomfort and weakness and stench and stains and embarrassing recurring episodes. The body would suffer from this cycle, long accumulating wastes before voiding them uncontrollably in spasms. Stinking noisy flatulence would accompany each part of the cycle, disastrous if discharged in company, and especially at dinner parties or dances. Fainting fits may have been induced to avoid such social catastrophes. Behind the fictional world lay the thwarted urge to be regular and the body's borborygmus against stasis. Underneath all the comedy and tears was a wordless groan.

---

[10] Merwin Peesley, "Nutraceuticals and Literary Criticism," *Post-Modern Q & A,* vol. 3 (Nov., 2009), pp. 86-101.
[11] Beard Pugh, "Victorian Toilets and Bathroom Habits," *Journal of Social Pathology,* vol. 9 (Dec., 2015), pp. 60-74; John Trench, "Why Go To the Bathroom?" *Aseptic Studies,* vol. 1 (inaugural all-toilets issue, Aug., 2017), pp. 1-2 et passim.

Faculty Club lounge
October 9

"You should've been at the Abercrombie's Saturday night. The new visiting professor, Colin Trott, was there. Sigurdsen showed up and got drunk and started talking about him. 'Look at that, monkey body, ratty beard, blue eyes on a mission.' Trott heard and came over. 'What did you say?' Trott's face was red. Sigurdsen laughed. 'You're still preaching the anti-industrial message in the computer age. Your favourite word, "plastic." I'm sick of your English prophet school, finding sexual salvation in the sacred temple of the body. Looking for an intellectually respectable way to have an orgy, transcendence through arousal, heaven on earth as your very own personal angel with genitals. Sex isn't holy, it's a hole. Any religious hermit eating flies could have told you that. You don't understand what every Roman aristocrat took in with his first sip of sin. Some of us do and others don't, some consider what others won't. That's why they're called the facts of life and not the principles. You're peddling bargain-basement metaphysics. Glimpse of heaven through a hole. You're a scholarship boy from the working class, full of sublimated rage. And you're maritally well equipped. Your mate is more than flat enough to be a martyr's wife. And wears enough makeup to look worse than if she wore none. Cotton underwear, I'll bet. Only white, covering upper thighs and buttocks.'"

"He's really lost it. What happened?"

"Trott and his wife left. Laura and Reid looked properly shocked. They don't like the Trotts. Had their fill of Colin Trott saying the department is 'acceptable' and the living accommodations 'adequate,' and as well his wife finding Prairie City 'quite a change.'"

"Why did they bother coming here?"

"Money. Makes more in one year at Prairie than in four at his Midlands red-brick. I don't think Reid wants another visiting professor. Between this one and Ashenden-Boyce he's had enough."

"Don't forget our previous writer-in-residence. The new one won't give him any trouble. They got him out of a nursing home. Wasn't there anybody else who was safe?"

"Selonica Dutts. Dozens of departments are after her. Woman, person of colour, bisexual and paraplegic. Can't miss. Creative Writing suggested her on the outside chance she'd consider coming here. But Reid wasn't interested."

"Why? Because. . . ."

"Yeah. And. . . ."

"Of course, I'm not. . . ."

"Me neither. It actually comes down to a. . . ."

"What's her stuff like?"

"Magazine verse. Original as tap water. She writes about metres. Never gets past iambic. Too busy explaining how complicated it is."

"I suppose for her. . . ."

"It would seem so."

Prairie Alumni
September

Appointment

The English Department announces the appointment of P. S. Smithson as its new writer-in-residence. He will be on campus beginning in November. A fixture in prairie literature since the 1930s, he is well known for his memorable tales of hardworking farmers and townsfolk. Their courage during the Depression is depicted in stories such as "Don't Hitchhike," "The Harrow Cuts Deep," "Drugstore Girl" and "Haywire Outfit," and in his novel, *Dust*. Regrettably, his stories and novel have been out of print for decades. But the new Prairie University Press commemorative limited edition of Smithson's works will be issued this fall. To those who have admired his writing, this has been long overdue.

P. S. Smithson succeeds the poet, Marlene Stumpf, who had to leave because of health problems due to injuries suffered in a vehicle accident. Afterwards, campus police had to restrain her forcibly when she attacked the driver of the car that backed into her motorcycle. The driver, Professor Peter Sigurdsen of the English Department, apparently made some remarks to her. Dismissing rumours, the chairman of the department, Reid Abercrombie, said the noise of traffic in the parking lot led both parties to misunderstand one another. "Professor Sigurdsen, who unfortunately received a couple of black eyes and a bloody nose in their altercation, actually said 'Unlucky bike' to Ms Stumpf and, a bit garbled in the heat of the moment, her words to Peter were 'You're a little quick, you shift, get stuck.'"

Dust

Chapter 1
The Storm Comes to Ryerson

The storm settled in over Ryerson Junction in the afternoon. From far away it looked like a dirty pillow smothering the land. As it got closer the sky darkened, then everything was brown dust in the eyes and grit in the mouth and the blowing noise of the wind. Women held onto their hems and hats, bending over as they walked. It was a hot Thursday in August, nobody was wearing a coat. Everybody hurried to get inside, mothers dragging their children or hollering at them to catch up or they would be blown away. It wasn't that windy but the kids got scared and caught up. Mothers fastened a hand and pulled, small shoes dragged, scraping dirt. One block long, Main Street was emptying fast. In ten minutes only a crumpled sheet of newspaper was tumbling in spurts along the dirt road.

"A little more hopeless in a big wide world of it," Maud Appleby said to her husband as they watched from the general store window. Thin and with a narrow face, there were streaks of grey in her hair, gathered into a bun at the back.

"I guess," Jonas Appleby said. He was a bald slack-bellied man in his early sixties who wore no jacket that day but red suspenders with a tan checked shirt and brown pants.

The Applebys owned the only store in that town of less than five hundred. Besides food and clothes, they sold harnesses and farm implements. There was a bigger store in Bettersley, a larger town about twelve miles away. But local people liked coming in to Ryerson and buying what was available and ordering other things. A train came through once a week on a spur line, a mixed freight and passenger service. No one could remember how the place got its name. It wasn't a rail junction. Someone made a mistake or had a strange sense of humour. Somebody remembered somebody saying a junction was planned but never happened. The name stuck, though everybody around shortened it to Ryerson. Both names appeared on the faded signboard hanging outside the one-room station a block off Main Street. The Applebys were born on nearby farms. They bought the store from old Andrew Macphipps fourteen years ago. An uncle had died, leaving Jonas some money. What they got for their farm made up the rest of the purchase price. The Twenties were good but now in 1933, nearly four years into the Depression, they were barely making a living. They looked on silently for a while, the future seeming as bleak as the storm swallowing up their store in dusty obliteration.

"Where's Blessed Thanks?" Maud Appleby suddenly asked in her sharp-edged voice.

"Darned if I know. She sure gets around."

Blessed Thanks Leah Ruth was their daughter. She was called Leah by almost everybody except her parents. She had been a child of their middle age and they had unabashedly put their gratitude into her first two names. Seventeen now, she was the belle of the town and the surrounding area, a dimpled blonde with a lissome figure and the prettiest of faces. At the Saturday night barn dances she was in demand by all the young men. She played no favourites and teased them all. The other girls envied her. They would imitate her slow fetching walk and the way she dressed in the bright-coloured clothes sewed by Maud. She would be finishing high school next June, her parents planning on sending her to teachers' college. Leah was not sure about that and yet did not say anything to them. She worked at the small soda fountain in the store, gathering the young men and girls around her like flame-transfixed moths. She dreamed of leaving, but not to return as a teacher in the small schoolhouse, as her mother and father wished. That was not the future she wanted. She was going to be a great actress far away in a big city. Late at night Leah would stand in front of her dresser mirror in underclothes and look at herself, wishing for more opulence in her youthful figure of soft swellings and protruding angles but not too dissatisfied with the girlish beauty she saw blossoming in the flattering glass. Photographs from movie magazines framed her image, smiling faces tucked between the mirror and the wood frame. It was no good telling anyone how real the dream was. Nobody would understand her feeling of knowing what was bound to happen.

"Should be home, out of this. I don't know, I really don't."

Maud turned from the window and looked at her husband. Meeting her gaze, he tried not to think about declining trade and unpaid bills.

"No need to fret. Most likely she's staying at a friend's."

It was hard to see across the street, but out of the blowing dust a figure emerged.

"Here comes Shabby," Maud said.

Sure enough, it was Shabby Gunderson. In bib overalls, hand clamping a straw hat onto his head as he leaned his bulk into the wind, he was making his way to the store. The door opened and he brought the dust and whistling wind in with him. He used his back to force it shut. He took off the hat, showing cropped and greying hair on his large head. His voice was light for a big man.

"Did Fred show up?"

Jonas shook his head.

"Don't guess he will now."

"Elsie had, you know, her heart set on getting those new patterns. I come all the way in for them. Started before the blow. Had to hitch the team up at Johnson's. Walk the rest of the way."

"This will finish the crop," Jonas said. "What's left of it after the drought."

"Farmer gets little enough for his grain nowadays, anyway," Shabby said. "I'll go on back to Johnson's."

"You're welcome to wait here till she lets up a mite."

"Thanks, I'll wait there. Elsie will be wondering about me."

Shabby made a farewell gesture with his hat and they nodded. He put the hat on, held it firmly and turned the doorknob, its white enamel worn down around the rim to the dull metal underneath. The door burst open, banging against him. He grabbed it, forced himself into the opening and pulled it shut behind him. The Applebys felt a blast on their faces. Moments later a bulky shape disappeared into the brown wind. Along the tan linoleum floor, beginning where frame moulding and door met, a pale triangle of dust expanded towards Maud and Jonas.

"Imagine coming all the way in through this for patterns," Jonas said.

"You know Elsie Gunderson," was the dry response.

A few miles outside of town a beige sedan was parked at the side of the road. Anybody passing by would have seen through the murky air a faint outline that looked like a large stranded animal huddled against the grey planks of weathered fencing. On the rear seat and in the trunk were suitcases. A man in his early thirties and a girl of seventeen sat apart on the front seat. Dark and sharp-eyed and with a pencil mustache, Fred Salter was a travelling salesman with lines in ladies' notions and fabrics. He came through town every couple of months with merchandise and samples to take and fill orders. He glared at the girl. She stared out of the windshield at the brown whirling air as she heard him.

"Why not?"

"Don't feel like it."

"You said you would."

"I changed my mind. I can change my mind."

He leaned over and put his arms around her and tried to kiss her. She pushed him away.

"Let me go."

"Come on, honey."

"I'll get out."

"In this wind? Try it."

"I will so."

"I brought the necklace. The one I told you about."

"Keep it."

"Be nice." He put his arms around her.

"Stop it. I'll open the door."

"Somebody's going to be first and it might as well be me."

He grabbed her and held her tightly, shoving her back into the seat cushion and forcing his lips down onto hers, and her lips squirmed and she brought up her hand like a claw and scratched the side of his face.

"Ow. You bitch."

He felt his cheek and she opened the door and was gone.

"Better come back," he yelled, the answer coming in a shrieking howl of wind.

The storm lasted until Saturday. Then word got around Leah Appleby was missing. A search party went over the countryside. On Sunday morning her body was found. She was lying almost covered with blown earth in a field, her mouth in a last effort to find breath open and filled with dust.

Seminar in Prairie Literature
Katie Krips' house, Belvedere
November 15, 7:00 p.m.

"Is everyone here, Carmen?"

"All ten of us."

"If you would place your cushions and pillows in a semicircle. You can put your drinks on the floor. We can get started. Tonight we are going to welcome to Prairie University a pioneer in prairie literature, P. S. Smithson. By the way, they're hoping to get the limited edition in the campus bookstore by the end of the month. I've been on to the university press about the delay and they say there's a backlog of other stuff. Until we get the new edition, we're going to have to share my old copies of the collected stories and *Dust*. Please be careful of the binding. Some of the pages are loose. Don't spill anything on them, mark them up or turn the corners of the pages. I asked the university library about copies but they don't have any. They had a copy of the stories years ago but it's gone. Same at the city library. I had planned to show you the film of *Dust* made in the Sixties by a local theatre company with a federal cultural grant. I was going to have the national archives make a copy of theirs but was told it isn't in a fit state to be shown. It's deteriorated beyond saving, something to do with acetate or humidity. There could be another copy somewhere, but if there is it's probably beyond repair, too. I remember seeing the movie when I was an undergrad. Made me aware of heartland life. I went into grad studies, did my MA at PU on him. Before P. S. Smithson there were only—I shouldn't say only—the journals of Harriet McGinty, that wonderful pioneer woman. His was the first work of the modern era to depict truthfully the lives of farmers and people in small towns. Anybody writing today about heartland life owes him a debt. Enough of this, you came to hear the man himself. The best way to begin is to have him give you an overview of his work, and you can ask questions afterwards. If you'd. . . . Where did he go?"

"I think he's in the bathroom, Katie."

"I'll get him. P. S.? You in there? Something wrong, P. S.? We're waiting. You need help? Carmen."

"What's wrong?"

"Not sure. The water's running. He's locked the door. I'll get the key."

. . . .

"Finally found it. Let me get this open."

"He's halfway out the window."

"Get down from there, you'll hurt yourself. Help me drag him in. Don't fight us, we're trying to help you. Let's put him in the bathtub for now."

"Doesn't he realize he'd freeze out there?"

"I've given up trying to figure out what he realizes. I'd have left him in that home if I'd known this was going to happen. I thought I could look after him. But it's too much for me. Nobody mentioned his writing there. I've brought it all back. When I mention *Dust* he gets a faraway look in his eyes. See what I mean? Stay right where you are, mister. I'm tired of chasing after you."

"What are you going to do?"

"Put him in the university hospital. They can send him back."

Prairie Herald-Times
November 19

Writer Missing

P. S. Smithson, prairie novelist and short story writer, left his bed in the university hospital Friday night and wandered away. He was wearing only pyjamas. The university's current writer-in-residence, he had been admitted for a rest. Katie Krips of the English Department said the duties of his position had exhausted him. She expressed concern because of his age, 101, and the recent plunge in temperature. "He's from tough pioneer stock, so I'm hopeful," she said. "But his pyjamas aren't much against this cold."

Prairie Herald-Times
November 20

Missing Writer Found Dead

Writer P. S. Smithson was found dead Saturday morning by the side of the freeway on the outskirts of the city. Two boys found the body on their way to a skating rink. He had frozen stiff and fallen over, right arm still extended, the hand in a fist and thumb raised in the traditional hitchhiking position. Wearing only pyjamas, Smithson wandered away from the university hospital Friday night. He had been admitted for a rest. When informed of his death, Katie Krips of the English Department said, "It's a very sad day indeed for all lovers of prairie literature as well as a great personal loss to those who knew and admired him." The way Smithson died reminded her "ironically and poignantly of his short story, 'Don't Hitchhike.' It's my favourite for so many reasons." She believes that he was trying to return to his home town, Smithers Junction, disincorporated in 1933 because of depopulation and the discontinuation of rail service. Smithson, 101, lived in a nursing home for the last five years.

Dust

Chapter 15
The Last

Almost everybody had left Ryerson Junction. The schoolhouse was closed because there were not enough children. The café and the blacksmith's and both boardinghouses were closed. No trains came any more. The general store was open only two days a week for a few hours. Hardly anybody bought anything. The Applebys did not seem to care. Maud did not appear in public. Jonas had stopped ordering stock. The Presbyterian and Anglican churches held shortened Sunday morning services for the few members left and Sunday school classes had been cancelled. There was some talk of combining the small congregations but that had not happened. There was talk of disincorporating the town. Most of the first families to settle there had departed: the MacDonalds, the Woods, the Duncans, the Johnsons, the Greys, the Thurlows and the Farnsworths. Most farmers in the area had given up their drought-parched, eroded acres and gone elsewhere. Debts had risen, mortgages went unpaid, foreclosures fell thick and fast and wagon and tire tracks marked for a last time the desperately arid and forsaken earth. They had arrived a couple of generations earlier. Now the land had let them down. But the land was not inexhaustibly fertile and the weather attacked a soil depleted after too many crops without a rest. Some departing went to rural areas elsewhere but many went far beyond the prairies. Under that wide tall sky and creeping along the flat ravaged earth, modern wagon trains trailed away into an uncertain sunset. An invisible substance began covering Ryerson, the dust of despair.

Shabby Gunderson came by the store for the last time. Maud was too sick to see him or Elsie and the kids. Jonas stood behind the scarred counter, with its jars of candy and cut plugs of chewing tobacco. Leaving Elsie outside, Shabby came in to say goodbye and the men shook hands.

"Fellow don't know where to go these days. Seems like it's hard for most everybody. We'll head for the coast. I'm pretty handy around machines, after fixing my old tractor and jalopy and others around these parts. Something probably turn up."

"I guess," was Jonas' slow answer, and seeing the children sitting beside their mother, "Take some candy to your boy and girl."

Afterwards he went to his wife, lying in their bed upstairs. She barely moved her head when he came into the room. He sat on the edge of the bed and looked at her, the wasted face and sunken eyes, the faint line of a mustache on her lip. What was left except to watch her die? He spent hours like that every day, watching and waiting for more than a stare. When getting into bed at night he moved carefully so as not to disturb her, even though he knew nothing would. It was part of making himself believe she would recover. That belief seemed to grow stronger as she was weakening, as if he was trying to compensate for the strength slowly ebbing out of her. The doctor, who came in from Bettersley, said she would probably recover if she went somewhere else. As he sat looking down at her, he thought about the doctor's warning about her dying unless a move happened fast. They would have to leave everything except what could be carried in their car, because no one was buying anything now. The bank would get the store and the land it sat on, an auction the answer for the rest to bring in some money. Very little, considering the few who came to the store lately and what they bought. People were making do with almost nothing, were trying to survive after years of loss and want. Patched clothes covered the rumbling in their bellies. Moving like scarecrows in a faint breeze, not caring whether others noticed listless limbs and gaunt faces, the constant thinking about food making everything else unimportant. They appeared to grow out of the parched and drifting soil, a crop of beings not quite whole in body or spirit.

Outside the wind increased, picking up dust and whirling it into eddies and small tornadoes, filling the empty street and the abandoned yards. Making doors and shutters creak and bang on deserted houses, it whistled through bare branches of trees. Like the people, the earth was moving. It was a blind flight to nowhere.

Shabby Gunderson stopped a mile from town. He was heading west, towards Bettersley, where some cousins of his wife were going to put them up for a few nights. He turned off the engine and it chugged to a final shudder. Elsie waited for him to speak.

"She won't last," he said.

"Don't I know. Leah done it to her."

"That was hard for her to take. Leah dying like that."

"It wasn't that. Not all of it. Those movie star dreams fixed Leah. And Salter."

"What did he have to do with it?"

"Didn't you see him at the church picnic last year? Playing up to her. Answer me this. What was she doing all alone out in that field?"

"Never thought about it."

"Didn't Sergeant MacAllister say at the inquest that her dress was torn on the left shoulder and her mouth had a bruise on it? Dr. Cunningham couldn't guarantee storm did either."

"Coroner said death was due to natural causes. Used a long word. Meant she couldn't breathe. She was out there at the height of the storm."

"I remember the word. Asphyxiation. More to it than that. Why hasn't Salter come back?"

"Because nobody's buying nothing."

"Nobody's bought much for a long time and he still come. For Leah."

"How do you know?"

"Leah told me. She couldn't tell Maud. You know what Maud would've done about her sneaking around with Salter. He wanted her to go away with him. Said he was going to get her into the movies. The day before the storm she come out to our place and asked me what to do. I told her, 'Don't you ever believe him.' She told me she was going to say no, and I sent you for the patterns to see if he was there. I got to thinking he might convince her. Thought maybe seeing you she'd be reminded of what I'd said."

"Seeing me? If she wanted to run off with him, she'd have done it."

"I suppose. Can't help blaming myself, though. Guess she liked him enough to say why she wouldn't go. And I guess he tried to get what he could and she ran out into the storm. She was lost."

Shabby looked at the brown pillow of dust on the western horizon.

"We better go. Another storm coming. Seems though it's never going to stop. So long, Ryerson."

The engine shook roughly, blurting its rude exhaust. The battered and heavily laden car moved off in a groaning and tipping crawl. Bald tires left faint tracks in the dirt. In minutes the wind blew them away. Everything faded before vanishing in the dust.

Mailbox, Alison Janeway
Main office, English Department
February 13
Untitled, written in red ink

> Beauty, speak thy fame/claim.
> Thou takest vanity
> For another name/dame.
> The prize be forfeit
> And the loss no shame/blame
> When thou seest
> They are not the same/game.
> > Be seeing you, anon.

Mailbox, A. Janeway
October 30

> Love and hate are much allied;
> The one is mistress to the other's pride.

Prairie Herald-Times
November 29

Suicide in University Area

On Sunday Alison Janeway, a professor at Prairie University, was found dead in her garage. She was sitting in her car, windows open and the engine running. A passing neighbour saw exhaust coming from under the garage door and called the police. An apparent suicide, she died from the inhalation of carbon monoxide. Police didn't find a note. Janeway, 46, lived alone in her small house in Belvedere. Neighbours said she didn't entertain and kept mostly to herself. She taught at the university for nineteen years. Chairman

Reid Abercrombie of the English Department said in a statement, "Alison was a dedicated Old English scholar and a valued member of our staff. She was generous to students with her time and support. She will be missed by them and by her colleagues."

From the Sigurdsen Notebooks
Critical Tales
January

Holy Texts

And it came to pass that the word was given to certain holy men and these men did preach to the multitudes that did gather unto them. And these prophets did speak of wondrous things, of an understanding that passeth peace, and said it would be given to those whom these lords of understanding did so wish at certain holy places of sacred trust in the true word. At such places the prophets stood on high and delivereth the word that had been given unto them, and the faithful gathered round about did inscribe these truths on tablets, to utter to the prophets whensoever those holiest of men wished. The faithful were told of distant lands called Versa and Talesia, Dramalan and Novelitica, where there was great travail and sacred and profane love and some indiscretions. Such things were in strange tongues and only those holiest understood when they went to those places.

Returning therefrom they spoke in the common tongue and with a great cunning to tell of those distant lands, and then were the holy texts written and were preached, and the true believers did receive them with unbounded joy, giving many hard years to study the word and not caring for worldly pleasures, the false delights of Sensuelle. For neither in fleshpots nor in vain pursuits could the word be heard, but only when the voices of those holy men, prophets of wisdom, did speak.

It so happened that the prophets grew exceeding wroth with each other and fell out of friendship. Then was brother against brother, the faithful dividing into camps that made war each upon the other. Each claimed the word unto itself, and verily a great din arose to the heavens. The several tribes journeyed unto lands of silk and money and great was the rejoicing. And in each did men erect a temple and builded in it a shrine of numberless rooms to their one true prophet and some became disciples to know the true sayings of the peoples in those distant lands, their chants and tales, and unto disciples of exceeding devotion was given a coat of many colours, the bamaphd, scarlet and blue and gold and lined with purple, and these fortunate ones did verily rejoice in the word and from them a shouting as of thunder arose out of the temples to the joyous heavens high and mighty, resounding to their worship of the truth.

And soon texts begat Techs and ITs and A and Ms. And great faith did abide in each tribe of the bamaphds. As each held its sacred text holiest, so amongst the brethren were more and more wondrous things being gathered from it. For they did verily believe that to go unto the distant lands was to make a perilous journey without the word. The word, all bamaphds said of their own, madeth the passage easy and the crooked line straight. The peoples in the distant lands did then no longer seem strangers. This gave cause for rejoicing, so the word begat more and more. And so it seemed the word must spawn its own kind for ever and ever without end. And on the tongues of the devoted rested words of weight. Great wisdom must surely be the result thereof.

Genesis
There was a darkness over the land
and FOG said, Let there be enlightenment,
and brought forth all manner of genius,
granting the manna of silk and money
and so it came to pass there were made
great works to see and hear and to read
and this was art and music and prairie lit
and so there spread the tribes of artists
over the land in colonies and workshops
and a great din rose up of many voices
heaping praise on them for these works
and FOG looked and was pleased
and said unto the people, thou shalt
have none but these to worship,
and the people builded temples

wherein there were coats of many colours
and the sounding brass and the word
of the FOG was spread by these voices,
who spake of the wonders of art
wherein the enlightened
told of the land and its people,
of the greatness of that land
and of the sins of its people,
for they would not hear the tongues
of those profit voices telling them
of the way of enlightenment
in paint tings and muse sick,
sacred songs of glossy-what-ails-ya
and epic cures of prairie lit,
he woes and her woes
from plaster aints to the pleasant,
for the people were deep in sinning
from sod homes on to tomorrow
and they were unafraid of this
army a get-ons and pocked lips,
and FOG thus declared unto the profits
and the tribes of enlightened,
Be fruitful and multiply, and
taxes begat taxes begat taxes begat taxes
begat taxes unto the generations of men
by Federal Order of Government.

The Fable of Adjectiva

In the land of Academe there lived wise men and women, and the wisest of
them taught all of the secrets of language to the young and to merchants and
housewives in regular and extension courses in the great school of Grammare,

famed in sundry lands. And the most illustrious of these teachers were husband and wife, Gerund and Verba, and had many followers spreading the word to run and jump and come and go and do all manner of things because this was the true message of the word, and never to be debased by the abominations of those who did not these things but spent their days in the gathering and storing up of words. For this was a waste and saith nothing of the true spirit of the act. To utter unto others whether in speech or by inscription must in no wise ever be more than the correct and spare use of exactly the right words, for so by their words as by their actions shall ye know them. None should say aught but the exact word and must be judged by it.

Great fame came to Gerund and Verba. Then a desire grew in them for increase. And they did use conjunction and soon Verba was with child. And there was unbounded joy in the house of Gerund. But when Verba's time came and she was delivered of a babe, the poor child was puny weak sickly talkative Adjectiva. Scorning her was Gerund's response. "Bearing such is like spawning an indefinite article. Doing anything with that one would be impossible."

Verba cried. When she at length arose from her bed she vowed to rear her child in the spirit and truth of the word. Right anon began the teaching of saying the act and no more, and speaking in the voice of one who does, and all such things. But pale little scrawny chatty Adjectiva could only lisp her long list of words for any occasion.

"You must learn the right way," Verba shouted. "Say as you do and no more."

Such was the strife between mother and daughter, teacher and pupil, for many years. There grew a great distance between them and each was exceeding sad. And runty skinny bony loquacious Adjectiva grew tall and graceful and comely and bright. But none among the young men came to prize her. They saw her as wordy and wasteful. She thought, I will surely die here unwed, a slave to these ways foreign to mine own. And more of her years she spent in drudgery, pruning words to the bare branches of knowledge. She came to know all manner of things, from the ways of the priestly scholars, the Diatribes, to the fiery dis-missals of labourers by merchants, the sundry busyness of letus and memobrandas of much report, and gladvertisers that praised without end. After much study she came to know how words were judged to be right and how it was always that the best way to say and to write them revealed a truth that served the ends of those who used them. There was no one true way, there was only a best one for each time and purpose. This be so, she thought, I shall make use of mine rightly. And the clever resourceful imaginative indomitable Adjectiva wove a long rope of verbiage and one night let that fall outside of her window in the school of Grammare and climbed down and fled the dominion of her mother and father to unknown lands far beyond. Her journey was hard, into and over and under and across the land of Prepositions. Sometimes she was helped by Adverbs, a tribe of outcasts who took her in and gave her modifying advice, told her to seek others of their kind. After much travail on the trail she found herself one day in a new land, and it was the land of Renoun. There lived there the Prince of Renoun, beloved by his proper and common subjects alike. He travelled among them to know of their troubles and did give generously of benisons and boons. It was a substantive land of ilk and sunny, and on none was ever passed the grim short sentence of death. Be fruitful and multiply within thy means was the Prince's commandment. By happenstance one day as he visited his subjects he saw the stranger and asked her who she was and from whence she had travelled. And sore afraid of being banished from that good land, she knelt before the Prince.

"I am homely gangly garrulous repetitive Adjectiva."

But he was much taken with her as she bowed, arrayed in her modesty.

"Nay," quoth he, "only beautiful befits thee."

And they became betrothed, and ever after she was known by a single true word.

The Committee

It was grow-up time for writers. Go stand in the corner. Who likes getting dumped on? That goes double for put-downs from smartasses who think they can mouth off any old way about anybody they want to. You'd think they'd know better. But when you're ethnically-challenged to the point of brain-dead, then it's more than smarts. We're talking about insensitivity. Big letters here, marker pen. So the old guys didn't know.

Classics and such. Gimme a break. Racism, sexism, elitism, classism. Stereotypes. Stomp on ethnics. Nobody called them on it, that's all. It had to end. How much of that can anybody take before it's show time? The word went out. Pay attention. Stick to your own turf. We're not here for anybody's amusement or dumbass ignorance either. So who's making the rules now, huh? It's payback time. Like those guys on the committee. Awareness. About time. Proud to be what we are.

"This committee is meeting to discuss complaints from various groups. They object to the author in question writing about them. Their claim is he couldn't understand their point of view. Didn't share the same racial or cultural background. The tragedies, for example. He wasn't Scottish or an ancient Briton. Or a Moor or a Danish prince. As for the rest. He wasn't Italian, Ilyrian, Greek or Egyptian. To take it further, with the histories. He wasn't an aristocrat. It's pertinent to mention also the fact that he wasn't from the lower classes."

"Ban the performance of his plays and restrict the circulation of copies to university libraries. Access would be limited to scholars, who would study them for their historical value."

"It's a shame, isn't it? He was middle class. A merchant's son who went up to London to get involved in the life of the theatre. If he'd written about that, he might have done something that would still be readable and unobjectionable."

"Dramatists in his day wrote about other cultures. Today they use their own experience and you know what you're getting. Unless they label their stuff 'fantasy' and then nobody is pretending to know anything."

"Hardly anybody attends his plays. The language is out-of-date or sounds overdone. He gets some of his facts wrong. Cannons before they were in use in England. Clocks in ancient Rome. I'm surprised various groups objected."

"They want no exceptions for historical, traditional or any other reason. He has a reputation. Nevertheless. Exempt one and where do you stop?"

"And there's something else. Always a chance a writer could get carried away reading that stuff. That would never happen with academics. Nobody reads scholarly journals except scholars."

"We have to be sensitive to the pain of various groups at some depictions, artistic or otherwise. They're invariably not done by one of their own kind. Where there's a shared experience. Common understanding."

"How can you see through someone else's eyes? And there's always the danger of getting your facts wrong. Making mistakes. Letting your imagination run away with you."

"We're all agreed then. I'll inform the various groups we're issuing a ban and restricting circulation."

Dick Meagher On Line
January 27

"Good morning. This is Dick Meagher. This morning's guest is Professor Peter Sigurdsen of the English Department at Prairie University. Professor Sigurdsen has announced that he will not give out any more essay assignments or set exams. He says it's his protest against what he calls 'academic sterility.' He's in the studio with me. He's wearing what looks to me like a toga and has a wreath of some kind of leaves in his hair. I assume that's part of your protest, sir."

"Yes."

"We've done shows about you and you refused to appear in person or come on the air because the moon or a certain woman said not to. But this time it's all right."

"Yes."

"What made you reject essays and exams?"

"Artemis pointed the way."

"I'm guessing she's the woman I mentioned. How did Artymiss show you?"

"She quite literally pointed out I was stepping in filth, droppings, ordure, dung—beep, beep."

"All right. So you were teaching for years. All of a sudden everything is wrong. But you don't quit."

"The filth of conformity sticks to us."

"I'm still in the dark. You'll have to explain."

"I have wronged the innocent."

"The innocents were students?"

"Forcing them to do that manual stuff. I said it was the rule with me or else and insisted, despite their protests. The young women I hurt. I can't forget them. Those innocent eyes haunt me."

"Does the department chairman know about this?"

"Doesn't matter. It's done."

"What about the administration at PU? Does anybody there know?"

"I have achieved my own awareness."

"Awareness? For something like that? I mean, come on. You're supposed to be an English professor."

"Ultimately, only I can deal with my own failure, but I will stay on to protest the abuses in post-secondary education. Madame has told me."

"What's this about a madam?"

"She has said I must stay. To teach and write."

"You listen to some madam? In connection with your profession?"

"She is my guide."

"Girl students and a madam. We're opening the lines for calls. Stay on the line. We'll get to you. All right, sir. You've lost me. Tell me exactly what and why you're protesting."

"Marking leads to conformity. By getting students to accept the idea that everything must be graded, those who mark ensure that students will never question the examination process. They are too busy competing with each other as well as searching for the ideal answer to do anything except comply. They never get to see what's wrong."

"There's got to be some way of finding out who's smart and who isn't."

"Those are irrelevant categories. Ability is manifest, even to a moron. A system that uses numbers, letters, categories and percentage points to distinguish ever finer degrees of correctness and incorrectness leads to the absolute authority of the system. It breeds conformity by failing the nonconformists and ensures that society will continue to be run by those who accept the idea of grading. Grading degrades to get rid of troublemakers."

"You can't pass people without giving them exams to see if they know their stuff."

"We don't have incompetent doctors?"

"The system isn't perfect."

"It is perfect. That's what's wrong."

"See it your way."

"Original minds are used to that."

"You're listening to Dick Meagher On Line. This morning's guest is Professor Peter Sigurdsen of the English Department at Prairie University.

He's said he's no longer going to assign essays or set exams. It's his protest against the whole system of giving grades. You can speak to him and give him a grade. Your chance to get back at the teacher. Go ahead, you're on the air."

"Come on, Dick, this is a new low for you. As low as your ratings. I thought the hermaphrodite pandas was the worst. But this guy is crazy."

"Next caller, go ahead."

"I don't see why we're bothering about professors. I don't know what they do, anyway, though they must do something, and we've got these universities."

"You're on the air. Go ahead."

"Aren't the hookers on?"

"They're going to be on tomorrow. Next caller, go ahead."

"Mr. Meagher, your guest is obviously an atheist. He preaches the Devil's message. The word of Satan. I'm surprised at you. I'm phoning the station manager."

"That's your privilege, ma'am. Goodbye. Are you an atheist, sir? I'm asking because you don't seem to believe in anything."

"I worship in the temple of Artemis."

"You mentioned this Artymiss earlier. The woman who tells you what to do. Is she the madam? I'm kind of confused."

"Madame is my earthly guide. Artemis is the director of my soul."

"What is the difference?"

"Madame is gifted with supernal powers. She probes for what I seek. To use a vulgar analogy, she has the ability to receive spiritual frequencies, by which she relays thoughts and occasionally a personal message or warning. She communicates with the realm of divine mysteries, beyond the fabric of ordinary sight. My goddess I may worship but dare come no nearer, but she may vouchsafe me some revelatory insight into the murkiness that is life."

"It's not getting any clearer. Guides, goddesses. I mean, come on. I've never heard anything like this since I started in radio. You're on the air, caller, go ahead."

"I don't think you're being fair to this gentleman, Mr. Meagher. He's trying to make a statement about how society runs. All you can do is get personal. His religion is his business."

"Maybe you should put on a toga and join him and Artymiss."

"Better than a dunce's cap. Professor Sigurdsen, I'm president of the Salamander Society. We believe in social adaptation to suit the occasion, but be true to yourself. I'll send you some of our pamphlets."

"They're coming out of the woodwork. Next, you're on the air."

"Where're the strippers, Divinity Fudge and Angel Cake?"

"They'll be on next week."

"Could you have a show on drag racing? Or like, classic cars?"

"I'll think about it. Next caller, go ahead."

"What's a toga, Dick?"

"It's like a robe. Covers your whole body."

"That guy's head should be covered."

"Next caller. You're on the air."

"What do you think, Dick? Can we survive the drop in the market?"

"We're having a financial expert on tomorrow. Next caller."

"Yes. Tell me, professor, how we're going to have schools or universities or classes without exams? That's the only way you can find out if students are learning. Your idea sounds stupid."

"I'm protesting a system of grading that coerces conformity by enforcing adherence to its standards. It degrades through numbers games instead of using colloquy and written intercourse to disseminate concepts. Obvious morons would expose themselves and drop out. Then the less talented, leaving the best students. Including the very best, who wouldn't have survived or tolerated the games."

"I still think it's stupid."

"Perhaps the more intelligent in the audience understand what I mean."

"You think I'm dumb because I won't see it your way."

"You're a moron for your own good reasons."

"Hey, I'm not the one walking around wearing a blanket talking like a crazy person about goddesses."

"Don't befoul the air. You couldn't possibly understand."

"You know you're completely off."

"To the great class of the intellectually benighted I must seem so."

"To anybody who's close to normal, you mean. Guys like you should be put away."

"We must finally get to that. I expect calls for me to be pilloried or even burnt at the stake. The answer to all innovative ideas has initially been to muzzle the purveyors of them. One must expect a grim denouement."

"You think because you know a lot of big words you're smarter than anybody else. You think it gives you the right to act superior."

"And you use 'think' too much for someone who doesn't."

"Hey, I can say anything I want and I don't think I have to beg your pardon. I couldn't care less what you think."

"We'll take the next call. Go ahead, you're on."

"Whoorrshis—sish—rish—worsh—sh."

"Next caller. You're on the air."

"I've got the answer to the riddle."

"You're supposed to fill out a card at the supermarket and drop it in the special box."

"Don't cut me off. I got the answer."

"We'll take one more before the break. You're on the air."

"My brother phoned in before the last call and you went and cut him off. He's got a speech impediment."

"I thought he was drunk."

"He doesn't drink. He gets nervous when he's speaking in public. He wants to say something. Can he come back on?"

"If he can control himself and make sense."

"You're making him nervous."

"I got a program. I can't wait till he calms down."

"He's slumped in his wheelchair."

"Put him on. I won't cut him off."

"He's coming over. Is it all right if he brings his little puppy?"

"Great. And people wonder why my hair went grey so soon."

"Here he is now, Mr. Meagher."

"Whoorrshis—f—beep, beep."

"We'll take a break. Don't go away, because when we come back we'll have two members of city council who have opposing views on the new downtown parking regulations."

Friends, when you speak the words of the Lord, when you mouth the sweet vowels of sacred song, are your teeth what they should be? The Lord gave us pearly whites and pink gums, a sweet-smelling mouth. Have you kept faith by keeping your teeth? Or have you, as so many others, let your mouth become a place of corruption? White and pink, my friends, not red gums and yellow, brown or black teeth. These are the colours of oral corruption, of Satan's work. He speaks with foul breath, the stench of hellfire and decay. Is he on your breath? Hm? Do you have spotted gums, are you a self-inflicted victim of gingivitis and pyorrhea? If so, you are an offence to the Almighty, polluting His words with your breath. Do not be mislead, the way of salvation is not through the partial plate. That is only the road to falseness, uppers and lowers, the clackers of deception. The final abomination for the eternally extracted. For they shall speak falsely when they have no roots in the Lord's truth. Before it is too late, protect the Lord's gift to you. Eat of the trees of righteousness the fruits thereof, and mouthfuls of the crusty baked loaves and corn on the cob. Partake of the unadulterated goodness of the earth. For in the sound of such chewing teeth is the praise of His bounty. Take unto yourself these blessed offerings, manna from Heaven, avoid novocaine and nitrous oxide, the so-called laughing gas, playthings of an idolatrous world, the easy way out. It is not too late. If you act now to save yourself and spurn those sugary blandishments Satan offers. I will smile for you, I will pray for your teeth.

You have been listening to Brother Ralph, the praying dentist. He offers a complete line of dental and health care products, including the only foaming tooth gel containing strontium fluoride for strong enamel and rich in both titanium dioxide for whiter teeth and formaldehyde to ensure an absolutely sterile oral environment. Brother Ralph will be at a mall in your area soon to conduct one of his famous clinics, watch for him. He's saved countless sufferers from tooth decay and gum disease. Many have come forward to seek oral hygiene and sat in the singing chair, the chair of hymns, while he performed his miraculous laying on of fingers. Many who had believed their teeth were lost beyond any hope of redemption have received instant caps and crowns and a sudden end to their pain and misery as they lay there and looked up at the giant floating balloon with the picture of Jesus. Those miraculous fingers sought the abscesses and cavities of corruption to clear the way to dental health. Watch for the notice of his appearance at your mall.

Friends, a final word. Your mouth is for heavenly praises and for the chewing of all righteous food. Don't destroy a blessing. Go the way of righteousness. There is no such thing as a dirty mouth, only a sinner in sore need of salivation.

Brother Ralph will be appearing this Sunday at Middlegate Mall. Don't miss your chance. Your teeth are too important. The full range of Brother Ralph products will be offered at specially reduced prices, and bulk rates are available on those days.

Prairie Herald-Times
February 4

Search Uncovers Fake Doctor

A routine check of the academic records of the Dean of the Faculty of Medicine at Prairie University uncovered more than expected. It exposed the completely bogus background of Lansing Beestrop, who has held that position for seven years. A reporter from this newspaper made the discovery while researching a feature article on the faculty, celebrating its tenth anniversary this year. When the universities Beestrop claimed to have earned degrees from were contacted, all denied he had attended. Harvard replied there was no record of him as a student. Dartmouth and Yale issued the same response. Further investigation revealed Beestrop dropped out of high school and never attended college or university. His curriculum vitae, listing degrees and other qualifications and experience, was faked. The selection committee that recommended Beestrop's hiring did not check his background, and those nonexistent degrees are listed in the university catalogue. When the university was told about the spurious degrees, President Meakin's office issued a statement. "This matter will be investigated by the appropriate body of inquiry and handled as expeditiously as possible." Asked about procedures used by hiring committees to verify credentials and references, the office had no comment.

Prairie Alumni
April

Appointment

The new Dean of Arts will be Jurgen Nagel, Chairman of the History Department. Dr. Nagel, 34, came to Prairie University two years ago. He will be the youngest dean ever of any faculty here. Considered a wunderkind by his colleagues, he has published a landmark study on the Congress of Vienna. His book on the Revolutions of 1848 will appear this year. He has also written many articles and reviews. He held administrative posts at Princeton and Harvard before coming here.

Prairie Dog
February 8

Dean Needs a Rest

Jurgen Nagel, the Dean of Arts, was admitted to the university hospital on Sunday morning. His office gave the reason as overwork and said he had recently come down with a virus. A hospital spokeswoman said he is being treated for nervous exhaustion and general physical debilitation. During his absence the acting dean will be Reid Abercrombie, Chairman of the English Department.

Prairie Dog
February 22

Dean Dead

Jurgen Nagel, the Dean of Arts, left his fourth-floor ward at the university hospital Saturday morning and ran through a window at the end of the hallway. He landed in a dumpster. The fall broke his neck. Nagel had been admitted for nervous exhaustion two weeks ago.

Prairie Alumni
June

Appointment

The new Dean of Arts will be Reid Abercrombie, Chairman of the English Department. He has been acting dean for the past three months. Sure to be a popular choice, he has been a familiar figure on the Prairie University campus for almost two decades. A noted Middle English scholar and excellent administrator, he seems the embodiment of a concept he lives by, the well-rounded academic as dedicated researcher and enthusiastic teacher.

Faculty Club lounge
February 28

"I'm buying. I got that job I applied for on the coast in September. I told Reid last week. He'd already hired my replacement. He was sure I'd be hired."

"Uncanny, isn't he? What happened out there?"

"You give a lecture in front of the whole department. Those who want to attend. Next step is to be interviewed by the selection committee. Turned out to be most of the department. The interview is in a large committee room, people sitting beside and on three sides of you at tables forming a square. Redundant and useless questions. They're sizing you up. Figuring if you fit into the mix of sexes and ethnic groups. I was lucky. They hired a woman last year. And a gay Polynesian before that."

"Who's the chairman?"

"Nestor Silbery. Little fat guy with an MA. Strings of hair covering his baldness like a wet mop. Written some radio plays. They have a revolving chairmanship, two-year term."

"What about your colleagues?"

"Dull after this place. No Sigurdsen or Mulcahey or Bowness or Skinner or Braun. Even a MacWhinnie or Biddle. A few like Dave, though."

"Reid's picked Dave as his successor. The coronation will take place at the next department meeting. I met your replacements at the Abercrombies' on Saturday night. The Brinkers. A husband and wife team. She's got an MA. She's starting an extension program downtown for the business crowd. The department is renting a couple of floors in an office building. The party was a disaster. Sigurdsen turned up, got drunk and started insulting the guests. Went after Denise Brinker. 'Shakespeare on the rocks. Advanced primer on writing more powerful English. Ten ways to better résumés, memos and reports. You're a squatty version of success, chopped hair, choppy legs. Life full of small victories. Getting yours.'

"He went after Dave. 'You and your lousy articles. Down the black hole. Like the rest of them. Making scholarship seem important. The canon is sacred. At our carrels in the drafty scriptorium we of tonsures and woollen robes—vestments, gowns, cassocks—huddle over the vellum and paint crushed lapis lazuli and cochineal, or is it only vermilion?—good old mercury sulphide—and lay thin floating shimmers of gold leaf on our Gothic script. Why do so many of us look as if we eat paper instead of write on it? We digest whole libraries through our gut and out come the droppings. Some are dumb or arrogant enough to believe what they write, and others are merely standard grade manoeuvrers collecting a pay cheque. The cover for it all, a factitious worship of ideas. Ideas, the half-man's excuse for not having feelings. Not wanting to deal with the experience of the flesh. We mortify it intellectually under the guise of unimpassioned observation. Rejecting the body as inferior to mind, which oversees everything with cool sarcastic disgust elevated into a fetish of inviolable truth. Apply your correct code, some pseudo-technical puzzle solver to explain away what the mind will never come to understand without the body. The worm threads its way through the word.

"'We're supposed to be a community of scholars. We're the most useless timeservers in the world. Sometimes when I walk through Mackerness Hall or the Arts Building and they're empty I think about that, what teaching English means. Rows of open classroom doors and empty seats, half-erased words on the blackboard, scribbled thoughts. Janitor's cart in the hallway, outside a door. Brooms, mops, rags and pails. And the sound of a broom inside, knocking against a desk leg.'"

"He's completely out of it."

"He's alienated everybody. Not rational any more. Doesn't show up unless he's got a class. The whole department avoids him. Laura told me he works in his office late at night. She has no idea at what, but he said that his pen is busy. Probably cleans out his ears with it. After he left the party Laura said to me, 'Peter's got plans.' She doesn't know what they are but she thinks he'll be leaving. He'll be doing the department a favour when he goes."

"I'm not surprised. At anything he does. He's been going that way for years. Reid won't be there to cover up for him any more. Dave certainly won't."

"Different in McGinty's case. At least he didn't make trouble for anybody."

"Sigurdsen has made us the laughing stock of the university."

Prairie Dog
March 10

Bank Tragedy for Professor

A man was detained for questioning after he walked into the campus branch of Prairie Savings Credit Union wearing a mask. According to witnesses, as he stood in line waiting for a teller he chanted something in what sounded like a foreign language. Campus police were called to the basement of the

SUB by alarmed Prairie Savings officials. The man, later released, turned out to be Professor Peter Sigurdsen of the English Department. He explained to bank officials and police that he was wearing the classical Greek mask of tragedy. He was showing how he always felt when in a bank. That was why, he said, red tears had been painted on it. Professor Sigurdsen had already been questioned last week about appearing in the Campus Market wearing the classical Greek mask of comedy. He had explained he was laughing at the high prices and mountains of junk food. The professor has been duly warned, Officer Beedey said, that if he appears again in a mask in a public place of business he will face charges. Various campus businesses have been notified about the masked professor.

Prairie Dog
March 15

Professor Calls for Lottery

Professor Sigurdsen is calling for a campus lottery, winners receiving free tuition. In a letter to this newspaper he writes, "This is a fair answer to the much higher tuition fees of recent years. Everyone would have an equal chance and the price of a ticket would be low. None of the profits would be needed for advertising or salaries. All money raised would be used for the benefit of the students." He sees such a lottery as "symbolic of the lottery of birth, which determines those in our society who are able to go to university." Among other features, his plan includes a limitation on the number of tickets a student could buy, to lower the risk of lottery addiction, and a compulsory deduction from the salaries of faculty and administrative staff to help share the cost of supporting this venture as well as foster a sense of solidarity in the university community. As an incentive towards the adoption of his proposal he suggests subsidiary prizes, such as free books. But his personal choice would be trips to classical ruins. No one contacted in the administration or among arts faculty would comment on his idea.

Prairie Dog
March 18

Letter to the Editor

It is time for the poisoning of graduate student minds to stop. In the ostensibly sanitary confines of the modern academic factory, graduate students are force-fed a diet of processed thinking in scholarly books and articles. Packaged in the latest academese, this mental nutrition is an accumulating disaster. An analogy comes to mind. Besides grains, broilers and laying hens in factory farms are fed an assortment of meat, bone, feather, offal and blood meal. Levels of pesticides and herbicides, synthetic fertilizers and antibiotics imbibed from these animal byproducts are passed on to succeeding generations in increasingly toxic amounts. Such chickens and their eggs are nutritional disasters. The various doctrinal poisons fed academic poultry produce the same effect. Is it surprising they all squawk the same? Schools of criticism wear different coloured feathers merely for show. Debeaked and imprisoned behind their invisible bars, they can only gabble, gobble and lay.

We must break this cycle of poisoning. Broilers and pastured hens fed organic grains and no antibiotics or animal byproducts are producing meat and eggs free of toxins. Must our academic flock keep poisoning itself? An 8-point program should be implemented immediately. (1) Scholarly books and journals should be ignored except as objects of ridicule. (2) Tenure should be abolished. (3) In my own sadly lacking discipline prospective employees should be asked to produce a creative work (poem, novel) before being hired. (4) In other disciplines original work should be mandatory, no bloodsucking. (5) A student falling asleep in a lecture should mean the automatic dismissal of the lecturer. (6) No research assistants to do the faculty member's own digging, and no more digging. (7) No symposia, colloquia or other subsidized gatherings for chewing the scholarly cud. (8) No sabbaticals, grants or other paid excuses for touring Europe.

The promise of education is not to create a subspecies, an insect that can only feel with antennae what it cannot see.
Sigurdsen

Prairie Dog
March 24

Letter to the Editor

Many species are territorial and mark boundaries. I see no reason why this cannot be applied in academe. With so many specialists in every department, there should be a foolproof way of ensuring no trespassing on another's privileged domain. The rubbing of a gland secretion would be preferable to the spraying of urine but we do not possess such a gland. I would not, though, recommend the unseemly spectacle of academics peeing on fire hydrants. Perhaps the Chemistry Department or an enterprising private laboratory could create an artificial substitute that could be bottled and supplied at reasonable cost to scholars. Pump or aerosol for ease of application. It could be used in the stacks to mark those special or rare volumes the scholar prizes. Whole shelves could easily be protected this way. Chairs and tables in the Faculty Club would be other desirable objects to be marked, first sprayed, first saved, a discreet spritz on a leg quite sufficient. An identifying tracer could be added to each user's bottle, ensuring there would never be two or more claimants to the same book or chair. Other possible applications include chairs at departmental meetings, favourite class and seminar rooms (a spritz on the door), library carrels and desirable walks on campus. Mating would be simplified and more immediate, as would separation and divorce. And in all instances the message to interlopers would be: piss off.
Sigurdsen

Dick Meagher On Line
March 30

"Welcome to the show. My guests this morning are two students at the university, Kelly Ripton and Megan Pisarchik. They're here to talk about something that's been getting coverage in the campus newspaper and the *Herald-Times*. Professor Sigurdsen—and if you've been a regular listener over the past two years you know who that guy is—is stirring things up again. He's had booths set up on campus, where his English students, dressed in costumes, are offering services. My guests are involved in this. What's going on over there, Kelly?"

"We're in Professor Sigurdsen's English 200 class, which is a survey of English literature. Instead of writing essays and exams we're offering services to students. I'm part of the Jane Austen Marriage Bureau. Our motto is, guaranteed results."

"I take it she was a writer."

"Yeah. In her novels people usually end up getting married to people they didn't like at first but get to know better."

"Sort of a happy ending."

"Yeah."

"So what kind of service are you offering?"

"We dress up in Regency costumes, high-waisted gowns and such. And we offer advice on dating and picking a marriage partner. We quote from her novels to support what we say. Or make up stuff that sounds like her. It's not hard if you've read everything and get some practice."

"Tell me about some of the advice you've given out."

"Sure. Yesterday a girl came to the booth and said her brother got her a date with an older guy who's a grad student in physics and isn't that great looking but all right and she didn't know if she should go out with him again. We read her some pages from a novel that seemed to apply to her situation, where the girl ended up really liking an older guy. Last week someone came and said that a guy she's involved with is from a wealthy family and is stuck on himself. So she didn't know if she could put up with him. We told her about a character who knew a guy like that. Turned out he was acting stuck on himself and she couldn't handle the fact he was wealthy. Sometimes the problem is modern— like drugs or sex—and then we have to think of what Jane Austen would say. Like about kicking a habit, bed-hopping, putting out, wanting a relationship to be permanent. We tell them basically to be sensible, not flighty or a coquette. And read a novel of hers, because everything turns out so well."

"You seem to be good at this."

"I've read tarot cards and palms and this is easier. Only thing is not to get too personal."

"What sort of service are you offering, Megan?"

"I'm part of the Charlotte Brönte Domestic Agency, and our motto is, plain women with big hearts. We try to help women students who are going to be teachers, particularly in kindergarten and primary school, and those who'll be going overseas. For anyone going into private tutoring, we have special advice. Our support is based on Charlotte Brönte's novels. In Charlotte's novels we've found really good advice on a teacher's relationship with her employer."

"What's some of the advice you've given?"

"Well, a couple of days ago an education student wanted to know about teaching in Europe and we read her passages about a teacher having trouble there. She falls in love with a married guy who rejects her. Now she doesn't know if she'll go. And last week a student told us she'd read about a position as a private tutor to a rich man's daughter at his estate in the country. We told her about a woman who had lots of trouble in a similar situation, except things finally were all right. If you don't mind being married to a blind guy. She said that's fine, if he's rich. The important thing we've found is, if you look you'll find the right story for each person."

"You like doing this?"

"Yeah."

"You don't think you should be writing essays and exams?"

"Professor Sigurdsen lets us hand in papers. We can select the topic. He writes comments on them but doesn't give a mark. We can write something to do with the course material or what's going on at the booths. Almost everybody is writing something about the booths."

"Suppose a student doesn't turn in anything?"

"He says he doesn't care."

"Yeah, but he's got to turn in marks so a student gets a grade."

"Everybody gets an A."

"He's gives out As? For nothing? The guy's about as loose as fifty piglets in a mud hole. I mean, come on."

"We don't mind."

"I guess not. We'll let the listeners have their say. Whether they like what's going on in a certain classroom over there. Go ahead, caller. You're on the air."

"The big-hearted one, what's her name?"

"Megan Pisarchik, and I'm way ahead of you. You're gone. Go ahead, line two. You're on the air."

"Hey, Dick, can anybody get their advice? I got a problem. It's about my girlfriend. She's got, like her, it's too big."

"Sorry, they're not here to give advice. Line three, go ahead."

"Hey, Dick, I can hear your ratings slipping."

"Line four, go ahead."

"There's gonna be an earthquake. My cat's under the bed."

"Maybe you should get under there with it. Line one, you're on."

"Your program is more ridiculous than usual. I never thought I'd phone but this has forced me to. How anyone can take your guests seriously is beyond me. I've been a teacher for twenty-eight years and I've read and taught Jane Austen and Charlotte Brönte and this mockery degrades them. Your part in it is insidious. Those young women are the playthings of an insane man. And you're using them. If you felt any shame you'd stop your crude showmanship."

"I think you're overreacting. Ma'am? She hung up. Line two, you there?"

"Is that me?"

"You're on the air."

"Hm hm."

"You have a question for my guests?"

"Hm hm."

"Obviously not. Line three, you there?"

"I'm line three. I'm waiting to get on."

"You're on."

"I'm still here. Holding on."

"Line four. Go ahead."

"They should not be giving advice. They're not qualified as professional counsellors."

"They're not acting as professional counsellors. It's a class project."

"They're giving advice."

"They're advising about dating and about teaching careers, that's all. They wear costumes and read out of some old books."

"Doesn't matter."

"We'll take a break."

How important are your loved ones to you? If they were in danger you'd want to protect them. The fact is they are in danger from the poisons around us. There are deadly toxins threatening us daily. They are the price we pay for the world we live in. Is there any hope? Yes, there is if you act now to protect yourself and your loved ones from poisons in the air and water. And in our food and homes. Yes, even there, from solvents and glues and lawn fertilizers and weed killers and fibreboard and rug and carpet and floor cleaners. There is no safe place except the one toxin-free zone on the planet, certified by third-party verification. The Church of Vitamin C. It is nondenominational, has no walls or doors but the purest water, cleanest air and risk-free food. Because the best vitamin C in the world is processed from the purest citrus fruit, the choicest kumquats and blood oranges, citron and Mediterranean lemons. Grown in our Fields of Plenty in the Holy Land, which assures you of the finest quality. Available in the form of easily absorbed mineral ascorbates, our vitamin C capsules are a potent weapon in the fight against free radicals produced by environmental pollution. The body is the temple of the soul, the holy vessel. Resist corruption. Sin begins deep within, at the cellular level. Fields of Plenty offers you a complete line of health supplements. Starting with the all-powerful vitamin C. Available at select health food stores or order online @ www.whollycit.com.

Tired of veggie burgers? Tofu wieners? Cheese slices? The yuk of yogurt? Do you hunger after protein on the hoof? The whiff of the hunt, the spoor of the beast? Is red and raw your style? Could you go for a glass of blood right now? You're looking for Meat Axe. Wholesale butchers for those with a taste for wild meat. We specialize in fresh kills. All game is fair game. Our game-farm network is the largest and best in North America. Government-inspected plant and storage facilities. Prime cuts, organ meats. Absolutely no processed meat. Two-day delivery on reserve orders. Old-fashioned butcher's paper and twine available for traditionalists. Plant tours available, with fresh blood on tap. Send for or download our newsletter, *Slaughterhouse Views*. Reserve your favourite cuts today. You can find us online @ www.meataxe.com.

From the Sigurdsen Notebooks
April 2

On academe

Anything that is treated seriously can be made to seem important.

There are always a lot of flies around dead meat.

Society's first line of propagandists, the teaching orders.

Educational institutions teach how to please the teacher.

At the level of nothing, the clones and drones of academe.

Scholarly=oxygen-starved and academic=dead on the page.

The critic must have an excellent second-rate intelligence: all the hard work has been done.

English courses: a fartless world of porcelain figurines.

There's Shakespeare.

There are no classrooms, only empty spaces.

On language and art

Language begins as grammatical error, incoherence on the edge of worship.

Grammar is an etiquette obsessed with correctness.

Beware the scalpels of linguistic coroners.

We are not ants. There is a world above the sidewalk of common speech and the tunnels of academese.

Be as active or passive as you please but only plural, never the singular one, remembering the dangerous ones go singularly.

Humans do not communicate, they approximate.

Never accept one way of saying anything.

Words are personal, like your skin. Go naked into the wind's embrace.

Art mimics the abstruseness of human experience. Anything definite is a failure.

No great work of art can ever be fully understood, nor should it be. It is a monument to limitation, a perfection of failure.

If art teaches anything it is humility in the face of chance. Into its lacunae continually fall and disappear the blindly solipsistic syllogisms of academic exegesis.

Poetry is a handrail in the dark. A novel is an elevator that ends up in the basement.

Proverbs don't apply at 4 a.m.

Sigurdsen's laws

Man is not a rational animal, man is an animal that rationalizes.

If it has to be advertised, you don't need it.

Our lives are a trail of body parts and junk.

We are beleaguered by vague and not-so-vague urges.

Humanity is a victim of its ideas.

Most people want their thinking done for them before declaring it to be their own.

The devoutly modern see life as a puzzle for science and a problem for technology.

Understanding is the greatest of all human fallacies.

Sigurdsen's rules

Don't ever read anything beginning with "free."

Don't eat packaged foods with more than four ingredients or with anything unpronounceable in them.

Things to avoid: speeches of any kind, critical reviews, tributes and testimonials, interviews with public personalities, newscasts, editorials, bestsellers, mass transport with stanchions, supermarket music, pop music (tautology), commercial television, professional sports, blockbuster films, name brands, anything that needs a refill or a new battery.

Respect: gravity, dark matter, weeds, garbage that doesn't smell too bad, insects that don't intend to devour you, animals that don't chase you, anyone who ignores you, and a woman offering you unleavened seed bread by the mouthful with her fingers.

Make peace with any spirit accosting your presence, especially at night, anything under the bed, all constipating foods, creatures living on or inside your body.

Professor Peter Sigurdsen
April 29

Dear Professor Sigurdsen:
Huggett Publishing Group has decided not to accept your novella, *Onderby*. The style and subject are literary, not suitable in the current market. The big sellers are fantasy, romance and the paranormal, sometimes in one work, and often in a series with one word repeated in every title. Check to see what's being published and get yourself an agent who is 100% enthusiastic about selling your work. I might add that it does no good to condemn readers before they look at your work. Words such as "moron" and "cretin" in a letter accompanying a manuscript are uncalled for and can only hurt your chances. Nobody, at Huggett or anywhere else, likes working with a difficult writer. Rejection is based purely on the needs of the publishing house and the demands of the market. Please keep that in mind.
Good luck,
Tissa Taubman

Discovered Clarissa Frothingham-Deville, author of *The Heart Will Decide*, a bestselling romance series of 25. The only known antidote has been found to be large excerpts from the biographies of serial killers. Real name: Elspeth Froggart. Residence: the Lesser Antilles. Fruitarian. Fasts regularly. Must be within lurching distance of a toilet. Dictates from her bed to an amanuensis.

Professor Peter Sigurdsen,
English Department, Mackerness Hall
January 21, 20—

Onderby

Put your derby on, Onderby.
    Schoolyard bully with pimples.

Pay on time or you pay with the rest of your life.
    Joey "The Enforcer" Magliotti

It helps if you're stupid.
    Crown Prince Franz Rudolph

If we could be what we want, we would not be what we are.
    Some schoolteacher.

The tenets of belief must contradict the urgings of time.
    Teniers de Louys Hoogman

Preface

I, Sigurdsen, eschewing the puny, the intellectual weeds, the feces who write theses, the coarse grass, for those flowers, sad-faced girls with severe implications, have as the prof aloft irreversible thoughts every so often, more every than often—an intellect you can respect, one with the received wisdom—will not venture into morondom, i.e., e.g., paranormal romance (ghosts grappling in the dark trying to find missing body parts), or the domestic that sticks to your fingers like jam, or feminimisery (she looked low on all essential fluids) or the rusty armour of fantasy (t'will/t'won't) or war as the ultimate insanity of order, but to any reader who may hap perhaps along will appeal to one of the less densely populated areas of the brain.

Everything disappoints after you dream it up. Time has a wrinkled posterior, but the beauty of before. If there were only goddesses reeking of pleasant odours that you could swipe with your PIN numberless times, Amen. You could package that and sell it over the counter as eternity. They rise among the flowers, our disputed selves, bound to wage rage age sage diss en gage. Never to try the tire-caressing roads of the too highly rated imaginative. Be irreverent but pray, and may the orisons of young brides be with you.

Any resemblance between the characters in this book and actual humans, though in some cases that's stretching a point, is purely intentional.

Norton Onderby, prime specimen of the uninspired yearning for relief. Switched from pre-med to English in his third year at university. After BA came MA, then off to England for a PhD. His MA supervisor, Fred Shackleton, since retired, had recommended him for an assistant professorship at Prairie University while Onderby was writing his thesis. That was almost six years ago, and aside from publishing the usual doctorate-derived articles in fairly reputable journals, he had tread water.

Something was wrong. He had been telling Jane for months. An assistant professor, Jane Merton was quickly becoming an authority on the Middle English lyric. After publishing a number of articles, she was preparing a full-length study. She and Onderby had paired three and a half years ago. From a red-brick in England, she had considered the possibilities in the English Department, decided on Onderby. A robust Saxon blonde with skin that reddened easily and agate blue eyes, she was quietly sexy.

Their first conversation had been in the faculty club over a drink. Onderby had invited Jane ostensibly to discuss a guest lecture on the Middle English lyric to his second year survey class.

"You're staring."

"I was admiring your hair."

"I'm an English blonde. The best kind."

"How so?"

"We're not the half-blondes of the south. Or the pale blondes of the north. We're perfection. Golden hair. Creamy skin. And our rosy pink faces show the temperateness of the English climate. Altogether unmatched."

"No mention of peaches with your cream."

"I do not indulge in clichés, Professor O. Hyperbole, perhaps."

"Especially about yourself."

"Hard to avoid, wouldn't you say?"

"Was I boxed into a corner. You believe in that Arthurian stuff?"

"You want to play Lancelot and Guinevere?"

"What I'm getting at is, do you think that passion is necessarily destructive of the social order, as exemplified by Camelot?"

"No, what you mean is, would I be your Guinevere in the complete sense of the word?"

"What word?"

"Would."

"Well, would you?"

"Let's leave it at could. For the moment."

"This is bantering, isn't it? Love it even if it isn't. Incidentally, I always thought 'Lance-a-lot' a perfect toy for the psychoanalytic bunch. I'm getting poetic. Or something. Must be the coffee. And the cream."

"We haven't discussed my lecture."

"Oh, screw the lyric."

"I shouldn't like that."

Onderby's office was at the end of a hallway on the top floor of Mackerness Hall, an old wooden three-storey building where the English Department was located. The main office, on the second floor, was far enough away that Onderby and Jane could talk without worrying about eavesdroppers.

"Why am I tired of this dilapidated dump?" he said one afternoon at the beginning of September, two weeks before classes began.

"Because it's a fire trap?"

"That has a positive side. If it burnt down, we'd be free."

"To do what?"

"Teach."

"In a tent. Not very comfortable in subzero temperatures."

"We could fly a kite."

"And live on what?"

"There's always a practical answer to everything. Keeps us slaves. Those invisible chains. Ties that bind. We're the high priests of some kind of knowledge that supposedly justifies our existence."

"Some would say we've got it easy talking about books for money."

"If we all disappeared, what would happen? Those who like books would read them. Those who didn't wouldn't. Literature would survive."

"But we wouldn't."

"That's self-serving. Doesn't negate my point. This department is a collection of tenth-rate pedants who should be kept as far away from the written word as possible. Who decided that the Great Plains needed more than basic literacy, anyway? We're footnotes to footnotes, like brown slush on the roads."

"Norton and his hair-shirt routine," a voice said and a brown brogue pushed the door, which had been ajar, slowly open. Edging himself in, mock scowl, hands in the pockets of his corduroy jacket, was assistant professor Hardy Kruger, big and rough-faced. He came from a family of ministers and corporation lawyers and had a simple philosophy. "We're bags of shit. We carry shit around with us, dropping some occasionally, but still having to make more. We're born like shit and when we die we turn into shit." "Happy old Hardy" Jane called him and he referred to her as "Blonde Beauty." After being exposed for a couple of weeks to his cynical appraisal of humanity, she asked him why he held such a saturnine view.

"As your English barristers say, let me put it to you. . . ."

"Don't bloody patronize me."

"All right. Let's say—this is a wildly unrealistic assumption—that a man running for the American presidency read Thucydides and Herodotus, listened to Mozart and liked sweet potatoes. Which of them do you think the American media would highlight? Right. Not only would there be stories about his gustatory preference but pictures of the candidate, along with his wife and children, all eating the stuff. The public would be assured that these were home grown, not imported. There would be an immediate rise in sales. He would receive hundreds of recipes for the golden tuber. And statues and busts of him carved out of it, slightly mouldy naturally by the time his campaign workers received them and threw them out. Television talk show hosts would interview nutritionists about the dietary value of sweet potatoes. They would make jokes about sweet talk and politicians. There would be naysayers. Some would think he wasn't manly because he liked something called 'sweet,' inferring that a real man would eat plain potatoes, preferably barbecued, and with ribs naturally. Political commentators who make their bread wry would smirk about him getting to the roots of problems, being a man of the soil, unearthing the goodness in the country, and not forgetting from where the American Dream springs, and so on. In a rational world, Jane, there would be an interest in Thucydides."

Kruger slumped into a chair and tapped his brogues together.

"What's behind all this? Don't tell me you've reached a new level of despair. This place isn't worth it. I've got an unopened bottle of Scotch, if you two would care to partake."

Onderby waved the suggestion away.

"I'm applying for tenure."

"This is news to me," Jane said.

"Don't start anything domestic or I shall depart," Kruger said. "Nothing messier than close contact spats between beloveds."

Onderby frowned at the ceiling.

"I've been here long enough that if I want to continue on in this place, and that's an open question, I should be applying, anyway. But the problem is Skinner and Braun are the senior members of the tenure committee and I'm persona non grata with both."

Kruger nodded.

"Join the lineup. Skinner, a peculiar man in any department. Skinny little bastard, hair plastered to his head, whistling as he slinks along the walls, feeling his way to his office. That gum chewer's never been known to look anybody in the eye. Not surprising after dumping his wife for Caroline, pushing her doctorate through her committee, getting her hired against regulations and giving her a graduate seminar. He teams up with Braun on committees. They self-righteously wreck the chances of doctoral candidates and tenure applicants. They're the best arguments against tenure I can think of. Her motive? Sex-starved and envious. One of the brides of academe. When two of her students held hands in class, she failed everybody. Abercrombie had to get the finals remarked. He's been covering up for her for years. If you were a geek or a nerd or stuttered or limped, you might stand a chance. Paired with Jane, you're a doomed man, unless—. You've talked with her?"

"Once. Had to see her about something."

"She offers visitors a cigarette. Did you take it?"

"I told her I don't smoke."

"Should have taken it and put it away. Said you'd smoke it later. Outright refusal to a chain smoker whose only lip service is tobacco, that's a hanging offence. A plea for mercy would only excite her."

Kruger laughed.

"I made Skinner squirm once, the first time we met. I went to see him when I became a member of the permanent committee he chairs, the one dealing with course suggestions. It's useless, does nothing, and that's why he created it. Adds to his workload, letting him pretend he needs help to do his work. On my way to his office I used the washroom, hadn't dried my hands after washing them. I was already late, a mortal academic sin. His door was open, I tapped on it and he lifted his head from something he was deliberately reading and stared. I walked in and introduced myself and said I was late because I'd been in the washroom. He stood up, extended one of those limp hands and I shook it with my wet one. He jerked his hand back as if he'd put it into a toilet bowl. He reached for a box of Kleenex on his desk, pulled one out and dabbed his hand with it and dropped it into his wastebasket. For the rest of our talk that hand remained in midair. I, of course, remained standing. The chairs in his office aren't for sitting. They're for gathering dust, the same dust settling on Mackerness Hall."

Kruger stood up, hands in his pockets again.

"I'll try to come up with something that might help. In the meantime, pray. Braun does. Doesn't seem to help her."

"Take her for a drink," Jane said after Kruger left.

"She'd probably order a Bloody Mary, made with my blood. Make a change from her menstrual strainings."

"Don't be disgusting, Norton."

"We're not disgusting Norton, we're disgusting Braun."

"And you're disgusting, period."

"Good, Jane."

"No good Jane would say that about herself or any other woman."

"Or man of wombman born, except when spurned, as I have been. The lady doesn't like me. I don't think she likes herself, but that's her problem. The lonely female professor crawling between the covers of a book. A nun of academe with none of the sacred virtues."

"You're wasting your time thinking about her. Your problem is Skinner. If you don't rile him too much, you won't have a problem. I've heard he's difficult. But surely you can manage if you try."

Luck seemed to be flirting with Onderby a week later. Ruth Braun came to his office. She knocked lightly, entered after his brisk invitation. She looked around. "Your office is quite large. Good view up here." Onderby winced. Comparing offices. "Not much heat in the winter. Loose frames let the wind in." She wasn't listening. He had a habit of putting his feet on his desk. She was peering around his shoes. As he realized he should take his feet down, she moved towards the door. "I came this morning to remind you that your list of publications for the committee should include work in progress as well. Each member should have a copy in the next couple of months. No hurry yet." "I was going to include that." Wrong. Shit. Should thank her. The door had closed.

"We not only consider published work for tenure, but take into consideration tasks performed by the aspirant. Jobs that aren't popular but necessary for the functioning of the department. Anything in that direction would help you. We're not considering your application for a few months. Plenty of time to add to your record."

Reynard Skinner was talking to Onderby, or more precisely to the light switch near Onderby's left shoulder. He as usual was standing as he listened in Skinner's office to this suggestive encouragement. It was a week after the encounter with Ruth Braun and he was looking for a way to improve his chances. See what the idiot suggests.

"If there's anything. . . ."

"There may be a couple of things. I'm busy with my edition of Phineas Fletcher's *Purple Island.* Takes all my time. Profound, that man, and unrecognized for so long."

Get to the point. What kind of donkey work do I do?

"The department is presenting a reading near the end of January in Bassett Hall to mark the tenth anniversary of the death of Edward Blaisdell. First poet in residence here and a graduate of this department. I'm supposed to set it up. You could look after it. Wouldn't be much. Some phone calls. A little coordinating. Picking up people. That's all. And I'm supposed to come up with some ideas for new courses for the committee vetting them. Back from my sabbatical. All my research to do. You've probably got some ideas. Submit a few to me for my presentation to the committee. Drop them in my mailbox."

Pompous fraud. Research students are preparing the edition of Fletcher. One of the academic experts at letting others do the digging. Tired of standing here, the whole schoolboy routine.

"I'll need some details about the reading."

"Get them from the office. Another thing. Tenured professors do not wear blue jeans. I suggest changing your attire. Before."

"I wear what's comfortable. Dress shirt, blazer, jeans and sneakers, and hiking boots during the winter."

"The rest is passable, the footwear exigencies of this climate, I suppose, but I would suggest an appropriate tie and different trousers."

"Trousers?"

"You object to British usage?"

"On the prairies? Is it appropriate?"

Throwing Skinner's word back at him.

"It's perfectly serviceable. To an English scholar."

"I can hear icy wind blowing through it."

"You write poetry?"

"No."

"Good." Skinner turned away to open a book.

"Hi—ee," in a screech from Caroline Adair Skinner as Onderby was leaving. He winced instinctively to avoid a slash and stun job from one of her hands as it waved close to him. Ruby claws and a bucket full of stones came within two inches of his face. Skinny and balding, with a wispy sun-bleached blonde thatch and the tan face of an old doll, she zipped past him.

It was Monday evening and he went to the Arts Building for the first meeting with his new Prairie Literature class. Unlike his other courses, it began at five o'clock, met once a week for three hours and concluded at Christmas, with the next class beginning in January. He entered Room 216 and everything was comfortably familiar and somehow curiously like a home. A green chalkboard ran along the front of the thirty by forty foot room and a foot-high platform extended five feet from it, with a lectern at the front of the platform and a desk and chair at the side. There was a wall of windows hung with white venetian blinds and a roomful of pale wood-veneered chairs with trumpet-flared steel bottoms painted blue and screwed to oatmeal-coloured linoleum, each chair having a paddle-shaped arm on which students could take notes. Rows of fixtures of fluorescent tubes hung from a white ceiling. Opposite the windows and at the back the white walls were partially covered by panels of what Onderby took to be pressed wood fibre and there for soundproofing or to be used as noticeboards, he could never figure out which, except he had never seen any notices pinned on them. Not knowing was part of an ignorance he cultivated on many large and small technical things abounding in the world and most of which to know about would add absolutely nothing he felt to his appreciation of his own or anyone else's existence. About two-thirds of the class was there, with others drifting in as he put his briefcase on the desk. He took out a folder of notes, sat down and looked through the notes as he waited. Within ten minutes the rest of the chairs were filled. He glanced at his watch and went to the lectern, put the folder on it and took off his watch, placing it beside the folder.

He noticed a student in the first row. A couple of inches over five feet, red-haired, she looked in her late twenties. She was dressed in a cardinal red blouse and bib overalls of black velvet, and there was a large black bow in her upswept hair. Her black patent leather purse was on the floor next to her black patent leather shoes, and the binder she had opened was a hard-backed three ringer and covered with fluorescent red plastic splotched mercilessly with stickers of cartoon characters. Her pen was large, orange and topped with a plastic butterfly. Some of the students had looked at her and at each other with head tilts and grins. The others were so self-absorbed that if she had come in naked they would not have noticed.

Onderby repressed a grin as he looked down at his notes. That pen and binder belonged in elementary school. And what was she wearing? But she sat there determined to learn, seemed the only one in the class whose mind was uncluttered with academic junk. This would all be fresh to her.

Onderby had noticed women in his other classes. It was natural, he told non-teaching friends, for a teacher to look at the beautiful and the sexy, even the pretty. That Childress girl two years ago pulling up her dress to scratch inside her thigh with one hand as she continued to take notes with the other stayed in his mind like a painting of a goddess caught in the bath. But he had not gone beyond looking. There was something of the Puritan about him. And even when a woman, as a few had, hinted that she wanted more from him than literary insights, he had restrained himself to a few remarks and a farewell drink to mark the end of the course. He also felt he could not betray Jane. Was that faithfulness or stodginess or what? Who cared as long as he was happy? And he was, wasn't he? Yes, he decided, he was. And she was better looking than any woman he'd seen since they met almost four years ago.

Prairie literature, a desert with aimless tumbleweeds. Poetry of the obvious, prose of the prosaic. The stepchild of the department. He got stuck with the course because nobody else wanted to teach it, especially at that hour. A week's teaching in a single evening. Would that help him in his application, or mark him out as a drudge unworthy of tenure? How to make it interesting? No need. The students were looking for an easy credit, a soft option. The classes were all the same. The usual half-asleep eyes and bored faces, with a sprinkling of intense note takers. A rumbling stomach from a missed dinner, a suppressed fart from a gobbled one.

Get on with it, Onderby. No need to introduce himself, he was listed in the catalogue and the undergraduate student guide, which gave him an instant and forgettable fame.

"The course texts are in the campus bookstore. They're together under the course name. For any of you who may be new at this, a note about taking notes. You don't have to write down everything. That may seem like good insurance but it's not necessary. They're called notes for a reason. They're what you should remember. They'll help you remember the rest."

The redheaded woman's hand shot up. He pointed at her, nodding.

"How are we to know when you're saying something important?"

"I'll tell you or infer that it's important by the emphasis I put on it, both in tone of voice and amount of time. Generally I'll begin with an important point, and when I conclude a lecture or section of a lecture, I will stress the important point or points again."

"How do you know what the important points are?"

"That's why I'm up here and you're down there."

A few students grinned.

"So when you think something's important, we should too?"

"Not because I say it, but because of my training and experience."

"Pardon me, but can you be wrong?"

"Possibly."

"If you don't know when you're wrong, how are we going to spot it?"

Onderby looked at his watch.

"You'll have to trust me, believe I know what I'm talking about."

"So we should accept everything you say, even if some of it could be wrong."

Onderby smiled.

"You'll have to take it on faith I'm almost infallible."

"You're saying we've got to believe you."

The class was very quiet, with a growing interest in the exchange. Onderby stalled, trying to end it.

"Look—I'm sorry, I don't know your name."

"It's Pookie."

A few smirks, a giggle, a muttered remark. Turning, she spoke to the class.

"It's short for Virginia."

Everybody laughed.

Until the coffee break Onderby spoke about the syllabus and schedule.

Afterwards he glanced increasingly at his watch as he listened to himself droning on in detail about the genres to be covered. He thought of a man dying of thirst scrambling across hot sand trying to find a waterhole. Grateful as always for eight o'clock in that course, he packed up quickly but when he looked up, there was Pookie.

"I'm sorry, Professor Onderby, but I have to say what I think. Is that all right in your class?"

For a second Onderby thought his happiness hinged on the answer.

"Sure, but try to focus your questions. Be specific, and don't worry as much about who's right or wrong as about the spirit of the work we're talking about."

She hesitated. He noticed her hands, clasped together holding the binder, fingers slender and palms narrow. They would be very soft to touch. But that jarring note of her pointed nails, as if they had been dipped in dragon's blood.

"I didn't understand a lot of what you were talking about. I've been out of school for years. This is my first year. I don't know if things will work out."

"Give yourself a chance. People who've been out of school a long time or lack much formal education tend to be leery about coming back. Don't be hard on yourself. Do your reading, take notes."

"I've never taken notes. I don't know what to write."

"If you like, you can show me your notes in a week or so. My office is in Mackerness Hall. Hours are posted on the door. Drop by and discuss any problems you have with the course. Or see me after class."

"OK. Thanks a lot."

He lugged his briefcase to the stairs, trod down to the first-floor exit in the almost empty building and pushed one of the large metal doors open. As he walked to the parking lot, he noticed the night air was getting cooler.

At the next meeting Onderby read a short story by Pensive Chambers, a native woman who became a prostitute, alcoholic and drug addict before she found Jesus. After reading "To Cry Out Loud" and talking about the use of a writer's life as a subject for fiction, he asked for reactions. A guy at the back raised his hand. In his late forties, he was the oldest member of the class.

"She can't face life. She goes from one drug to another. Lots of people need something to get them through. Not strong enough themselves."

Ready to rebut, a woman had raised her hand before he finished.

"This was written in the 1970s. Nothing's changed. Know how many native women go missing every year, are never found? Abuse leads to self-abuse."

"They're not like anybody else. Sex, liquor, drugs come easy to them and they never want to quit that kind of life. This one found Jesus. Another drug."

"What do you mean, this one?"

"Indians. What do you think I mean?"

Pookie had been sitting quietly, dressed in a white sweater and jeans, a plastic lily in her hair. She raised her hand, turned and looked at the man.

"She was trying to find herself. Thought good times were the answer. I think she's wonderful for coming through it all and finding what she really wants. If that takes religion, I've got nothing to say against it. Eight years of screwing strangers is an awful lot of dead meat."

"How would you know?"

"I've done it. You earn your money most nights. Other nights aren't bad. Sometimes you meet a nice guy. It doesn't mean anything because he's got a wife and kids and he's with you to get some excitement in his life. It's a thrill for him. And believe me, most nights the thrill is all his."

"Don't tell me you had to do it. There's a lot more opportunities for women now. Thanks to your feminists always complaining. That's why lots of guys are opting out. Carry the load we've been carrying. See how you feel after a while."

Pookie smiled at him the way someone who knows the truth does at someone who's talking theory.

"I know women who got a bad break, like being beaten or molested or thrown out when they were kids, and got into sex work. It doesn't mean they're angels. They like to spend on their rotten pimps, and some are dumb. But they didn't put that thing between a guy's legs. Or what's between theirs. People with money and good families make mistakes. But you'd obviously know more about that than I would."

Nobody wanted to take her on after that. Onderby filled in the rest of the time with a lecture on first person narrative technique, relating it to how Pensive Chambers tells her story. He wondered what kind of bad break made Pookie begin. After class she was there, with her direct look and lively eyes.

"I'm sorry I kind of took over for a while, Professor Onderby, but when I know something about something, I've got to say it. That's all right, isn't it?"

"You added a lot to the discussion."

She brought her fluorescent red binder up to the level of her breasts, which in that white sweater seemed like hills freshly covered with snow.

"You said you would look at my notes? Do you have time tonight?"

"Sure."

One corner of the binder pressed into her right breast. He braked his train before it disappeared into an avalanche. She opened the binder to her pages of notes and handed it to him. Her delicate handwriting looked like calligraphy written with a paintbrush. Every few lines appeared the phrase, "Professor Onderby says," and every few lines after that, "I think." Onderby read that sometimes she disagreed with him and sometimes agreed. Occasionally there was a large question mark in the margin.

"You don't have to add those phrases. You can assume I said all that and add your comments without saying 'I think.'"

"I like to make things clear to myself. Your name reminds me I'm hearing your opinions. When I'm more used to taking notes, I'll drop that. Did I write down all your important points?"

He handed the binder back.

"You've done a good job. In two classes."

"Thanks. Goodnight."

Pookie placed the binder on a seat behind her, put on her white trench coat, picked up the binder and walked out of the room. As he watched her without seeming to, Onderby noticed that he was beginning to see her differently. She seemed taller than her five feet, two inches, her clothes appropriate and even necessary. His concern, almost pity, for her lack of academic skills was evaporating, replaced by admiration for the strength and intelligence that insisted on a particular way of expression and would not be compromised by the petty needs of an institution. He had the strange feeling he was encountering a force older and stronger than academe, even society, and that beguiled him.

Perhaps the feeling had something to do with his job. What was that job, and what was he supposed to be? He knew what the department wanted: no trouble and the usual percentage of failing grades. What did he want? It had been easy to slough off classes so he had time for articles and for Jane. Not that he was negligent. He saw more students outside the classroom than most of his colleagues. He never used his position as a way of intimidating students. But he had to admit that, despite his yearnings to be different, his classes were almost identical in method to those offered by others. He had really dared or changed nothing and accepted almost everything. He was like hundreds, even thousands of others across the continent.

Why not change things? After the third class Onderby asked a favour of Pookie.

"Do you think you could bring a hooker friend of yours to class so she could tell everyone the truth about life on the streets? It would bring Pensive Chambers' story up to date, give it life."

Pookie was not enthusiastic.

"I'll try, but a lot of the girls I knew have disappeared. By the way, Professor Onderby, they call themselves sex workers now."

"Let me know if you can. I think it would work."

She let him know about five minutes before the next class began. She was waiting outside the room. With her was a large woman who seemed to be in her late twenties. She had a fleshy face with dimples. Her lipstick was a glaring orange-red and her blue eyes were unfocused and yet wary. A mass of blonde hair exploded over her head and drifted down her back. She wore a black leather skirt, very short, and a pink sweater. Slung from her left shoulder was a pink purse on a strap. A black leather jacket was draped over her right arm. She looked like a wilted orchid.

Pookie introduced her as Venus. Her voice was businesslike but surprisingly young.

"I get two hundred an hour."

Onderby bargained, aware of the irony.

"I appreciate your coming but I can't pay that much. I'll give you a hundred."

"Since Pook drove me and is going to take me back, I'll give you half an hour."

Onderby paid her and said to Pookie, "We'll start right away. Next week, I'll fill you in on what you missed." They walked into the room and he let Pookie introduce Venus.

"Professor Onderby asked me to bring somebody who is kind of an up-to-date Pensive Chambers. She can tell you more than I can. I been out of the business for years. And I wasn't on the streets, anyway. Anyhow, this is Venus."

Pookie stayed with Venus at the front for the half hour.

"I work on the street. I charge $200 an hour. That includes when we start talking. Prices are set, no bargaining. Cheapest is a hand job, $50. To go down, $150. Usually takes fifteen minutes. Regular sex is $200. Takes about half an hour, usually less. I got a couple of things I can do to make the guy finish if he's slow. I carry condoms. Most guys take them. Some don't want to and I take a chance if the guy looks OK. Get myself checked by a doctor pretty regularly. Workers in houses charge $250 for regular sex. For $300 they offer 'girlfriend extras' with it, like cuddling and spooning. That's not going to happen in a car."

All the questions were asked by women.

"How did you get started?"

"My father left my mother for another woman. My mother got a boyfriend and he used to get her drunk so she'd pass out, so he could screw around with me and my little sister. We told my mother and she told him. He said we were liars. She wouldn't do nothing. Me and my sister ran away. I was fourteen. She was twelve. It was hard. We hung around pubs downtown and guys would buy us meals and get us drunk. They'd screw us in a room or even in back alleys. After a week we met a pimp. Said he would look after us so guys would pay for sex, and he would buy us clothes and we'd live in a good place. So we went along. But he got us on stuff. We were high all the time.

And he beat us if we didn't turn enough tricks every night, no matter how we felt. One night a john cut my little sister so bad she had to go to the hospital, and when I got there my sister was dead. I got another pimp now. He's better to me. He doesn't hit me. Only when I deserve it."

"How old are you?"

"I'll be twenty in two months." The surprise was audible in the room.

"Do you want to do this for the rest of your life?"

Venus smiled sarcastically.

"Probably won't be long, anyway."

"Are you bitter?"

"I got stuff for when I get down. My guy looks after me pretty good and most times I don't think about things."

"What do you think of your customers?"

"The johns? It's business. I get paid. Even if they only want to talk."

"Have you ever been beaten up?"

"Got hit once. Not real bad. I think about the chances of some guy cutting me up, though. Others besides my sister have been cut so bad they died."

"Do you do anything your customers want?"

"Anything but let them hurt me. If they want me to hurt them, I don't mind."

"I heard hookers don't like to be kissed."

Venus made a face. Pookie stepped forward and spoke.

"You have to keep something for yourself. Kissing is personal. Men don't understand that. Most don't care about kissing. It works out. Don't believe what you read about sex workers who say they're having a great time. I haven't met any. Streetwalkers don't talk that way. They're bored or high or worried about who's in the next car. It's business. Some who work in houses and have clients who are businessmen might say it's great. They could be kidding themselves, like anybody else. When you sell your body, you sell more than your body. And maybe it doesn't matter to some women as much as it does to others."

Onderby had a question for Venus.

"Do you ever think about leaving?"

Venus shrugged.

"Sometimes I think about meeting a nice guy and getting married and having a family. Most times I don't."

He thanked Venus and she and Pookie left. He thought he should sum up for the class what had been a positive experiment.

"Pensive Chambers' story is more than a story. She is alive today and on the streets of this city."

After a few minutes of self-congratulation, he paused. A woman raised her hand.

"I don't see how listening to a streetwalker talk about her tricks teaches us about a story. That's like social work or sociology. And we've seen that kind of stuff on TV. If we were reading about people working on a farm, we wouldn't get a farmer to come and talk to us about tractors and fertilizer."

"I'm trying to shake up your assumptions that books are only words and don't refer to real people and the characters in them are in another dimension. Literary characters and reality are obviously different, but there is a connection, and I want you to be aware of it. Pensive's story is a part of the life around us. Venus has shown that."

Nobody looked convinced. Take a gamble.

"How many of you think bringing Venus here was a bad idea?"

Slowly but insistently, like spikes of mould in a rotten apple, hands rose until almost all of the forty students had shown their rejection of his experiment. As Onderby was counting there was a knock on the half-open door. Pookie had managed to get back before the class was over. He motioned for her to take her seat. He noticed that at her re-entry some of the hands had started retreating back to their owners. He smiled at her.

"I asked the class if bringing Venus here was a bad idea. You saw from the raised hands that most thought so."

"I thought so too, Professor Onderby. It was showing her off as if she was a freak."

"As I told the class, I wanted to show that Pensive Chambers is alive today, not between the covers of a book."

"Using her to explain something about a book, you forgot her feelings.

She's screwed enough without coming here and being screwed again."

"She took the money."

"What did you expect? She's a whore."

Onderby's eyes unfocused until all he saw was her bright red jacket, which she hadn't taken off, and the plastic rose in that fiery hair. Her face, a blob of impertinence to him now, stayed stolidly in front of him.

"I think bringing her had value as a lesson in linking books with life."

"OK, but as an old whore I can tell you we know when we're being screwed."

Pookie spoke to him after class.

"I met a friend who was returning to the city and she took Venus back. I was lucky."

"I wasn't. Why did you let me invite her?"

"You're the teacher, you asked. I knew if I told you my feelings, you'd still want me to do it. I was hoping that you'd see why it was wrong, but you didn't, even after the class saw what you couldn't. So I had to try and make you see it. Am I talking too much, Professor Onderby?"

"No, I always appreciate your comments, even if we disagree."

"Always appreciate" had a note of condescension neither missed, and "disagree" was a last try at saying he was right, though both knew he wasn't.

One experiment fizzled, try another. Go see Katie Krips, in charge of prairie lit because nobody else wanted to be. On the warpath promoting local writers. Ready to praise the mediocre if it was arrogant enough. Her seminars never dull, except the writing. Onderby had attended one. Several poets read their work. She sat next to him at the back of her living room, hands inside the pockets of her billowy green pants. Every so often, moved by what she heard, she would utter a sharp, "Oh." He glanced over and could see her shuddering, wondered how literally she took her own advice about coming to the point. He had shown her a short story of his and she had read it quickly and said, "This stuff is obsolete, Norton. You write like some constipated Englishman. Don't be obvious about your theme. Let your metaphors do the damage, pulverizing the readers for the final barrage of truth, get rid of those semicolons and colons and don't bother hyphenating anything. Instead of worrying about punctuation, leave out a period or a comma, wake 'em up. You're competing with romance shit and TV. Blow the bastards away."

There was one thing in her favour. Had no use for the creative writing department.

"Those assholes. Jonathan Scavell, the limey con. Wears cravats and farts in rhyme. He writes worse than you. Janice Blastoff fucks crocks in rest homes. Think they're being examined by a nice nurse. Easiest pay cheques on campus."

He hadn't been to her office in over a year. He repressed a grin seeing again its walls decorated with photos of soiled doves. Lifted petticoats showing gartered hose and chubby thighs. She saw him looking.

"The joy girls. The West couldn't have been won without them. Grab a chair. What's shaking your shit, Norton?"

"I need a local writer, Katie."

"Stuffed shirt like you. Maybe you'd like her in leotards and long hair, holding an espresso and spouting."

"Spouting poetry for my class in prairie lit."

"Oh yeah, you got stuck with that course."

"Who've you got?'

"I'm not a madam."

"You're prairie lit's soiled dove, sacrificing for the cause."

"I don't know if that's an insult or lame praise."

"It's probably both. You said I can't write."

"OK, we'll put it down to lack of talent. I can get you Karen Westerberg, young, good-looking, feminist with trimmings. I've heard her. She'll shake 'em up. Especially any fathead guys lurking in there."

"Next class?"

"She'll be there."

She was waiting outside the room at eight. Square shoulders, blonde hair cut short, snub nose and provocative eyes. Her figure and body movements said she worked out in a gym or jogged. She wore a canvas-coloured poplin jacket over a pale blue denim shirt, indigo jeans and grey sneakers. She walked into the room and introduced herself. Onderby appreciative. Those semi-teardrop cheeks and that slight hip flare and soft stretchy cotton that sighs over them, the luckiest fabric alive, except for silk, of course.

Onderby sprung his surprise on the class, which didn't look surprised or that interested. Some relaxed. At least they weren't going to be examined on this. After introducing Karen, he asked her to step up to the lectern. He returned to his desk and sat down. She seemed a veteran of poetry readings. She spoke in a firm voice, undaunted by facing forty people.

"These are poems about an independent woman being herself, expressing her spirit. After I read through a poem, I'll stop if anybody has anything to say."

She put her sheaf of poems on the lectern and stepped back, arms close to her sides, fingers curled, as she spoke. Her voice became louder as she pumped emotion into it.

I am not pink
I am not your baby
I am not your blanket
I am not your giggles
a tickled pink dimple
not a pink rose
not a pink dress
there's nothing pink
about my intentions
I am the colours
of all humanity
a sunset a dawn
every shade of water
and flame
there's a tiny piece
of me you could find
the only pink I have
not the birthday
party ribbon

or the pale strawberry
birthday cake
but that pink
I was born with
and flushes red
and dark to a hot
snug crimson
even there I will not
stay pink for you
I am my own colours

When she finished the class was quiet. She waited and turned over a page.

there's a man I've ironed
or getting all the bulges out
too many propositions
about himself directed at me
so much inadequacy
puffed up swollen
like a finger at me
too many times
one muscle too many
so I pressed him in his suit
with steam and steel
he flattened the air went out
he went down to the width
of a comic book and I laughed
he didn't when I reached for scissors
now he's the paper cutout
I've cut out of my life

Silence followed this poem, too. Karen turned another page, waited a little
longer than the last time and read the next one.

my mother the everyday saint
wants an everyday daughter
to pray for the martyred her
Dad's dead I told her
dump him out of his rocking chair
get your own ideas now
you're as drunk as he was
with your rosary of sacrifice
how much did you put up with
how much did you do for us all
tell me again in screams
get that husk of widowhood
off your back
you don't fool me
with that uniform of saintliness
Mom-and-me-in-the-mall memories
no thanks
I'm not buying shoes with you
I'm stepping into my own life
and walking away
saints don't suffer
like their daughters do

Again silence after she finished. She turned a page and looked at the class for a second before continuing.

they don't advertise my thighs
they don't know my size
why don't they realize
they're selling TV lies
how many legs
can I buy for my life
how much is it worth

to cover them up
with dollars of dolors
stretch the internet
one crotch one world
every tidbit's tiny
prophylactic profligacy
want to turtle in my soup
want to rub up against the truth

After Karen finished a hand went up. The man in his forties who had jousted with Pookie spoke snidely.

"You're one of those feminists. You believe it's all men's fault for everything that's happened to women."

She focused on him the way a hawk eyes a rabbit.

"I'm a woman who won't believe a bunch of bullshit. I want to be empowered to live my own life. I don't want a man telling me what to do. Or what I should think."

"You really think that men deserve all the blame for what's happened to women? None of it's your fault?"

"Men have always had power over women. You can't see us as anything but victims because that's what we've always been. And you don't want to see anything wrong with that because it lets you keep dominating us. If you'd listened to my poems you'd know I don't want to be part of your world. Some women try to be man copies, lose part of themselves, but they're never accepted as men. When they make it they get the worst of a man's world, like cancer and heart attacks. Not power."

The man was red-faced now.

"All I heard from you was nothing but hate for men. Speak for yourself, but don't tell me you're speaking for all women. Don't tell me all your problems are caused by men. Dumping everything on guys. You're looking for an excuse for yourself."

Karen stared. "Somebody like you. . . ."

"What do you mean, somebody like me?"

Onderby wondered if he should jump in to prevent an argument from becoming an exchange of insults. Let things go, he decided, but tensed when Karen stepped in front of the lectern.

"You'll never accept a woman as equal. You like everything as it's been, as it is, because you feel threatened by women."

The man straightened up in his chair and leaned back, his hands pushing at the paddle-shaped arm.

"I've never felt threatened by any woman. Castrate your boyfriend. Hate your parents. Sexiest thing around. You got problems."

Karen put her hands on her hips. She walked to the first row of seats, ten feet from him.

"So I'm a thing. Gave yourself away, didn't you?"

Onderby stood up quickly.

"Perhaps we should get back to the poems. This serves no purpose."

Karen stared at him, returned to the lectern, picked up her poems and as she walked towards the door a voice said, "You want another woman's opinion?" She stopped, turned around, and holding her poetry like a gift that had been refused and then asked for, was undecided. Pookie didn't give her time.

"I really liked your poems. I haven't read much poetry. Don't know much. Can I ask some questions?"

Karen walked stiff-legged back to the lectern. Pookie had saved the class. As usual, she sat in the front row. She wore a grey sweatsuit, the top emblazoned with a grinning open-mouthed tyrannosaurus rex, its teeth an array of butcher knives.

"I think someone who says as many angry things as you do has given a lot of love that didn't work out. I'm not saying you can't speak for more than yourself. Women have always been shit—oh, excuse me, Professor Onderby— dumped on. If anyone's seen too much of the wrong end of a man, I have."

In her quiet even voice she asked several questions that brought the discussion back to the poems. Several others became involved, but the man who argued with Karen spent his time writing a letter. The discussion was so intense it went over class time. If it hadn't been for some rather loud packing up sounds and ostentatious putting on of coats, Onderby wouldn't have noticed how late it was. After quickly dismissing the class, he saw Karen and Pookie say something to each other before coming over to see him. Conspiracy of grins and nods. The poet appeared satisfied.

"Thanks for staying out after we got things going again. You ruined it by getting between me and that asshole. It turned out pretty good. I'm glad I came."

Onderby heard a duet of "Goodnight" as the women left.

Without her binder Pookie was waiting for Onderby the following week outside the classroom.

"I'm dropping out of university. Ever since I started me and my boyfriend have been having arguments. They've been getting worse. He thinks I'm wasting my time."

"What do you think?"

"I don't think so."

"Did you tell him that this is important to you?"

"He won't listen. There's something else. I don't know if I can write anything. The only writing I've ever done is on Christmas cards."

"You're doing extremely well in class discussions. I'm confident you wouldn't have any trouble. If you drop out, you probably won't return. It's none of my business but it seems your boyfriend is thinking of himself instead of you. Perhaps I should talk with him. Does he come to the university?"

"Sometimes he picks me up after class. Like tonight."

"Why don't you attend class? Later we'll see him together and I'll talk with him."

At the beginning of class Onderby reminded students they had the choice of writing a term paper or doing a class project. Each would be worth half the course grade, the other half their mark on the Christmas exam. For the term paper the subject would be up to the student but had to be based on the works studied in the course. The project would be read out in class and could be a story, poem or essay, but related to prairie life. He had offered this choice to every class in this course and ninety-nine per cent had always chosen the term paper.

With borrowed paper and pen Pookie made notes as Onderby talked. After class they walked to the student parking lot, where her boyfriend was waiting in his car. He started the engine as they approached and revved it several times. He scowled at her.

"Where ya bin? I been waiting an hour."

She walked up to the driver's side window.

"This is Professor Onderby. He teaches the English course I'm taking and he wants to talk with you."

"I'm busy. We got to go."

"No, we don't. Turn the engine off. You can listen to him. Professor Onderby, it's cold standing out here. I'll sit in the back and you sit in the front."

"Shit." The driver turned off the engine. The car was parked near the street, close by an arc light. A closer look at the driver revealed a T-shirt, a black leather jacket, a shaved head, tattooed neck, wristbands and broken knuckles. Onderby smelled cigar smoke.

"Mr. . . . ?"

"His name is Zachary Hobb. But he doesn't like anybody to know about the Zachary, so call him Hobb."

"Jeez, Pook. Can it, will ya? You want to know my take on this? She works in a clothes store. Why does she need more education?"

"Because she may not always want to work in that store. In my course she'll expand her vocabulary and ideas, learn how to write better and to speak confidently in group discussions. In other courses she'll be learning other things to help herself. Gain confidence in her abilities."

Onderby doing PR for PU, unpaid, on his own time.

Pookie leaned forward and put her head between the bucket seats.

"I'm not saying our life is bad, but I want to improve and you should let me."

"We got to go." Hobb started the engine.

"You can go without me." Pookie opened the rear door.

"Ain't coming?"

"You heard what I said."

"OK, shut the door."

"I can keep going to school?"

"Yeah."

Pookie shut the door and Onderby opened his and got out. She smiled.

"Thank you, Professor Onderby."

Hobb mumbled "shit" as tires spun and the car jumped away.

At the next class Pookie almost ran into the room as Onderby began his lecture. She slapped her binder and pen down on the arm of the chair and slipped off her earmuffs, woollen scarf and padded jacket—it was a late October evening and outside the earth frozen and grass white and glittering under pinpoint stars—and dropped sideways into the chair. Her feet were in the air when her backside hit the seat with the soft smack of denimed flesh on varnished veneer. Her grin said she was six and in toyland at Christmas. And the man she came to hear was Santa and his beard had better not fall off. After class she told him she had decided to do a project. But she had to clear the subject with him first.

"I want to write about my life as a sex worker and read it to the class."

"Sure. Everybody else will be doing a term paper. You'll have plenty of class time to speak. Late November would be best. Let me know when you're ready and I'll reserve an hour, or more if you need it."

As he lay beside Jane that night he thought about Pookie jotting down random bits of memories. Or one uninterrupted sentence punctuated by moments when she stopped to breathe. He dreamt he visited an amusement park. She was behind a ticket window, pasties covering her nipples. She wiggled her tongue and said, "Wanna buy a ticket for the big titties?" His hands held a heap of coins. They spilled on the ground and all over the counter and the man behind him in the lineup laughed and shouted, "He can't pay her." Head like a shrivelled white balloon splotched with fungus, the man was trying to shove past him. Onderby woke up and saw Jane's left shoulder and arm covered by a blanket. He realized she had never appeared in any dream of his and he had never mentioned any of his dreams to her. What did she dream about? He had never asked her.

Writing about prostitution was less painful for Pookie than telling people about her childhood. Her mother, severely retarded, became pregnant after being raped by a pensioner neighbour one afternoon when Pookie's grandmother was out shopping. Pookie was the result. Eventually her mother had to be sent to an institution. She was raised by her grandmother. She told her the story after both the pensioner and Pookie's mother had died. Her grandmother, Sally Korn, named her Virginia, "Pookie" being the name her mother Iris called the baby. No one knew why. "Tatlow," the surname Pookie adopted, was an old telephone prefix. She had seen it in a tattered, decades-old phone book when she was a teenager and preferred it to "Korn." Her memories of her mother were few and called to mind a slack mouth and a stare. Gentle hands felt the child's face and arms each time as if it were the first. In the beginning Sally would bring her in her arms, and later by the hand. Pookie was a little frightened at first but almost immediately began to feel the attachment between them. "Here's your daughter, dear. Here's Virginia." Iris' hand would slowly stretch out towards the girl and sometimes she would whisper "Poo-kee." The child would learn about the unspoken in eyes and fingers, hear it speak past age and words, the spaces between bodies and minds.

Sally, whose husband had died years before, was in her eighties and growing absent-minded. She began to leave the front door open when she went shopping and would forget her purse on the checkout counter at the supermarket. One day she wandered out in her nightgown, hat and purse. The store manager brought her back. He saw taps running, the furnace at full blast and windows open, and a half-naked four-year-old playing on a kitchen floor littered with dirty saucers. He notified social services. Sally began receiving daily help from a government care worker.

Betty Petrovich was a cheerful woman who did more than she was paid to do. She ensured that Pookie and her grandmother could stay together. She would drive them on Sundays to see Iris and afterwards to a mall or out for a drive into the countryside. Sometimes they would sit on a log beside a lake and eat ice cream, and Betty, who had been widowed early and never remarried, would tell them about her childhood on a farm, with the hard work, the cold that made her hurry between the buildings and winter nights with little else but laughter. "Boy, did we eat a lot of potatoes and cabbage. Not like this stuff." She would take tissues and wipe the ice cream from the redheaded girl's chin and then the bottom of the soggy cone in her hand. She told her about the Northern Lights. "Like green flames all over the northern sky. And sometimes waves of white silk. You'd think there was a woman over there doing a dance. That's what I thought when I was a little girl like you."

When Sally died Pookie was twelve. Without a husband Betty couldn't adopt her, and within a couple of years was diagnosed with bowel cancer and died soon afterwards. Pookie had no other relatives besides her grandmother and was sent to a foster home. She had to face the horrors alone. At the first home the man molested her until she ran away. At the second the woman thought she was trying to seduce her husband and would beat her. At fourteen she ran away again. The third pair of foster parents were indifferent and wouldn't feed her. They left the city and her behind. The fourth pair got divorced. She was sixteen, got a job as a waitress and dropped out of school. At her third waitressing job she met Danny Brancusi, who said he wanted to hire the eighteen-year-old as a secretary in his trucking firm. When she told him she had never used a computer, he had laughed and said, "Listen, beautiful, you'll do all right." He broke her in as an entertainer of clients and occasionally would lend her to friends in other businesses to perform the same service. Years later she heard Brancusi was killed when a jack collapsed and dumped a truck axle on his chest as he was repairing brakes.

"I suppose it was quick," she said.

When Pookie found out what had happened to Betty she visited her grave, and every year since took flowers on her birthday. She honoured her mother and her grandmother the same way. They were the special women in her life. Sometimes she cried with loss and longing remembering their unlucky lives and the bits of love they managed to give her. Each time she would rededicate her efforts in her own struggles as a tribute. This was too personal to share with the other students. Wouldn't they laugh, or worse, pity her and pretend to understand. She wouldn't risk that.

At the end of the next class she told Onderby she was ready to deliver her report in the following one. Mid-November was waiting for Onderby as he left the Arts Building. Every star in the universe seemed to be trying to outshine all the others. Artemis, the huntress, caught him periodically with her quick, bright arrows as he walked along a line of elms to the parking lot. He looked up once. In front of her and outlined by her pure white glow slim greyhounds drifted across the blue lawn of the sky. So the stars were flowers after all. And what would be the message from the official virgin to the frozen places of the heart? Were the desperate disparate? As he drove through the parking lot and home to Jane, silver arrowheads bounced off his car.

Onderby was planning his own destruction. He didn't know it yet. It would grow out of his aimless dissatisfaction. Teaching English was part of the education industry, a contraption for helping to mass-produce graduates. Why should students care about literature? They were the television and computer crowd, with everything spelled out for them in colour. A page was old-fashioned, a story with ideas took too much time. The world was going by too fast to decipher print. Headline nonstop news at the top of every hour, with the usual quota of politicians smiling official smiles and telling official lies, while special interest groups with as much interest in democracy as in Babylonian astrology plotted their compromises in private, and with the usual quota of dead and wounded shown on stretchers and being carried away from the rubble of explosions set off by groups with "liberation" and "freedom" in their names and propaganda. Words meant nothing and they meant too much. Released from books of religion, economics and science, thoughts in the cell walls of syllables floated, and airborne viruses and bacteria infected the self-deluded and their followers. Wrong bred wrong until large sections of the world were the decaying parts of one body, blue-black swollen flesh putrefying with germs spreading into fresh areas through the navigable blood and creating strange alliances and monstrous wars against the body's defenders, white blood cells, T-cells and phagocytes, mimicking friendship and planning destruction as impersonal as the power of a machine that will use the last bit of its fuel to reach the rust and silence of extinction. From space any strangers would see the always-grinning skull, the perpetual joke, too far away in time and too lost as a lesson, if they needed one, for them to know about parochial politicians who had sold humanity and the world out for a chance to preen themselves in public for a few moments.

In the next class Onderby told students that Pookie would be delivering an oral report, the only one to do so. She stepped up to the lectern holding her notes, some of them underlined so she wouldn't forget. She was dressed all in black, tight sweater and miniskirt slit up her right thigh. She wore huge hoop earrings and lipstick so red her mouth looked as if it were bleeding. Her upswept autumn red hair was held in place with black barrettes and that rare shade of sunset green in her eyes looked more intense.

"First, about my situation. I was sent as an escort to customers by the guy who employed me as a secretary. I was sort of a part-time call girl. Though I knew pretty quick being a secretary wasn't my real job. My boss wasn't a regular pimp, so I didn't have to deal with booze or drugs and he never touched me. When I wanted to leave, I could. But it was still sex work, giving my body to strangers to keep boss and customers happy.

"People think sex work is bad or glamorous. It's neither. It's sex, that's all. But sex with men who are unsatisfied, even after they leave you. I'm going to tell you how knowing them helped me to quit. I'll tell you about some of the most interesting clients I had. First, I want to mention George, who was a salesman. He wanted me to let him pinch me everywhere and with my clothes on. Most of them were soft, but when he pinched me on the bum he did it hard. After the first visit I got some soft latex and put it inside my skirt or dress. After that I was fine. He never caught on. But I mention him because of why he wanted to pinch me. He told me that when he was seven he was at his cousin's birthday party. She was turning eight and he liked her. He pinched her a few times, first on the arm and shoulder and finally on her bum. His mother saw him and pulled him up out of his chair and slapped him hard a few times in front of the other kids and mothers and told everyone what he'd done and said he was filthy and bad. George was so ashamed he ran out of the house. His cousin's father found him a couple of blocks away and brought him back, but he wouldn't go into the house. After that he thought there was something wrong with him. But he needed to do it even more. Later he lost girlfriends because he was more interested in pinching than in kissing or having sex. He got married and his wife threatened to leave if he didn't stop pinching her. So he went to prostitutes.

"So what did I learn from George? Sex is more than physical because our minds are part of it. And to cover my ass. Well, I got one laugh tonight, anyway.

"Philip taught me something different. He was an engineer and he wanted to tell me about his wife and all of his old girlfriends and about arguments with them and the gifts he had given them without getting anything back, including any love, he said. Finally one night I asked him, 'Philip, why do you think you got no love?' He said, 'I didn't deserve it, I guess.' I told him he didn't get any love because he was looking for it. It doesn't come in a box. He laughed too, and I thought I'd repeat it tonight. Anyway, I made him see love isn't a big thing, yes, laugh again, but a bunch of little things that, if you want you can call love. But you can't go looking for it like a rare animal in the jungle. I learned that by telling him.

"I want to mention Tony, an Italian guy. He liked small redheads with big breasts. He wanted to marry me the first night. I said, 'I thought Italians liked blondes. There's got to be a reason for you to like me.' He told me I reminded him of his brother's girlfriend years ago who he was crazy about. So I said, 'Hey, how do you think I feel about that? What are you going to do, rub out my face with an eraser?' Tony accepted that I didn't want to be anybody's fantasy girl. And I began to see that I was sort of a fantasy girl to all those guys. And not there only for sex, or whatever. I thought, what about my own fantasy? What do I want? That was the beginning of my leaving.

"But so you don't think this was all comedy and good times I want to tell you about Lester, a big guy who also told me he liked redheads but didn't tell me he could really hate them, could change his mind in a couple of seconds. He was all right until we were lying there afterwards and he said, 'Don't think I'm stupid. I know about it.' I'm thinking hard, what does he know? He grabbed my wrist and squeezed it until it really hurt and I yelled, 'Hey, cut it out.' He put his other hand over my mouth. I could hardly breathe. I pulled his hair. He took his hand from my mouth and put it around my throat and started choking me. I thought that if I didn't do something I'd be dead. I hit him with my fist three or four times and finally I poked his eye hard. He screamed and let go. I got up and ran downstairs naked to the hotel clerk. He got the cops. They ignored my almost being killed and the marks on my wrist and throat. They treated me like a criminal because I was a sex worker. I had to ask a cop to go to the room and get my clothes. I heard later they were pretty sure he killed two street girls, but that was never proven. When I was putting on my clothes I felt a horrible pain in my hand. One of my fingers was covered in blood and crooked. It was broken and never did heal properly. It still has a slight bend in it.

"I hope this has given you some idea of what that part of my life was like. Between discovering my right to what I wanted and surviving those guys who hurt women, I had good reasons to leave. I got this body back. It belonged to me all along."

Pookie sat down to applause that lasted for half a minute. She kept rearranging her notes as she stared down at them. At the end of class Onderby went over to her. She smiled and spoke before he could.

"Whew. That was one of the hardest things I ever did. Tried my best. Got some laughs."

"I've taught this course more than a few times and I enjoyed your report, and learned more, than from any other."

"Thank you sir." She almost giggled.

A week later there was a letter in Onderby's office mailbox. Skinner wanted to see him.

"You should be aware by now that this is a conservative campus. Inviting a prostitute to speak to your class is not what we expect from a staff member."

"I was teaching a story written by a woman who became a prostitute, alcoholic and drug addict."

"In turn or all at once?" Skinner's snake grin.

"She became a Christian and found her self-respect."

"I understand a member of that class was a prostitute and read a report about her life. What's that got to do with prairie literature?"

"I give students the option of writing a term paper on course material or delivering an oral report about something connected with prairie life."

"I suppose that's her area of expertise. Nonetheless, something more literary would've been more seemly."

"The class enjoyed her report."

"No doubt."

"She overcame a troubled childhood."

"Don't they all."

"Why am I talking to you about this? Shouldn't the chairman be the one to speak to me, unless of course he thinks it insignificant."

The snake coiled.

"He knows you're applying for tenure and thought the matter more within my purview, and so passed the complaint on to me."

"Complaint?"

"One of your students wrote a letter complaining about your teaching, including your seemingly inordinate interest in prostitution, for one thing."

"What about his interest in denouncing mine? And since when are staff members grilled about their teaching, based on student complaints? There have been complaints in the past. None have been taken seriously."

Snake grin sour.

"You mean the student guide, those sophomoric appraisals? This was a serious letter."

"You're comparing a letter from one student with a guide detailing the evaluations of hundreds."

"I'm not going to debate the merits of undergraduate guides based on juvenile grudges."

"You don't think this is a grudge?"

"There's no evidence of that."

"Besides not wanting to hear about prostitution, what else is there?"

"The writer thinks you favour a certain student, namely the reformed streetwalker."

"The evidence?"

"The student claims you let this woman take over the class and you pay her an undue amount of attention."

"So this amounts to vague allegations and an aversion to prostitution."

"We're simply bringing this to your attention. I'm sorry you're taking it this way. Still wearing jeans, I see. Merely an observation."

"I've taught here more than five years. This is the first complaint from a student of mine. The student guide rates my classes as excellent. The guide has no malicious intent, unlike whoever wrote the letter."

Skinner frowned. Onderby stepped towards the desk. Skinner jerked backwards in his chair. Onderby dropped a crumpled napkin into the wastebasket beside the desk.

"I have no malicious intent either. And clothes don't make the man, the real fabric is inside."

In his office that afternoon he spoke with Kruger, who mentioned the student guide to undergraduate courses.

"It always rates Skinner among the worst profs in the university. Your reference to the guide wasn't appreciated. I recall some choice epithets directed at him. 'Sleeping pill, loose binding, cold toast, glue hairdo, wall slider.' Why did Abercrombie pass the letter on to Skinner? It should have been given to you or thrown away. Disgruntled students have been known to complain and make up stories. There's no allegation of sexual misconduct. You're doing everything out in the open. And since when does a prof openly play favourites in class? Quickest way to lose respect. The short story covers you on the prostitute and your student's report was boffo. So what's going on? Who's the shit disturber? Bumped into Katie last week. She said you got a hot little redhead in your prairie lit. She didn't say it as if you were getting a bit of the old extracurricular."

"Recommended a poet I brought in to read. Poet must have told her. She and my student are friendly. Pookie saved the reading from a brawl between Parnassus and some oaf at the back."

"Pookie. Sounds cute."

"Yeah. Boyfriend twists spines for exercise."

"So you've met the beast. Otherwise?"

"Remember Jane?"

"You lucky bastard, who could forget her? I'll nose around, see what I can find."

Jane was in the office when Kruger returned two days later.

"Friend of mine in admin ran a check on your class. Looked up their other courses. A guy in your prairie lit is in Braun's second year survey. Older guy."

"He's the one who argued with Karen, the poet who read."

"There's your culprit. Talked with Braun. She goaded him. He wrote Abercrombie. I'll bet her panties were steaming."

Jane winced.

"Hardy."

"Pardon me, milady, but I forget your ears have never been profaned by curses or foul thoughts."

"What's this about Braun?"

"Norton's been accused of impropriety, to wit, inviting a prostitute to speak and of paying too much attention to a student who was one."

She looked at Onderby. Explain.

"The guy is a suit. Three-point snotrag in the jacket pocket, French cuffs, attaché case. Middle-aged business type. Fat face, overweight brain."

"What about the student thing?"

"Nothing to it. She's got a boyfriend. Tattooed neck. Knuckles like walnuts."

"Or what?"

"That was Hardy's reaction. Doesn't anybody believe in my pure intentions?"

"Are they?"

"Absolutely."

Alone later Onderby thought about ending up with the likes of Skinner and Braun in a lost corner of the academic world called Prairie University. The universe was luck. The best and worst of it would merge, like two lines in time into one inevitable nothingness. Meaning and significance were pretence. Any meaning out there among the cast sand of stars would be too much for us, though perhaps he didn't so much disbelieve in some ultimate meaning beyond the limits of human intelligence as to think humans were unworthy of it. The hero had died in him as it did in everyone, with no sign and on no special day or occasion. Everything was a business now. Life was a business, to do efficiently and on time. But sometimes that programmed inevitability didn't seem to exist and the lungs filled with blue sky and the veins pulsed like filaments of red root, and airy flesh and nerves felt joy in a whole universe of possibility, earth heaven and heaven earth and fiery water flowed as cool fire into the one river of never-ending sunset. And always denial afterwards, as if it was the only deception to be avoided.

Like his other courses, prairie lit went on punctually to its predestined end, a kind of pedagogical illusion reducing the amorphous meanings of words to the litany of a lecture providing certainty at the cost of professed ignorance, the beginning and end of all thought. More poetry and short stories, a play and a novel and it was done, the last class, outside the subzero first week of December. At the end Onderby and Pookie were alone, he standing and putting papers into his briefcase and she scribbling last-minute notes in her binder. They looked at each other and Onderby shook his head.

"And you thought you wouldn't do well."

"It was my first class, how was I to know? And I still have to write the final."

"You don't have anything to worry about. By the way, I gave you an A for your report."

"Oh," she said with real surprise, tossing her head and grinning. "Thanks."

"No thanks needed. You deserved it."

"I'm going to miss this class. If you don't mind, I'd like to sit in on a class next term."

This was a lie and they both knew it. He nodded.

They walked out of the room and down the hall and out into the freezing December night. Wisps of snow floated down from a sky that seemed immediately above their heads. Neither said anything until they reached the corner where she would leave for the student parking lot and he the faculty one. As they came to it, she suddenly reached up and kissed him on the cheek.

"What?" His audible surprise.

"Because you'd never. It's something that I don't have much experience in, so I'm getting in a bit of practice."

"You're teasing me."

"No. The best kisser I ever knew was a boy and we were both seven."

"I don't want to be nosy but what about your boyfriend?"

"Hobb? Oh, we're like partners. We do a lot of parting but it's never permanent. He's really desperate for somebody to make him feel good. I'm desperate for somebody to need me bad."

"That's hard to believe."

"Why? Because I answered a lot of questions in class I'm not supposed to know the answers to?"

"Of course not."

"There's more to life than a classroom. Because I did well in your class doesn't mean I do well at everything."

She had been trying hard not to shiver since they stopped walking. Onderby knew he couldn't keep her any longer. Wavering flakes tumbled through the pale amber corona of the streetlight and hovered around her for a while in their slow descent. A few crystals landed and melted on her upturned face.

"Well, Merry Christmas, Pookie Tatlow."

"Merry Christmas, and thanks for everything."

Onderby reached out and hugged her before he knew what he was doing and she hugged as hard as he did for those few seconds.

"Goodbye." He was the first to speak.

"Bye." She quickly turned and walked away.

He watched the pearly glow of her parka disappearing into the swirl.

Pookie wouldn't talk much with Hobb during that week as she prepared for the exam. When he touched her in bed she wouldn't respond, and when his touches became aggressive she spoke in a pained tone he had never heard from her.

"Cut it out. I need sleep."

Five days after the final class, on a Saturday morning at a quarter to ten, Pookie waited in a silent crowd outside the university auditorium. Cirrus clouds chased each other in games of tag across a pale blue field. The auditorium was an old structure built in the 1920s, its stucco walls gone grey and covered with masses of ivy. Pookie had only eaten a slice of toast. She was too nervous to have anything else. Because she didn't know if she could leave the exam in case she had to pee, she had drunk only two sips of coffee. She was thirsty already but that was better than peeing her pants or having to leave and not being allowed back. About five minutes to ten, the brown double doors opened and the crowd began filing into the interior, the size of a dozen tennis courts. Pookie looked at the twelve-foot wooden walls and the large exposed beams in the rafters as she walked on the oak flooring. Examinations in four courses were taking place. The other three were Christmas exams for full year courses. Signs with course names directed students to various rows of seats where their particular exam sheets and writing booklets were waiting. She found a seat in her section. When it was ten on the clock inside the entrance doors a voice over the public address system said, "You may begin. All examinations are of two hours duration. Please place your booklets in the appropriate pile on the desk near the door when you leave." Monitors stood in the aisles. She heard her beating heart as she turned over the exam sheet. There were two sections to the exam. In each were five questions. Candidates were to select a topic from each section and write an essay on it. In the first the questions were about prairie life depicted in the various forms studied. She chose to write about Pensive Chambers' story. The second section dealt with the relationship between form and content. She wrote about how Karen Westerberg's poetry reflected her moods and ideas. She wrote quick outlines on the question sheet, as Onderby had instructed the class to do when he had discussed the exam. After finishing the second essay Pookie looked at her watch, saw there were two minutes left, walked to the desk and placed her booklet on the pile.

Walking out into the cold sunlight, Pookie felt a release of the tension and sadness she had been feeling for the past couple of weeks. She was glad that Onderby hadn't monitored the exam, a job done by instructors from various departments. She realized she hadn't spoken to anyone from the class. She didn't remember recognizing any of their faces. There were midterms in her other courses. But this was her first final, the exam she wanted to ace. That night she sat on Hobb's lap as he was watching television. Putting her arms around him she whispered, "Hobb, let's go somewhere." His hands were on her breasts as she finished the invitation. They went into the bedroom.

She got an A.

January. Another message from Skinner. No invitation to see him this time but a reminder of the poetry reading coming up at the end of the month. Onderby tossed it into the wastebasket and closed his eyes. He leaned back in his office chair. Kruger tapped on the door, walked in and sat down. Neither spoke for a while. Kruger guessed.

"Skinner?"

"A reminder about the reading he dumped on me to honour that fart Blaisdell."

"Prairie lit's poet laureate of pig shit. Never had to soil my brain teaching it."

"I've avoided it. One thing about that prairie lit I've been stuck with. Free choice of texts. I went to the department library today. Took a quick look at his stuff. Worse than I remember. 'Prairie moon, floating orb of night, harvest of our pioneers' hopes and griefs, companion of dusky wanderers asleep in teepees and dreaming of buffalo hunts, shine through this blizzard burying my thoughts in white despair as I plod lost and alone over this wintery expanse.'"

"Plod is right. 'Dusky wanderers'?"

"You heard it. The first edition."

"There were others?"

"Let's hope not. Waste of paper."

"What's the plan?"

"I'll go see Katie."

As he appeared at the open door of her office she was trying to look sympathetic as she listened to a student reading a poem. A fledgling Blaisdell, Onderby thought. "Norton," Katie said as if she had been expecting him. She shooed away the poet with an encouraging smile and invited Onderby to sit down.

"What do you think of Blaisdell?"

"I don't."

"I've got to set up a poetry reading in Basset Hall at the end of the month commemorating something about him. His passing from us, I think."

"Best thing you could commemorate."

"Skinner palmed it off on me. Any suggestions?"

"I hear Karen's reading worked out. Why not get her again? Give me a few days to think of some others. I'll drop a note in your box with a list. At such short notice they won't be the pick of the crop. It's Blaisdell, who cares? Let Karen steal the show. Shake up Bassett Hall."

A few days later Katie said in her note that she was only able to get two poets, Hugo-Ron Marsden and Evan deCoupe Grese. They were locals, so he wouldn't have to pick them up at the airport. Onderby phoned and filled them in and invited them for a drink at the faculty club the evening before the reading. It was noon when he phoned Karen Westerberg. The call woke her up.

"Blaisdell? Who's he?"

"Somebody you don't have to know anything about."

"Yeah, OK, sounds fun. Anything I want?"

"Anything you want. I'm inviting the three of you for a drink the evening before."

He mentioned the others.

"Fuck, no. Not those assholes."

"That bad?"

"Worse."

"We don't need to meet. Katie recommended you and I've heard you read. You tore up the class. It's January 30. Make sure you're at Basset Hall by seven."

"Sure." She yawned.

Kruger dropped by.

"The girl, hot stuff. The first guy sounds like a pretentious prick and the other guy's name sounds like an immigrant asking for a lube job."

Later that afternoon Onderby put into the department mailboxes of the five members of the tenure committee an envelope containing a list of his published articles and work in progress, double spacing between both the published and unfinished works to make the list appear longer. During the next two weeks he posted notices around the campus advertising the reading and sent an article promoting it to the campus newspaper. He put Karen's name at the top of the list of poets. He reserved Basset Hall for that evening. At the faculty club he met the poets. Marsden was short, heavy and balding, about fifty and wore glasses. His leather jacket had studs, his jeans tears and his boots chains. He seemed to like rings as much as Caroline Skinner, but his were jagged chunks of metal.

"Here's to that shit, Blaisdell. Pardon me if I don't mention his name tomorrow night. This wine's good. I'm getting another."

Grese looked mid-twenties, hair crew cut and both sides of his head shaved and everything he wore denim except his earrings.

"I'm multimedia. Books, movies, synthesizers, computers. You friends with anybody in creative writing? What do they pay? Make fuck all from readings."

Basset Hall was half full the next evening at seven. Less than a hundred people had shown up for the tribute. Onderby was perversely pleased. On a platform at one end he sat with Marsden and Grese, along with Edward Blaisdell's widow, Enid, and the president of the university, Dr. Philip Meakin. Proceedings were due to begin but Karen Westerberg hadn't arrived yet. Ten minutes later his confidence in her was evaporating rapidly. Meakin looked at him and shrugged, stood up and approached the lectern. Scrawny, with a weak voice and wisps of white hair like cotton candy, he coughed for silence.

"Thank you all for coming. Basset Hall has seen many an event in its long history but I doubt one as significant. This is indeed a wonderful occasion, for the university and literature. Edward Blaisdell was important to the life of this place. His was and is the voice of this part of the country. I knew him both as colleague and friend. This night gives me great pleasure, the more so as his dear wife Enid is here to share in the recognition of his stature."

Onderby glanced at his watch. Marsden stifled a yawn. Grese had made eye contact with a woman in the audience. Enid Blaisdell looked frail. She was ninety-seven. Meakin whispered for another few minutes. Then it was Onderby's turn. He thanked everybody for coming and began a summary of the poet's career, from his birth on the east coast to his travels in Europe and on this continent, and followed with a survey of his work, listing the titles and dates of publication of his various volumes. As he was talking, Onderby imagined himself with the head of a donkey, braying. How could he enthuse over couplets on prairie sunsets seen from Lone Man's Bluff in Nineteen Thirty? Nature poetry by someone whose dull nature deadened everything he wrote.

"Edward Blaisdell's evocation of steam locomotives pulling carriages of immigrants through the immense new land, comparing them to caravans plodding through the Sahara Desert. His eulogy to hawks boring—I mean soaring—overhead as the sun shet, shat, shit, sat, set."

A couple of people in the audience laughed. Others were restraining themselves. What a pointless, stupid thing this was. Onderby felt laughter shaking him low inside. He tried to keep it there, squeezing the sides of the lectern. It began to totter. He almost fell over with it into the first row.

"I'll conclude by noting that years before they became movements in modern poetry, Blaisdell produced concrete poetry and performed sound poetry. His concrete poems are in his last volume, *Prairie Forms.* Because my time is limited I'll only mention the letters of 'love' shaped by twisted thorny stems of a wild rose bush. In sound poetry he has few equals. In recordings he imitates the sound of a steam locomotive leaving the depot and skimming across the prairies in "Choo-choo Woo-woo." He imitates the sound of Indian drums in "Boom Da Da Boom." These were recorded by the university and are in the archives. Unfortunately the old LPs are too scratchy and warped to be played."

He saw Karen, dressed in black, standing by the double doors at the back of the hall.

"That's all the time I have. We'll now hear from poets who are carrying on the traditions established by Edward Blaisdell."

Onderby introduced Marsden and sat down. Marsden offered bitchy fangs: "Is a rat two-footed? Does it paint its toenails? You should know." He concluded with an account of a sexual journey through Eastern Europe, mentioning only the names of the countries he visited. "Rom—mania, Bulg—area, Pole—land, Hung—gary, hun hun hun hun, uh uh uh uh, Slo—venia, Czech, Slov—akia, Czech Czech Czech, slo slo vak—ee—aa."

He's literally an asshole, Onderby thought, as Marsden sat down to bits of applause. Grese sauntered up to the lectern. Like Marsden, he made no reference to Blaisdell. Meakin looked uncomfortable at the omission. Enid Blaisdell looked as if she were waiting for a bus. Grese began in the middle of something. "Should not be interfaced with your modem. Rubber verbs incontinent. Allow ample drying time. Sins of alliteration breed contempt. Christ loiters. The gates of the mansion. Phalanx, philately, flagellate. In phenomenal doses. Like a means of. But let's not. Lethargic latitudes. Desktop liaisons. Crunch cupids in numerological onrush. Is that a dactyl, slant meridian, you wiped from your eyes?" An embarrassed giggle drifted from the audience towards the platform. Onderby made puffing sounds with his lips and looked at his watch. Why doesn't this guy hand out encyclopedias and dictionaries, so we can bore him by showing off with stupid word games? The non sequiturs finished, more bits of applause.

Karen was moving slowly towards the platform. Onderby remained in his seat, knowing she wouldn't want to be introduced. He noticed a group of young women dressed in black and advancing with her to the front. They took empty seats in the first few rows as she stepped onto the platform. Black jeans, sweater and sneakers, she walked to the lectern and spoke from memory. Her voice was darker than Onderby remembered. This was a public reading, not prairie lit, and the occasion was all hers. Something seemed to whisper in Onderby's ear. This had happened before and the result had never been good. Karen's voice rang out.

> it's over
> not begun
> but it's happened
> already so many times
> I'm finished fucking with you
> bastards who think
> you're too good
> to have come out of a woman's body
> whining with child puke

the green stench of promises
tomorrows weddings disasters
stillbirths
the oh baby lies
don't rummage in me
for beginnings straining
for the spilled boast
fucking me so good
I would die with come
drooling out of my wound

I've put a razor in my cunt
and you can slice
your stubs to bloody slivers
and I bloodwashed risen
fondled by your glances for a while
and beyond your touches
every step forward
will not look back
at the fallen dreams
like corpses
littering my life

The women in the seats began chanting: "Our bodies belong to us." Several people stood up and left, some with walkers or canes. One muttered as he walked out, "What's this got to do with Edward Blaisdell? I took a chance catching my death of cold coming here." A large man in an overcoat and muffler stood up and Onderby recognized him as the man who had argued with Karen in class.

"I've had enough of women's rights. It's all about blaming men. And abortions on demand. Know what you are? Murderers of unborn life. Abortion clinics sell infant body parts. I lost my son. My wife had an abortion to get back at me. Heartless bitch. I'll never see my son. You goddam fucking bitches."

The chanting became louder. The man in the overcoat wiped his eyes with the end of his muffler.

"My son was chopped up and sold like a rabbit. Crazy bitch laughed at me. 'Go get your son. He's in a garbage can.' I tried to strangle her. The court ordered me to stay away. I'll kill her if I ever find her."

"I know you," Karen shouted. "You're that guy in prairie lit. You knew I'd be reading tonight. You came here on purpose."

The chanting stopped. Karen was right. Onderby remembered her name was on the posters he had put up around the campus. Everybody was staring at the man in the overcoat standing in the third row. Onderby looked around. No campus police. He wasn't carrying a phone. Best thing to do was end the reading. Defuse the situation. He went to the lectern and stood beside Karen and smiled.

"I'd like to thank everyone for coming tonight. It's been quite an occasion."

"We haven't finished," Karen said. "It's a performance."

Still trying to smile, Onderby whispered without moving his lips.

"There'll be another performance if he's carrying something."

"Ask him to leave. Phone campus security."

"Sorry, I'm taking charge."

Karen shouted at the man in the overcoat.

"Satisfied? You've ruined our performance. Typical male bullshit. Blame us for everything. Our bodies belong to us."

Slowly the chanting began again, Karen leading from the lectern. One of the performers came to the front and began dancing. She stripped until naked, still moving slowly, bare feet and arched back a single curve. "You're Satan's whores," the man hollered and reached inside his coat. "Somebody call campus security," Onderby yelled and pulled Karen down. The man took out a paper bag, threw it in the direction of the platform. It hit the lectern, splattering its contents. Marsden was first to react. "Shit." He and Grese left and Meakin escorted Enid Blaisdell away. Onderby stood up behind the turd-splotched lectern. The performance had stopped, the women arguing with the bag thrower. "You'll never leave us alone," a woman said and punched him in the face. "Satan's bitches." He pulled her hair and she screamed. Other women jumped him, riding him to the floor and one yelled, "Castrate the bastard." Campus police arrived and began to separate the squirming mass of bodies.

Most of the crowd had made for the exits but a few were recording the melee on their smartphones as Onderby handed the naked dancer her clothes. He slipped on a turd and fell with the dancer onto the floor, taking her with him. The phones caught Onderby sprawled on top of her, hands on her breasts, as well as an officer questioning him later. The next issue of the campus newspaper published photographs and printed a story that took up the whole front page: "Poetry Orgy in Basset Hall." Onderby's name was sprinkled throughout the story and he was mentioned as the organizer of the event. Among others questioned was Onderby's turd-throwing student. He was taken into custody and charged with creating a public disturbance.

In his office two days later Skinner looked like a man having a hard time pretending he's not enjoying an execution. He spoke to the ceiling as Onderby stood in front of him.

"I shouldn't have to tell you what you've done to the reputation of the department. And to yourself as well. All you had to do was arrange a poetry reading. We've had hundreds of them at the university and never an incident like this. It makes me wonder about your judgement. The department felt I should be the one to inform you of its disappointment. I told Reid I had nothing whatever to do with this mess but had in good faith entrusted it to you. I don't know what else there remains to be said."

"I didn't know a fanatic was going to show up."

"Which fanatic do you mean? I understand Ms Westerberg was very late, didn't even bother when she finally arrived to condescend to sit with the other participants. And that she brought a bunch of women to perform with her in a kind of travesty of a Greek chorus. I've been told her poetry, if it can be described as such, made a mockery of the tribute, showing a sheer lack of respect. I can tell you Dr. Meakin and Enid Blaisdell were upset by all of this. Didn't you impress upon her the significance of the occasion? Your poet encouraged the reaction she got. And you watched a naked woman perform some grotesque gymnastics, signifying who knows what, and did nothing."

"It was part of the performance, a kind of theatre to involve the audience."

"It certainly did, but not in the way any responsible person would expect or enjoy. And that's where this question of your judgement comes in. I told you when I entrusted you with this assignment this department values unselfish contributions as important considerations in determining whether tenure is granted to an applicant. You were enjoying your poet's performance while neglecting your duty to the department, Enid Blaisdell and the memory of Edward Blaisdell."

"I wasn't pleased with everything, but I felt I had to give Karen artistic licence. She's a poet, agree or disagree with what she says."

"Look where your attitude led."

"I'm not a mind reader. I didn't know a mentally unbalanced man would go berserk."

"I know. But again, judgement. Common sense should tell you somebody as unorthodox as your poet requires careful management, not simply respect. You're not there as a fan of hers."

Snake jaws parting. Skinner grinned up at the ceiling, a slow, almost unconscious stretching of the lips. "The grin of death," Kruger called it. "You're within striking distance. The end cometh."

"Have you done any work yet on suggestions for new courses? I'll need something in the next month. For that committee. I've got to get it out of the way before the tenure committee meets."

Lying beside Jane that night Onderby said he thought his career might be coming to an end.

"I can imagine what the bastard said to Abercrombie about the reading. I don't have a chance. Skinner and Braun are out to get me and they will. May as well face it. Bye-bye to PU."

"Skinner can't do you in unless you allow him to. I've looked at your articles. They're good. The course guide always gives you high ratings."

"Teaching counts for nothing. He's waiting for more mistakes. If I don't make any, he'll find some. With that bitch's help."

"You've got to forget them." Jane rolled over onto her left side and fell asleep.

Onderby dreamt that Skinner welcomed him into his office with his snake grin, the forked tongue flicking up at the ceiling. A naked Ruth Braun was waiting for him with a bullwhip. He hobbled in leg irons, his hands behind him in handcuffs. She sneered, fresh blood smeared over her mouth. "We're giving you a new curriculum vitae." He turned to open the door but there was a heavy bar across it. Skinner, crouching behind his desk, peered over the top with a smartphone as Ruth Braun advanced towards Onderby, swinging her whip. She flicked her wrist and the whip curled around his neck, tightened and began to strangle him. He woke. He felt his neck, drenched in sweat.

A week later Onderby met Helmut Meinsdorf, a friend of Kruger's. They had drinks in the faculty club lounge and Onderby talked about Skinner and the poetry reading. Meinsdorf was a big-boned man with a shaved head and staring eyes. A painter, he listened to Onderby's complaints before delivering his verdict with a heavy accent.

"What could you expect? Your English department is a museum and you are curators. You think I would ever, even for the money, work in such a place? Art must live, breathe. You know nothing of art."

"I write short stories," Onderby said, vaguely uncomfortable admitting this.

"I bet they stink."

Remembering what Katie had said about the story he had shown her, Onderby remained silent.

"Sure, I am right. So, Norton, are you going to stay in this the rest of your life? Praying over the literary gods you display to your students? Because this is a religion. And you all are told who is good and who is not and everyone is too scared to say anything different. You know why Hardy is my friend? Because he takes none of you seriously. He told me about your tenure shit. He will never apply. It is a joke to him, as it is to me. Are you ready to try something different, something none of your colleagues would ever do?"

"Like what?" Onderby was afraid of what he was going to hear but wanted to hear it.

Kruger, smiling, was more than slightly drunk.

"The ruin of one career coming up, or maybe the making of a writer. Who the fuck knows? Put your future in the hands of this guy and you may find out, but a warning, he's as nutty as a squirrel with both cheeks full. Do you matter that much to hesitate, or are you like the rest of them, bullshitting their egos they're too important to literature to recant. Is the world of Skinner and Braun too much to lose?"

Kruger downed the rest of his beer and slammed the stein on the table.

"May I assume your silence means assent? Go ahead, Helmut, ruin this pedagogue's life. One dead flea, like the rest of us. Put an end to bloodsucking the life out of words."

Meinsdorf stood up and pointed at Onderby.

"Be ready. I will let you know."

He left and Onderby asked Kruger about him.

"He's a waiter at Chickie Dee's, a coffee house where avant-garde artists— dare any other kind show their face?—hang out. He was vegan for a few years. Now he eats raw meat. The rest is prehistory."

"What will Jane say?"

"What any woman would. He's crazy and you're crazy. Women don't understand what makes men crazy. Because women don't go crazy, they get bitchy."

"Women have gone insane."

"Only when driven to it by men. A disease contracted from religious and political gurus, cult leaders, anything faintly human holding an electric guitar or appearing daily or nightly on television or in movie trash or in any of the other fetid spawned manifestations of mass culture. Get in on the fame game, you have to beat them off with a stick. Has to do with the male bird with the brightest plumage, that kind of thing."

Kruger stared into his empty stein.

"What if I told you universities could be guilty of murder?"

"Not directly, I'm assuming."

"Let us say guilty of self-induced, deliberate blindness. Whilst undergoing the forlorn experience of doing my first degree here, I picked up a few stories.

One was about the head of the botany department in the '80s, a Dutchman who turned out to be a German. Got into the country after the war with a phony passport under the name of August Koopman. Real name Reinhard Kastenmeier. A guard at Flossenburg. The bureaucrats at immigration back East found out his passport was phony. He had disappeared by that time, surfacing out here, where he spent thirty years growing flowers, and whatever else botanists do. He was in charge of those greenhouses at the university farm. Became an authority on potatoes or something. He was eventually recognized and the student newspaper published a picture of him along with the story. When I heard about him I searched through back issues of the paper and saw the picture. White crew cut, round spectacles, arrogant glance. I could, without too much imagination, see him swinging a bullwhip.

"There are two more parts to this. He wasn't your regular camp guard, with Alsatian and rifle patrolling an electrified fence, or up in a watchtower with a machine gun, siren and a searchlight. He beat and tortured inmates. Middle-class background. Fresh out of school, too. How does one so young become so cruel? Proud of his SS uniform, apparently. And headed for bigger things if Hitler had had his way with the world. But, handcuffed to destiny, he was fated to sprinkle roses with water instead of blood. So what to do? He was close to retirement age, so the university pensioned him off. I should mention that, according to the sworn testimony of eyewitnesses before an allied tribunal, he had shot, beaten, stabbed and strangled dozens of inmates to death. He was high up on the list of Nazis the authorities wanted to have a talk with. Extradition, you say, and that's where this story gets interesting. Germany applied and it was turned down because at a hearing Kastenmeier's lawyer said his client was terminally ill with liver cancer. No medical exam to determine if he was telling the truth. The university authorities took Kastenmeier's side, saying most of his accusers were dead and the memory of those who weren't couldn't be relied upon after many years. A lawyer representing the university appeared at the hearing, argued against extradition and submitted letters from several university officials praising Kastenmeier's character. So a sadistic murderer who entered the country illegally escaped punishment. And concerning Kastenmeier's health. When I read about the case, twelve years ago, I did some digging and found out he was still alive and living in Mexico.

"Leaving aside the appalling nature of the man and his crimes, what accounts for the university's attitude? Ivory tower syndrome, or defending one of its own, regardless? Where's the commitment to truth, or at least the seeking of it? Instead of thinking of his victims, his defenders in the university community saw him as the victim. Of what? They're insulated against everything except dry rot."

Onderby flicked a finger against his stein.

"None of that surprises me. He'd become a botanist and that's how they saw him. Academics see degrees, or the lack of. They're like seals of approval."

Kruger drained his stein.

"A Nazi wouldn't have a degree in botany, unless he thought he could prove that white flowers, and especially German ones, were superior to all other colours."

"It's the title. Professor of botany. That did it. He'd been accepted. A homicidal botanist? Never. Except to weeds."

"So let's say you were something really innocuous and dull, a professor of library science, you could get away with anything."

"Are there?"

"Bound to be. There are professors of everything."

"What about being a professor of everything? You could get away with everything."

"Wouldn't work. Too much trespassing on other guys' territories. You'd be condemned as a generalist. A dilettante."

"Think of it, though. BA in everything. MA in absolutely everything. PhD in everything beyond. What are you studying? Everything. I've submitted an article to The Journal of Everything Studies. They accept everything. If, of course, you've got degrees in everything. No triflers."

Onderby picked up his stein and turned it upside down. A couple of drops fell onto the table.

"Who knows anything, I mean, ultimately?"

Kruger turned his stein upside down. No drops fell out.

"My ministerial relations would say God and my lawyer relations would say the law."

"That's it, isn't it? You are what you believe and believe what you are."

"That has obvious limits. You may not understand what you're doing, psychologically or morally. Most people live in ignorance. Whatever that ignorance is, to them it's true. Beyond is the scary place where you have to start thinking for yourself and take the consequences. Hardly anybody can and that's the almighty trouble. It always has been."

"Where's truth in all this?"

"Still looking for it."

"Maybe nobody ever will find the damn thing."

"I have another story for you, of more recent vintage. It happened the year before you arrived. It also has to do with extradition. The outcome was different."

"We need more beer."

"We do."

Kruger brought the refilled steins back and continued.

"Why do the amorous and the murderous so often intertwine?"

"Not to romance novelists."

"They're hacks. Almost as ridiculous as English professors who think they can write novels. The answer to my question lies in delusion. Love is a temporary delusion, and what most call love is infatuation compounded with lust. When it inevitably wears off there's a reaction equally intense, a mingling of boredom with distaste or disgust and sometimes even hate. Hate can give rise to murderous impulses. A case in point, the current dean of the Faculty of Education."

"Disagree. Enrollment in or being on the teaching staff of the Faculty of Education automatically disqualifies you from either love or hate. Schoolteachers are naturally immune from deep feelings of any kind. They're born to be propagandists spouting platitudes. Their function is to indoctrinate."

"All right, we're talking about getting a new piece of ass. We're in the gutter so let's get comfortable."

Kruger drained half his stein.

"The dean's dream piece is on the staff, teaches physical education. One of those morons who climb ropes for a living. She knew the ropes when it came to getting him off. Gives another meaning to her BEd. But the problem for the dean was he was married when he met her. Teachers aren't supposed to be inventive or daring or anything except good with chalk and other mentally inert things like kids. So why not divorce? Because adultery sounds good in court when a wife claims the moral high ground. Psychological abuse and so forth. What does the dean do? Takes his wife to Switzerland on a vacation. Must have convinced her he'd broken up with the rope climber. Told her his was out of bounds except to her. What happens in Switzerland? The wife dies in a car accident. Apparently lost control of the wheel on a mountain road. The dean wasn't even injured. He wasn't in the car. If you have an evil mind like mine you begin to think bad thoughts. The Swiss police, a rather phlegmatic bunch one surmises and not possessed with overactive imaginations, began to have such thoughts, too. Very thorough, the Swiss. After examining the wife, they examined the car. They found the brakes had been tampered with. Something to do with a perforated brake line. Their experts said the crash wouldn't have accounted for it. They arrest the dean on suspicion of murder. He denied the allegation, contacted his pals at PU and they went into action."

Onderby laughed.

"Sounds like an old movie. Husband plots wife's demise, carries it off but makes a mistake spotted by a clever police inspector."

"Movies, like detective stories, tell half the truth. The crime, the solution, but not what the ending would actually be. The authorities don't want the rabble to get the idea they can get away with anything. But among the authorities, in which I include our woeful bunch, the law is slippery and justice falls on her ass."

"Do the guilty sleep well?"

"Very well. They don't believe they're guilty. The law has a wonderful excuse for them. It's called extenuating circumstances. Means no one is guilty of anything except anonymity or poverty."

"What about the dean?"

"He married his beloved. They climb ropes together."

"What ropes were pulled to get him off?"

"Meakin and the deans signed a joint letter to the federal government demanding it get him extradited. They didn't deal with the case at all. As if it was beneath them to discuss mere facts. All the usual crap. Eminent scholar, outrageous charge. If the victim were Swiss, the Swiss wouldn't have gone for it. But international relations being what they are, and with the fussing over a dead body of a foreign national bound to incur expense, they opted for frugality. They released the body and the prisoner."

"Come on, Hardy, there's got to be more to it than that. Why would they all line up in support? Academics live in wormholes. They don't agree on anything except how important their own specialty is. And they secretly believe the other guy is their intellectual inferior."

"You're right. A dean of education wouldn't rate notice except among the aggies. It all had to do with favours. I was able to piece a lot of it together. It begins at the top, with Presidink Meakin. His daughter got a teaching position in the Faculty of Education six years ago. Not surprisingly she's a moron, but that wouldn't have disqualified her. She has a history of drug abuse. The dean overlooked that. She was picked over several more qualified candidates. She's still fighting her addiction, has lapses, and he covers for her. There's a certain federal politician whose son was accused of date rape by another student, and Meakin apparently talked her into dropping the complaint. That politician was the point man in pushing the feds for the extradition proceedings. Incidentally, the student who alleged rape was an English major. After dropping the complaint, she was awarded a scholarship by Abercrombie."

"So the dean was simply the biggest offender."

"It's survival. All the legions of puny academics whose titles are an intellectual pretense are part of the larger pretense that is universal education. Seems like a great idea. Doesn't work. All you have to do is look at mass-market culture. There are hundreds of colleges and universities across this continent and their impact is nil when it comes to public enlightenment. Why? The public doesn't want it. It wants to be entertained. And that means it can be conned by the authorities, including us. We're part of the con. And intellectually respectable enough to cover up for Nazi botanists and profs who do in their wives."

Onderby told Jane about his upcoming venture.

"You're making a mistake."

"Maybe I want to make a mistake."

"Watch yourself with Skinner and you've got a fair chance of getting through this. This waiter-artist isn't an academic. What does he know about your life? Stay away from him."

Two weeks later Kruger came to Onderby's office.

"The word has come. You are to meet him on Saturday at the coffee house. Beyond that, I know nothing. Be there at seven. Which one of the twin gods of time was it, a.m., p.m.? The latter. Be punctual, he's German. It's how they almost conquered the world."

On Saturday Onderby told Jane he was going to a coffee house with Kruger.

"To meet his German pal?"

"Want to come along? Make an evening of it."

"No. You know what I think."

"It doesn't do any harm to listen to what the man has to say."

"This will not end well."

Chickie Dee's was on the south side, the oldest part of Prairie City, had been a Chinese restaurant, a pizza place and a laundromat. Not far from the university, it attracted students, artists and writers. There were regular poetry readings and occasionally showings of artists' work. The noticeboard inside the doorway was covered with slips of paper advertising rooms and suites for rent, second-hand books and CDs and free puppies and kittens. The lighting was dim, the talk quiet and the air smelled of espresso and the kind of cosy pretentiousness coffee houses seem to create. They sat at the only free table. Kruger looked over at the bar, against the opposite wall.

"The voluminous blonde is Chickie Dee, real name, Natasha Fyodorova. She and Helmut are lovers. That's how he got the job. Sort of an audition. He passed muster."

The woman grinned on seeing Kruger and came to their table twirling a towel. Onderby noted curves almost out of control. Ample, not sloppy. Made for comfort. Kruger introduced Onderby, who grinned and received the same, as well as a twirl of the towel.

"I have a surprise for you, Hardy. A Russian girl."

"A hottie? For tonight?"

"Be serious. My niece is coming here in two weeks to stay with me. She is a student. I will introduce you."

"You'd better send her my picture and tell her I'm not rich. I want her to see and to know what she's not getting."

"She is a nice girl. She is not after money."

"Next time I come take a picture and send it, prepare the poor girl."

"All right. What can I get you gentlemen?"

"We'll have espressos and anything still crunchy. Where's the man of the hour?"

"In the back. I will get him."

They watched her walk away. Kruger gave a low whistle.

"Wow. If sex had a voice, it would be singing about that ass."

"The rest of her isn't bad either."

"Careful, man of Jane. No pulling at the leash. Lustful thoughts not allowed. Only I, a prowling bachelor, may praise such cornucopian pulchritude."

She returned from a room at the back, made and brought over two espressos from the bar and a flaky pastry filled with cream. The pastry was for Kruger, his usual order. Five minutes later Meinsdorf came out of the room at the rear. He was holding a smartphone.

"We are going to fly."

"Wait till I finish this." Kruger's mouth was full of pastry, his grin covered in flakes.

"Not you. Norton. I have the route planned. Here, look."

He held up the phone. In the dimness Onderby couldn't see anything except its outline.

Kruger swallowed.

"Ah, my literal German friend, vouchsafe us the purpose of all this, come clean."

Slipping the phone into his shirt pocket, Meinsdorf sat down.

"This will be something. I have got us a plane for tomorrow. We will be flying over the city. And to do what? To deliver a story you, Norton, will write as we fly. In the sky your thoughts will be uplifted, you will be inspired. This is the best part. I will throw the pages of your story out of the plane."

"It's a new kind of rejection, I suppose. Reject myself."

"No. This will be your gift to the people, the word from above, godlike and almighty."

Kruger shook his head.

"Metaphors are our business. Don't meddle with the meddlers. You're an artist, do the shit you do, throw it out of the plane, parachute down from on high and sell it when you land. Tell the media first. They'll cover it and you'll get publicity. There, I've planned your route to fame. And millions, if that's important. Leave this poor guy and his miserable life to rot."

"All right. You want to be like the rest of your kind, bookworms afraid of the light."

Onderby drank the rest of his coffee and put down the cup.

"I'll do it."

Kruger stared at him.

"Must be the caffeine. Wait till it wears off. Go for a walk, get some air. This is—."

"Insane? I know. So what? I work with neurotics and sociopaths. What else do you expect after all this time with the impaired?"

Meinsdorf stood up.

"The airport tomorrow at twelve. Go to GA. I will be there. Bring felt pens and packages of paper. Coloured is better. Plan on nothing. It must be of the moment."

Kruger cleared his throat.

"You may be charged with littering."

"Details. Bureaucracy. By-laws. You are not an artist."

"A minor benefit is I will probably never see the inside of a courtroom."

Jane's reaction was predictable.

"Hardy's right. What possessed you to agree?"

"I don't know. But I'm not backing out."

On Sunday Onderby drove out to the international airport, south of the city in a semi-rural area. The GA section was for airplanes not used for scheduled or commercial flights. Small jets and propeller-driven aircraft were lined up near a hangar. Meinsdorf was talking to a man who had a white handlebar mustache and was wearing goggles and a fleece-lined leather jacket. They were standing beside what looked like the oldest prop plane there. A hang-glider with wheels Onderby thought as he carried a knapsack containing several bundles of orange paper and two felt pens with black ink towards the men. Meinsdorf saw him and flicked a thumb at the other man.

"This is Buzz, who is our pilot."

Onderby said hi and nodded at the plane.

"It's a two-seater. Can it carry the three of us?"

"I've carried four small." The pilot sounded tired, yawned.

Small what? Monkeys? It occurred to Onderby that nobody had mentioned payment last night. Should he, and now?

"What's this going to cost?"

"Don't worry. He owes a favour."

"She wasn't that good," the pilot said.

"Good enough for a quick flight in this old thing."

"Want a shot before we take off? Got a bottle of demerara."

"For later I have weed and sandwich crèmes. I lick the centres. Norton, I will sit in front with him and you sit behind on the floor. Up there you will be inspired, I promise. Write and hand me the paper and I will throw it out. All great works will finally be lost. Why should yours be different?"

Onderby climbed into the back with his knapsack. The pilot started the engine, radioed the tower and taxied over to the runway, waited for clearance to take off and did so with what Onderby thought was the limit of the plane's ability to keep from disintegrating into propeller bits and shards of metal and glass. The shaking continued as the old plane climbed and banked steeply to the right but when it levelled off vibration and noise died down. There appeared to be so little plane and so much blue sky around it. The pilot headed for downtown and Onderby took the bundles and pens out of the knapsack and considered what to write. He looked at Meinsdorf, who had lit a joint and opened the window beside him a little. The smell of marijuana smoke drifted back from the cockpit. The pilot looked at Meinsdorf and took a squat brown bottle out of a paper bag and drank from the neck of the bottle. Prairie City a smudge on the horizon. Onderby wrote.

"I'm in the hands of the gods, two idiots in a crate probably half a century old and held together with fibreglass and wire. I'd rather be in Jane's arms now. That's a lie. I'd rather be here on the edge of nothing, flying nowhere. I don't want the comfort of sex for my invisibility. I'm invisible except to me. What does the life I lead have to do with me? I am defined by things that describe me, people that name me. And I name them. We define everything and everybody to make ourselves believe we know them. This is our reality. It's as fragile as this envelope of air I'm travelling in and as unknowable as my destination. Uncertainty is the beginning of knowledge, and certainty an admission of ignorance. Believe what you will. But know that your belief must be the beginning of your understanding, not the end. When you reach that state you understand what binds us to ourselves. This is our fate, to stand before the mystery, amazed."

He gathered the sheets and handed them to Meinsdorf, who fed them into the air rushing past the slot of an opening in the window. They streamed away, fluttering over the suburbs of the city, idling down to an oblivion of isolated phrases lost in the backyards and streets of common sense.

Closing his eyes, Onderby leaned back against the side of the fuselage. A few minutes later he felt a blast of air and noise. The pilot's side door had sprung open and he was gone. Onderby yelled over the noise as the plane became unsteady, losing altitude.

"Where'd he go?"

"Who?" Meinsdorf was licking the cream between the separated halves of a cookie.

"The pilot."

Meinsdorf looked.

"He fell out. He won't feel anything. He was drunk. No loss to him or to anybody else."

"Grab the controls. Give it throttle and keep the nose level."

Meinsdorf crawled over to the pilot's seat and began thrashing around. Onderby looked through the open door and could see they were over a park, with stunted trees, bush and battered grass. There was a small lake near the middle and they were headed for it. The plane wavered, almost stalling, the engine coughing, the wings unstable. As Meinsdorf's hands blindly pushed and pulled, the plane lurched in its descent, plopping into the lake. The water came in fast as the plane sank, Onderby squeezing by the pilot's seat to get to the open door. Meinsdorf was there and helped pull him through and out. The lake was only a few feet deep and the plane didn't sink completely. They waded to the shore. People in the park were recording the event on their smartphones.

The incident was featured on the front page of the *Prairie Herald-Times*: "A Stunt Ends in Disaster." Above the story was a picture of the plane, wing sticking out of the lake. It didn't help that Meinsdorf, in an interview at the scene with a reporter, declared the purpose was freeing literature from "the stinking hand of the university. What I threw out was useless like all writing, but that is art, being useless but necessary. Gesture is everything. Bold strokes. Nothing held back. Teachers are failures. Bunch of flops. Sucking the blood from art." He got in plugs for himself and Natasha Fyodorova ("my paintings will be showing at Chickie Dee's—the best espresso is there—next weekend at good prices"). When reminded of the pilot he had said, "I did him a favour once and he pays me by getting drunk and falling out of his plane. He told me the door latches needed to be fixed. Art is not well served by such people."

"So you've decided to commit suicide, have you?" Jane said to Onderby as she drove to their apartment. She had picked him up at the lake after he had used a bystander's phone to call her at the university library. A friend had driven her to the airport. She had picked up their car there.

"You've never dealt with Skinner and Braun. And if and when you apply for tenure here you'll have published your book. They won't be able to touch you. If they sabotage you because of jealousy, neither one having done a book, you'll be able to go somewhere else, anyway."

"Who else is on the tenure committee?"

"Mulcahey, Krieghammer and Harlan Priskey."

"You don't need a unanimous vote for your name to be sent to Abercrombie. The majority rules here. Krieghammer has published several articles. He must surely recognize your work. I understand Mulcahey and Priskey have published something as well. They may side with him. The others will back down, make it unanimous."

"'Precious Priskey,' as Hardy calls him, the English Department's gourmet/gourmand. He'll be retiring, after four decades of waddling around department hallways picking up gossip and boring students with his fat lazy voice. Why would he care about taking my side? And what about the naked dancer and my belly flop?"

"They shouldn't have anything to do with it."

Onderby's inquisitor this time was the chairman of the department. Kruger called Abercrombie "the best used car salesman on campus. He fronts for damaged goods and he knows it, and that smile is so platinum-plated you could sell it as precious metal." Onderby entered the chairman's office with a sore back, a bruised forehead and little hope. The note in his mailbox that morning telling him to see the chairman as soon as possible had not been signed. Abercrombie was leaning back in his leather-upholstered swivel chair, smile on hold. His intertwined fingers rested on the vest of his three-piece plaid suit.

"Have a seat, Norton. Let's get down to it. This plane business puts the department and the whole university in a bad light. This is the second time in a few weeks you've been involved in an event that's created adverse publicity for us. The reading could be seen as a fluke, something that got out of hand. This other is different. What happened? Were you on drugs? You may as well tell me because these things have a way of becoming known."

Onderby knew he was looking at a future dean of arts and university president. In his crazy way Meinsdorf was right. When you stripped the ivy from the ivory tower, what was left? A series of poses. Behind the propriety lay pretense. Not a pretense based on ignorance but on the assumption that the answers were in that tower and known to a privileged few with degrees banning ignorance. That was the agreement. You paid, you learned, and most of all you learned to lie. And that helped you believe the rest. Always the solemn intoning of propriety.

"You've applied for tenure, Reynard tells me. These things don't help your application, though strictly speaking they're not academic. We're not private, with rich alumnae, charitable trusts, foundations and corporations to support us. We're a public university. Student fees don't make the grade, if you'll pardon the joke. Government funding depends to a not negligible extent upon good will. That good will could easily vanish if behaviour by staff is perceived as counter-educational."

"Counter-educational?" Kruger laughed out loud. "From an English professor. It's Prairie University, but still. What did you say?"

"The usual. Under pressure. Didn't know it would turn out that way. Temporary lapse of judgement. Shit, I hate myself."

"Self-flagellation isn't the answer. Realpolitik is."

"What are you getting at?"

"Realpolitik would advise go see Ruth Braun."

"You've got to be kidding. Besides, I couldn't be unfaithful to Jane."

"As I thought, a man of principle. You're doomed in this place. Shouldn't have applied for tenure. Accept uncertainty, as I do. I'll find something somewhere. I won't have wasted my time and degraded myself playing their game. The letters say it, PU stinks. Suppose you please these neurotic halfwits, what's waiting for you? Two decades of freezing weather. Committee and department meetings with people you wouldn't say hi to anywhere else, and a few crass manoeuvrers like Caroline Adair Skinner and Abercrombie. It's the deadest of dead ends, the academic middle of nowhere on the Great Plains. Anything but a belly laugh and a dirty gesture is too much praise."

"You're a born nihilist. Jane and I are going to get married. I'd like us to have enough certainty to plan a future. Maybe it wouldn't be much here but it would be a start, if nothing else. I don't need advice from a cynic."

"People like you call people like me cynics when you don't want the truth. I told you that adventure with Meinsdorf wasn't in your best interest. The problem is, you see what I do but you tell yourself that you can stomach it. At the same time you hate yourself. So you throw paper out of a plane."

243

"It was wild up there. For a moment I was a free man."

A conspiratorial silence of one.

"Hardy, would you, could you—?"

"Absolutely not. Martyrs don't get substitutes. Lying there in the altogether twiddling her nipples. 'Ruthie, old Norton needs a break on this tenure thing.' The very thought appals moral sensibilities, not to mention physical ones. Besides, I'm currently eyeing a visiting professoress in Romance Languages. A Brazilian with Natashaesque abundance."

"You've never mentioned her."

"Nothing is certain yet. But one has hope."

Jane entered the office.

"Hope, Hardy? I thought you were hopeless."

"Ouch. Me misanthropic vitals have been pierced. Cleverly too. A double hurt for a wordsmith."

"Don't overreact. It ill becomes you."

A glance at Onderby as she sat down.

"I've been getting sympathetic glances all day. As if my dog died."

Onderby grinned.

"Despair not. The department rates dogs more highly than humans. Unwavering loyalty. Obedience to the call of the master."

"You guys having fun?"

Kruger stood up quickly.

"I think I'll leave."

The next afternoon he returned.

"I have another criminal case for you. Saved the best for last. It's an unsolved murder. Alison Janeway."

"She committed suicide last year."

"That's what it looked like. But in my perambulations I bumped into Beedey, of campus security. Had to do with talking myself out of a parking ticket. I'd parked in front of the library, left the motor running and rushed in and grabbed a book reserved for me. Came out and there he was writing out a citation. The one thing he's ever been quick about. Told him why I'd parked there, that I'd been a minute. Didn't work. Decided to outflank him. 'Guess

I'm not as quick as you guys solving cases, like our late prof.' Stopped writing. 'Don't know about that one. Neighbour saw exhaust leaking out of the garage and called right away. We were there fast. Doctor too, and he said she'd probably died within the hour. Said carbon monoxide was the cause of death but she was so pickled in booze he couldn't figure out how she got to the garage. She was sitting upright, hands on the wheel, head back against the headrest, eyes closed. No scrapes, cuts or bruises on her. She wasn't wearing panties or a bra and had no shoes on. After the engine was turned off and the exhaust fumes went out the main and side doors, you could smell the booze on her. The coroner's report said there were traces of semen in her vagina. I figure the inquest called it suicide because the monoxide was the direct cause of her death. That's the way it went into the records. But there were sure as hell questions about the whole thing.'"

"Did you get a ticket?"

"No. He put the book away and we talked. I asked a few questions. He didn't know much more."

"Any other ideas besides it being murder?"

"The obvious question is who? Alison Janeway was one of those anonymous drab women that work in libraries or teach. I never paid attention to her, even spoke to her. She was a department fixture."

"I spoke to her once, when I was with Jane. They talked about something to do with *Beowulf.* I mentioned something about Grendel, I forget what. She had this pathetic smile. I felt sorry for her, as if she needed a date. Spend your life teaching *Beowulf.* Dismal."

"Ever since that talk with Beedey I've wondered what happened. How did she go from being nobody's to getting drunk, being raped, if she was, and murdered? That kind of thing is not supposed to happen at Prairie U. What would be the motive of the murderer? He didn't want it known he'd been desperate enough to go after Alison Janeway? Lots of other questions. Was the killer insane? Did he know her? Was he a student or a member of the faculty? Was he invited or did he break in? The only fingerprints the police found were hers. So we could be dealing with a very clever man or one that was lucky. She wasn't the type to pick up a stranger in a bar. I think she knew her killer, at least well enough to let him in. None of it points to an anonymous intruder."

"So the guy is most likely on campus, maybe a member of this department."

"It all comes together and then none of it makes any sense. See what I mean?"

"No."

"I've been thinking about the case, on and off, for months. It can only make sense if it doesn't. To figure it out you've got to consider everything that's illogical. Put all of the illogicalities together and you've got the answer."

"Maybe there's a missing piece of evidence that would explain everything. Without it, you'll never be able to figure things out."

"Suppose we could work out what that missing piece of evidence is? Factor it in, get the answer that way."

"You're proposing an intellectual exercise. There's a moral question. The woman is dead. Why not let it go? What will this do for her memory?"

"We're after a murderer."

"If she was murdered and we can prove somebody did it. Are we after a murderer or the answer to a puzzle? That's the problem with detective stories. They're a form of play, making a game out of tragedy or circumstance or farce or whatever you want to call it. It's a reduction of what we understand as reality to a comfortable kind of absurdity. Over it all is the problem solver pretending to a kind of insight that makes crime a matter of outthinking the criminal. The moral conundrums involved in any crime are ignored or deliberately misconstrued or made light of or used as stage machinery or misused to assist the plot. The whole thing is a kind of fairy tale for adults who want easy solutions to what is after all unsolvable."

"This isn't a story. It happens to have happened, excuse the prose. Granted, I see it as a kind of puzzle. But there would be satisfaction in figuring it out, and more importantly, justice in tracking down the clever bastard who did it. A battle of wits and a foray into the realm of psychopathology. It's different from the other two cases. They were a matter of escaping justice. This is a matter of finding it."

"Are you prepared for failure?"

"My life is a failure. What else is new?

"Anything to get us started?"

"The house is still on the market. Death makes the rounds. Sounds like the title of a bad mystery. Or is that tautological? We could have a look at the house and garage this weekend."

"I'll have to tell Jane. She'll find out anyway. We could get a psychic to pick up any random vibrations, voices from the beyond. Alison's ghost screaming for vengeance. Perhaps drop us a clue."

"Ghosts tend not to be specific, I understand. We may get the scream but not the clue, at least not in a form that's decipherable."

"Think of the drama. And the whole thing may come to nothing."

On Sunday afternoon Onderby met the others at the house. Others because Kruger decided to bring Meinsdorf. It was open house from noon to four. The realtor was talking with two couples on the front lawn as the newcomers eyed the property. Mainsdorf walked onto the lawn and spread his arms wide.

"I call upon all spirits to welcome us. We come in peace. To learn what happened to the woman that was killed here. I am not a believer in any of that junk, but if something would happen I could be persuaded to rethink things."

He walked back to Kruger and Onderby.

"That should do it. If it's bullshit, nothing."

One of the prospective buyers, a middle-aged man, came over to Meinsdorf.

"Was a woman killed here?"

"She was murdered in the garage. There could be curses and stuff. I wouldn't touch the place. I am here to speak with any dead that show up."

The man went and spoke with the others. The realtor began talking fast and smiling but the buyers went to their cars and drove away. The realtor, a pudgy man with a round face, stared at Meinsdorf. Frowning, he walked over.

"Thanks for ruining a sale."

"You're selling a murdered woman's house. People should know, if they believe in that kind of stuff. Like ghosts coming in the night because they can't rest until everything is straightened out. If we brought a medium there could be ectoplasm floating around."

"We'd like to have a look at the house," Kruger said.

"You're not serious buyers. You're here to poke around."

"It's open house till four. If you give us any trouble, we'll phone your company and complain."

The house was a white stucco bungalow with two small bedrooms, a kitchen, bathroom and a combination dining room and living room. The one-car garage, also white stucco, was separated from the house by a sidewalk merging at the front with the driveway. The house had been cleaned but the furnishings not changed. The realtor sat in the living room talking on his phone and occasionally checked on the three as they wandered through the rooms from front to back. The last were the bedrooms, one converted into a computer room and the other with a single bed, a bureau and a night table with a lamp. Like the rest of the rooms, this one seemed to convey nothing but anonymity. The single personal touch was a small framed picture of Alison Janeway on the bureau.

"I have seen her," Meinsdorf said, picking up the picture. "Last year at Chickie's. It was a Saturday night in November. We were busy. She was alone. I talked with her. Buzz showed up. I called him over, introduced him. I had things to do and they talked by themselves. They left together."

"That pilot?" Onderby said. "Did you ever see the woman again?"

"No."

"Do you remember what you talked about?"

"It would be the same old stuff I say to any woman. You have such pretty eyes. You look great in that outfit, like a fashion model. You could be in movies. TV. Are you old enough to be out tonight? I have always preferred— what eye or hair colour they are or what skin colour. All that bullshit. Women love it. You guys know."

"Did he say anything to you about her?"

"We never spoke about her, except what you heard at the airport."

"You said you did him a favour and he said she wasn't worth it. Like a bad one-night stand."

Kruger shook his head.

"We don't know what happened after they left the coffee house. Where they went or what they did. There were no marks on her, no evidence of a struggle. Whatever happened, there's no motive for the pilot to do anything drastic. Except for the sex, none of it connects up with him. Even that is conjectural. All we have is, the time frame fits. She died in November, on a Sunday."

He looked at Meinsdorf.

"Do you remember the date?"

"A Saturday, that's all."

"There doesn't seem to be anything else here. Let's have a look at the garage."

They went in through the side door, which was unlocked. Inside Kruger pressed the electronic pad to raise the main door. The interior was unfinished, the walls shiplap and 2x4 fir studs, and the roof exposed joists, beams and shiplap. A garden hose lay coiled in a corner. Cardboard boxes were stacked in another corner. There was no car. Dark patches from years of leaking crankcase oil formed a rough oval where the front of the car had been parked.

"We could come at night and see if there is a spirit here," Meinsdorf said.

Kruger rubbed his shoe along a patch of dried oil.

"Daylight or darkness, there's nothing here. An empty life, an empty death."

"You ready to give up?" Onderby said. "What about your illogicalities adding up to something?"

"All right, let's list them. A pilot who wouldn't have killed her. A faked suicide for no good reason. A suicide too fake to be true. A murder that doesn't make any sense."

"And maybe she couldn't face her life any more after an empty one-night stand. Got dead drunk and staggered in here and had enough left to start the engine. There, I've solved it for you. Let's give this up and go."

Kruger stared at the patches of oil, like drops of dark paint.

"Maybe some crimes are meant to remain unsolved. They're more than simple crimes, they're moral puzzles with so many angles they cancel each other out. There's another way to see this. We've taken into account the motives and psychology of two people. We started with one. Today we added another. But we've gotten no further. Suppose there's someone else behind all this, cleverer than us? Clever enough to make things confusing for the authorities so they'd render the obvious verdict. And smart enough to trip up anybody who happened along later and got curious."

"You're saying there is a murderer?"

"All I know is there has to be somebody else. I don't know if he's a murderer or an accomplice to something."

"What would be his motive?"

"That's where he's got us. We'd have to be able to see into his mind. We don't know him. And we probably haven't got sufficient evidence to figure out his motive or motives. We're finished."

Meinsdorf's voice rang out.

"You academic people, making everything too complicated. She got drunk and fucked and died. Why? Who cares?"

The agent came to the side door.

"I've got to lock up."

"So that was Mind-dwarf's contribution to the discussion, was it?" Jane said.

Onderby had told her everything over dinner. She skewered a pink sliver of steak with her knife.

"Having read the interview he gave at the lake after the plane crash, I expected as much. He has no clue as to how arrogant he is."

"What do you think of Hardy's idea about Janeway?"

"Not much. He's probably been carried away by the oddness of her death."

"Oddness?"

"Well, it was odd, but that could be all it was."

"No mysterious third party?"

"Probably not. Ironic, isn't it, that she achieved more attention from you guys dead than alive. Alive she never got a second look. Dead she becomes interesting, and in Hardy's case even alluring. That detail about the semen must have piqued his interest. And the fact that she was without her panties, bra and shoes. In his bother about puzzles and quest for justice, I wonder how much salacious content there was? The old maid who actually has sexual feelings and for once doesn't keep them repressed. Why go to the house? Did you find the missing panties in a deep drawer somewhere? I wouldn't be surprised if he sniffed them. Beware of men who seek justice when it comes to women. Sometimes there's something else, a prurient interest, behind the urge to play detective and find the truth."

"I suppose you're including me along with him. I tried to argue him out of it."

"Going to the house was ridiculous. Mind-dwarf showing up is proof of it. Incantations on the front lawn, calling to spirits. The man is obviously an egotist, and conceited enough to believe that he's infallible. Superstitious into the bargain. He does and doesn't believe in the occult, taking both sides and doing it like a clown. It's a wonder the real estate agent let you inside. All of you blithely assuming you're on the track of a murderer. While probably secretly after more juicy details. Except the infallible one reduces the whole thing finally to his gutter view of existence. I excuse him because I have nothing but contempt for him. From you two I would have expected more. Hardy, and you by going along with him, violated the one thing she had left, her dignity. She had decided, for whatever reason and whatever the circumstances, to end her life. There may be more to it, even criminal, but it is nothing compared with that. You should have let her alone. She at least deserved that."

"I don't think we were violating her, at least not consciously. Did you know her?"

"Not really. Old and Middle English meet but don't mingle unless they're taught by Abercrombie, who preaches his special brand of social and academic togetherness. Everything must be relevant. Consummate politician."

"Spoken like a specialist."

"And you must secretly want to be one of those popular lecturers who try to wow impressionable students by relating everything to everything else. No thanks."

"There's an academic law. The higher you go, the less you know. But you make that little bit justify spending your life knowing it. And you end up like Alison Janeway."

"That's not Jane's way."

A week and a half later Kruger entered and plopped himself down in a chair.

"You remember the Russian girl I was promised by Natasha? She's arrived. A holy horror. With fangs yet."

"Ugly?"

"No, I could cope with that. Not being much myself. She's possessive. Of things. A complete plutocrat in the making. And for some reason she thinks I'm better off than I am."

"You're not obligated."

"Natasha and Helmut are good friends of mine. They seem to think it's a perfect match."

"Tell them the truth, and tell her."

"That's where you come in. I want you and Jane to have dinner with us. Help me break it to her. So she won't say anything to Natasha."

"It's that bad?"

"I do not exaggerate except for the poetic licence I carry in my wallet, allowing me to bluff my way through life."

"I'll tell Jane. Dinner where?"

"Anywhere cheap or she won't believe us."

"I've never seen you like this, Hardy. You're usually cynically blasé about women. Sure you aren't getting cold feet about her? A bachelor's final refuge, picking a supposed irreconcilable difference as an excuse."

"When you meet her you'll understand true trepidation."

"You could do this a lot quicker. Be rude, act like a slob, scratch your ass, pick your teeth, spit out gobs of mucous."

"She'd tell Natasha, who'd catch on to what I was doing. This has to be a smooth operation."

"She could fall for you, forget about money."

"She's incurable, trust me."

"What's her name?"

"Valentina."

"Pretty name."

"Pretty greedy."

Jane was doubtful when Onderby told her at dinner in their apartment.

"Hardy's exaggerating. He doesn't want to get involved and doesn't know what to do. He's using us as accomplices to get rid of her. Bloody fool."

"She's a leech."

"So he says. Look at the man. His clothes are messy. I've never seen him without his shirt collar ends curled up. The leather elbow patches on his jacket are coming off. Does he have more than one of anything? He's gotten comfortable living the way he does."

"This woman might think he's a miser with piles of gold."

"His only piles would not be gold."

"Even if she's not as bad as he says she is, he obviously doesn't like her, so let's do what he wants. Couldn't hurt either one."

Late the following Saturday evening Onderby and Jane met Kruger and Valentina. Onderby had chosen Bonnie Jean's Quick Eats, an all-night restaurant downtown where university students, artists down on their luck and various night crawlers gathered. It was cheap, the main items on the menu scrambled eggs, hash browns and sausages. Slices of anonymous pie were stacked with iced squares of cake on plastic shelves at the end of the counter, along with pots of coffee. Always crowded Friday and Saturday evenings, the buzz of conversation was punctuated by sounds behind the counter as staff prepared and served the food. Dress was fashionably down-at-heels, denim jackets with corduroy collars mingling with designer silk scarves. Customers kept coats and jackets on or draped them over their chairs. Tables were close, patrons back to back.

Kruger smiled when he saw the long lineup outside and the packed crowd inside. Introductions were made in line. Valentina was in her early twenties, of average height and figure, with pale hair, eyes and skin. Conventionally pretty, not a heart-stopper, Onderby decided. Jane was polite, too polite, and he didn't know if it was sympathy for Valentina or she was bored or offended by the whole thing. The conversation between the four moved as slowly as the line. The early spring weather made the wait easier. Once inside, Kruger found a table with room for four, commandeered a stray chair and used his frowning bulk to warn others to steer clear. The limited menu made the choices easy. Everybody chose eggs and hash browns, avoiding the pale glutinous gravy, the greasy onion rings and a mound of leftover side bacon scraped together. Onderby and Kruger opted for sausages instead. Jane, wanting something sweet, selected a piece of iced cake. As planned, the men shared the cost. Good strategy, they had decided. The eggs and hash browns were acceptable, the sausages not, and the cake harder than it should have been and the icing even harder.

"Oh well," Jane said.

Time for Kruger to intone.

"On the limited budget of those of us lowly who toil in the fields of academe, this is our humble lot. Be grateful."

"I thought you were a professor," Valentina said. "You work in a field?"

"Figuratively speaking."

"You mean you do exercise. Work out. To keep yourself in shape. That's good."

Onderby's turn.

"We toil in classrooms too, with scant reward."

"How much is 'scant'?"

"Very little. You've seen our cars and clothes, and now our meals."

"You are joking with me."

"I wish I were but the truth is, professors don't make the money people think they do. It's the satisfaction that keeps us going. And the fact that we're useless otherwise. Did you enjoy this slop? I can't remember the last time I had a decent meal."

Jane made a face. Customers stood up to leave and a coat sleeve brushed against Valentina's hair and was dragged away.

Valentina stared at Kruger.

"Didn't you go to Oxford?"

"Not guilty. I know someone who did. Does that count? Boise State, anybody, Texas A and M?"

"You went to such places?"

"No. I simply mention them as educational institutions in good standing in the wide open spaces."

"What's A and M?"

"Agricultural and mechanical."

"Agricultural is farming. You said you worked in a field."

"So I did."

"I took a Cambridge course. From the extension department."

"In what, pray tell?"

"Economics."

"You majored in bank accounts, wallets, stock portfolios, mansions, Paris fashion and the allaroundgoodlife. Pretty soon the planet is going to run out of stuff to please you people."

"I have read Shakespeare."

"I'm sure he would've appreciated that."

"So you're not a rich man?"

"That's what tonight has been all about. You're looking at a peasant. I live here among all the other peasants. You came a long way for nothing. You won't find any wealthy men here. They move to warmer places. We are wasting each other's time."

"In my country the professors are not rich."

"And neither are we. We'll drive you to Chickie Dee's and say goodbye there. Sorry to disappoint you. Have a nice trip back."

"I'm staying here. I have a student visa."

"Natasha didn't mention that. Not taking any English courses, are you?"

"No. Graduate studies in economics and computer science."

"Wonderful combination. You'll rule the world. Yet another billionaire. I'll have to elbow my way through you people to pick up my unemployment cheque."

A final mouthful of eggs and hash browns.

"Sooner or later we'll be rounded up as terminal cases. No need to teach the wealthy, and teaching peasants verboten. Mass entertainment for everybody. The unreal too-real reality of reality TV, a gutter crawl. Sitcoms and fantasy romance, or romantic fantasy. Which came first, the sword or the ring? For all those males with teenage minds, comic book superhero macho drivel. Literature on the endangered list. Politically incorrect, by definition. Can't have that."

Jane picked apart the remains of her cake with a fork.

"Finished, Hardy?"

"My family are preachers. Those that aren't lawyers."

"Think of what the legal profession lost when you turned it down."

"It turned me down. Unfit for legal combat. Something about ethics. I had a bad case of them."

"So I've been hearing."

It was a quiet ride to Chickie Dee's, Jane silent beside Onderby, who drove. As they passed the dark streets of Belvedere and the university area, Valentina frowned. Kruger kept his eyes closed the whole way. It was after midnight when they arrived, the coffee house had closed. Meinsdorf convinced them to stay for a drink. Jane said no but Onderby said one wouldn't keep them long. Kruger agreed. Natasha brought out a bottle of Russian vodka. Jane and Valentina didn't want any so a coffee liqueur was offered. Natasha made Jane agree to a sip. They all sat around a table at the back, the lights even dimmer than usual. The drinking proceeded apace except for one.

"You are not having much fun," Meinsdorf said to Jane.

"No."

"A one-word answer. You are trying to be so English. Reserved. With your stiff buttoned-up lip. As if you still have an empire."

"I don't have to try. I'm English. Proud of it. What's bloody having or not having a bloody empire got to do with it?"

"I am German. I know you."

"German. Another word for arrogance."

"The English always think they are too good for Europe. Always trying to fuck us up."

"You did a good job of that yourselves. Losing two world wars. Dancing to Hitler's tune. Murdering tens of millions of innocent people. We've never done anything like that to Europe."

"I knew you would mention that. One mistake and we are forever punished."

"You call it a mistake? As if you cut your finger or stubbed your toe? It was a nightmare. If you hadn't been stopped, we'd all be living in concentration camps."

"The world has become one big concentration camp and you cannot see that, with your superior pretensions. Bowing to your kings and queens and royal and honorary whatevers. Prince Twitface, Duke Damnitall, Sir Shitstain, Lord Pompousass. You are a joke."

"I support our institutions, about which you have absolutely no idea. If we hadn't taught you democracy after the war you started, you would've remained Nazis and communists and slaughtered each other. I wonder how the rest of Europe would've felt about that? I've had enough of this, Norton, I'm leaving. Norton?"

"He has passed out. Good vodka."

"When he comes to, tell him I've gone."

"He will see that."

"You're an insufferable ass."

Jane's exit was quick. Kruger's red face showing the effect of the vodka, he roused himself to speak.

"Was that necessary, Helmut? She's a good sort, as the English say."

"I know you like her, Hardy, with your sentimental schoolboy mind, but I see something in her. She plays by the rules, no matter what they are. In one way or another people like her survive, so don't feel sorry for her. The world will die because of obedience, the curse of the inferior."

After a few minutes and another glass of vodka, he paused to look at Kruger, now passed out on the floor. The women, woozy, were resting their heads on the table.

"Now that we have gotten rid of the English we can enjoy ourselves. Only their upper class enjoy themselves, the rest told they don't have a right. Have you seen their newspapers? And we are told the Nazis invented propaganda. Jolly old England beat us Germans to that by many years."

Meinsdorf stared at the empty bottle of vodka. Natasha raised her head from the table.

"Where is Jane?"

"She left. She doesn't like us."

"I could see. Why?"

"You would have to be English to understand. It's about who is best. They are not any more. It's hard for them to see that."

"You didn't insult her?"

"I was honest."

"Your honesty insults. So it didn't work between Valentina and Hardy?"

"I told you he is not interested in a woman who thinks about money. He needs a woman like you but he is too blind to see that. He lives like a rebellious schoolboy and keeps a picture of an impossible girl in his heart. She will always be there."

"I will talk to him about her."

Valentina lifted her head and felt sick. Natasha took her upstairs to her room in Natasha's suite. Minutes later Onderby and Kruger roused themselves and got up and sat at the table. Onderby asked about Jane. Kruger put a hand against his forehead.

"What's in that vodka?"

Meinsdorf grinned.

"It's Russian. You are used to beer."

"What's the time?"

"Almost two."

"Time to retire, I suppose."

"Why? Don't go to bed. Stay up for the dawn. An act of disobedience is an act of freedom, always."

"Here's a lesson for you, Helmut. Freedom has limits, like anything else."

"They are artificial, imposed."

"Go without sleep and you'll find out what's artificial and what's real."

"You are not an artist. Maybe Norton, who thinks of himself as one, can understand. Art is a kind of insanity, pushing against things to see what will happen. Art is daring or it is nothing. Life is the same way. Accept and you die. Rebel and you live."

"If you can get away with it. Rebelling against a political or social system is a lot tougher than splattering a canvas, chipping a stone to pieces or making blatant noises. The pushback is poverty, prison. It's the old status quo."

"You are part way there. The most dangerous art is that of words. Not because of what they say. Because some dare to say it. Everybody knows the truth. Even the stupidest know some of it. Saying it is rebellion. Writing it treason. Silence is obedience. It's living to many. It's death to art."

"You're being too political. Humans adapt, consenting or rebelling according to circumstances. Nothing to do with art. Art is a luxury for those who practice it, essential for aesthetic reasons, not utilitarian ones. It's useless to everybody else. It's got nothing to do with truth except in its most primitive form, propaganda. Newspaper headlines, television news, and political speeches, posters and commercials. Lying words and images. You think everybody can see at least some of the truth. Nobody knows what the truth is, including you."

Onderby put a hand on his belly and groaned loudly.

"Between the greasy sausages and that rubbing alcohol I drank, I have had it. Give us a lift, Helmut."

Kruger shook his head.

"A taxi, even walking, would be better. You've never been in a car with him at the wheel. Take the word of a survivor. Believe me, once is enough."

"I have improved lately."

"Pardon me if I doubt that. You drive as if nobody else is on the road."

"Nobody is."

"You see? Beware, Norton."

"I will drive you. Early Sunday morning. Streets are empty. What could happen?"

"Don't listen. He's impulsive. He'll suddenly decide to do something crazy. You'll be trapped."

"I'll be too tired to think. Or care."

He stood, groaned again. Meinsdorf got up and looked at Kruger.

"Natasha said she is coming down later to talk seriously to you about Valentina. Natasha believes you do not understand Valentina's purpose."

Kruger made it to the door first.

"All right. One more time. Borrowed, I suspect. Lead on."

Meinsdorf drove an ancient Mercedes sedan with suspect brakes and a worn-out standard transmission that balked and clunked with every shift. Finding the right gear with the shift lever, on the steering column, was a guessing game and sometimes he guessed wrong. The lever flopped and wobbled, and occasionally sagged as if tired out. The odometer had broken, Meinsdorf said, at a million miles. Nobody else would or could drive his car and he was proud of this. As he drove he would make comments to his passengers, who were always first-timers. Kruger's second trip was a first.

"Don't worry, we will stop. I calculate the distance."

"Everything works, and I don't ask questions."

"Good radio, very clear, especially for Mozart."

"This car will survive any existentialist bullshit."

"The rhythms of the universe are built into these four wheels."

"This will be the last one that runs."

"No car survives its driver, or should."

But what set Meinsdorf off from other drivers was his belief in what he called "predestined destinations."

"Where you are going, you have already been. The journey has been made. If your body doesn't get there, through choice or by accident, you can make that journey over again if you wish. There is an element of choice here. Some keep making the same journeys and some are never aware of how many they have made."

After his first trip with Meinsdorf, Kruger had a question.

"How did you get your licence?"

"I was very friendly with the woman who tested me. I passed the test."

"You're a traffic menace. You should be off the road."

"I should be the one who is driving. My destination is greater."

"Whatever and wherever that is, you will never get there."

"I am already there. You don't understand, Hardy."

"Yes, I know, I'm not an artist."

To Onderby Meinsdorf's car looked too low or lopsided or something that wasn't right. In the glow of a nearby streetlight the cream colour was pale. At a quick glance no rust. He wouldn't chance more than that. It was a short distance, a quiet night.

"There is a way of doing this," Meinsdorf said as he slid behind the wheel.

Onderby sat beside him on the bench seat.

"Way of doing what?"

"The last few times it has been hard to start. If I play with the shift lever as I turn the key, it usually works. Or hitting the dashboard. After that I must communicate with the car."

Kruger sat beside Onderby.

"I told you a taxi was better."

Meinsdorf shook his head.

"You are too negative. Our positiveness must flow into the car."

"Positiveness?"

"It is a word."

"I know, and clumsy enough to be German."

"You are lucky I am not one of those political correctness people. I would sue you for defamation of language."

"German is the ugliest language alive. Sounds as if you're clearing your throat, spitting, angry or insulting somebody."

"Careful, Hardy, or I will challenge you to a correctness duel."

"What's that?"

"We must think of personal things to condemn in each other."

"I would beat you."

"Shouldn't we be going?" Onderby said, thinking of Jane and wondering what mood she would be in waiting for him.

"This will be quick. Helmut, you are reality challenged, common sense challenged, humility challenged, hair challenged."

"I am proud to be, even the hair. You are artistically challenged, positive challenged, vodka challenged and girl challenged."

"Guilty except for girl challenged."

"Valentina?"

"Money hungry, not for me."

As he jiggled the shift lever, Meinsdorf turned the key and the engine started.

"You see? I have defeated your lack of positive energy."

He found first gear, released the clutch pedal and its inch and a half of travel engaged a worn clutch, the car easing away from the curb. The dashboard lights flickered uncertainly before settling into a dim glow. A low growl came from the differential. At the shift into second the transmission made whizzing and grinding noises, as if the gears were being chewed to bits. Meinsdorf didn't chance a shift into third, the car settling into thirty kilometres an hour.

"Looking for a parade to join?" Kruger said.

"It will get us there."

"I should have a nice beard by then. It's worse than last time. Not only are the synchros shot, along with the crown and pinion gears, the ignition switch sounds as if it's one start away from oblivion. Show some mercy and have this poor beast put down. The salvage yard beckons."

"Never. The car will outlast me."

"You must be terminal. But no. I can see you at the ultimate moment of ascension steering up into the clouds to Valhalla. A hero's farewell. Death in battle against the hordes of troglodytes. Those aesthetically blind, deaf and dumbed down. A gesture of triumphant despair."

"Perhaps you are right."

"No perhaps about it. German engineering has reached its limits with this pile of junk."

"Tonight is as good as any other."

"Everything's closed. Do it next week."

"I have decided. It must be done tonight. My life and the car's. My final ride. An artistic farewell in flames."

"What exactly are you planning? A head-on against a freeway pillar? Old hat. Driving off a cliff—older hat. Parking near the down-and-outs and getting mugged, with all the trimmings? Not the artist's way. Floating in a flaming raft with your car down a river or across a lake? We're getting warmer. I suggest you take some time. Think about the glorious possibilities."

"It must be tonight. I am ready."

"Think about Natasha. How will she feel?"

"She will understand. She's Russian."

"I sense that you're looking to make a grand gesture. How about doing us a favour and burning down Mackerness Hall? It's an old pile of wood. Should burn like a torch."

Onderby intervened.

"What is going on between you two? Suicide? Arson? I'm getting out and walking."

Kruger shrugged.

"I am merely saving the blissful relationship between two friends of mine at the expense of a desiccated academic dinosaur. The symbolic significance alone is worth it. The only casualties may be a random rat and a few bookworms. Hardly worth bothering about."

"He'll go to prison."

"He can plead temporary insanity or egomania. Either will work. All his attorney has to do is put him on the stand and get him to talk about art and artists. Absolutely guaranteed."

"It's crazy."

Kruger leaned back against the seat and smiled.

"We'll need gas and rags. A couple of burning piles should do it. Helmut's got a lighter. We'll watch from a distance, safely away from campus security."

"Leave me out of it."

"What have you got to lose except seeing our nemesis go up in flames?"

"It's an old building."

"It's a symbol. As a member of the Union of English Profs, PU local, you are required by statute to recognize a symbol."

"You won't accomplish anything."

"That's the point. A nothing act for a nothing symbol. Nothing equals nothing. Helmut would agree."

"Agree with what?" Meinsdorf said, steering through the dark streets.

"Will torching Mackerness Hall satisfy your need for a personal artistic statement? For the moment?"

"It will do."

"Done. I've saved a relationship with an act of academic defiance. Academic defiance? That's an oxymoron."

Onderby made a final gesture.

"In burning the building, you'll be burning books. That's a crime to anybody who's civilized."

"Mostly books and articles by profs. That's all to the good. For any Shakespeare texts lost in the blaze I will do a personal penance. Inflict a random page of a paranormal romance on myself. My expiation will be to buy a complete edition of the Bard's works and beg for forgiveness. For some in the canon profuse apologies. The rest are stationery."

They went back to the coffee house. The women were sleeping. Meinsdorf picked out some old towels and shirts and stuffed them into a shopping bag. He used a hose to siphon gas from his car into a glass jar. At the last minute he remembered his butane lighter and as an afterthought included a few joints. No one said anything on the way to the university. Meinsdorf parked a few blocks away on a side street. The area around the main campus buildings was dark and quiet. There was nobody around as they walked to Mackerness Hall. It stood out darkly against the night sky like a decayed Tudor manor house. Not completely dark though. There was a light on in an office on the second floor.

"Somebody here on a Saturday night?" Kruger said. "That's done it."

"It's early Sunday," Onderby said, feeling tired. Like the voices of the others, his was a harsh whisper.

"Splitting hairs, are we? Maybe somebody left a light on. Can't take a chance and have a look, I suppose. Hold on, there's next door."

Next door was Grumman Hall, the former graduate women's residence. Built at the same time as its neighbour, the wooden structure had been closed down a couple of years ago as a fire hazard.

"Yes. Grumman Hall will do nicely."

"Not the same," Meinsdorf said. "Your symbolic stuff doesn't work."

"It's a gesture of defiance."

"Defiance? Burning any old building?"

"We'll make it an offering to Hymen. At least we won't have burnt any books."

Onderby's whisper became harsher.

"We're standing out here in the middle of the night debating whether or not to commit arson. Let's do it or leave."

"It's up to Helmut," Kruger said. "Throw the gas and rags away or light up the sky."

"I will do it. How do we enter?"

"Besides the front entrance, there's two others, one at the side and another at the back, below ground level, I remember."

"How do you know this?"

"It was my misfortune to attend a dance here once. Desperate women fighting a best-by date by trying to snag a nerd."

"We will try the back."

Meinsdorf led the way along a sidewalk between the buildings, past the side entrance and around to the rear one, two steps below ground level. The door was locked. He put his shoulder against it and pushed and the rotten wood holding the lock gave way. They entered and he flicked on his lighter and in the flame-lit darkness they could see a basement with a timbered ceiling. A stairway led to the first floor, with a reception desk and rooms strung along two hallways on either side of it. On the two floors above were more rooms, like the others stripped of furnishings. The wooden floors and stairways creaked under their shoes as they followed the tiny flame. Their voices echoed through the empty silence.

"Can you smell it?" Kruger said. "It's dry and faint but there, lingering. Decade after decade of vanished people and silent voices lost in these bare walls. A hundred years of prairie life in a musty odour."

Meinsdorf inhaled deeply.

"I smell something. Cunt, but stale. Old maid stuff. Bony, and white cold skin. Lots of heavy underwear. Books and glasses and science notes. Really homely broads."

"Get your nose out from between a woman's legs and sniff the grand old air of history. We are about to erase it. Show a little respect. Perhaps a moment of silence?"

"Are we here to burn this place down or to make speeches?"

"Your German sense of order. Duty calls. Valhalla awaits. Proceed."

"We should start fires in rooms on the first two floors, near a wall, and open windows for a draft to feed the flames. The fire will move up and set off the top floor."

"Soak and set. Norton and I will open windows."

Within ten minutes fires had been lit in four rooms, two each on the first two floors. Old plaster walls and ceilings fell away as the dry lath and timber burnt quickly. On their way back to the car they stopped to look and could see flames and smoke spurting out of windows. Sitting in the car they heard sirens, by which time the building was a bonfire. Kruger's voice punctuated the silence.

"We're lawbreakers. I don't feel any different. We haven't hurt anybody. I've never rated crimes against property as highly as crimes against people. Rich people have made property crimes more important. Not all crimes are created equal, are they? Are they?"

Onderby's snores filled the silence, along with the smell of marijuana smoke.

When Onderby got to the apartment it was almost dawn and Jane was asleep. He slept in till late on Sunday. She was up and working at her computer when he awoke. He ate brunch alone. Jane was in one of her silent moods. He went to see her. His smile was meant to be apologetic.

"Passed out. Didn't wake up till almost daylight, got in late and didn't want to wake you."

"Thanks."

"You left early."

"Yes."

"Bored?"

"Yes."

"I suppose the whole evening was a bore for you. I wouldn't have suggested it except as a favour to Hardy, who wanted a foursome as backup. At least we did help him get rid of her. Not his type, anyway. Well, I'll leave you to your work."

Kruger phoned that evening.

"Seen the paper? Made the headlines. And the TV news. Total loss. It was going to be turned into a heritage building. Monument to feminist prairie spinsters or something. How's Jane? I didn't tell you. She and Meinsdorf had an argument. The English versus the rest of Europe. He went full German on her. Quite bitter exchange. She left steaming. I don't blame her."

After the call he went to see Jane.

"Hardy told me about the argument you had with Meinsdorf. I'm sorry you had to go through that. He can be too much sometimes. At least he's an antidote to the phoniness of academic life."

"You may find him an antidote, but I find him toxic to any reasonable discussion and personally repulsive, a breast-beating ape."

"He's got a different point of view. It can be aggravating. He's a nihilist who thinks he can get away with contradicting everything he encounters. Listen to him long enough and he's predictable. Another artist looking for excuses to explain why he's a mediocrity."

"So you do understand him."

"I'm another mediocrity, but lack the nerve to pretend I'm something more. Too bad I wasn't able to defend you. Not that you needed defending, from what Hardy told me. Did he say anything in your defence?"

"He was drunk, ready to pass out. His face was red. The vodka, no doubt. And I don't think he wanted to offend his friends."

"He loves you, you know."

"I know."

"From afar. It's part of his trouble with women. He's already smitten with mine. Please excuse the possessive. I can't help it. Grammar. Let's drop Meinsdorf into the trash."

"I'm fine with that."

On their way to Mackerness Hall next morning they saw the ruins. A heap of scorched and charred timber lay at jagged angles on the concrete and grey stone foundations of Grumman Hall. Late in the afternoon Jane came to Onderby's office with a copy of the student newspaper, dropping it on his desk. The headline read "Arson Suspected in Burning of Grumman Hall." He pretended to read the story carefully. He blinked once, when "Hall" looked like "Hell." Jane stood over him. Hoping she didn't see his momentary grin, he shook his head.

"Too bad."

"What do you make of the jar?"

"What jar?"

"The one they found in the ruins."

Kruger appeared at the door. He saw the newspaper.

"Hi, Jane. Sorry about last night. Meinsdorf gets carried away. Teutonic arrogance. And too much Russian vodka."

Jane remained standing, resting her thighs lightly against Onderby's desk.

"Hello, Hardy. Sit down. You may as well get in on this. I was asking Norton about the jar they found after the fire."

"Jar?"

"The police say it contained the petrol used to start the fire. It was a large sauerkraut jar. The label was still on it. I don't want to think what I'm thinking. Am I wrong?"

"What do you mean?"

"I mean, sauerkraut, German, egotistical bastard, Meinsdorf."

Onderby's turn.

"He does weird stuff, like the plane. But why burn down an abandoned building? The man's not delusional. What would be the point?"

Kruger's turn.

"There are a lot of Germans and Austrians in Prairie City. In the surrounding area, too. Lots of people besides Germans eat sauerkraut. I eat it—sometimes. Not lately. Torching a graduate women's residence. Sounds like a fraternity stunt. The kind of thing their juvenile minds would think was cool."

Onderby's again.

"I had passed out and apparently was joined soon after by our friend here. We didn't wake up till almost dawn. So unless he sneaked off and did it himself, which is unlikely, the fire was started by somebody else with a taste for sauerkraut. All I've ever seen him eat is pizza and borscht."

Kruger's again.

"Russian vodka is unforgiving stuff, knocked us out. By the way, we shouldn't be too quick to stereotype people. Automatically link a certain food with a certain race or nationality. That's playing identity games. That's what Meinsdorf's ranting amounted to last night."

Jane's face relaxed a bit.

"If you're lying, I leave it to your conscience to bother you. If not, sorry but I am English."

She left. Each took a deep breath, exhaled like the soft sound of a friendly breeze.

Sitting in his office the next afternoon, Onderby thought about the suggestions for new courses. He remembered flying high above it all, when he wrote like a man released. After typing the suggestions on his computer, he made five copies. He put each copy in a separate large brown envelope, wrote the committee member's name and the name of the committee on each envelope. He sealed them and put them in a desk drawer. As he shut and locked his office door, he heard a doorknob being rattled at the other end of the hallway. Assistant Professor Blair Newell was leaving his office. Obsessive-compulsive, he would lock and unlock his door at least a dozen times when he left, and then shake the doorknob. He took his own towels and soap to the staff washroom. Each visit would last for up to half an hour. He would plan his trips there around teaching assignments and staff meetings. He would take off his jacket and roll up his sleeves and lather arms as well as hands and then wash off the soap and begin again. The skin on his hands was cracked and raw and he had to wear bandages. He avoided shaking hands or touching anything he had seen handled by anybody else and could talk about germs for hours. His fiancée had had a mental breakdown trying to cope with his disorder and finally left him.

Of those who knew of his condition many believed it to stem from Newell's difficulties as a doctoral candidate at another university. He never finished his thesis. He was applying for tenure at the same time as Onderby. His chances didn't look good. He was depending on committee work and being helpful to department members.

Ruth Braun was holding Onderby's publications list and saw Skinner's copy in a tray on his desk. She was sitting, the only faculty member ever offered a chair. She had dropped in unannounced. With her usual bluntness, she skipped pleasantries. "Professor Onderby's list seems thin." Skinner's eyes momentarily left the ceiling fixture to glance at the tray. Her stare caught and held him and he blinked before looking away. "I'm going to photocopy a journal article of his the library has," she said. "If you wish I could drop off a report summarizing my conclusions." She knew it would be impolitic and too obvious to mention the poetry reading or the plane crash, and knowing Skinner, unnecessary. He felt that Onderby was easy prey now if Braun or any other member of the committee wanted to reject him, but he wanted those course suggestions. "You might drop off a copy of the article, in my box, but that's all I'll be able to find time for."

Two days before the meeting of the committee that considered new courses Skinner left a note in Onderby's mailbox reminding him about the suggestions. Onderby replied with a note he was busy and the suggestions would be in Skinner's mailbox during the noon hour before the committee met. At 12:30 on that day he put the envelopes into the mailboxes of the committee members. The meeting was at one o'clock in a seminar room on the top floor of Mackerness Hall. Skinner skittered into the main office at 12:55, snatched his envelope and hurried upstairs. The other members had theirs and were waiting. The envelopes remained unopened. Opening them before the chairman of the committee arrived, especially a full professor, would have been a breach of academic etiquette. Scurrying in, he sat at the head of the long conference table. As he opened his envelope, the signal for the others to do so, a thin-lipped grin engraved itself across his lips.

"These are some random ideas I've jotted down. Worth considering, I think. Let's have your thoughts. Spare me no criticism."

Skinner pulled out the sheet of paper. His grin faded as he read Onderby's suggestions.

1) The medieval mystery play and the genesis of detective fiction.
2) Themes in children's literature: sex in the sandbox.
3) Comparative rhetoric: Gothic novels and television talk shows.
4) Climate change and infidelity in the romantic novel.
5) Folk tales, life insurance commercials and soap opera, an ongoing dilemma.
6) Heart valve action in traditional heroines a medical problem finally?
7) Colonic irrigation and textual irregularities in paranormal fantasy.
8) The evolution of censorship as revealed by the rumpass curve.

"Hm," Skinner said to break the silence. He kept staring at the paper shaking in his hands. "Haven't seen these in a while. Seems I've forgotten what I wrote."

The other committee members were looking sideways and across at each other, eyebrows raised. Various grimaces and shrugs. The truth comes more slowly to some, but within a couple of minutes everyone had come to approximately the same conclusion. One knew absolutely everything.

"Would you explain the rumpass curve?" Kruger said.

Skinner was now staring out of the leaded windows running the length of the room. He spoke to a cloud as it disintegrated.

"That would take some time. I'm sure I've got notes somewhere."

He dashed out of the room, leaving the envelope and suggestions on the table.

"I've sent my copy to the student paper," Kruger told Onderby later in his office. "He'll be the campus idiot for a while. You're finished here after this. He and Braun will stick the knife in and Abercrombie will look the other way."

"I wouldn't have gotten tenure, anyway. Don't say anything to Jane."

At his request Skinner met Ruth Braun in her office a few days later, she not surprised, having seen the latest issue of *Prairie Dog*. The sole staff member who read it regularly, her primary interest was in photos of male athletes. The headline on the front page in the latest edition: "Prof's Strange Suggestions Suggest Something." She handed Skinner an article by Onderby. He pretended to read it as he talked.

"Judging by this one it's obvious his level of scholarship doesn't measure up to our standards here. I think I'll have a talk with Harlan."

Hands clasped on his bulging belly, Harlan Priskey was gazing at a poster on his office noticeboard. A map of the cheeses of France showed tiny wedges placed according to their area of origin. He was thinking about dinner, filet mignon with mushrooms and petit pois and a warm sourdough bun, along with a couple of glasses of an excellent Merlot. As he lapsed into a doze, Skinner's knock awakened him.

"Come."

Skinner's head eased around the door, plastered hair, staring eyes, stamped grin.

"Harlan, I'd like to discuss the upcoming tenure committee meeting, if you've got the time."

"Certainly, Reynard. Enter and sit yourself down."

Skinner fidgeted in his chair.

"Ruth Braun and I were thinking we should be quite thorough in our evaluation. It's a poor choice this time around. And considering the number of tenured professors we already have, I wonder if we should be in a hurry to grant it. Especially with candidates who aren't absolutely of the first rank."

"Got to go through the motions, I suppose. I thought I'd evaluate their records next week."

"Seen much of the other members lately?"

"Not really. We're all busy, aren't we, Reynard?"

Skinner took the hint.

Ten days later, on an ambiguously cloudy afternoon, the tenure committee met in a room in Mackerness Hall reserved for important committee and department meetings. Oil paintings of former chairmen hung on the mahogany-panelled walls. "The deadhead gallery," Kruger called it. As committee chairman, Skinner took his place at one end of the long oak table that had served the department for almost three quarters of a century. To his left sat Krieghammer and Mulcahey, to his right Ruth Braun and Priskey. Each member brought a folder and Priskey a cup of coffee. Skinner was in a hurry.

"Let's begin, then. The candidates are Norton Onderby and Blair Newell. You've been provided with a list of Onderby's articles and his work in progress. You also have, courtesy of Ruth, Newell's record of service. Anyone care to begin?"

He looked to his right and Braun took the cue.

"I wasn't overly impressed with either candidate, although Blair Newell has certainly been a workhorse for us, if that matters very much. Perhaps it should."

Krieghammer broke in.

"I did some checking. A couple of colleagues in eighteenth century at other places say Onderby's work is good. The other guy is a no-show as far as I'm concerned. Who is he?"

Skinner grinned.

"Blair Newell is a conscientious person who, ever since he came here six years ago, has helped with things like picking up department guests at the airport. He's our liaison with the arts faculty. He works with the alumni association, supplying them with information and keeping us up on happenings there. And he's supplying Betsy Card with archival materials from the department for her history of the university."

"Sounds to me like a gofer, some kind of public relations guy. Is this an academic meeting or a cheerleaders' awards panel?"

Mulcahey laughed.

"I don't want to take sides, but I have to agree. Onderby's record looks all right. It's probably as good as some others who've been given tenure here. As for the other guy, he doesn't even have a doctorate."

"This is not about taking sides, Dolan," Skinner said, with a snap to his voice. The heads on the wall were smirking.

Braun tried to save the situation.

"I think it would be better if we toned down the rhetoric. There's no hurry. We could meet again. We haven't heard from one of the members."

It was up to Priskey. He rubbed his right index finger around the rim of his cup.

"If one were to insist on the highest level of scholarship, neither candidate would do. Onderby may be acceptable. Liaison, picking up guests? Not the usual criteria. One hesitates in the matter."

Krieghammer shifted in his chair.

"It can't be that difficult. You're not judging Camembert versus Brie."

The smirks on the wall disappeared.

Braun and Skinner talked as they walked downstairs to the main office after the meeting.

"I'll get the letters out this afternoon," Skinner said. "No sense in keeping the candidates waiting. Too bad about Newell. It's a shame the other members wouldn't agree."

Onderby found a letter in his mailbox the next morning.

Dear Professor Onderby:
I regret to inform you that your application for tenure was unsuccessful. I speak for the other members of the committee in wishing you well in your future endeavours.
Yours sincerely,
Reynard Skinner
Chariman, tenure committee

Ruth Braun drank espresso at the small kitchen table in her apartment. It was a ritual, as was the bitter chocolate she bought in slabs and broke with a knife into chunks to munch with her coffee. An hour ago she looked at her naked body in the bathroom mirror after taking a shower. She touched those large breasts she covered with sweaters and between which she draped crosses. Through the ragged greying bush she had fingered herself between her scrawny blotchwhite thighs that she wound with tight wool skirts. She was alone as usual. There was a friend in the Middle West, a travelling companion who like her needed not to be alone during vacation. They took pictures at all the tourist sites around Europe, but never of each other. She finished her coffee and chocolate and prepared to go to early mass. She picked her largest cross, a plain silver one, for her dark green sweater. She would smoke her first cigarette of the day before leaving.

Although expecting rejection, Onderby was surprised at how angry he felt looking at Skinner's signature. That black wriggle of ink made the whole matter more personal than Onderby had wanted. That inevitability he had almost sought distanced the conflict, made it symbolic, as if he and Skinner and the others had taken part in a moral drama. The signature was a reminder of Skinner's power, of neurotic mediocrities punishing the victims of their delusions. After his anger wore off, he understood there was an impersonality about the conflict, but it was not what he expected. Rather than being of Olympian significance to cosmic intellects, with some side bets on the outcome, it had been something microscopic in a tidal pool. Grabbing a slimy rock and holding on as waves pulled hands away. Keep a tight grip or be washed off and carried out with the ebb tide. Who cared which it was? Theoretically everybody who bothered about what was right, but in reality only a few friends.

When Onderby told Kruger in the afternoon about the letter, he slumped into a chair.

"It was to be expected, but still. If I get the story, I'll let you know what happened. I'm guessing it was Priskey. They got to him. Probably bribed him with a fondue pot. Or gave the asshole a new recipe for mince tarts. What are you going to do?"

"Work out the rest of my contract here."

"And go where?"

"Maybe the Gulf Islands. Write something."

"I'll dig into the academic ash heap, see what I can find. What about Jane, or shouldn't I ask?"

"I feel bad."

That night Jane cried openly for the first time since Onderby had known her. He didn't see the tears. She had her back to him and was looking out of their living room window. Her shoulders shook a couple of times and he heard sobs. When she spoke, her voice was tight.

"That's the end. I thought we might get through this but I was wrong."

"You were already applying to other places."

"I would've stayed if you had gotten tenure."

"You didn't have much faith that I would."

She turned to face him.

"Norton, you're as inevitable as a Greek tragedy. And I don't fancy my life as one. I warned you but it was useless. You're a little boy who thinks of the world as heroes and villains and you're the one to rescue it from evil."

"Lancelot, remember? To your Guinevere."

She went into the bedroom, slammed the door. Onderby drank a couple of glasses of wine and left. He went for a walk. When he returned he opened the bedroom door. Jane was half asleep, her hair tousled and spread across two pillows. He went to her, bent over and kissed her forehead. She opened her eyes and blinked at the light behind him.

"Sorry," he said. "Sorry for everything."

"Me too. God, Lancelot. Get some sleep. But not in here tonight."

Less than five months later Jane was hired as a lecturer at an English university. She had to leave almost immediately on receiving the news. Onderby helped Jane pack her things. Kruger came by the night before she left. As they stood in the apartment doorway after a farewell drink, he kissed her cheek.

"I'll miss you, Blonde Beauty."

"Hardy, do I detect emotion, uncynical emotion in that statement?"

"Damn right you do. There's so much crap in the world. Someone like you is rare. Too rare for me to pretend any more. Look after yourself."

He walked to the elevator, stopped and waved and was gone.

The next morning final goodbyes in the departure lounge at the airport. A plane taking off as they were getting out of the car reminded Onderby of the crash.

"Write when you can," Jane said.

It felt like a last embrace. He was bothersome and burdensome. She was heavier to him. Her body had gone to that slightly cooler but always noticeable temperature of friendship and was an entrance no longer but closed to him now. He walked her to the departure gate. Jane breathed one of her large sighs. He squeezed her hand, felt the pressure returned. She walked up the carpeted gangway and disappeared. It's often the little, silly things that linger. Onderby knew he would never see Jane's belly button again. Or brush his finger around it, tickling her. Professor Merton and Professor Onderby. What did that come to? Two kids playing in a sandbox with pails and shovels, throwing sand in her hair, and the world when she cried.

Onderby's contract ran out that spring and was not renewed. Kruger found him an instructorship at a northern college beginning that autumn. Well into the summer Onderby was debating whether he should go into the academic wilderness or let his life take another direction. His strongest desire was to go to the Gulf Islands, away from the morass of formal education. He wanted to postpone the decision as long as possible. His final day in the department was a lesson in anonymity. The secretaries were more polite than friendly. His mailbox was empty except for a reminder to renew his parking space for the upcoming session. The hallways were emptier than usual, most staff on vacation. His one friend dropped by to say farewell. Everyone else shunned him. Being seen with him was risking infection by what Kruger called "*institutorium ostracismo,* damn the Latin, and worse than the bad breath of gossip."

Finally with his bulging briefcase and shutting his office door for the last time Onderby felt the loneliness haunting such places. The hallway looked like a series of cells with doors and nameplates, for monks or for prisoners? How many of these people knew, let alone liked each other? This so-called community of scholars was a warehouse dispensing public education, an excuse for masters of minutiae. These followers of various codes of criticism followed them into oblivion. They had their few years of walking those corridors, like so many anonymous others, and retired with the delusion of having been a scholar. As for being teachers, at least there was no pretence.

Onderby drove away from the university in late afternoon sunshine. He looked in the rear view mirror and saw the dust his tires spun into the air. Each speck flashed a golden second. The universe passed us by once and we are still falling to our rest. He had seen the dust dance.

An hour after Onderby's car left the boulevard, Pookie Tatlow emerged from the Administration Building. In her handbag was a university catalogue. As she walked past Mackerness Hall and the SUB to the boulevard, she thought about which courses she would be taking in the upcoming session. Hobb's car was parked up the road in a no parking zone. The engine was running. She saw him walking in the other direction. "Hobb." He kept on going.

Prairie Herald-Times
September 10

Professor Trashes Publishing House

Peter Sigurdsen, former professor of English at Prairie University, entered the New York offices of Huggett Publishing Monday afternoon and began attacking office equipment with a club. A secretary and a computer serviceman were injured slightly before Sigurdsen was subdued by two security guards. Dressed in a dark suit and tie and wearing sunglasses along with a false mustache, he had limped into the offices using a cane. After unbuckling his belt and dropping his pants, he pulled a wooden club from two strips of cloth tied around his leg. He battered desks and computer terminals before swinging at the door of senior editor Mitchell Dibbleston and smashing the glass panel. Witnesses reported hearing him yell, "You want trash, I'll give you trash." When the security guards grabbed him he offered no resistance. Handcuffed, he waited quietly until police arrived. Before he was taken away, an officer pulled up his pants and buckled the belt. In a statement issued later, editor Tissa Taubman said the former professor "couldn't take rejection." He had written in a letter accompanying manuscripts that he resigned his professorship to devote all his time to writing fiction. On the title page of each work submitted he had written, "If you reject this manuscript you are a certified moron." Upset by rejection slips, he had repeatedly telephoned and sent email, using abusive language. Ms Taubman said other publishing houses reported receiving similar calls and mail.

Prairie Herald-Times
September 13

Professor Committed

At his pretrial hearing in New York on Friday Peter Sigurdsen, formerly a professor at Prairie University, was found incompetent to stand trial for creating a public disturbance, carrying a concealed weapon, uttering a threat and malicious damage to private property. Sigurdsen used a club to batter the office equipment at Huggett Publishing on Monday. Rejection of his novels was apparently the motive. A court-appointed psychiatrist who examined the accused testified he was a psychopath subject to severe paranoid delusions about academic life and his own literary talent. He had no previous criminal record and had been under a great strain because of a change in careers, Sigurdsen's lawyer told the judge.

Officials from the Palinka Asylum at High Prairie attended the hearing. They presented papers signed by Sigurdsen's relatives committing him to that institution. One of the officials, Dr. Hobart Blember, testified that after having examined the accused in jail he concurred with the court-appointed psychiatrist about Sigurdsen. He called him "a textbook paranoid with a persecution complex and delusions of grandeur, living in a world that rarely connects with the real one." The judge placed Sigurdsen in the custody of the Palinka representatives for the trip back.

Sigurdsen showed no emotion during the proceedings. Before they began the judge ordered a court officer to remove a strip of paper attached to the back of Sigurdsen's jacket. Written in red ink on the paper were the words, "Not a responsible person." His lawyer told the judge this was a prank played on his client by some joker with a twisted sense of humour. No member of the administration or teaching staff at Prairie University contacted about the former professor responded.

From the Sigurdsen Notebooks
December 1

Her letter said this evening around five. Taking a long time. I should cook something. Can't cook. Don't know what she'd like. New England specialties? What do they eat back there? Baked beans, chowders, corned beef and cabbage. Not a big eater, judging by her photograph. Small in that dress. Buttoned to the neck. Sardine sandwich. Something special. Oysters, lobster. She a vegetarian? Eggs would be safe. An omelette. Melt cheddar on top. Coleslaw. Some fast chopping. Throw in mayonnaise. Lots of toast and butter. Then coffee to finish. Start with? Eyes sherry-coloured. What kind? Medium dry. This reminds me of your eyes. As I'm filling her glass. Have my poems ready. Nothing about love. Too personal right away. Nature's good. Have to be careful. Not as good as yours. They're not that bad. Some of hers like coy shorthand. Familiar with God the Father. Rebellion against her own. Couldn't openly oppose him. Big lawyer. The college. Kept her in the house. Didn't want to go out much, anyway. Needed time to write. She probably wouldn't want to eat right away. Want to take a nap. Sofa would be best. Clean this place, vacuum, new towels and soap. Hair on the bathroom floor. Ring around the toilet bowl. Scrub everything. If I could watch. Girl legs and cotton drawers. Snowy. Make her legs look creamy. Drops of rain on a fuzzy apricot. Pale pink cleft split. Try saying that fast. Don't. I'll drive this pen right through the paper. A few sheets left. Never get enough. Pulling up pouched cotton over a satin pouch, flattening her chestnut curls. Homemade pad. Soaked drops of scarlet. Odour like rusted iron. Itch of the unused, seep like a wound. Virginal at her age. Literary none. Seamed from lips to bum. I appreciate your coming. I know you don't get out much. Long way from home. Came by train? Four days. Take the plane next time. Less than a day. Come in. Sorry to leave you standing out there in the hallway. Take your wrap? Shawl. Sit down. Sofa's best. Like a sherry? No? I'll take a quick one. Burning? What's burning? That's only the omelette. Forget it. Not worth eating now. Have a look at these. I want your opinion. I'll open a window to get rid of the smell. Peanuts? Got salted and unsalted. Chocolates? Some have liquor. Some have nuts. No hurry. And don't be afraid to tell me what you think. Bards of a feather critique together. Sharing is the best beginning. Away from the interference of inferior minds. We'll indulge in the lonely accomplishments of art. The bathroom? That door over there. Fresh towels. Extra rolls. Those eggs don't look right. Demon with yellow stare. I'll cover them with cheese. Goddam finger still bleeding. Oozing out, sopping red fin. Goddam cabbage. Hard to slice. Got to hurry up. No mayonnaise. Put a few drops of vinegar in it. Toast's burnt. Who got away with my loaf of bread? Butter's gone. It was there. Coffee's gone. I put the sherry on the table. I know I did. Can't see it anywhere. The glasses are here somewhere. I saw them yesterday. Nothing's anywhere. Where is the frying pan, the cheese? Won't be able to finish. Leave the lights on. I have a guest coming. Show some consideration. You have no right. I can't see anything. What should I call her? Be informal. Emily.

From the Sigurdsen Papers
Archives, Prairie University Library
Untitled, undated 400-page manuscript

I[1]

---

[1] Meaning me, part of the phenomenological parameters of established entities.

Northern Lights Quarterly Review
Fall, 20—

The Book

Kudos to Marantz Publishing for issuing Peter Sigurdsen's *I,* four hundred blank pages prefaced by an untitled page with the first person singular pronoun and a footnote. The editors of this tiny nonprofit press in High Creek discovered the manuscript among the former professor's papers, donated by his family to the Prairie University archives. It's difficult to know where to begin praising this masterpiece of omission. Stripping away all convention and literary baggage in this landmark holograph, the author has reduced language to the solitary presence of human consciousness asserting itself. On a technical level the sheer brilliance of white pages, each a sonorous and concatenating contrast to the one exception, is astounding. To take only one facet, distance from the pronoun heightens the sense of isolation from that stark and universal declaration of being. For it is the universe we are dealing with here, the cry of the ego against the blank truth of nothingness. With cosmic significance the author speaks for all of us, the plural reduced to a singular naked fact embodied in one syllable. Linguistically, the reduction is revealing. The sound of that single letter, a muted utterance of pain or assertion, makes for an aurally symbolic lessening of personal significance. True, figuratively the upper case is a pillar, as substantial as a column in a Greek or Roman temple, but inherently a ruin also. That surely is the message behind its being alone on that page except for a footnote far below, making the capital letter appear groundless, floating. Nearby there is only the footnote number, an irony seemingly whispering in its ear. Number one is one alone. Each one is merely an addendum, a footnote. The truth is after all embodied by the lower case i, the dothead ego separate from the straitjacketed body and plunging with it through time and space. This book, nothing less than the ultimate book, is what language is all about.

From the Sigurdsen Papers
Archives, Prairie University Library
Undated manuscript

The Face in the Mirror

There hadn't been any business that day or the day before. Hadn't been any for two weeks. I leaned back in my swivel chair, feet on my desk. I thought about having a cigarette but told myself I'd given up the habit. The door to my inner office opened and my secretary came in. I like 'em big and busty, with a nice ass and a little sass. Emily is short and skinny, dresses like a Victorian spinster. But I don't pay her much and she's a quiet one. Came to me a while ago looking for a job. Sat there talking about a fly buzzing around the office. Started in on snakes and worms. Not standard issue, I thought. She's no decoration but does what work there is and when she isn't working writes notes on scraps of paper and stuffs them in her desk drawer. She gave me the news in the peculiar way she has.

> The lady has a message
> Too secret for me to tell.
> I think you know the type,
> Brainless, all body, so well.
>
> I said I'd intervene,
> Stand before you with this plea
> To listen to a mortal—
> Though it's only little me.

Any job is better than nothing and a good looker is well worth a gander. Let's see her, I said. She comes in like the answer to a wet dream. A pair from a tropical melon plantation, ass that talks dirty, waist your hands could get around easy and legs that would look good in any position. All wrapped up in midnight blue with slits. Beauty is only skin-deep because that's all it has to be. Did I say she was blonde? And not a cheap bottle job. Usually I don't stand up for introductions. I did for this one. The lump in my throat was choking me. That always happens when I see a woman who makes me think about women all over again.

She looked ready to fall over, but only if the mattress was soft enough. A mouth made for deep kissing said, "Mr. Quester, I need help."

"That's why I'm here. C. Quester, a modus operandi for every occasion. Cradle the keester. Spread out the lard."

I sat down and flicked a thumb at a chair. She dropped like a soprano after hitting all the high ones. She opened a handbag you could have packed twelve loaves of bread in, pulled out a wad of tissues and dabbed each eye once. I got the sweet one, the broken smile. I've seen it too many times but it still gets me.

"I've lost Poochie."

"I don't look for dogs."

"He's my husband. We've been married eight years."

"You can find them in the catalogue. Under made-to-order robots."

"You don't understand. We love each other."

"A big word. Everybody has a piece of that one."

"Something must have happened for him to disappear like this. Will you help me?"

She gave me saucers with doves in them.

"I'm not living high off the hog now. What's the tag?"

"What?"

"Name."

"Regine Raskolski."

"Phone number, address?"

"290-0120. 1794 Elmwood Terrace. You can fax me as well. Send email."

"I can't afford fancy stuff. It's feast or famine with me."

"I noticed your office was a little bare."

"Let's have some details."

She perked up a bit, but not enough to ruin the act.

"Ivan disappeared a week ago. Didn't come home Wednesday night. I phoned his company, Brickward Business. They said they haven't seen him. He's the manager of their Prairie City branch and a major stockholder. Stationery and office supplies. Ivan's relatives back East own the parent company, Brickward Mills. Pulp and paper products. Have you heard of them? That doesn't matter, I guess. I'm sorry about going on like this. I'm worried about him."

"Anything happen between you?"

She shook her head.

"Everyone's got irons in the fire. You've seen the secretaries at Brickward?"

"He'd never—."

"Go for a joy ride? You're the best looker I've seen come down the pike in a long while. Maybe you got bed-stale. Could be he's after fresh stuff. Middle-age dork-squiggle. Thinks he's missing something by not shoving it into young upsy-daisy. Forking a piece in some last-chance motel. My advice is, forgive him when he comes bouncing back in with the roses. Or get yourself a shyster. Hack his balls off with a dull machete."

"If that's true, why isn't he more careful? It doesn't make sense for him to disappear."

"When legs get tangled in bed, nothing makes any sense. He might fill up good and drop her. You'll get a story about temporary amnesia. Took the wrong plane to the wrong city. Working too hard lately."

"Should I wait?"

"Up to you. Sooner or later you'll be getting all his earthly goods. End up in a warm climate and get fondled on a beach. Unless the babe has sharp hooks, is not as dumb as she is young."

"I think you should find him for me."

Thought that would do it.

"I got a beagle, Eddy the Nose."

"Couldn't you handle this personally?"

"I don't peek through keyholes. Eddy gets a thrill out of it. Makes him good. Great sense of where to find the quarry. Got all the latest equipment and he's reasonable. I'll have something for you in a couple of days. I charge $40 an hour plus expenses—Eddy's fee, travel time, mileage. I'll need $1000 as a retainer. It goes towards paying for the job. If the final bill is less, you get the difference."

I took her cheque and handed her one of my business cards. She stood up a lot faster than she sat down. Everything shook the right amount. Not bad for someone in her waning thirties. In love, sure. The only thing I would have believed from her was that she never used a padded bra. On her way out she let her rear view say farewell. When the jasmine or whatever faded, I asked Emily for her appraisal.

> Such divinity of simper,
> Magnanimous of smiles and pouts,
> One would think she had to whisper—
> But I'm a woman, have my doubts.

"Says she's in love."

> I live in principalities
> Where love takes forms of grace,
> Trees and brooks and meadows—
> Wanton nature gives them place.
>
> Hurrying by now,
> Slips over frogs and mice—
> Touches a sunset with brass,
> Blaze of oriental spice.
>
> Cumin, cinnamon, turmeric,
> Cayenne on the edge of the bowl,
> Such taste in the ingredients,
> A kitchen as big as the soul.
>
> I, rooted in a back garden,
> Wear my April crocus cup,

Shivering, a saffron maid
Dropping a curtsey, looking up.

"Don't tell me you've never been in love?"

I had a friend once years ago,
A Pleistocene it seems to me.
Glaciers have rubbed the years away,
Yet among rubble and scree

A weed of thorny reach,
Spines to make my fingers sore—
Wifely duties dressed in lace—
Besides, the fellow wanted more.

"What do you do to occupy yourself?"

I knit and sew, darn what's reft,
Embroider and crochet—
Things a heart has left
When wearing time away.

Emily went back to her desk in the outer office and put her notes in the drawer. She sat down and I could see her eyelids droop. Sometimes when she's finished reading she sits quietly for a while, her eyes almost shut, her hands together on the desk. Thinking up the next batch, I guess. None of my business.

I got Eddy the Nose on the job. He came to the office two days later at five. Emily had already gone to feed some pigeons or something. We sat in the inner office sharing a bottle of Old Dixie. Eddy is a little guy who stutters when he gets excited. He'd found Ivan Raskolski easy. Where was the surprise.

"He's shacked up with a babe out by the university. She's a member of Delta Psi Pi sorority, name of Thela Crammond. What a body on this one.

293

She's got b-boobs, 38 d-d-d double D easy. And the rest is a match. They get together at this apartment on 103rd Street, near 72nd Avenue. University Towers, suite 506. Got some pictures through the living room window. Nothing raw. But they'll do the trick."

He handed me a large brown envelope. Inside were four shots, five by eight. Raskolski and the babe in the foyer. The couple heading for the living room couch. And two on the couch. Kisses and cuddles in one. Serious grappling in the other. The babe's décolletage déshabillé and posterior at risk.

"Excellent. Quick too."

"I tailed him from the job. The employees were covering for him, lied to the wife. That's not unusual. I did the stakeout from an apartment building across the street. The university leases it for grad students. There were a couple of empty suites. One on the fifth floor. Said I was postgrad, here to look at Prairie University. Phony ID. They don't check. Rented it by the day. Got lucky. Snapped them the first night. Almost a direct line of sight."

"Have another shot. Eight-year bonded bourbon."

"I've had two, Charley. That's my limit."

I'd forgotten that Eddy passes out if he drinks more than two of anything, weak or strong. Usually drinks pop. I'd had to fill his glass with water both times. He'd added enough whisky to make the water look dirty. What a waste.

After he left I phoned my client, told her I found hubby. She sounded careful behind the happy noises. Invited me out to her place in Whitby, the most exclusive suburb in the city. Gates, private cops, guard dogs, cameras, high-tech security. I'd been there once tailing a woman whose husband wanted to know where his inamorata went when he was away on trips. That was years ago, before I stopped doing keyhole business personally. Driving along tree-lined streets in early twilight, I wondered what Regine Raskolski had in store. She probably guessed I wasn't a patsy, wouldn't fall for a setup. I decided to let the chips fall where they may, and if anything wasn't right I'd put the kybosh on the job. The stunted no-name trees gave out at wrought-iron gates and I called from a phone in one of the stonework posts. A maid with a foreign accent high-pitched enough to alert any guard dogs around opened the gates. I cruised past wych elms up a curving asphalt driveway that went on for not quite as long as a keynote address. When I got there I was looking at millions in white stucco fronted by columns. On the rising slope of lawn you could have staged a nice quiet cavalry charge. To my touch the front doorbell answered with silence, but after a couple of seconds the maid of the mill, import style, opened the door. Her face as nail-scraping as her voice, she wore a black dress with buttons everywhere. None I'd want to push. Her eyes, blacker than the dress, bored into my dirty schoolboy mind. She promptly slammed the door after I had the gall to tell her my business. The missus must have scolded her because she returned lickety-split. She ushered me into a drawing room left over from a movie set, plush couches, ceiling-to-floor velvet drapes and toe-deep rugs on a parquet floor. Pictures of dead millionaires hung on the walls. Even the silence sounded expensive. The Raskolskis had more than enough to keep a pack of divorce lawyers happy.

She swung in in something so tight she'd have to peel it off later with hot wax. Giving me the big smile, she came within kissing distance. I wasn't bothered too much but I wondered about those millionaires. They looked permanently disappointed. My corpuscles were panting but I ignored them. When I'm on a job I concentrate, which sometimes means I lose free stuff. At the time I figure the job has to come first. Later on I'm not so sure, except maybe a woman didn't make a sucker out of me. This one figured to be tricky and maybe even dangerous. Danger never looked so good or so easy to get into. Electric blue silk cupping the bottom of those creamy nippled pears and whipsnug to a ripe ass. Bait, and I'm the hungry trout to gulp it down, only I'm thinking I got some time.

Something she'd drenched herself in, probably distilled from Venus flytrap for a Shanghai brothel before the Second World War, began to make my eyes water. She squeezed a few tears into her voice.

"You've found Poochie already?"

"You better sit down."

"I can take it standing up." Obvious double entendre if you've got a dirty mind like mine.

"Your hubby's playing footsie with a babe. A student. He's got a suite at University Towers. (Another one.) I brought some photos."

I watched her eyes. Nothing changed. Same deadpan stare. She already knew.

"Don't play dumb, Mrs. Raskolski."

"It's Wanda."

"Thought it was Regine."

"Wanda Regine."

"This whole deal stinks. You're too upset at the wrong time. When you get the bad tidings you're a dead fish. Open up."

"I don't know what you mean."

"Cut the crap."

She moved closer. The Shanghai Special had a foreign accent but I understood. A woman can hint so hard she's got neon in her eyes. But I hadn't tumbled onto Wanda Regine's game. That bothered me, so I kept my hands from overhauling her keester. Her lips were swollen welts and red as a wound. I'd be wrapped up in the softest web in the world. It's a kind of dying, losing yourself so deep you don't care any more. When you come back to your body after it's over, a night or a year, it's like it never happened, only it did, and you're not sure how much you had to do with it or what any of it meant. The crease in view was a ripe slit and had a match below with curls. The deal is to keep you from thinking. Screw thinking, I grabbed her. All her curvy softness collapsed and she began crying into my lapels. I got a mouthful of golden tresses. Softspun silk. A moan. It made my corpuscles tingle, as if sex and pity were the same and it's right to feel mixed up instead of stopping to figure things out.

"I'm a lonely woman."

Music.

"So lonely."

Heavenly music.

"I have to fix my husband, he's a real bastard. Will you help me?"

"I've never seen the like of you."

She drew her head back and laughed and I got a whiff of chocolate mint.

"Do I shock you?"

"Not unless my finger's in the socket."

She laughed again and it was definitely mint. I tightened my arms around her and kissed her hard. She returned the pressure and it was a contest, lips against lips. I did pretty well until she put her fingers inside my shirt. I'm ticklish and that broke the spell. Almost. She sighed, playing with my chest hair.

"That was nice, Charles."

"Charley."

"Are you with me?"

"Not till I get to the bottom."

"Don't joke. You don't trust me."

"Don't push it, honey."

"I can kid around, too," and she took me literally. "That feel good, darling?"

I didn't let that fizz on me. Maybe Raskolski couldn't cut the mustard with her any more. Picked the babe because she'd have less of a track record and dollars would help bring her home moaning in fine style. A bit of faking in one so young is not unheard of. And that would be grist to my mill. Luscious would be dragging me under the covers. I had to be careful. I hadn't yet seen hide nor hair of her game, so I decided I would give my gonads time off until the situation became clear.

"Oh, Charley." I was getting the Swedish massage treatment low down and nature was being obedient as per usual. Nice, even standing up. But I can get groped and think at the same time. Or at least try.

"Cut the feelies for a bit, Wanda Regine. You've got to let me in on what's the trouble or I take a hike."

She grabbed my cheeks and pinched them. Nothing fizzed on her. A pout that promised everything and nothing made me a little crazy. I grabbed a fistful of her hair. She kneed me. Not quite hard. A woman of her own. My arms went elsewhere automatically.

"You won't help?"

"I'm not a sucker."

"I am. You'll love it."

"The truth. Before we play."

"He's a rotten bastard. He mistreats me."

"I'll bet what you spend on your gorgeous face and figure is more than some national budgets."

"You don't understand. He's kinky. Whips, canes. Golden showers. And worse."

"Why stay?"

"Prenuptial agreement. Divorce, nothing."

"Why did you sign it?"

"He was nice back then and we were in love."

"He was so nice he brought a contract to bed."

She backed away and sneered at me, so I sneered back. When a woman is trying the confuse act, best thing is to confuse her.

"Don't try to make a prize monkey out of me with this vomit material. You want me to fix his wagon but I've got bigger fish to fry."

"What are you talking about? You all right?"

I had her flummoxed. I kept sneering. Sneering works for a while. But you can suddenly look like a gink. That's fatal. I eased off to a leer. My lips were getting stiff.

"But me no buts, beautiful. There's something you've got to tell me."

"I was wrong about you, Charlie."

"It's Charley."

"All right, I know about them. Brickward is losing money. That bitch has something to do with it. Get more dirt on them. I can be so grateful."

She brought those pouting lips to mine and touched them. A whiff of perfume from her hair drifted over me. I wanted to throw her down and peel off that silken layer of cling wrap. She pulled away and whispered. It wasn't goodbye but wait till next time. She left and I stood there wondering how she had outflanked me. The maid returned, glad to show me out. As I was driving away I realized I'd forgotten to show Wanda Regine the photos and she hadn't asked to see them.

Using her number in the student telephone directory, Eddy had been able to find out the babe was sorority and an honours student in English. He also found that Brickward Business had a contract with Prairie University as the exclusive supplier of stationery and office equipment. Wanda Regine said the babe was behind the company's losses. I decided to check on the connection between Brickward and the university. On Monday I went to the English Department at PU. The head was a guy named Allardyce. Beefy face heart-attack red and tweeds on a bouncer's body. Smiled like a poisoner watching your first sip.

"How may I help you, Mr. Quester?"

"My client is the wife of the manager of Brickward Business. The company that supplies your supplies. It's been losing money lately. She's asked me to look into a possible connection between the losses and a certain coed, an honours student in this department."

There's a look between men when talking about another man getting extra. It passed and he got back to the business at hand.

"The department doesn't have direct dealings with companies. Office supplies are requisitioned from the university stores. They're part of the annual budget. Authorized by the administration after each department submits its estimates. Students have nothing to do with it."

"That's what I thought. Mind if I look around, ask questions?"

"No, but be discreet."

Allardyce got up as he said this, a guy who liked to look busy. We left his office and went through the main office to the open doorway. He walked behind me, a tweed-clad arm raised and hovering behind my shoulder in a scholar's version of the bum's rush. A couple of strange ones were in the hallway, a gink in an oversize safari jacket, his back sliding against the wall. Stiff-legged, as if he'd filled his pants, he had the stare of a lizard. The other was aesthetically challenged, a face disappointed by too many mirrors and a pair of bean bags weighing her down in front. She followed him into an office, twitching as if she had to scratch somewhere soon. They left the office door open.

"I'll start with those two."

"Remember my caution about being discreet. My colleagues wouldn't enjoy being bothered unnecessarily."

"I'll use the same gloves you use on private investigators."

He pretended not to hear, posing in the frame of the doorway. I headed across the way. The slider was seated behind a desk. The twitcher stood beside it. I wandered in and they stared at me.

"I've seen Allardyce and he says it's all right if I ask you questions about a matter I'm here to investigate."

He began to stare at the ceiling and she gave me death rays, as if I'd been rummaging around in her underwear for a winning lotto ticket.

"Your credentials?"

I took out my investigator's licence and she glanced at it.

"Not good enough."

"It's genuine. Check with the police."

"I'm not satisfied."

"I have doubts," he said.

"Unsatisfactory," she said.

"I'm beginning to have serious reservations," he said.

"You'll have to try again," she said.

"After you've thought about it," he said.

"I told you, I talked with Allardyce. Your honcho."

It was useless. They were mannequins after closing time and I was wasting mine. I put the licence away. Editorialists routinely pay lip service to the idea of higher education. I can't see it. Not when mutants crawl out of the holes. The slider was still looking at the ceiling when I left and the shortchanged beauty was rubbing her crotch against the edge of his desk. Two bugs on the edge of the cosmos. Only it's the tire of a giant earth mover spinning in a mud hole in slow motion. I was more philosophical once, before people got to my good nature.

I walked down the hallway. A couple of office doors were open. Inside of the first was a guy picking his nose. He seemed the kind that would keep a pet chrysanthemum. He had the longest crew cut I've ever seen, five inches of grey straight up. His nose looked whittled from a wormy piece of driftwood. Stacks of what seemed to be thick paperbacks covered his desk. I stepped inside and could see "manual" and "bibliography" printed on some of them. He frowned at me. I'd interrupted choir practice by coming in late.

"Yis?"

"I need some information about an honours student."

He took his finger out of his nose.

"Try the main office."

"I did. Allardyce said I could ask around."

"Not here. I'm busy."

"Nose still full?"

I left and entered the other doorway. I walked into a nightmare of tartan wallpaper and upholstery. Confronting me was a death's head topped by an enormous black wig with sausage curls. She attacked me with a Scottish accent from a bad commercial.

"Wha' are ye doin'? Ye hae nae business heere."

"I'm trying to get information about an honours student in this department. Could you help me?"

"I dinna ken yeur purpose. Yull haf ta try elsewhere."

Her r's came rolling at me on the high tide. I ducked out, suffered from plaid blindness for a few seconds. A door opened and a willowy floater came out, an apricot pouf tucked into his lilac jacket. He passed, giving me a lingering stare. He wouldn't have known anything about a coed. As I walked by the main office on my way out, the two prizes I started with were in the hallway. Eyes-on-the-ceiling was chewing gum and whistling and not doing either well. Nobody's choice fixed me with death rays again.

"You still here? Your credentials are inadequate. Unsatisfactory. You're wasting everybody's time."

"Mouth on a hinge."

"I have grave reservations," Eyes-on-the-ceiling said.

"Don't let me keep you."

As I was saying, higher education is not all it's cracked up to be. What looks from the outside like an industrious collection of hermits comparing notes on how to fast and meditate turns out to be a sanctimonious assortment of crazies, stuffed-up assholes and by the numbers intellects who think the best way to get and hold onto a job is to act as if they're members of an exclusive religious order with ordained insights and only one of orthodoxy deserves the privilege of knowing the truth. Quester demurs. A lonely right.

Wanda Regine was turning out to be as slippery as bald tires on black ice. A beautiful sexy liar. There are worse people. Much worse. But working for someone like her means you've got to watch your client and the other party. That calls for ad hoc manoeuvring, outguessing everybody, including yourself. The babe was my next stop. I drove over to Delta Psi Pi sorority house and a member sneered and told me Thela Crammond had moved out. I asked at the administration building for her address and was told she was living in Ordway Hall, the undergraduate women's residence. The receptionist there said she wasn't in, check back at four. In the residence cafeteria I bought a sandwich. Some kind of greyish pink meat lurked inside. The sandwich had the blandly stale taste of institutional food. Trying to forget it afterwards, I phoned Emily to see if anything had stirred the office dust.

> There is a time
> You know well,
> When afternoon,
> A tolling bell
>
> Of lingering swing
> And brassy hue
> Tips up there
> And stars come true.

I took the hint and told her to go home. At four I returned to the reception desk and another receptionist called up to the room and handed me the phone. I told the babe my business and she said to wait in the common room. Common was right, judging by the brood of young women sprawled on a long leather couch in front of a TV. They were chewing on chocolate bars as they rated the anatomy of a guy in a soap. Five minutes later and Thela Crammond came in, making Eddy the Nose's photos look like mugshots taken at a police lineup. You couldn't have put together any better from parts of all the other women in the building. Looking like a slightly wised-up angel, she walked over to me. I felt it was some kind of honour even to be seen with her. Her body tight in blouse and jeans, she made love to the conniving air, her face looking soft enough for a touch to bruise it. Lower lip curved like a rose petal, nose almost perfectly straight, large eyes gentian blue, hair sunlight streaming down through a forest. Skin pale blush and cream. I had the feeling I was seeing her at a moment she would never repeat. Something sad about that. All beauty has a sadness to it. Makes it more beautiful. Quester, the broken-down connoisseur.

She smiled and waited for me to speak. Her smile was as good as a lot more from most women.

"Ms Crammond, I'm Charley Quester, private investigator. I'd like to talk about a personal matter, somewhere private."

Ms Crammond surprised me. Her voice went with the wised-up angel look, a little on the tough side.

"Sure, come up to my room, Mr. Quester. You don't look too dangerous."

There was something a bit risqué about following her across the common room and foyer. I felt eyes on us right up to the elevator. Being with her inside was like touching her. She smelled like popcorn, hold the salt. When we got to her room she left the door open. She told me it was the rule with male company. The room was the size of a small bedroom, a single bed against one wall, a desk against the opposite one, next to a closet. A window filled most of the wall opposite the door. There were two chairs, an upholstered one she offered me and a wooden one she sat in. No stuffed animals or other fuzzy things, no pennants or banners tacked on the walls. Books, papers, a cell phone, a laptop and a wallet were on the desk. A small suitcase lay on the end of the bed. She saw me looking. Her voice sounded less tough.

"I moved in here last week, after I left Delta Psi. I was lucky, another girl went home the day before I asked over here."

"Tired of sorority life?"

"Tired of the rah-rah snobbery. As if there's anything to be snobbish about at Prairie."

"Why did you join?"

"My friends were. They kept asking me, so I said yes. I started talking sorority after a while. Getting excited about frat boys, pledge week. All that bullshit. I'm going to transfer to another university. PU to PU. What did you want to see me about?"

"My client thinks you're having an affair with her husband and ruining his business."

"I'm not having an affair. Who is she?"

"Mrs. Wanda Regine Raskolski."

"Wanda? She's my stepmother."

Wanda Regine obviously had a low opinion of my intelligence. Or a high opinion of hers. A lot of people think if they can get you cheap you can't be much. Sometimes they're right. I happen to be an exception.

"Why is your name Crammond?"

"I had my name changed. Crammond is my mother's maiden name."

"So the man you've been meeting at University Towers is—."

"My father. You've been spying. Wanda's using you to get his money. She'd do anything."

"She told me there's a prenuptial agreement. She gets nothing if there's a divorce."

"She's been trying get around it ever since she met him. He had everything, she had nothing, so she signed, planning from the beginning to get something on him so she could dump him for a big settlement."

"She said he's mistreated her."

"She would. Probably didn't tell you she gets everything if he dies."

I didn't say anything.

"I knew it. She'll confuse and use you."

So much for the client-operative relationship I'm supposed to protect. But Wanda Regine didn't seem to need any protection or deserve it.

"Thanks for talking to me."

I stood up and looked at her. She had crossed her legs, bringing out the swelling contour of her right thigh, caressed by the soft cotton of those faded blue jeans. Her eyes stared past me, seeing someone else. Her tightened lips drawn down, she looked older, a bruised angel in a world where angels are supposed to keep their feet off the ground. I didn't wait for an answer.

I phoned Wanda Regine and told her I had information. She invited me over. After a shot of Old Dixie I left the office and grabbed a salmon sandwich and some oily fries at a dump on the way out there. That brought on the runs. There's nothing like sitting on a toilet in a restaurant washroom hosing the bowl with the raw sewage of your mistake and feeling your ass splashed by the crapshoot of contaminated water as you wait for claws tearing at your guts to stop and your balled fists bang on the cubicle walls. You swear for the umpteenth time to eat better and know it's a lie. Walking carefully to my car in the parking lot I let out a few duck farts and then a loud long one sounding like a leaky muffler on a getaway car and some snoop bitch with a pocket dog on a leash gave me a dirty look. As if she never farted. I was going to say something personal about her plumbing but didn't want to excite myself and have to head back to the washroom. The ride settled my guts. It was dark when I got there and my headlights picked out the open gates and I drove through wondering why they weren't closed. The post lamps at the bottom of the steps and spotlights high up between the columns of the portico were on. This time she opened the door, wearing a scarlet and black silk dress slit top and sides to show how much fun the right guy could have. Her eyes looked yellow, her lips red as a bow on a box of chocolates. She smiled and my libido crouched at the edge of its lonely cave in case she decided to give to the poor.

"Come on in. I have a surprise."

"I've seen it."

She grinned, Her Ladylikes acknowledging a compliment before leading the way along the entrance hall to the rear and through a pair of glass doors to a glassed-in annex attached to the back of the house, where among a grove of potted orange and lemon trees there were a couple of wicker chairs beside a round table.

"I'm having late supper served in the orangery."

"Thanks, I've eaten."

"You're ruining my late supper. Try the pâté?"

"I'm here on business."

She sat down and motioned with a sweep of her hand for me to sit. I reached inside my jacket and took out the envelope with the photos, leaned over, handed it to her and sat down. She took out the photos, glanced at them and slid them back. She tossed the envelope over to my side of the table. She wanted to hear me first.

"I tracked her down. Sorority, but she's moved into the women's residence. We had a talk. She told me he's her father. Thanks for not telling me she's your stepdaughter."

It's been my experience that when they're exposed in a lie, contradiction or misrepresentation, people will try to ignore or sidestep it. Wanda Regine was an expert sidestepper.

"She's not related to him by blood. Do their embraces look like father and daughter?"

I tried to remember. It seemed I'd looked at those photos weeks ago, not a couple of days. The ones of them on the couch. Too intimate to be filial. Wanda Regine was resting her hand on her chin and grinning.

"You surprise me, Charley Quester, being taken in like that."

"She said you'd do anything to get his money, including using me."

"You believe that?"

"I believe my client, until I have reason not to."

She picked up a small brass bell from the table. It tinkled and a tawny-skinned maid in a black dress and stockings and white apron and cap came in carrying a tray and set down some covered silver and a silver ice bucket with the neck of a bottle sticking out of it and left. Unpretentiously pretty, and quite a change from the other maid. Nice calves, the right amount of muscle knot and curve. Wanda Regine took the covers off the silverware, picked up a rye cracker and smeared what looked like liver sausage on it and nibbled. Classy but not fussy. I felt a little shaky down below but it wasn't serious.

She finished and looked at me, yellow eyes of a hungry cat.

"Some investigator you are."

"What she said threw me, especially about him being her father. But it would've helped if you had told me all the truth."

She flicked a finger at the bucket, an imperious move.

"Do the honours."

"I'll pass, thanks."

"You're a downer."

She stood up, eased the bottle of champagne out of the crushed ice and unfastened the wire and peeled off the foil. Using both thumbs and alternating the pressure from side to side, she popped the cork. Nicely done, muted pop and a bit of spray for show. She poured bubbles and foam into two narrow glasses as she licked her upper lip with the tip of her tongue.

"Have a sip of champagne. And don't tell me no."

I stood up, reached over and picked up a glass, bubbles rising in strands of tiny pearls. We faced each other. She sipped as she looked at me over the rim of her glass, those feline eyes shiny with something I couldn't know. I sipped, felt fumes tickle my nose and the dry wine fizz in my mouth. I swallowed and took another sip and a violent cramp made me bend over.

"The bathroom."

I dropped my glass onto the table and she put hers down and rang the brass bell. The maid who had answered the door on my first visit appeared. Her lips creased into a sneer when Wanda Regine told her. Clutching my belly, I followed her out and along the entrance hall to a side corridor and down to a door. She left without a word. I banged into the door opening it and staggered into darkness, swearing and groping for a light switch, hoping I'd make the toilet in time. My fingers found a switch, slapped it and a light came on. I was looking at a clutter of brooms, brushes, mops and pails. There was a small washbasin in a corner and I lunged towards it, tearing at my pants and hoisting myself onto it. My shorts were still half on and the blast filled them and soaked my ass. Some of it was trickling down my pant leg into my sock. I kept groaning into the rising smell filling the broom closet. Afterwards I used a brown bar of laundry soap to clean myself and my suit pants and socks and threw those shorts into a pail. In damp pants and wet socks I walked carefully back to the orangery, where Wanda Regine was still sipping her champagne.

"Feeling better?"

"I'm leaving."

"You are going to keep working for me?"

"Yeah." I picked up the envelope and left.

Driving away I rolled down the window, letting the breeze air out my clothes and my brain. Two women with different claims on the same guy and both lied. But it's easy to get fooled until you look closely enough. The trick is to concentrate on the facts, not the person. A good-looking woman can be fatal to finding the truth. Love is the best liar. It's you lying to yourself.

The next morning I ate a light breakfast and got to the office after eleven. Emily had been there for two hours. She's punctual. If I'm more than an hour late she gives me that schoolmarm look that says you'll never amount to anything unless you mend your ways. I gave her a rundown of yesterday's events, leaving out unimportant details like the broom closet, and she shook her head.

> I saw a robin yesterday
> Grip a thin fellow with his beak,
> Who twisted and squirmed around to know
> What fate does to the small and weak—
>
> There wasn't much delay
> Before redbreast swallowed him whole,
> A gulp to end the blind thing's woe—
> To serve for wings, a higher role.

"What's that got to do with anything?" I said, and she smiled. In the inner office I took out the bottle of Old Dixie. I reached for my glass but decided not to have a drink. Something was bothering me besides my guts. First thing to do was find out if Raskolski had a daughter. I phoned Eddy and had him check. He's good for digging as well as stakeouts and tailing. In an hour he got back to me.

"He had a daughter but she died. Twelve years ago in an auto accident, along with her mother."

"No chance of a mistake?"

"She is d-definitely dead."

Two liars and one was paying me. I needed to know why I was needed any more. There wasn't anything to do except tail the wayward quarry. There wouldn't be much more to find out. I wanted the money if I could get it without playing Wanda Regine's game, whatever it was. I made a call. She answered, told me she was at poolside. We were having a warm April. Warm for Prairie City, which means an ice cube will melt at noon on the sidewalk if you hang around long enough. Wanda Regine was sexy and beautiful and smart. That's where my always too willing imagination lets me down with women. All it could see were drops of water evaporating among goosebumps on bikini-tight flanks. A voice full of thawed-out sunshine prepared to be a bit amused.

"Found out anything?"

"What is it you want me to do?"

"Keep after them. Get more pictures. I need evidence of adultery. I'm leaving him."

"What about the prenup?"

"He was unfair, forced me to sign it. I had nothing back then. I was a single mother, desperate. I found out later he didn't list all of his assets. When I told him he laughed. 'So what? You get nothing unless I'm dead.'"

"You didn't tell me that your husband had a daughter."

"He doesn't."

"I said had, beautiful."

"I didn't seem important after all these years."

"It would be nice to be told things."

"I like to be told things too, the nice ones."

"It's hard to keep from playing with that keester of yours. I'd better keep my distance until I finish the job."

She cleared her throat softly and I could hear ice tinkle in a glass. I thought of her belly and sunlight licking into its button shadow.

"Don't wait too long."

I kept holding the phone after the call, decided I would see Thela Crammond again. Wanda Regine didn't have to know. She wanted more pictures, I wanted the truth. I phoned Ordway Hall. The receptionist said

Thela Crammond was out and would be back tomorrow. I felt much better. That's when you should be careful. I'd forgotten the first rule of an investigator, don't turn a feeling into a fact. Nothing had gone amiss yet. I'd let myself believe nothing would because big surprises don't usually come from small lives.

An hour later a guy came in and wanted me to deliver a package to an old house near the river. He wouldn't say what was in the package. I told him I had to know. He said it was none of my business. I told him if I was dumb enough to carry anything illegal or incriminating and the cops picked me up I'd be in trouble. He said that's why he was paying me. I told him he couldn't pay me enough for doing anything that abysmally stupid. All six and a half feet of him got up and he glared, his gorilla knuckles bulging. I leaned back and put my feet on the desk and told him to go and die somewhere, dig a hole and bury himself. He thought about doing something, turned and left.

Somebody from my bank phoned and wanted to sell me life insurance. I told her my life wasn't worth it, try the suburbs. A fly blew in with the breeze through the open window and landed on my desk, fluorescent green with a head like a black button. It took off after preening its wings and began inspecting the office. I knew if Emily heard it she'd be in talking about flies. I decided to leave early. It was after four, anyway. When I opened the door she heard buzzing and gave me her prim glance, the Puritan Maid one that says, you're not fooling me. I was going to say, I'm hungry. But I'd learned never to argue with Emily, it's a losing preposition (being too clever by half). I decided to pass up my usual dinner of steak and fries and instead had a mushroom omelette at Monsieur Andrés. Even ordered a salad. I felt like a vegetarian. Next thing, I'd be drinking parsley water like an invalid at the Buddhist restaurant down the street.

It was after five when I left the restaurant, a string of romaine caught between my teeth. I decided to visit the third party in this ménage à trois (not quite describing the situation but sounds artsy) before seeing Thela Crammond again. I drove over to University Towers, found a parking space within hiking distance and pressed the 506 suite button on an intercom beside the entrance door. The guy that answered sounded cocky enough to give you pointers on the stock market while he was getting out fast. I identified myself and said I had a message from his wife. His voice got cautious, like a cat on a rotten fence, and then I heard the buzzer signalling the door was unlocked. I rode up in the elevator with a woman who kept glancing at me as if I might be dangerous in a confined space. She jumped when I belched the omelette and tossed greens. I thought about blowing my nose but figured that might give her a heart attack. At the fourth floor her nails clawed the doors open. I stepped out on the fifth onto a carpet of no discernible colour and looked down a hallway of dim silence. High-rise living, everybody in a sealed cubicle, as if that's privacy instead of a real estate swindle aided and willingly abetted by splintered lives.

I found 506 and knocked and Raskolski opened the door, looking as if he wished investigators were still in season. His face was meaty, with what appeared to be a permanent five o'clock shadow. He was bald except for a fringe of dark hair. His lips were pink, like flabby matching strips of raw pork. There was too much top and bottom to his frame and his shiny suit couldn't hide it. I wondered how Thela Crammond could go for him, but what some women will pick for a dork-squiggler confounds all reason. I've seen strange combos come down the pike. I figured she had kinks that didn't show at first sight. Or maybe I was too busy ogling her. With a fat man's sneer Raskolski put on the tough act.

"Say what you have to."

"Your wife hired me, she knows your situation."

"What situation?"

"The babe in arms. Your piece on the side."

"You son of a bitch."

"Your wife's ready to gut you unless you give her everything she casts a possessive eye on."

"She won't get anything."

"She has adultery and eight years of being a perfect domestic angel."

"Rotten bitch."

"You can tell me inside."

"Five minutes."

He opened the door enough for me to step around him. I smelled sweaty cologne, eau de lime à la garbage can. The living room was straight ahead and large. A big window gave a view of other grey apartment dominoes. Without asking me to sit down, he lowered himself onto an upholstered easy chair. I took the sofa opposite. On the coffee table between us sat a Roman oil lamp with a spout in the shape of an erect phallus. Several DVDs lay piled on a table beside his chair, "sex"—something—in red flames on the case of the top one. Behind him on the wall hung a reproduction of an oil painting. A naked cutie with cake-eater's hips couldn't make up her mind whether she was getting into or getting out of a bathtub. A thinner, much younger babe hung on another wall, lying back on a couch and showing her teenage pointers and fuzz. Second-hand culture and stale ideas. They went with the silk suit and the loud cologne. He rubbed a bloated hand over some bald skin before roaring like a dyspeptic walrus.

"Well?"

"Your wife didn't send me. I'm here looking for the truth in your domestic mess."

"You goddam lying bastard. Get out."

He got up, not fast, face of a politician who'd lost an election because he told the right lies the wrong way. I grin whenever a loudmouth challenges me and I can handle him.

"Give me any trouble, I'll put the boots to you. You're the lowest of the low. I wouldn't give you the time of day. So sit or I'll ram your teeth down your throat."

He stared and sat down.

"Tell it. Keep to the straight and narrow without straining your brain."

Nice bit of assonance. Emily might have appreciated that. Raskolski gave me his business tone, the one to make the world hurry up. But there was a hint of a personal gripe larded in there.

"My beautiful wife is suspicious and greedy. I didn't know till I married her. My relatives convinced me to have a prenuptial agreement drawn up. Wanda signed, said she loved me. Right away she started accusing me of sleeping with other women. For years I argued with her. I finally gave up.

We've gone our separate ways since. She won't give me a divorce because of the agreement. She's tried to get around it. I'd have to be dead before she'd inherit my estate. As a divorcée she'd get enough to live on from me, but the way she lives it wouldn't be near enough. I haven't filed for divorce because she'd contest it and she'd use lawyers and judges the same way she's using you. Tears and skimpy clothes. She does well by me. If you've been to the house, you know that already. But she won't give up and doesn't care what she does."

"That's the story I got from your daughter."

"My daughter's dead. I don't know who you've been talking to. I should've known. Wanda wouldn't have hired you if you had any brains."

He laughed, with enough dimples to start a doll factory. He crossed his pork hocks and began to rock back and forth, a life-size windup toy in a fat man's store. I let him unwind. I thought things out. No need to tell him Thela Crammond said she was his daughter. Why had she lied? She knew I'd find out. I had to. The motive? Not clear, but money was part of it. She wouldn't love Mr. Chops enough to forget about finances. Sorority babes, self-defrocked or otherwise, are ace sniffers no matter what they have to sniff. Nothing is too low for them. Unless you're the one who happens to be smitten with her. Then it's love. Proving a guy is a fool. Some of us admit it.

"You've had your five minutes."

Making with the tough again. I glanced at my watch. Past six. Was he expecting her? Maybe she was there. He hadn't wanted to let me in. The doors to the other rooms were closed. I'd had enough of the businessman's hideaway and his stink-killer, anyway. I stood up fast. His eyes got big. I was going to say boo but didn't want to look for the smelling salts. Thela Crammond could pick them.

The next afternoon I was at Ordway Hall. The receptionist phoned Thela Crammond, who told her to send me up. When I got to her room the door was open and there was a note pinned to it: "Back in a minute." I took the same chair, waited fifteen. She came in wearing a pink terrycloth bathrobe, pink slippers shaped like bunny heads and was drying her hair with a beach towel. She pushed the door with her heel, leaving it half open. She gave me an offhand smile laced with enough exquisite boredom and latent interest to boil the corpuscles of an octogenarian monk with the mange. When she turned to hang the towel on the doorknob the lapels of the robe fell open. Her honeymelons, softly weighted, were almost round. Pert budded nipples tilted up slightly. A negligent toss of her head and those tousled strands, almost curly now, danced. I was going on automatic pilot.

"I felt dirty, had to take a shower."

Using the side of her lower lip, she blew a strand away from her eye.

"I can't imagine you being dirty."

Topping that was easy. She took off the bathrobe. I don't know what Jason was after. I found the Golden Fleece. She tossed the robe onto the bed and picked up a pair of panties lying next to it and slipped them over her thighs. I'd seen that done but not like she did it, as if the centre of the universe was between her hips. She bent down again, this time picking up a brassiere. She fitted the cups over her breasts. Turning away, she showed off her tapering back and softly rounded shoulders, lifting the straps along her arms until I could feel them pulling between shoulder and collarbone. Reaching behind, she took the two ends and hooked them together. The satin fabric tightened against her skin, still damp from the shower. She was testing me, seeing if I wanted to get into the queue behind Raskolski. One grab, even a lingering finger, and more than my hand would be caught under the bra. She was playing the surprise gambit, stalling so I could think of nothing else. I crossed my legs. If she was disappointed, she didn't show it. Those slightly chubby cheerleader legs did a barefoot two-step over to the small open closet. The light picked out the downy blonde hairs on the back of her thighs. Rummaging around, she gave me a good look at her backside, maybe plump for some. I like a bit of crease and fold. She snugged herself into a pair of sotight jeans that looked glad to be home and warm again, and buttoned up and tucked in a white cotton blouse, leaving her breasts showing like the twin lobes of a cream heart the cupids were promoting as a hands-on valentine. Her back against the door, she went through a medley of moves with her feet and legs in putting on white socks and sneakers with enough of an awkward touch to make you want to help her, then rip everything off. My gonads were in shock. The rational part of my brain was like a man crawling over hot sand towards an oasis he's trying not to believe is a mirage.

"What do you want?"

She dropped into the chair by her desk. She picked up a brush and began pulling it through her hair. Sometimes a tangle and a groan in tugging it loose, that pout of slight pain mock agony of an almost erotic intensity. My brain was melting.

"You told me that guy is your father."

"Did I?"

She stopped brushing and her blue gaze locked onto mine. It was an act. She didn't want to talk about Hubbyhips. Her schoolgirl come-on wasn't going to flummox me.

"He's not your father?"

"Did I say he wasn't?"

"How about a straight answer? I have a client, your stepmother."

"That's no inducement."

"What would be?"

"There isn't any."

"You won't help?"

"Why should I? I don't have to tell you anything. You're here as her spy. I said all I'm going to last time."

She started brushing as if I wasn't there. I wanted to spank her with that hairbrush but it would've been pleasure and not punishment for me and maybe her, too. Another daddy. Let's play naughty little girl. Let's paddle her widdow wumbum. Beautiful girl. All female. But something had gone wrong. Maybe I was out of date. Babes did what they wanted to nowadays. Age of consent was a formality. It was the Age of Consent. I could stand up easily now. When I left she was examining her hair for split ends. The one I'd seen was out of sight.

I got back to the office at four. Emily was writing on a slip of paper in quick deft strokes with an old-fashioned wooden pen, the kind that has a removable nib. She uses it for office work, too. A computer? Ask her to fly to the moon. An individual, she is. They broke the mould when they made her.

I gave her a summary of what happened. I thought she smirked but you can't tell with her. Those eyes, hazel with a drop of maple syrup, saw things I never could. She had an opinion.

> The bonny flower blooming
> In Arcady or Samarkand,
> Plush meadow for a regal bed
> Or in such waste of sand,
>
> May wish for Inca heights—
> Donate the wind a seed or two
> After zephyr and scirocco—
> Seeking that lost Peru.

"What's that mean?" I said. She put the slip of paper in her desk drawer, stood up and put on her coat. She showed me a piece of junk mail, a brochure for a flower garden. She picked up a basket she'd brought that day and left on a corner of her desk. It was packed with her knitting and tiny jars full of honey. I figured she was going to feed flies and knit something to keep the bees warm during the long cold winter, when flowers are memories. Winter was months away but that's a lot of knitting.

After Emily left I sat in my office and tried to puzzle things out, which never works. I start to wonder and wander and end up wasting time. I have those middle-age thoughts, what's happened to my life, why haven't I done more with it? I think about being stuck in a decrepit office with a spinster and trying to do business with wealthy liars and other choice riffraff. The stuff that floats in the door and expects you to put your morals on hold and solve their lives for them. But don't leave dirty footprints on the rug. I think about the grey in my hair and my old car with its slipping clutch and assorted wrong noises that will mean more expense sometime soon. The rent on my apartment has gone up. Rent for my business premises hasn't because the neighbourhood has slid into down-and-out status. Hookers, addicts and pushers are part of the scenery outside. I get concerned about Emily being mugged. The building, four storeys of red brick, grey stonework around the windows, dates from the 1920s. Peeling paint and cracked linoleum in narrow hallways with rows of doors, flaking gold and silver lettering on frosted glass panels. Empty offices abandoned by shysters and alcoholic dentists. Others cheap fronts for phony importers or mail order fraud. Doors closing on anonymous silence. The janitor and the cleaning woman, a prehistoric married couple, monsters from a horror film, stagger around and reek of jug wine. A safety or fire inspection would mean automatic condemnation, but nobody ever inspects anything. Fire hoses rot on cast-iron reels, the sand buckets are full of cigarette butts, the ancient extinguishers came with the building. A wonky elevator but the door has always opened easily. Some tricky climbing when it stalls between floors. I'm on the second, take the stairs. I've heard that the owners are wealthy foreign investors who use the place as a tax write-off. Or an eccentric multimillionaire who sometimes visits late at night and sleeps in the basement. I mail the rent money every month to the address of a holding company in one of those glass and steel towers in the downtown business district. I figure if I open my mouth the rent will go up. It hasn't in the seven and half years I've been here. Before that I worked for one of those outfits specializing in industrial espionage, stealing corporate secrets by using the latest audio and video equipment and bribing executives. But I got tired of grey crime and its half-dirty dollars. I decided to be a private operator. It's not all it's cracked up to be. Mostly divorce cases, domestic stakeouts, shadowing cheating husbands and occasionally a wife. Once both husband and wife wanted me to spy on the other. Neither knew the other came to see me. A question of ethics but I was collecting cobwebs in my wallet. They both turned out to be wrong, a couple of paranoids. I saved that marriage from the shrinks and the shysters. A harder row to hoe than it looks but better than finding how company X has improved its latest gizmo from some guy who's tired of toeing the line and could use more of the folding or a pricey hooker who'll do things for him his wife won't. Or who'll jump onto a higher rung at company Y with his know-how in tow. Nothing grates too much with me now. I'm used to all the finagling and I won't take a lot of guff from either the hoi polloi or rich snots.

As I said, I tend to wander. Sometimes I end up thinking about women I've known, the best, the worst, the last, the first (been around Emily too long). I've seen more than enough domestic warfare to make me steer clear of anything permanent. Ideal couples are rare. Love? It's the first spring breeze, when everything is new and the air smells of blossom. It's the perfection and promise of something in her eyes. It's beyond fact, truth, reason and common sense. It's the biology of the soul, as rare as a pink kitten. I thought I found it once but she was a tigress in heat, a striped snarl, my jaws on her neck. A lot of great exercise and self-preservation. The best exit line when you're dumped is, "You're right, I'm being saved for a higher purpose." It works, stuns them. One time it didn't. She had the nerve to say, "It must be dog food." It isn't worth being civil to some women. They want unconditional surrender.

The phone rang and I let it ring, poured myself a shot of Old Dixie. I frequently imbibe before dinner, soaking my stomach lining with whisky. It's a precaution against what I'll be eating. Figure alcohol counteracts the poisons at the fast food dumps I'm forced to patronize because I don't have the wherewithal to hit the high spots. A decent dinner for me is something not wrapped or boxed in plastic and without enough grease to set fire to an unusually damp forest. It happens enough to make me try to remember the last time. Cash reserves being low, I was forced once to patronize a burger emporium where the cutlery tasted better than the food. I'd happened to prepare myself that time with too much protection and couldn't tell the difference between the meal and the utensils. The plastic beat the cheeseburger and chips, the fork being marginally tastier than the knife. But the napkin beat both.

After a while the phone rang again. I picked it up, waited. "Quester?" It was a man's voice, polite as it had to be and suspicious by nature. The voice of somebody who'd be suspicious if his shoelaces were untied. Kerry Grady was a detective with city homicide. I'd met him a few years ago. A man whose wife I was shadowing went berserk and killed her. She was sleeping with his best friend. They'd swindled my client on a stock deal. Grady had a college degree and thought it gave him star status in the department. We said hello and he got official in an offhand way.

"Drop by before you get too cosy with your pillow. A certain somebody had your card on him. That somebody is no longer breathing. Bullet in the brain."

"Care to tell me who?"

"Ivan Raskolski. Care to tell me why?"

I was sure I hadn't given him one of my business cards. As sure as I'd given a card to Wanda Regine.

"I'll be there in two shakes of a lamb's tail."

"You still talking like that?"

"You want I should talk like I'm full of constipated grammar?"

"You're out of date. Nobody talks like you."

"That should bother me?"

Twenty minutes later I showed up at Prairie City police headquarters. It looked like all police stations, a big dentist's office with holsters and handcuffs. Everybody busy making with the uniforms and official looks, as if crime is a business but none of the customers are willing. Grady's office was two floors up and down a quiet hallway, the usual ten square feet with a metal desk and padded metal chairs. The door was open. He was on the phone. I tapped on the door. He stopped jawing, nodded towards a chair and I sat down. His superannuated crew cut was going grey, a couple of shades lighter than his lead-coloured eyes. He liked to play smooth tough guy but he played it looking into a mirror. He should have been taller for his size and compensated with lifts. Push him and you got the punishment he had saved up from dealing with the morally deprived. I saw him take apart a guy with a straight right, an uppercut, right cross and finished off with a beaut of a left hook. A mean drunk and bigger than Grady, he made the mistake of taking a swing at him. Otherwise Grady was a suburban family man who took his kid to the game. He finished his official palavering and put down the phone. He stared hard for the record and gave up, knowing I wouldn't be reduced to gruel by any third degree routine.

"Tell it."

"It was simple till you phoned. His wife hadn't seen him in a while. Last Wednesday she hired me to find him. I found out he's renting an apartment near the university. Playing house with a coed. I talked with the babe, my client's stepdaughter. According to her, it's all innocent. I told his wife. She didn't go for that. I saw him Tuesday evening. Gave him my peregrine's eye view. Wifie going to use the babe against him. He dumped on her. The usual conjugal jungle. That's where it stood."

"He was killed with a head shot. Point-blank with a .22. Slug has enough power to get in but not get out. Ricochets around in the brain, tears it apart. No gun on the premises."

"The much underrated .22. Favourite of hitmen, assassins and intelligence agencies everywhere. Behind the ear for easy entrance. Not much recoil, get off a lot of rounds fast."

"You give him your card?"

"No. Can't figure how he got it."

"Any of it make sense to you?"

Cops can get tricky, hoping you'll oblige by tripping yourself up. They get to thinking crimes are like puzzles, even though their experience tells them different. They don't like thinking it's all animal stuff, at least their end of it. They're zookeepers cleaning up shit. Why shit happens, that's somebody else's lookout. They're not supposed to bother themselves about it. But they can't help thinking it's more than mops and pails. They look for answers that don't stink. But the smell goes with the uniform and being official. Try telling them that.

"Too hyper for a middle-age suit getting a piece on the side. Maybe he was into something he couldn't handle. His wife told me business was bad. It could be that."

"Anything else?"

"You want me to figure everything for you?"

"All right. But you better not be playing games."

"I'm too played out to be playing with cops, especially educated ones."

He thought about that and couldn't decide whether I was kidding or complimenting him.

"Take off. Let me know if you get anything, and don't leave town."

I took the cliché with a straight face. On the main floor a policewoman came out of an office. No uniform could hide her walk. There are things even whisky has a hard time making you forget. I was almost married because of a walk like that and all the accoutrements. Sometimes I think I made a mistake. I'll admit to being hardheaded about being hardheaded. Maybe the ones with the big price tag are worth it. I've made do with bargain basement. You don't get to the summit but you don't fall a long way either. As far as a dirty mattress.

Now what to do? One from three is two. Emily again. If I didn't watch out, I'd end up in the park feeding the pigeons. I got to the office early Thursday morning. She was scribbling on a slip of paper with her wooden pen. Seeing I wanted to talk, she put her pen down on a blotter and screwed the lid on the ink bottle. Methodical muse awaits news. Where were the breadcrumbs? Hands folded in her lap, she leaned back against her wooden armchair. I told her what was bothering me. She nodded, but you'd have to look hard to see it.

> A woman knows a woman better
> Than a man could know her
> Unless he read the secret letter
> Of her heart, that frequent debtor—
>
> Smoothed, creased and yellowed pages,
> Such memory of her ages—
> And he could see what fades
> With ink, work of no paltry sages.

"Could you speed it up?"
She frowned.
"All right, I'm sorry. I'm fed up with this case."
She looked at her fingers for a few seconds, making me wait. Don't tell me she isn't a woman.

Something gives
A heart away,
It may be love,
It may be play.

For what it is
And where it stays
You must know
The rhyme of days.

"You mean—pardon my crude language—put a tail on them." I was getting too polite. She does that to you. Could be the throat lace.

The hawk is a flier
I like to see,
So unannounced—
Unlike a bee.

"Ah, I get it. Careful is the word."
She looked up at the ceiling. I couldn't see anything.

I pick a flower
That has no name,
No pedigree
Or common fame,

No accustomed rose
In garden soil
Trowelled and mulched
And sprinkled royal,

No shady place
That's fenced the sun,

Placed planets on view—
That's a nightly run—

And randomly stars,
Constellations, too,
A moon coined silver,
The cushion dyed blue.

No pampered bloom,
Stilted, raised to be
A showpiece bowing—
The wind—majesty.

No budding petals
Where love is worn,
Calyx, rosehip,
The appointed thorn.

The flower I pick
Isn't known too well
Except to bees
And they don't tell.

I got up quietly and went into the inner office. She was in her writing mood. I phoned Eddy and left a message on his answering service. He called back in an hour. I told him to keep an eye on Thela Crammond while I shadowed Wanda Regine. I called Wanda Regine. I don't know what I expected. She didn't sound any different.

"I guess the police told you," I said.

"Yes."

"That's the end of the case. I'll send you my bill. Bit of a surprise. Him bumped off like that."

"I told you, Mr. Quester. He had business problems."

Whose business? I liked the "Mr." and her freeze-dried tone. But that's an old story. The ardently amorous woman trying to get what she's after. When she either gets it or knows she won't, it's the icicle dripping onto the back of your neck word by word. She got what she wanted. She was rich now. How did she do it? I knew Raskolski's death was no more connected with business than birds fly north for the winter. Or cops sit on rich people and ask nagging questions about murders. Money buys respect even without paying for it. She knew that already.

"Till when, Mrs. Raskolski."

"Goodbye."

I went down to the Prairie River to do some thinking. There's nothing else in scrub brush country except gopher holes and those flatiron miles. River? Sewage trickling along a gouge a large stick could make. A snake crawling through a slough to die. Prairie City. Summerscape, a mosquito swarm blown through dusty streets. Winterscape, brown snow chewed up for eight months by boots and tires. Bungalow suburbs, white on white. Wind biting at your face, ice cubes in your lungs. Downtown, freezing corners sharpened by the wind. A nowhere of bugs and ice to get lost in and forget the years. Why do I stay? For the same reason there are ruts in a dirt road.

I side-footed down the hill to the bank and sat on a tuft of weedy grass that looked like a bad haircut. Some locals had embarked on a beautification program: beer cans, condoms, plastic bags and junk food wrappers. A bunch of flies were having a party over a heap of dog turds. Other celebrations were going on at other piles and single droppings. All downwind. I checked the soles of my shoes to be sure. Something can look wrong because you're not seeing it right, and that was my problem. Why would a wife want her husband back when he's a turd? Because divorce means she carries away no loot. That's where I come in. Expose porkfork and youngstuff, wifie can claim infidelity. Bargaining time among the shysters. Flies over the turds. What was wrong with this was the daughter angle, disposed of, and murder because why murder tubby hubby when a private dick is set to expose him? So what was right? Let's go back a bit. To the daughter angle. If he was porking his own flesh, wifie and her legal sharks would be sniffing loot and trying to ace out youngstuff. So double nix on the rub out for spousie, which left me with Thela Crammond. Two things had to be right. I had a call to make.

Climbing back up I wasn't so lucky. I wiped my shoe on the mayor's face. Some slacker had thrown away a bunch of re-election flyers for Mayor Doppel-Gangrene or Syphilisovich or Pizzariaroski or Achooka or Dumbrae-Macswipe. They all have that self-appointed look you need to spend the public's money and edgy eyes from telling too many fibs. Small-timers who love welcoming titled obsolete jet-lagged touring dignitaries on the city hall steps and wear chains of office like a cannibal displaying his necklace of bones. They believe in sister cities and by-laws and real estate deals and shopping malls and the mill rate and the chamber of commerce and the better business bureau business and fraternal service organizations and pinning long-service badges on civic retirees and prosperity and parliamentary rules of order in mindless debates in council chambers and parades with grand marshals in convertibles leading drum majorettes twirling batons and in those low election turnouts that favour the incumbents. They are the minutiae of politics, as monotonous as a hooker's bedsprings.

At the office I sat wondering why I was still working on the case. Wanda Regine would be paying me off with a nice bit of change soon. But I couldn't walk away without knowing. Professional pride. Eddy called back and said Thela Crammond was sharing a basement suite in Belvedere, near the university. He gave me the address and phone number. I phoned the suite and a woman answered. I told her I was calling from the registrar's office. She said that her roommate would be in after four. I cleared up some correspondence and told Emily to bill Wanda Regine and drove over to Belvedere. The place with panache for the academic crowd. It had as much class as a plate of boiled potatoes. Identical streets of stucco bungalows punctuated by a few ranch houses, all close to the ground because of wind, cold and the heating bill. In newer suburbs, further out, the Cape Cod style was making an appearance but that heating bill was keeping them small. Only in Whitby could plutocrats like the Raskolskis flaunt their immunity to the windchill factor. Mansions on the prairies. The rest could drool.

The suite was in a bungalow two blocks southeast of the campus. I knocked at the side door and a plough puller of a woman opened it, breathing boiled cabbage and garlic on me. The smell of a gas stove floated from behind her. I told her I'd come from the registrar's office to see one of her tenants. She looked me over from crotch to navel. For a moment she appeared ready to haul me upstairs by her horse teeth and do something personal with my coccyx. When she stepped aside I could see where she stood was a landing between upstairs and downstairs. I slipped past her, brushing against two of the biggest and hardest I've ever felt.

"You like plum brandy?" she asked in an eastern European accent not quite worn away by grinding decades of prairie climate. "I bake plum bread. Very good." I wondered what else she did with plums.

I gave her a grin and walked down the stairs. At the bottom was the stove I'd smelled. It was against a short wall and facing the stairs. To the left and against a partition made of plywood were a wooden table and two chairs. Behind the stove wall were the gas furnace and hot water tank and a door to what probably was the bathroom. There was a door in the partition. Behind it would be the bedrooms and maybe a sitting room. I knocked and Thela Crammond opened the door. She didn't look surprised, invited me in. The sitting room was a couch and a coffee table. The bedrooms were on either side. The doors faced each other. The bedroom walls were bare plywood. The spitgrey linoleum was curling up in spots. Through an open door I could see there was barely room enough for the single bed and the junk store dresser. The window was a horizontal slit, would show somebody's heels passing by. A comedown for her. She asked me to sit, said her roommate was out. The couch was a faded brown, the nap worn away on armrests and cushions. There were slick marks on the seat cushions, like melted plastic. The rickety table was and smelled of glue.

We sat down and the seat cushions kept sinking into what felt like cardboard. When we stopped, the armrests were level with my neck. She crossed her legs, in those same stretchy wornsoft jeans, and flicked a sneaker toe at me. The rest of her was pale grey sweatshirt. She looked tired, eyes red from crying or lack of sleep. She was ready for whatever I was going to say. But she wasn't happy I was going to say it.

"I talked to him the night before he was murdered. What you told me about your stepmother and the prenuptial agreement is probably true. You're no bimbo on the make, some floozie on the fly, a chippie peddling her twat to some scrapehead cologne addict who loved shooting the cuffs and pretending he was a hot one with the schoolgirl set by shoving his spongie up the youngest hair pie he could get to take licorice allsorts off him. He wouldn't have thought of sex with his daughter as fouling his own nest. But all you'd have done in playing with pappasperm was give your stepmother ammunition—incest added to infidelity—in any court fight to get around the prenup. That you'd never do. Whatever went on, you're not his daughter. She died years ago."

She lay her head against the back cushion, closed her eyes and spoke quietly.

"I'm his stepdaughter. My mother died. My father married Wanda. They divorced and he took off. I don't know where he is. She married Ivan. She's my stepmother twice over."

She opened her eyes and looked at me.

"I don't know why you're interested, coming here with your zipper undone."

I had to look down. It wasn't.

"Don't tell me you haven't? Didn't she give the key to her chastity belt? She's paying you in dollars? Aren't you lucky."

"It wasn't luck, it was the toilet. I had diarrhea."

She laughed. It was the saddest laugh I ever heard.

"There was no money after the divorce. Wanda got a job driving one of those coffee trucks that go to where guys are working. She hated it, took me along with her during the summer holidays. She met Ivan on a construction site. He was looking over the new branch office his company was building in Prairie City. They got to talking. I was sitting in the front seat. He saw me and said something and she called me over to introduce him. I knew she was after him so I behaved myself. They started dating and he wanted to take me along sometimes. To the beach and the park, on car rides, stuff like that. He'd be friendly and kid around with me. I was twelve then. My father didn't even bother to show up, so this was different and nice. They told me they were going to get married, I was happy. I'd have a family again. Wanda was excited because he was rich. We were going to live in a big house, she said, with domestic help. There was a tennis court, pool, diving board. Wouldn't I like that? Sure. He likes you, be nice. Sure.

"A week before the wedding he came to the apartment. She said that she had to go out for something. He called me over to the sofa and put his arm around my shoulder. He kissed me on the cheek, and on the lips, harder. I tried to get away. He was trying to be friendly, he said. Didn't I want to make him happy and my stepmother happy? She'd set me up. He'd been after me all the time. I had nowhere to go. So I shut off my mind and pretended I had no body and let him do it. It hurt the first time. He was so excited, rough. But I didn't cry. I bled quite a bit. He said virgins did. He said we were going to be a happy family. He would be so good. Sure. Wasn't I happy about that? Sure. Wanda came back with a new dress.

"On the honeymoon he slept with me. She didn't care, she was buying clothes, getting her hair done and her fingernails manicured. He let her have whatever she wanted as long as he could have me. I was so sore I had to see a doctor. She told the doctor I'd been riding a bicycle and the seat was wrong. After the honeymoon he would come to my bedroom regularly during the night, when the maids and the cook were off duty. The house was big, no one caught on. I got pregnant when I was fifteen, had an abortion. I certainly didn't want his kid. He told me he loved me a lot. A lot is right. He'd go crazy sometimes, do it all night. I never got excited, even interested. Know what it feels like having a sweaty smelly bald slob of a slug on top of you sucking your face as he makes that same back and forth motion, as if he's trying to dig a hole with his thing. His pig stink was really bad and he had women's boobs, with hair on them, a blobby ass and hippo legs. I used to lie there thinking, what a pathetic asshole. I thought about stabbing him or running away but I never did. Guess I was waiting for something to happen. We took trips as father and daughter. He'd play Mr. Daddy in front of old ladies in the hotel lobby, saying my sweater was too tight or my skirt was too short. I wore a bikini once and guys came around and he dragged me away from the pool.

He got excited back in our room and tried to shove his thing up my bum and I ran out into the hallway naked and he came out with his pants around his ankles and said he was sorry, he would never do that again. The elevator doors opened and a couple of grannies came out. We left the hotel an hour later. The desk clerk asked why we'd decided to check out so soon and Mr. Daddy said his little girl was homesick. Wanda had a boyfriend by that time and didn't come with us. Wanda used me to get Ivan and he used the prenup to keep her from exposing him.

"Things changed when I started university. I joined a sorority so I could live in a house on campus and not be bothered. Hardly ever went home, never slept there. I won a scholarship, so I had money of my own. He didn't like it but there was nothing he could do. He'd come to the sorority, but I'd told them to tell him I wasn't in. He even tried to get up to my room once. They called the campus police and he was told to stay away. After that I didn't go home. He didn't do anything for a long time, even stopped trying to get me on the phone. Two months ago he moved near the campus. He left a message saying he had to see me and I went up to his apartment after I thought about it for weeks. I knew what he was going to try, but I had a surprise for him. He grabbed me when I stepped inside and I flipped him across the room. I'd taken a self-defence course and enjoyed it and started serious training. He got up swearing, ran at me and I gave him a chop on the side of the neck and he went down again. I sat on the sofa, asked what he wanted and he started crying, said he loved me. No, you never did, Ivan, you fucked me, I said. There's an enormous difference, a lot bigger than your prick. He wanted me to help him up, so I went over, held out my hand. He grabbed it and tried to pull me down and I stomped on his ankle. Took off my clothes and stood there. This what you want, Ivan? Come on. He reached out for my foot and I kicked him in the face with the other one. My heel caught him on the nose, he started bleeding and I got down close to him. Want to try anything else? I got him a wet towel and put on my clothes. Don't leave, he said, I've got to tell you about Wanda. I know all about her. She's bankrupting me, he said. How sad. No, it's true, she and that guy are embezzling company funds. Divorce her, accuse her of embezzlement and adultery. I would but she'd use you against me to prove I'm an unfit father. How true, but I wouldn't tell on you. Help me fix her. Fix her? Stop her from stealing. You expect help from me? Why don't you pay her off? Because she'd want everything. That's your problem. I'm going. All right, you won't help, but see me again, I'm lonely. I'm sorry for what I did. Sure, like tonight, when I walked in. He started crying again and said he had an ulcer, maybe stomach cancer, and he had glaucoma. He was so pathetic I promised I'd think about seeing him. Went up once more. He didn't touch me. We sat and talked and I left. Never went back. He didn't mention her or the business. Can't pretend I was upset when I heard he was dead. My name and my phone number at the sorority house were in his wallet, along with an old picture of me. The police traced me here. And that's it."

She uncrossed her legs and stood up. I surfaced too but slipped and almost sank back into the depths. I put out a hand to grab something. It turned out to be her thigh. She flinched as if she'd been scorched with a branding iron.

"Don't touch me. I know you didn't mean anything by it, Mr. Quester, but I don't like it, especially when it's an older man."

With one hand on the armrest and one on the back cushion I hoisted myself up and we faced each other.

"It was sheer desperation. This couch doesn't give up its prey easily. I'm used to short rations. Like milady's plum bread upstairs."

"You'd be wasting your time with her. She's not your type."

"You sure you're not a lot older?"

"I had to grow up fast in some ways, but in others I'm a kid. And I didn't kill him, if that's what you came here to find out."

"I didn't think you did."

She smiled a tired smile, her eyelids puffy. So sometimes I wish I were thirty years younger and still believed in love. We said goodbye and I walked up through the smell of boiled cabbage and garlic. And I breathed it in, like the fool I am.

I went back to the office, sat there with my feet up on the desk. Plum brandy. Ye gods and little fishes. I got out the bottle of Old Dixie and poured myself a shot and stared at it. If you put the skids under Ivan the Horny Toad

Raskolski with a head shot, why not make it look like suicide? The weapon in his hand, fingerprints his, and the police would draw the obvious conclusion. Hadn't the killer appreciated this cliché in movies and detective stories? That meant Lustbucket's no-return departure wasn't premeditated. A bottle of sleeping pills and a stiff drink would have been less messy, a trip through a window more dramatic. But both would have to be planned, and this wasn't. Whoever iced him had a reason for not using the suicide ploy. Traceable gun, fingerprints, panic, not able to think, and at this point I couldn't.

A store manager phoned, wanted me to catch a shoplifter. He said his chain was already paying for security that provided camera surveillance and store dicks but the thief was very good. His store was losing too much money. I told him it's always an inside job when they're that good. Replace any suspicious staff. We're a union shop, he said, I can't fire anybody unless I've got proof. He wanted me to hang around for a few days. My brain needed a rest after the Raskolskis, so I accepted. The store was one of those megadumps selling everything from auto parts to tomatillos but never exactly what you're looking for, especially if it's quality. This one catered to welfare cases and low-income pensioners who could get light-fingered around the organic fruit. I borrowed a cap, cardigan, windbreaker, baggy pants and crepe-soled shoes from Eddy, who keeps clothing of many kinds for disguises, and hit the place Friday morning. It was the size of an aircraft hangar, the shopping cart cost a dollar to borrow, returned when you took it back, and some veteran of a forgotten war was hovering inside the entrance as a kind of official greeter who would spot suspicious characters and notify the store dicks. The old duffer I saw couldn't have spotted the polka dots at a Polish wedding. I went to the returns desk and asked for a few locations as I cased the joint. I must have rechecked something because a voice that could've sliced see-through salami snarled at me out of the orgiastic ethos of that shoppers' nirvana.

"It's at the back. I told you that."

Customer relations. I took a gander. Nature hadn't been on her side for a long time. Keester six axe handles across. Skin rashes and facial hair. A nose trying to look at itself. Mouth for chewing cud. Dutch boy haircut by a homicidal maniac with a scythe. Longshoreman's arms. I rate the fair sex by how many drinks I'd need before they'd look good enough to hit the hay with. A beauty intoxicates with a single glance. For the dainty in front of me I'd need every distillery in the Highlands.

"You told me," I said. "And I can see why."

Leaving uglybitchinabadmood to the rest of her miserable life, I wheeled my cart like a gink, looking for somebody desperate enough to steal a tub of margarine. A fossil with a walker was cracking open and testing peanuts on his false teeth and an immigrant woman of some apparent European extraction tore the mesh open on a carton of organic peaches and took one out and slipped it into a plastic bag of poisoned ones. The employees looked as if they were on parole or had failed the entrance exam to kindergarten. A husky who was mopping the floor came over and asked if I was looking for something. She had the shortest pigtail I'd ever seen and wore a T-shirt with sleeves made for shoving a pack of cigarettes up and under. She had a skull and crossbones tattoo on the ham of her upper arm and smelled like an ashtray in a skid row hotel. I told her I was in search of the spermicidal toothpaste and erotic cling wrap. She thought about that, gave up and went back to her mop. She bent over, not a bad keester. Pretending to be lost, I entered the employees-only areas behind the produce and bakery sections. I saw lettuce leaves on the floor and stacks of cardboard boxes in one and giant ovens behind multilevel bread trolleys in the other.

I bought a loaf of pumpernickel and a carton of eggs and went to the nearest checkout. Swollen-ass women were unloading megabox breakfast cereals of wheat-dusted and oat-flavoured sugar and packages of belly bacon and minced pink steer's ass in plastic loaf pans and tubs of margarine sludge and ice cream and cans of hamburger goo and cheese goop in a bottle and torpedoes of diet pop and horse feedbags of chips and trays of ringsize powdered or pink-iced doughnuts and puffy cakes with hairstyled frosting sprinkled with something that glittered under a plastic dome and light salad dressings of flamingo puke and slugbelly creamsnot. Occasionally a beheaded lettuce wrapped in cling wrap would roll aimlessly along the conveyer belt like a mouldy casualty from the Reign of Terror. The bony cashier wore glasses last seen on nineteenth-century rural schoolmarms and she had thin lips made for scolding truant boys.

"You should have gone through express," she said. "You have two items."

"I like waiting, but don't take it personally."

Lips twitched, itching for the principal to wield the cane. Or maybe she would have enjoyed doing it herself, on the bare bottom, until welts rose like skinropes and the blood came. She rang me through and I paid. My change was slapped onto the counter.

"You need a bag?"

I passed that up and dropped a nickel into her bloodless spider palm and she tore a bag off the stack and tossed it in my direction. Bags cost in that store and you bag your groceries.

I was leaving when the Empress of China walked in holding hands with a prairie sodbuster, part of somebody's historical fantasy. I rubbed my proverbial eyes. She was an empress, indeed, younger and better looking than any I'd ever imagined. She moved as if the air around her was being given a rare privilege. Chin up, shoulders back and arrayed with her long hair, hint of a smile, regal eyes used to acres of peasants with their faces to the ground. I wouldn't have had the nerve to tell her this was a democracy and you had to be rich before you got that kind of treatment here. She was all female. She didn't carry herself the way most women do, as shifting sacks of cement. Her movements said having a woman's body was an infinite pleasure. It was almost indecent to watch her below the waist, her thighs teasing her backside forward, the slow rotary pull from side to side. The rube was a beak on stilts, forty years her senior and fresh from the manure pile. Now there was a mystery, if not a pardonable crime. I forgot about shoplifters, which is why I'll never get wealthy in my racket, if anyone does. I tailed the hick and his dear one, wheeling my cart the recommended distance behind. The hayseed was carrying a store basket with his other hand, his consort processional-minded and saunteringly bemused. I, student of geometry and applied physics, considered the changing diameters of circumferences of conjunctive female hemispheres in motion, as well as allied problems of the coefficient of friction, slip stress, resultant transference of heat and variable vectors of force studied intramuscularly and of the adipose tissue from lateral and vertical thrust. It was an exhaustive analysis.

I stopped. What was I doing? I'd become the gink I was dressed up to be. Tailing a Hong Kong cuddly and some stump ranch nosepicker who was paying lots to burp her. An enterprising young lady specializing in generous pensioners who were tired of watering geraniums and wanted to try out the nozzle on a fresh patch. Or maybe she was an immigration sidestepper who married the wad in his jeans to get past the twelve mile limit. He'd thumbed her snap in a catalogue at one of those marriage agencies offering Far Eastern brides for the ancient and ugly, the habitually lonely, the nocturnally weird and wet dreamers hankering after a harem of one supplicating suppliant who would do as she was sexually bid. I could see life among the groundhogs wouldn't suit this one. He'd had to get her away from the bunkhouse boys and bring in his treasure. If she hadn't yet, she'd get him to sell his bit of prairie panorama and move to the city, where she could spin-dry him faster before proceeding to other delights among the plainsfolk, or maybe go out to the coast and auction herself off among the jade fanciers.

I have no psychic powers. I don't even know what day it is. Luck is something else. I was about to turn up the next aisle when I saw the denizen of the wide open spaces slip a couple of tins of sockeye under his long heavy coat, a little out of season for the warm weather recently. I decided I'd hang around and see what else he fancied. Next stop was the cheese and several chunks went into his basket. When they were alone, or thought they were, under the coat. Same thing with the pepperoni sticks, aspirins, toothbrushes and vitamins. You've got to stay healthy to keep those fingers nimble. His lady fair was the lookout. But I'm a passable gink when I want to be. She never caught on to my bumbleability act. They bought a bag of peanuts and a bottle of mineral water. I headed lickety-split for the manager's office. A store dick nabbed them outside. Up in the office they said they had a right to see a lawyer. Next day the manager, who had been out at the time, phoned and thanked me. The couple turned out to be a retired machinist and a jewellery saleswoman from Shanghai. They had met and married two years ago. They'd come back from the coast because he had inherited the family farm last year. First offence, and a teary lawyer managed to bring in the bad smell of possible racial prejudice. They got off with a few weeks of community service.

Not the kind of case I like. But money is what it is, and I'd had time away from the Raskolskis. Overthinking is a mind trap. Leave something alone and it'll clear up, like a muddy pool. A day away and I was beginning to see clearly. I had some help from Eddy, who phoned me on Monday at the office. Thela Crammond's story checked. Her mother was dead and her father was last seen collecting welfare in Windyspot or Dryspit or some other prairie haven of the forlorn. Ivan the Abominable had been married to Wanda Regine for eight and a half years and leased the apartment two months ago. He and Thela Crammond must have been photographed together one of the two times she'd gone there. Wanda Regine had a boyfriend. He was head of the sales staff of Brickward Business. Name of Melvin Stoker. Anything? Wine snob. Expensive taste in clothes. Fast cars. I guess she liked them snotty and spoiled. She was trying to get him appointed boss of the local operation. Raskolski's relatives weren't buying it. I thanked Eddy for his usual excellent job. He was modest in reply, as befits one who is pre-eminent in his field.

After the phone call I leaned back in my chair and closed my eyes. I saw a face in a pool. A girl, and not a girl. A woman trying to look a lot younger. Thela Crammond said she made two visits to the apartment. She stripped the first time. When Raskolski tried to rape her. That must have been before the stakeout. I remembered the videos, oil lamp, arty nudes. Didn't suit her. Eddy caught somebody else. I phoned him, told him to make enlargements. Closeups of the face. Send them right away. He brought them himself an hour later.

"B-boy, Charley. You g-guessed it."

He dropped an envelope on my desk and sat in one of the old wooden chairs reserved for paying guests and for professional associates who work cheap. There were four enlargements. Everything looked familiar, apartment, furniture and couple. But the woman wasn't Thela Crammond. Somebody older, but how much it was hard to tell. She wore a blonde wig and dressed young. I asked him why he'd thought she was Thela Crammond.

"I waited to see if she was spending the night there. She came out and went to her car, across the street. It was dark. But she'd parked near a light. Used my telephoto lens. Got shots of her and the rear plate. Blew them up. Got the back of her head but the plate was clear. Found out who owned the car. Got a student directory and checked her photo in there. Those photos are small. Looked like the same girl. Checked again after I did the enlargements. They're different. By the way, the owner's address is the same as her stepmother's."

"She never mentioned a car. I'll bet she walked over to see him. When she stopped going home she probably left it there. Somebody else has been driving it and paying the insurance. A relative could do that."

"Could I trouble you, Charley? Rent and stuff, you know."

I made out a cheque. Usually Emily sent the retainer to his bank. My own account would be getting healthier, what with my fee for the supermarket job plus Wanda Regine's nice pile of change. Eddy left and I phoned the widow Raskolski. The snooty maid answered. She is not at home. No, I don't. She cut me off. I called back and said my lawyer was going to sue for unpaid fees. Wait, please. Seconds later Wanda Regine came on the line.

"Yes, Mr. Quester? I will send the cheque."

"You should hire somebody who can lie better. Like you. Your stepdaughter told me the whole story. Doesn't do a thing for your reputation."

"She's a pampered brat. Ivan spoiled her."

"That's not all he did to her."

"You believe her?"

"I've got no reason not to. Not as it stands."

I heard her take a deep breath.

"Don't know why I should bother. Ivan's dead, it's over with. I suppose I should clear things up. Come on out. Now would be best."

I'd gotten what I wanted and hadn't said too much. I put the enlargements back into the envelope, rolled it up and slipped it into the inside pocket of my jacket. On my way out I was going to tell Emily to take off early. But she was busy with some bills that had come in. A couple were overdue notices. I mentioned again the cheques we'd be getting. That didn't make any impression. Hand-to-mouth isn't her style. Solid upper middle all the way, comfortable money. It's nickels and dimes, I've told her. And could've added, not many a guy would put up with a secretary scribbling all the time. You get the help you pay for. But she doesn't run off at the mouth. She's never put a foot wrong. Keeps everything on an even keel.

Whitby's iron maiden answered the door. I hadn't forgotten the broom closet. I knew she hadn't either but her face was blank. I barged ahead down the hall. Hurrying after me, she let loose with fragments of curses in a foreign tongue. She caught up, out of breath, as I reached the orangery, and gasping led me through glass doors and out to a swimming pool. It was a tidy pool, its concrete border almost square. The turquoise paint gave the water a tropical beach look. Wanda Regine was at poolside, reclining in a padded deck chair, and wore the tightest stretchiest bikini her curves could handle. It was white silky fabric, with the trace of a lip crease in her crotch. A stray hair seemed to curl enticingly between pouch and thigh. But that could have been my willing imagination. She had a light tan, perfectly suited to her pale honey hair. The straps of her bra were undone. She wore sunglasses and a lazy expression reminiscent of post-coital dreaminess. That's about as roundabout as I get. None of this was for my benefit. That didn't stop me from appreciating the display. Sleek-faced and bulky, Stoker was sitting upright in a deck chair next to hers. Sweating into a cream summer suit, he looked the worst kind of salesman, arrogant about lying to make a living. He got his reputation instead of his hands dirty and believed it was no different. Guys like him make it tough for the others, who have to convince the public that there should be a competition between the best of them for a commission some people will persist in believing shouldn't exist in the first place.

The maid walked me up, nodded and left. Wanda Regine introduced her porker. He looked at me as if I should be exterminated with the ants scurrying along the concrete. She smiled the way a beautiful woman will smile at a guy who's not her boyfriend when her boyfriend is around. The maid returned with one of those metal-frame chairs with cloth back and seat, sort of a hammock for your ass. She plunked it down and made another exit. I sat. No preliminaries, no drinks. It was leftover business. And Wanda Regine didn't sound rehearsed.

"My stepdaughter is deceitful. A lying bitch might be a better way to put it. Whatever she told you is a lie. The truth is, she had an affair with Ivan that started years ago, when she was fourteen. She was my first husband's daughter and I didn't meet her till she was ten. I don't know how she was raised. I tried to do the best I could for her after her father took off on us but she never accepted me. She played up to Ivan as soon as she met him. He wasn't a strong man and was vain, so he didn't put up much resistance. She sat in his lap all the time or sprawled on him on the couch. I told her to behave herself and we had fights and I slapped her once. Nothing changed. There's a toolshed for the gardener. It's at the back of the estate. I kept an eye on her and I saw them go in there one morning. They thought I'd gone shopping. I'd forgotten something and gone back and saw them from my bedroom window, upstairs. I went out there and opened the door. They were on the floor. She had no clothes on and he was on top of her. When he saw me he swore and got up and tried to push me out. He said if I didn't mind my own business he'd divorce me and I'd get nothing because of the prenuptial agreement. She's not your daughter, he said. I said, I'm her legal guardian and she's under age. If you touch her again or try to get a divorce I'll get you thrown in jail. I said to her, Thela, put on your clothes and come with me right now. She didn't want to. He tried to interfere, so I slapped him. He wasn't much of a man. I pulled her by the hand back to the house. Threw her into her room. But I knew that wouldn't be the end of it. They'd find a way. Months later the head of her private school called to tell me Thela had a poor attendance record and maybe should board with them. I knew what was happening and confronted him and he laughed. Both of them wanted it. If I'd had him charged the little bitch would've denied it. They never did anything around me. It was over between us. I'd thrown him out of my bed. That didn't bother him. I think he'd been after her from the beginning, anyway. All kinds of presents, more than he ever gave me. He'd ignore our wedding anniversary. They went on trips together. By then I didn't care. She was sixteen, old enough to know what she was doing. We had one fight after that. About what he was spending on her."

She stopped and looked at her porker. I had an opportunity to study her neck. There was an oval hollow on the side I could see, a shallow dip of softly sculpted form near the collarbone. It was meant for serious nuzzling.

"Mel, bring out the drinks wagon, will you?" she said in an offhand tone.

"Get the help to bring it out."

His face was flushed. She looked at me.

"What'll you have, Mr. Quester?"

"Bourbon, if you've got it. Neat."

"I think we have. Scotch and water for me, and get something for yourself, honey."

She was still looking in my direction. He trudged off and her smile got warmer.

"I like service."

"So I see."

"Mel's all right. He worked for my husband as sales manager and now he's working for me."

"That he is."

"He can leave any time he wants. I'm not a hard woman. But I'm no sucker. It's taken me a long time to get all this. Not going to throw it away, especially on an employee."

She rubbed a palm down the side of her thigh. She was firm, her skin having an elastic give that tightened immediately. Her muscles were smooth. A woman's body, all supple and purr. But there was no pussycat in her eyes.

The hireling returned with the wagon and we sat there sipping. The bourbon was not the best but passable and he'd given me an adequate shot. She drank as if she didn't like the stuff and it wouldn't be good for her figure. She resumed speaking as if she hadn't stopped.

"He took her on cruises, to resorts, plays, concerts, and the opera. Bought her the best clothes, a sports car. He paid no attention to the company. The head office wanted to know where the profits were going. They sent a troubleshooter to find out what was going on. He should've been fired. His relatives protected him. He was warned, though. One night he came in, said I was spending too much. You're the one who's spending, I said, on your stepdaughter. Leave her out of this, he hollered. She was with him and we were standing in the hallway. It was snowing and they still had their coats on. I remember. I thought, what did I do to her to have her behave like this? Of course, I wasn't her real mother, so who knows what happened in her childhood? But I couldn't help thinking I'd been a bad parent. They took off their coats and went upstairs. That was the first night they openly slept together in her bedroom. She was seventeen by then and I didn't care any more. I knew I'd have the domestic help as witnesses if he tried to divorce me. I stayed because I wasn't about to make divorce lawyers rich fighting over the money. I liked him at first, and his having money didn't hurt. But after a few sweaty nights with him, I started looking at the ceiling. That little bitch saved me from being bored, if you know what I mean."

She laughed. The whisky was making her slightly drunk. Time for my act. I stood up and took the envelope from my jacket pocket and held it out. She handed her glass to the help and took the envelope. She pushed her sunglasses up onto her forehead, removed the enlargements and looked them over. Nothing changed in her face. She squinted at me.

"So?"

"You don't see anything?"

"All I see is that you've had enlargements made so their faces are clearer."

I felt my feet sinking into something a lot softer than concrete.

"I don't know what you're trying to get at, Mr. Quester. That's him, that's her."

"Thela Crammond?"

"I ought to know."

"That's not who I was talking to."

"You're not trying to kid me, are you?"

Still holding two glasses, the lap dog took his cue.

"You've got a nerve coming here and pulling this crap."

Right up my alley.

"It's the lady and me, so stop shooting off your mouth."

"Hey, you watch your mouth." He put the glasses down between the deck chairs and stood up.

I put my glass on the concrete and it got the immediate attention of a nearby ant. I straightened up in time to get a fist shoved in my chest instead of my face, where he aimed it. I'd been hit harder by air conditioning. I gave him a shot in the belly, hard enough to give him indigestion. I didn't want a manslaughter rap hanging over me for dusting off a cream puff. He folded, sucking air. I'm not that tough and I don't go looking for fights. There's always some guy out there who can rip your head off and mail it to you in a paper bag. But I've never liked showoff tough guys, especially those I can handle. She jumped in to save his honour.

"Sit down, Mel, before you lose those expensive caps and crowns. You're better at serving drinks."

He turned and walked to the house, but not very straight, and disappeared inside. She told me to get myself another drink and sit down. As I was pouring, we heard a car screeching down the driveway. She shook her head.

"He'll get over it. He went to a private school and thinks he's too good to look bad."

"Do you collect them."

"It's hard getting rich and staying rich when you've got a great body and a beautiful face. Guys think everything is between your legs and if they can get you into bed they're in, in a manner of speaking."

"Are you a little tipsy?"

"It's wearing off, so stop thinking what you've been thinking."

"I was beginning to like you before you said that." I drained my glass, swivelled around and dropped it onto the lawn behind my chair.

"Charley—I can call you that now that he's gone—why did you bring these?" She tossed the photos and envelope in my general direction. Etiquette. I reached over and picked them up, stuffed them into my inside jacket pocket.

"Mrs. Raskolski—I can call you that now that we're alone."

She picked up her glass and flicked it at me. Droplets landed on my face.

"We're even. But tell me why."

"I've already told you. The student I talked to isn't whoever that is in the photo. This isn't a shakedown. I don't have near the wherewithal to take you on. I'm trying to find a murderer."

"Am I a suspect?"

"Right up to your beautiful golden eyes."

"A man who can compliment you on your eyes when your whole body is on display is either very clever or impotent. Which are you? By the way, my eyes are greenish hazel. You're not very observant for a private detective."

"The hardest part of this case has been concentrating on your eyes."

"If I believe you, I mean about this mystery girl you've been talking to, then there's somebody involved we don't know."

"Unless you're lying."

"Why would I lie?"

"To cover up something. You inherit your husband's estate by his death. The prenup died with him. His natural daughter died years ago. His other daughter is your stepdaughter. There's no provision for her. No last-minute will has popped up. I'm guessing there isn't one. Which makes your story Swiss cheese. You say she was a willing sex toy. Why didn't he let her jump the queue ahead of you? She's in his apartment playing footsie with him. She gets nothing. You get everything, no matter who offed him."

Her voice got hard.

"He was worried about business."

"You exaggerated that. I checked. The branch out here is turning a profit. His relatives have always covered for him. They would have kept doing so unless he did something really stupid. Even he wasn't that dumb. You're a smart woman. When you saw the closeups you figured I'd stumbled onto something. So you pretended it was Thela Crammond. What woman couldn't recognize a wig, when a guy can spot it? She's not your stepdaughter's age. Not even close. You know her. You're not going to tell me who she is or how it all happened. And you're not afraid of me getting your stepdaughter to prove it isn't her in those shots. Means two things. You wanted to find out exactly how stupid I am and you can't be touched."

She flicked her sunglasses down over her eyes and lay back. I stood up and walked around the side of the house and drove away. Not as fast as her asskisser. The reason is always the same.

I phoned the basement suite and Thela Crammond's roommate answered. She told me Thela finished writing her final exams and had left the city to be interviewed for a summer job. She would be back on Friday. Routine business came in that week. A guy knew his wife was bedding down with somebody. He didn't know who. I handled the case personally. Eddy was busy working for other clients. The sleeping partner turned out to be an old friend. Not an uncommon situation. My client would've claimed adultery in divorce proceedings, his wife planning to allege he physically abused her. There was an out-of-court settlement. Two brothers who owned an appliance store were missing small items, toasters and blenders. I did a little surveillance. The night watchman was sneaking stuff out through the service entrance to a pal. The night I saw them they'd decided to pull the big heist, had brought a truck and were taking stoves and fridges. The watchman was fired and his last cheque used to make good some of the losses.

On Friday afternoon I drove to the bungalow in Belvedere. The plums opened the door. The garlic factory was going full blast. She grinned, probably had been keeping her teeth in condition by pulling nails out of the floor. With her was a sour-faced gink, suspenders over a faded workshirt and holding up his patched dungarees. He had the kind of face you'd see in a eugenics textbook as an example of mental retardation among the rural poor. One of the tundra gang, smelling of the meat they killed and the meat they slept with in sod huts with a tin pipe through the roof. Tired of frostbitten feet, caulking chinks and of farming soil meant to grow lichens, he'd come to the city for some steam heat and groceries. His eyes stared at me from the deep cover where his brain stem was hiding. I got the idea that his inamorata mentioned me and he was there to protect his proprietary interest in her virtue. I couldn't see the rose between her teeth. She'd probably eaten it.

"I'm here to see Ms Crammond again," I said, "to ask her more questions."

She stepped aside, he didn't. I looked for a rusty implement he might have been clutching but there were only empty hands three sizes too large, like dirt-enseamed brown gloves. He finally moved, scraping the stubble on his chin, his way of warning me in case I desired to trespass on ladyfair's sowbelly panties. Hiding any thoughts of such lechery, I squeezed past his stink and descended into the coed's quarters. The door to the bedrooms was closed. I knocked and Thela Crammond opened it. Before she could say anything I held up a hand.

"I had to smell your landlord to get down here, so go easy on me."

She smiled. She shouldn't have been there or maybe anywhere in a world that destroys such beauty.

"You met Mr. Wozenko. You poor man. Come on in. The air's fresher."

We sat on the same middle-earth couch. I pulled out the photos and handed them to her. She flattened them on her knee with her palm and looked. I could see she knew.

"I showed those to your stepmother. She told me that's you. You can save me a lot of trouble. I think you both know who she is. I'd never implicate you."

"I know."

Cautiously, as if she was talking to herself, she put her hand on my sleeve. She left it there for a few seconds before taking it away slowly, deliberately. I've touched women and they've touched me, in all the famous places, but those few seconds with her hand on my arm went somewhere nothing else did. I could say I loved her the first time we met. But what that could mean, even if she liked me and there was no guarantee she did, was very little because of what happened to her. We both understood and she was doing her best to tell me she appreciated what I felt. I don't know whether she knew all I felt but we were reaching for a wounded compromise. I never pitied her. She'd have hated that. But I'd have done anything for her I could, any time she needed me. She knew that, too. Wounded beauty is a terrible thing, the best gone wrong. Nothing can fix it. All you can do is look up at the everlasting stars and wonder why. That could take your whole life.

"I know her," she said.

She handed the enlargements to me while looking off somewhere, crossed her legs, ankle on knee, fingers playing with her sweat sock.

"She's a professor. I took her course last year. Old English. Her name is Joanne Ackermann. I don't know much about her. She looks different there. That's a wig. Those aren't her usual clothes. She dresses old. Baggy sweaters, wool skirts, heavy shoes. No makeup. Don't know how Ivan met her."

"She drove a car with plates registered in your name over to his apartment."

"Ivan bought me a sports car when I was eighteen. So I could drive around campus and home on weekends. He was trying to hold onto me. Make poor little me grateful. When I came to the university I left it behind. The smell reminded me of him. A glue stink. I guess he gave it to her to drive sometimes. Don't know how Wanda knew her. She still paying you?"

"She paid me off. This is on my own time."

"I thought so. Why?"

"Somebody iced him. I want to know who. Professional curiosity. That's all it could ever be."

"Not a sense of justice?" She made the irony obvious with her tone and I obliged her.

"Justice was done when he was pushed over the great divide."

She raised her eyebrows the tiniest bit. Anything more would have been a victory dance. When I got back to the office I left a message on Eddy's phone. It was sunset. Emily had taken her good leave hours ago. I swivelled my chair around, and feet on the windowsill I looked at the sun's gaudy ad for romantics and lovers whose eyes get above a crotch. Like a painter drunk on colour splashing the sky with everything he's got and letting it run, arctic river blue and lime green glow and ingot gold and scarlet blood soaking cloud bandages and brassy flame bronzing out, snuffed, and suddenly you're upside down looking up at crushed ice on a felt carpet of indigo. I got up and put on the ceiling light and all the drabness came back. The three straightbacked guest chairs, antiques with less wood than the wire holding them together, my swivel chair circa Wild West railway depot, the scarred oak desk, the landline left on it from somebody's past life, next to the box of pens that should but didn't work, and always the one you picked up, the half-empty filing cabinets with forgotten memos and reports, the wastepaper basket full of junk mail. I got out of high-tech detection for this. No Wi-Fi, no smartphone, no computer, no fax. I was pre-everything except cuneiform and smoke signals. And now I was looking for a murderer without being paid. I was breaking the rules. You had to get money to do something in this society. The widow Raskolski had closed the books but I was being stubborn. It would've been too easy any other way.

I got out a bag of smoked almonds from my desk drawer. They had gone stale. I put my feet on the desk, leaned back in the swivel chair and closed my eyes. The next day was Saturday, so Emily wouldn't be coming in and seeing me dishevelled and unshaven early in the morning. Too much of a shock. As I dozed off I wondered what she did with her weekends. Probably volunteered for duty at one of those animal shelters. Patching bugs. Tiny bandages, leg splints. Sewing up butterfly wings under a microscope. Using tweezers to feed tofu hamburger to little blind owls. Petting ladybugs that can't get off the ground. Trying to get the robins to go vegan, offering them granola worms. They'd have to listen, perched there with their wings bandaged. Sneaking food for the flies. Watching the sunset at a nearby lake (bound to be one), a sparrow sleeping on her shoulder. Getting ideas to jot down on those slips of paper. Not a bad life, considering. Beats sniffing people's dirty underwear. I told myself to get some sleep before I went completely off. The last thing I heard was the cleaning woman shuffling along the hall, dragging her cartload of dirty mops and pails full of crud. She never came around on those nights she and her janitor husband had a snootful. I told her not to bother with my office if a light was on, I was sleeping. I don't think she bothered most of the time, anyway.

I woke up at dawn with a crick in my neck. My head had flopped over to one side. The rest of me wasn't too limber. I stripped to the waist and washed and shaved, using the sink in the small closet next to the filing cabinets. I turned out the ceiling light and locked both office doors, as if there was something important inside like my reputation. I made my way stiffly to the coffee shop in the hotel next door. In semidarkness buzzing with worn-out fluorescent lighting I had a cup of their mocha drivel with toast and a couple of eggs over easy. The only thing easy about them was the way they bounced around when I tried to stick them with my fork. The toast, burnt at the edges, tasted like napkins edged with soot. The butter smelled as if it hadn't seen the inside of a fridge since the dairy and flies had staged a fertility rite on it. The middle-aged waitress looked tired, so I didn't say anything. The first light of dawn was a rising adagio outside, the decaying buildings and vacant lots of the old part of the city half-hidden and half-lit by a new day and looking the best they will ever look. At another table lounged three customers, down-at-heels high rollers, the kind that use hacksaw blades and tie bed sheets together to escape from institutions. Guys who think you're looking at them and reach for the shiv in their boot. They weren't there to eat, they'd be planning their next job, the one that would put them in the lotto winners' circle. The cops were already shining up the handcuffs for them. Dyspeptic but spine unpierced, I went back to my office.

Feet on the windowsill, I listened to the early morning traffic. I told myself I'd give the case a few more days. I've told myself lots of things I've ignored, a good way to make yourself feel better while you're secretly planning to keep ruining your life. Mine was a wreck. One more detour wasn't going to make much of a difference. I was dozing when Eddy phoned at eleven. The man knows no rest. I never take a Saturday off but I relax between snoozes.

"She's an associate professor. Been there sixteen years. She's forty-six. I couldn't get the other measurements. Ha ha. Never been married, lives alone in her house. Has a car and a cat."

After his call I thought and got nowhere. I took my car for an estimate on a new clutch. It was one of those franchise outfits, computers and coveralls. The manager had eyes that watched each other for a sneaky move. A grey goatee matched the widow's peak that was losing ground on his forehead. I should have left right away but I like getting bad financial news from an expert. Standing behind the counter, he pecked at a computer keyboard, and I knew the longer the pecking went on the worse it would be. He made faces at the monitor, like a lab technician considering test results, before looking at me.

"Parts and labour, total, would be $575 plus tax. That would include a new plate, release and throwout bearings and machining the flywheel. We change the transmission fluid. We replace all seals, everything right back to the differential. The pilot bearing, too."

"It's an old heap."

"It's driveable."

"To the salvage yard. For that price I'd rather junk it."

He thought about that and did some more pecking and took off $105. I said I'd probably be in next week.

"Go easy with it. If it slips as bad as you say."

I almost thanked him for being so thoughtful. I went back to the office and did some phoning, which is what I should have done in the first place. I got a price of $350 from a nearby garage. By four I was too hungry to think about anything. My stomach had recovered. I grabbed some ulcer food at a local mom and pop café. Mom and Pop had long since gone and immigrants ran the place. They'd been robbed so many times they'd put up a sign saying there was never any more than $200 on the premises. Wrong. In that neighbourhood $5 got you the attention of thieves, addicts and muggers. Nice turn of phrase, "on the premises." Not theirs. Maybe a relative who'd taken a law course in high school. It sounded dated and curiously appropriate to a flyspecked dump about the size of a lunch wagon. First-rate masochist that I am, I sat on a stool and ordered a steak and fries and ate them with a blunt knife and a bent fork. The steak was bone and gristle, the fat scraped instead of trimmed. Chewing on the nugget of overfried meat I finally found, I was reminded of the taste and texture of an elastic band. The fries were greasy enough to satisfy any heart surgeon with an itchy scalpel finger. I was going to smother everything in ketchup but I saw the lippy ring of coagulant around the top of the bottle and the watered remains inside. I decided to forego dessert after seeing what some plastic factory was turning out as pie with imitation whipped cream, guaranteed to gather dust forever without spoiling. Unless you have the misfortune to eat it.

I went to my apartment and lay on the sofa and fell asleep right away. I spent Sunday recovering from gastronomic disaster. I turned on the television. The religious charlatans were plugging in their direct line to God and pleading tearfully for more money to fight Satan with. Can't pay for television time by going around with a begging bowl. Those expensive suits cost money. Their teeth had to be perfect and polished so they could smile nicely as they blessed their video congregations, who'd never put up with a spiritual message from some guy with crooked teeth who dressed in jeans and a denim shirt. They wanted the absolute final truth and the overall purpose of everything from a guy who looked as if he knew. I switched on the sports. Endless uniforms and teams playing in swollen leagues for empty cups and pennants and divisional and world championships that meant nothing except to crowds that had nothing better to do with their leisure time than watch overgrown men playing boys' games for a mercenary's wages. It was delayed adolescence with macho-military overtones, laced with paranoia à la go ahead and barbecue ribs smothered in hot sauce but you'd better not bake cupcakes. The commercials were everywhere, a vision of life as the Big Sell. Spend yours buying junk you don't need. The super-technologized gadgets with manuals the size of telephone books and that cost much more and do about the same job as the obsolete stuff. Who decided progress meant more technology and society was a waste dump for it? They wanted to sell me junk food, cars, fast food, vacations and life insurance. They'd used millions of dollars and thousands of hours of labour to do that and I thought, I'm out of date, I don't believe any of it. I turned to Hollywood for an older brand of fantasy. But Hollywood can be depended upon to destroy your every wish for any kind of intelligent entertainment. The commercial-riddled affair I switched on expected me to believe that an aging gangster would go through heartrending nostalgia over the old days, when his type was above pushing drugs and only dealt in extortion, white slavery and contract killings, and shoved fork twistings of spaghetti between their mustaches and quaffed glassfuls of chianti from potbellied straw-bottomed bottles while listening to some tenor air out his tonsils on a windup Victrola. I reached for the remote before I puked. I thought about my last girlfriend. It took half an hour before I was able to quit and fall asleep. It had been a lousy weekend.

On Monday I got to the office early, called the English Department and asked for Joanne Ackermann's office phone number and the time of her first class. It was at eleven. I phoned at ten. Her voice surprised me, low and velvety. I identified myself and asked for an appointment. What about? Ivan Raskolski. There was the expected pause.

"Who?"

"He was manager of Brickward's. His company provides office supplies to the university. He died about two weeks ago. The Wednesday before last."

"What has that to do with me?"

Now the pause was mine. Pauses can be tricky. Too short, they're ineffective. Too long, it's dead air.

"I'm involved in the case. I talked with him the night before he died and he mentioned your name."

Like pauses, lies are a dicey proposition. They have to be the right size. Third pause. She bit.

"In connection with what?"

"I'd prefer to talk about that in person."

"Are you working for the police?"

"Not officially, but Detective Grady of the city police has asked me to look into the matter."

"May I have his number?"

I gave it to her. She'd phone back, she said. She called fifteen minutes later and agreed to see me at four. It could only be for a few minutes because she was so busy, she said.

At a quarter to the appointed hour I was in the English Department main office asking one of the secretaries for Professor Ackermann's office number. A chirpy young 'un, she gave it along with the glad eye as she swung her thinly sweatered breasts in my direction. I gave her the onthejobhoney grin as my corpuscles howled at the full moon. The hallway was empty and all the doors were closed. The inmates were probably being fed crickets enrobed in fondue by the medical staff. Or dressing casually correct to simper later on at a poetry reading where the writer ginks who don't want to be mistaken for cupcakes hold onto a can of beer and walk around with cigarillos in their sport shirt pocket and write about taking their son to the hardware store on Saturday morning, and where sometimes there's a notorious fossilizing fart who tries to lay as many bimbos as possible, babes who think getting dork-squiggled by fame is worth spreading 'em, even if it smells of slackmuscle underwear, and that slickprick braggadocio by a puffed up neonname is poetry because it makes their buzzers go off and they drop down wetpanty sacrifices to his fuck total, and he thinks this beats picking them up in bars, where his white hairwave, hand tremor, liver spots and upper plate would definitely be drawbacks. I found her door and knocked and that slinky voice said to come in. She was looking into a filing cabinet. On the phone she sounded as if she was spread out naked on a tiger skin rug. In person she looked as if she should be hiding under it. Nature lost interest when she came along. This poor schoolmarm had lost a girl guide troop somewhere. Her face was flat, the colour of old newspaper, her eyes a pale emptiness, her lips nonexistent, and her body had no discernible curves. Her hair was cardboard brown streaked moth grey. Never did a woman more deserve to be called a miss. The kind that sneaks peeks at guys and either gave it away once and was eternally burnt or yearns subliminally for love. That voice was an empty caress but it was still pleasant.

"Sit down, Mr. Quester."

She sat, I sat, and I'll be in grad school afore ye.

I had to be careful. Otherwise I'd be using up my small store of diplomatic language in a trice. I took out the envelope, slid out the enlargements and handed them to her. She had trouble keeping the photos flat. Nothing changed in her face when she looked at them. She glanced at me across the desk and didn't say anything. That's the difference with educated people, they know when to be silent. It comes from having answered a lot of examination questions. You're supposed to say enough of the right things in the right way and slip past as many of the wrong ones as possible. And if in doubt, pretend you know by sounding intelligent. Dwell in your written answers on the obviously acceptable but never make this seem easy. Silence is the last, best weapon of the ignorant academic. There's a dignity about it. And you'll never get yourself into trouble.

I also have a few tricks. They aren't much but they work sometimes. One is pretending to be after something different than what I want. That relaxes the other party. Another is sounding interested in whatever the other party says. People will respond to real interest. Makes them feel important. I didn't expect her to say much about the photos. Showing them to her was letting her know I knew the lay of the land. No big lies, please. I had to pretend they were the last thing I'd want to ask her about, and drum up enthusiasm for anything she told me. First, to get the keyhole scenes out of the way.

"Professor Ackermann (apple-polishing but a good starter), I showed you those without comment (nice turn of phrase) because they're private and should remain so (bit too fancy). They came into my possession (legal jargon but handy), I won't say how because it's not germane to my immediate purpose (don't fool with this guy), but they do prove you knew Ivan Raskolski (avoids the fastidiously indirect 'were acquainted with'). The police have asked me to investigate his death (merest hint of a threat). I asked around in his apartment building and someone mentioned seeing a striking (Quester, you bastard) woman enter his suite who spoke in an attractive educated manner like an English professor (may the clouds part and the sun shine on me). So I checked with the English Department. And here I am. Business associates say he was under a great strain lately (blowing his nose would have been a strain for him) because his company hasn't been doing well (tacking on 'financially speaking' would have immediately dumped me into the mutually inclusive businessman and educated moron categories). Could you tell me anything about that?"

How much any of that fooled her I couldn't guess. She wasn't stupid, but might be desperate enough for a man to notice her. I could merely hope that I'd driven in the harpoon deeply enough with "striking." She gave me nothing.

"The detective told me that, as far as the police are concerned, you're simply a private investigator working on your own. I really don't know why you're bothering me with this."

"It's not my intention to bother you. I was told, off the record, that the police are looking for any leads they can find."

She pushed the enlargements across the desk. I gathered them together and stood up.

"I'd better turn these in before I'm charged with withholding evidence."

I drew another blank. She sat there watching me sink into quicksand. I thanked her for her time and left. She obviously hadn't believed my story and had figured out what I was after. I remembered what Emily had said about a tight shadow. I found a pay phone and left a message for Eddy. I was starting to spend my own money. Professional sloppiness that could eventually mean mission food and shelter.

On Thursday Eddy phoned.

"You'll never guess."

"Don't have to. That's why I'm paying you."

"Shessssssssss—."

I waited for him to stop steaming. Emotionally involved in his work. Keeps him going. It's a personal thing.

"She's seeing a guy. I followed her car down a dark road. He was waiting. She got out, got into his car. They were in there quite a while. Something of a commotion. Used my best mike and camera. Couldn't get much. No light, damn radio was on. They were arguing. She was crying. She got out. The interior light went on before she slammed the door. I got a picture, not that good. But it'll do."

Professional modesty. And he was interested, brought the photo.

"This one is on the house, Charley."

I phoned the English Department, found out when Professor Ackermann would be in her office on Friday. At ten that morning I was there. The door was open and she was seated at her desk. I dropped the photo on it. This time I didn't say anything.

"You have no right to come in here."

"Talk or I see the law."

She looked at the photo.

"You've been spying on me. That's invasion of privacy."

"You've got it wrong. What you're looking at is conspiracy to cover up a murder."

"I happen to be having an affair. It's none of your business."

"I know who that is, and whose car you used to drive to Raskolski's apartment. The police might like to know why you're chummy with the guy who's sales manager at Brickward's."

She broke. She didn't cry or rave. But her hand nearer the photo trembled enough that I noticed it. I stuck my oar in.

"He's sold you a bill of goods."

I wasn't saying anything she didn't already know. I didn't know how much she'd kidded herself. You can kid yourself better than anyone else can do it. A sheepskin and mortarboard don't keep you from getting all hopped up when it's who's the one. But to the wrong kind of guy an educated woman is another piece of ass.

"I haven't done anything," she said.

Good sign when they say that. It means they have and they're thinking about how to cover up. A little push at this point invariably helps. I closed the door with my foot and sat down.

"You may be on the straight and narrow but you can never be sure what somebody else will do under pressure."

"It's over, anyway," she said.

Better. The instinct for self-preservation has set in and fair's fair. Expect raw servings of the former beloved's character. Time to be silent in the confessional.

"Wednesday night was the end. I told him I couldn't deal with it any more. One thing after another. I told him about you and the photographs. He said there was nothing to worry about, they didn't prove anything. I didn't care, I wanted nothing more to do with it. I'd done what he wanted, even the wig. He talked me into so many things."

She turned and looked out of the window. She was crying or going to cry and trying to hide it. At least she wasn't a phony using tears to get past me. Or maybe she knew I'd be thinking that. It's possible to outthink yourself if you're a crummy detective trying to keep up with people's tricks. Sometimes women don't know if they're tricking you or not. They're so good they can fool themselves. They call it instinct but I call it female survival. Best thing is to wait. The mood will pass and she'll get back to business. Joanne Ackermann took longer than usual, probably because she was educated. It doesn't look good to be quick in your moods or a guy won't think you're serious. Guys don't have moods. They're either too stupid to know one or they're cranky bastards.

When she turned back to me she was ready to talk again. Her eyes were dry, so she'd either held it in or been rerunning the video. It's been my experience that when people give you big news it's a silent explosion. No blast, no shell fragments. But you check yourself to make sure.

"He said Mr. Raskolski had a bad heart. If I could get him excited he'd have a fatal heart attack. He said Mr. Raskolski liked girls and I had a girlish figure. I suppose he meant I'm small-breasted and have a petite rear end. He told him I was a graduate student and was twenty-two and provided services to businessmen to pay my way through university. That he met me on campus when he was talking about stationery with the manager of the university bookstore, which is true. He came over to the bookshelves where I was standing and noticed the book I was looking at. He was interested in taking an extension course in English and would I give him some information? Of course, I knew he was trying to pick me up, but I'd seen him talking with the manager and he did seem like a nice guy. And interested in taking a course, too. That's how it started. About a month after we met, he told me he was going to lose his job because the boss didn't like him. His boss, Mr. Raskolski, was from a very wealthy family back East with various important business interests, and his relatives had sent him out to the Prairie City branch office of their stationery and office supply company, but he was incompetent. He was jealous because Mel was respected by everyone and practically ran the office. He thought his relatives were certain to find out and put Mel in charge. Mel said I had to help him. It wouldn't be murder because men have died while having sex or soon afterwards. After it happened I was to call him, he'd come over, fix things up and I could leave and wouldn't be involved. I didn't want to do it and said it was prostitution. He told me we'd get married as soon as he took over. I tried to get out of it. I said I was forty-six, not twenty-two. He said I looked a lot younger than I was and to wear lots of makeup and a blonde wig, and he'd get me another car to drive over there because somebody who knew mine might see and possibly recognize it. I told Mel to get another job. He said Mr. Raskolski would get him blackballed, he was so jealous. If he's got a bad heart he'll be too afraid to do anything with a younger woman or girl, I said. He said, I know something that'll make him forget his heart. I said we could live off my money until he got another position, or he could enroll and get a degree. Mel didn't want a wife supporting him and said he was too old to go to school. I was afraid of losing him, I agreed. But I kept putting it off and he kept after me, saying he'd be getting fired soon. How can you respect me, getting me to do such a thing? I said, finally. I should leave you. Go ahead, he said. I did, for a week. I was miserable and I couldn't think clearly. All I could think about was that I had a chance to be happy with a man who loved me and I'd left him. I didn't think I'd get anyone, or if I did, he would be a much older man. But someone who was younger than I was and very attractive to me, never. If you're a middle-aged professional woman who's not beautiful and has a moderate income, there isn't much out there and most of what is you don't want. I said yes, I would do it."

She stopped but only to take a breath, as if she'd been on a bus too long and didn't care about anything but getting there.

"I was so nervous I was shaking when I got to the apartment and had to keep my hand from trembling when I knocked on the door. When he opened it I was surprised. He looked healthier than Mel had described him. I didn't like him. He reeked of cologne. His hands were puffy. His suit was shiny. He played the debonair man on the town to the hilt. He told me to sit on the sofa and offered me a drink of wine. I drank it in one gulp and coughed. He offered me another. I drank that fast, too. His sofa was horrible red plush and there were tacky paintings on the walls. He wanted to play a video to get us in the mood. Anything to delay the moment, I thought. He turned it on and sat next to me, his arm around my waist. The video was old, the men wore striped bell-bottomed pants and the women wore miniskirts. The music was some earsplitting stuff and the camera would wobble. The sex was like bad acting. But nothing was very clear because the film was grainy. He said he liked old videos because they were more realistic. When it was over he put his arm around me again and I thought, here we go. There are some men that are repulsive. They make you sick when you get close. I asked for some more wine. I thought if I passed out and woke when it was over that would make it bearable. I had two more glasses and he had quite a bit, too. Before I knew it, he was sprawled on top of me and pulling down my panties and trying to get into my rear end. What are you doing? I yelled. Don't you take it up the ass? he said, surprised. I said it would hurt too much because I had bad hemorrhoids. I don't but that was the only thing I could think of. Mel had told me he'd want me to play a schoolgirl getting raped by the teacher, and maybe suck his thing if he wasn't dead by then. But he would be, Mel assured me, so I wouldn't have to do that. You're a prime heifer, he said. I thought, he's one of those barnyard guys, bestiality and such. Let's see if you're lying, he said, and started wriggling a finger up my bum. I could feel his fingernail scratching me. Stop it, I hollered. I sat up and shoved him away. I don't do that. I don't want your money. He had given me $500. I got to take a leak, he said. I thought he was going to go into the bathroom but he pulled me onto the carpet and unzipped his pants. He pulled out and rubbed his thing with his hand until he came, then peed on me. It fell on my stomach and my clothes. I felt like throwing up. He waved it at me. Give me an hour or two and we're back in business. I got up and left, drove home with that stuff soaked through my clothes. I took a shower and phoned Mel."

She wasn't looking at me any more.

"You said he'd drop dead."

"He would have, honey, but you didn't handle it right. Next time do it right and he will. I'll patch things up. Get a good night's sleep."

"You know what he did, what he wanted to do?"

"He's kinky, Joanne, honey."

"You didn't tell me everything. He tried to sodomize me. You know what it's like being peed on? He's disgusting."

"All right, calm down."

"I said I wouldn't go back and he said he'd get fired. He phoned me here the next afternoon."

"He said that you're long in the tooth. And your shanks are stringy. I told him you'd been studying too hard. He's willing to try again."

"Thank you both very much."

"Joanne, precious, do this for us and then we'll be together. I told him your ass is out but anything else is fine with you."

"What?"

"You want this to work out, don't you?"

"So I went back. I was in shock, the same as when I lay there on the carpet and didn't move as he came, then peed on me. Mel said it was a matter of working on him and it would happen. I'd never heard of anybody like this guy. He liked girls but he didn't want to buy them. He wanted to entice schoolgirls but he was afraid of being caught. So I was a substitute. I wasn't near the age he required but he wanted me to act like it. My body was like a girl's to him. But he had a problem with me, impotence. He said if I was young he wouldn't have had a problem. Because I wasn't he did, and so the peeing and the other were substitutes. The first night you tried to sodomize me, I said. He said he was excited. Because he'd never done that to a girl and was aroused by my body. He said he probably wouldn't have been able to keep his erection. So I had to talk and behave like a girl to get him excited. I used a lot of hand manipulation, and mouth too, to keep him aroused. My wig fell off once and he saw the grey in my hair and lost his erection. I said I was prematurely grey, it ran in my family. I didn't know if he believed me. And I didn't care. I loathed putting that thing in my mouth. We gave up and I went home and phoned Mel."

She took a deep breath.

"He's impotent with me, he'll never have a heart attack. He needs a girl."

"That's because you're not trying hard enough to be a girl."

"I'm an English professor, not a whore."

"Read him some love poems, or something from a book about young girls and dirty old men."

"Oh yes, my shelves are full of that."

"Try again, Joanne, honey."

"There were two more times, no better than the first two, though I wore a padded bra. I was finished with the whole thing, I'd been degraded enough. Mel knew before I told him. I was spending the weekend at his apartment. He said he'd probably be fired any day. I said there was nothing I could do. He said there was. He's terrified of guns, can't even watch a movie if guns are used in it. When he was a kid he found a gun in his parents' bedroom and fired it accidentally and shot off a toe. We could scare him to death easy with a gun. That's murder, I said. Not really, he said. We're not using bullets, we're using psychology. Would you rather I was fired and had to leave to get a sales job somewhere else? All you have to do is take a gun with you next time and pull it out and that should do it. Suppose it doesn't? I said. I'll be standing there holding a gun. Don't worry, it won't be loaded. He might go crazy and attack me. I'll go with you, wait in the hallway. When he drops dead you call me in and I'll fix everything. If there's a problem, holler and I'll come right in. Why don't you frighten him with the gun? I said, leave me out of it. He wouldn't go for it, honey, because I joke with him all the time. He'd never expect something like that from you. You can walk right in there and tell him you've got a surprise that'll get him off. He'll be so excited it'll be easy. There's nothing to worry about, precious, it can't go wrong.

"It's hard to describe how I felt. Right and wrong didn't mean anything any more. I wanted an end to it, no matter what happened. I hadn't much left. I hated myself and yet was fascinated even as I was repelled by my shame. It's hard to want for so long and have nothing but lecture notes and a class schedule. To get stiff, to get middle-aged, moth-eaten and eccentric about things that don't matter because the ones that do are beyond you. You can see it all and there's nothing you can do about it, the wanting of what isn't and can't be. He saw and knew enough to use it to destroy me. Sometimes I wonder if it was more than using me. Maybe he was enjoying manipulating an educated woman. But I'd be flattering myself. He's too selfish to think of anybody else. I loved a man who loves only himself. You have to accept what you're not going to get, otherwise you'll get what you can't accept.

"He didn't come up to the suite with me, he gave me the gun in the car. He said he'd stay in the car and park a block away. Somebody might notice it parked near the building. He showed me how to take off the safety catch and fire it, to look more authentic. It wasn't loaded, anyway. It was small, shaped like a capital L and fit easily in my purse. And I had my phone, so I could call him in case anything went wrong. He kissed me, said this would do it. We'd be married in a few weeks. I was in a trance. I rode up in the elevator with a married couple who were holding hands. They looked at me once. I felt they could read my mind and knew what I was going to do. The feeling was so strong I felt like going down again.

"When I knocked he opened the door right away and said Mel had told him I had a surefire way to get him hard and get him off and I thought, dimly and not quite consciously, if Mel's in danger of being fired why is his employer so willing to use him as a pimp? The doubt was there but it never quite became an idea. While he got us drinks I pulled out the gun and pointed it at him. He turned with the glasses from the bar, which was at the side of the living room. When he saw me standing with the gun unsteady in my hand he laughed."

"What the hell is this? You going to scare me into a hard-on? Oh, I get it. I'm supposed to be firing bullets into you. That might work out, strip and get on the sofa. We'll play with the barrel. That bastard think of this? No wonder he's the top sales guy on the prairies. What would I do without the son of a gun? Even the wife is crazy about him and she's a hard bitch."

"At the mention of his wife my hand tensed on the handle of the gun and my finger jerked the trigger. Mel had left the safety catch off. There was a noise and the gun jumped in my hand. Mel had lied about it not being loaded. A bullet hit Mr. Raskolski somewhere and he made a sound, as if he'd been shocked by touching a live wire, and fell down. He lay on the carpet with his mouth open, his eyes staring at the ceiling. I looked at the gun as if it had tricked me and threw it down. I phoned Mel and he was there in five minutes. He went over to Mr. Raskolski and knelt beside him. When Mel looked up at me it was like looking at his face for the first time."

"He's breathing. I can feel a pulse."

"Hurry up, call an ambulance."

"You got his head. That should finish him."

"We can't let him die. That's murder."

"He's going to die, anyway."

"I don't want anything to do with it."

"You have no choice, precious."

"The way he said it I knew the hunch I had about Mr. Raskolski's wife was right. He went to the kitchen and brought back a roll of paper towels and tore off some. He picked up the gun and wiped it and put it into his pocket. Mr. Raskolski's scalp was torn near his forehead and there was a hole but it was hard to see because blood and something else was oozing out. His mouth was still open, his eyes staring. Mel wiped off the entrance doorknobs and flushed the used towels down the toilet and took the roll back into the kitchen. He kept a couple so he wouldn't have to touch anything with his hands when we left. I stood there watching him, couldn't do anything."

"Come on."

"We can't leave him if he's still alive."

"They couldn't save him, his heart's weak. He'll be dead in an hour."

"Check his pulse again."

"But he wouldn't listen. He grabbed my arm, pulled me to the door and opened it. We didn't say anything on the way to the car. He drove me home. When he dropped me off he kissed me and said he'd phone the next day. Stay with me, I said, I don't want to be alone tonight. He said he couldn't because of a meeting with a client. It would look bad for him if he didn't show up. That night I couldn't sleep till almost dawn. I kept thinking of that poor man dead up there. It's strange how even a deviate can arouse your pity. I dreamt he was standing beside my bed, face covered in blood. He bent over to touch me and I woke up.

"It's crazy when I think of it but during the ride to my house I didn't remember Mel saying the gun wouldn't be loaded. I didn't think of that other woman either. All I thought was, I've killed somebody. And Mel, instead of being the cause of my trouble, became a support for me. I needed him to get me through what he'd done to me. Ironic, isn't it, how your destroyer can become your deliverer? In the state I was in, after the nightmare of twisted sex and the shooting, he was the master of my life. I hated him by now, and loved him still, in the half-light of bitter nocturnal sex, as if our bodies knew the hateful truth that he partially understood I like to think and I refused to see and save myself because I wanted the last little bit of his lust and my longing for it. This was what my life was going to be, working out the love through hate, and my suffering for what reason I couldn't see but some mindless necessity forced upon me because I wasn't the beautiful answer to any man's dream. Punishment for no reason, or rather the one I gave myself by wanting what I shouldn't have. And in reaching for it I brought down on myself the double injustice of want and retribution. What was I guilty of except the natural sin of loneliness? I had to pay for that by being me, and when I wouldn't, when I wanted, the payment became too much. He stepped in my way and I wouldn't ignore the challenge, but he did it to use my desire to debase me. I could see him as an evil agent of some sort if I believed in that kind of thing, but he was worse for being nothing more than a salesman, selling a few dozen hours in bed for what he wanted. The dirtiness I was made to feel was no more to him than a salesman's commission for cheating some woman into paying for what she shouldn't buy. I bought him and his lies. And he, the con man who can't see life any other way played his tricks because that was all he knew. He's pathetic, needs to cheat. He's a sneer and a snicker. And that's what I bought myself for wanting him.

"We met the next evening on a deserted road. He said the body had been found by the cleaning lady. The police had notified Mrs. Raskolski and come to the office and asked questions. It was important for us not to see each other for a while because the police might be watching and anything unusual would be noticed. I knew he was beginning the process of getting rid of me. I couldn't let him think I was that much of a fool. And I couldn't be alone with what I'd done, so I probed hopelessly into my own disaster."

"You didn't tell me the gun was loaded."

"I didn't know it was, precious, honest. I got it off a guy and he showed me how the thing worked."

"He laughed when he saw me with it. You said he was afraid of guns."

"That's what I heard around the office. Ask anybody there and they'll tell you."

"Are you sure you didn't hear it from his wife?"

"His wife? She's wanted to get rid of me as much as he did. She won't even talk to yours truly. Had it in for me from the beginning."

"He said you were the best salesman on the prairies. He depended on you."

"That's what they say when they're going to get rid of you. You don't understand business."

"I think I do. I learned it from you."

"Don't talk that way, precious. If we love each other, there's got to be trust."

"If?"

"You know what I mean. Don't twist my words."

"Don't you mean untwist them?"

"Now don't start that. I didn't shoot him."

"No. You'll never be guilty of anything except lying."

"Did I lie about him being weird? It's not my fault things went wrong."

"It's never your fault. That's why I'm here."

"He said we were going to get married but would have to postpone it for a while. Driving home that night I had to pull over to the side of the road. I cried for what I'd done, all of it, and mostly for not being able to see the truth from the beginning. Though I understand why, I can't forgive myself. It's ego, I guess. You never think there's a fool inside of you until it shows. The one comfort I can take, and it's small, is that I hadn't been tricked by someone of my intellectual calibre—unfortunate choice of phrase. Only a man so foreign to me that I couldn't see the cheapness of him, the moral emptiness, could have tricked me. His lies were too big, too unsubtle for me to accept what they were. I suppose my pride would never let me believe I could be involved with such a man. That's a kind of hubris, I guess. Even before you showed me those photos on Monday, I knew everything was over. But I had to see him once more, to let him know how I felt. It was also revenge because I wanted to make him sweat. He did, and he did what I expected. He tried to shift all of the blame, and the guilt too, onto me. I should have given Mr. Raskolski a heart attack the first way. I should have kept my dumbass finger off the trigger. You were hoping I'd pull the trigger accidentally. I'll have a nice story to tell if this comes out. And for the first time he wasn't sure of me. He even raised his hand to hit me—pure acting— my turn at snickering. That detective knows more than he told me. He'll be back, so you'd better kill me. But I'm safe because you're too gutless to do anything yourself. He'll go to Mrs. Raskolski now and she'll protect him. I'll find my own way."

She'd finished with herself and with me. Class dismissed. There was nothing I could say. Telling her she'd eventually have to go see the police was like telling the tide that it had to come in. She'd have some explaining to do. But once she brought in her plot-happy accomplice she wouldn't have a tough time pasting that paper cutout to the wall. She'd get a lot of sympathy and little if any jail time. That wasn't what bothered her. It was facing what she had left. I reached for the photo, rolled up the loose scroll. As I shut the door I looked back. She was staring into that distance between lives.

To get Joanne Ackermann off my mind I went to a club that night. I needed a diversion. Sex is a good diversion. Unless you make it more than it is. It's like salted peanuts. After a while all you taste is salt. With my luck in clubs I usually meet women when they've turned interrogator, looking for what is known by the professionals in the field as a relationship. That means sharing the rent and payments for a few years or until the gonads give out and you end up holding hands on a park bench. Trouble with me is I can't resist turning truth into a joke. Lost a lot of women, especially interrogators. The deadliest are the ones who've decided they must be married by the end of the month.

"What do you do?"

"Neurosurgery, specializing in front end lobe jobs."

"Is there much money in it?"

"Millions."

"I went to my friend's wedding last weekend."

"Hooray."

"What university did you go to?"

"Harvale A and M and Camford Tech."

"Never heard of them."

"That's why they're so famous."

"Did you study for a long time to be a neuro—whatever?"

"Until I got tired of second-rate intellects teaching third-rate minds."

"Have you ever been married?"

"Only in my dreams."

"I guess you haven't got any children."

"I've never asked what happened after I've deposited the installment."

"I don't understand that."

"Nobody does. It happens."

"Thanks for the drink" (if they're polite and haven't seen another potential at the club, party, museum, gallery, reception, banquet, dog show, freeway accident).

I inevitably encountered several Euros over here for the loot. Expensive hookers out for a no-cut contract with a bankruptcy buyout clause.

"My girlfriend married a doctor. They live out on the West Coast, in Snotsure Properties."

"My last boyfriend was the son of the ambassador from Buenas Noches. He drove a Pusillami Fugatso."

"There is no art here, no culture. My father took me when I was a girl to the Eurogallerie of the Finezarts."

"I am an interior decorator. Women here are so backward. Their husbands always say they are beautiful. They have no taste."

I got as far as the parking lot with one of the Euros and saw the rust holding her car together. She told me it was a classic. How does a piece of old junk turn into a classic? I had the insolence to say. That was as close as I got to her good taste. Wrapping her dyed muskrat pelts around her, she drove off with a leaky muffler banging against the asphalt and blurting out clouds of soot. Every one of them gets married eventually. That's the end of somebody's dream.

Glutton for punishment, I went back in. It was getting late. The marriage-minded had gone, leaving the field to the detritus, the castoffs of meaningless campaigns. Inevitably, there were those conversations you get into without knowing why.

"What sign are you?"

"I'm the blue and white one as you turn off the highway."

"A comedian. What's your name?"

"Charley."

"I thought so. You're an Aquarius. I can tell. I've lived with four Aquarians who were Charleys. Broke up with the last one a few months ago. Sorry, Charley, bye."

Another one.

"Can you see it? My black eye? My husband hit me. I wanted to get pregnant. He doesn't want a kid. First time he ever hit me. I'm filing for divorce. He's sending me flowers, trying to get back. It's too late. See that woman over there? She's only known her husband. I had my fun before I got married."

Then there's what the other side offers, the professionals with three-piece suits and one-piece minds who try to smile their way into a woman's crotch and the guy who'll jot down a phone number and take her out and pay for the meal with coupons and the drunk who tells you he had the alcoholic blonde propped against the bar and the middle-aged businessman's face who tells you what a beauty he picked up last time and the guy who calls them all douche bags and the runt who says he's a professional athlete and will be leaving for a party where babes are waiting to spread their legs and the wolf face lingering over a drink and waiting for closing time to pick up the last of the losers and the immigrants from southern Europe who'll try to get some bitter divorcée drunk and gang rape her on a deserted beach.

I left, tired of the lost battalions of the endless marital and sexual wars. You wouldn't think something as simple as sex could be messed up by so many. But any time randy animals get together they're going to be pulling at the pantyhose. And when they're told that sex is supposed to be special, and most of them about as special as a bunch of toads, you're bound to have a lot of sweaty exercise going on between a lot of hot bodies. Trying to find what? They couldn't tell you. They're itchy, and rather than figure things out they do the obvious. They're looking for something extraordinary but they're only capable of the ordinary. They have enough brains to be dissatisfied with that and not enough to know they shouldn't be. It's a waste of breath telling them.

At my apartment I got steamed up. After a few shots I fell onto the bed and looked at my watch. It was after four. I was up at eight to drop my car off Saturday morning. Installing a clutch takes up much of a working day, even at an honest garage. The garage was a couple of blocks from my office. I decided to walk back and spend the day there. When I opened the door I didn't smell the usual musty air. On Emily's desk wild flowers filled a small narrow-necked vase. She does that sometimes. I went into the inner office and saw a flower in my whisky glass. She'd never done that before. A message from her personal temperance movement. Or maybe she figured the case was getting to me. I didn't have a drink that day. Couldn't remove the flower. I put my feet on my desk and considered the view from the office, as it were.

Something was still wrong. There were holes in the professor's story. I didn't doubt her feelings but I didn't trust them. I've never met an honest person. Everybody lies to suit the occasion. It's called an explanation. Her story was too smooth and camouflaged by her feelings. She was using them to cover up the facts, hoping I'd be sidetracked by emotions. People are all the time. Expert liars know that. Most of us are amateurs. She had flipped over the salesman and agreed to delve into Ivan the Unable's underwear. She wouldn't lie about that. No woman values sex as much as a man does. She may go in for anonymous calisthenics for a while. But that's generally because daddy did the baddy or she's trying to ape a man by showing she can be as randy on the spot. But the great majority of women wise up sooner or later to the fact that most men are good for nothing else. Women want love or a reasonable facsimile thereof, which means they've got you by the short hairs. The saddest hooker has a dream about marrying a decent guy who loves her truly. It was obvious from the professor's story how much smarter she thought she was than her beloved. Any roadkill would have more usable brainpower. I didn't go for the trance stuff. No matter how much she daily doted on him, she'd never do anything she knew was stupid. Going there with a pistol to shock Ivan the Incapable would be proof of retardation. Safety catch on, safety catch off, loaded, unloaded, the only thing loaded was her story. He wasn't shocked, he laughed. That was to throw me off, because having me believe he'd deflate like a punctured tire at the sight of mademoiselle holding a cute little pistol in her pinkies would be too much to expect, even from a dumb detective. He might drop a glass, but hands over the heart, no. She was testing my brains by using all she had. She dumped on her beloved, hiding him under a load of crap. He used, tricked, insulted, humiliated, betrayed her. From what mouldy tome did she get "precious"? Wanda Regine's keester fitted nicely into this because whether she got her boyfriend to remove hubby, or he got the prof to do it, she got rich. Would the prof protect Stoker if she thought he was fondling another woman's goods? Telling me she suspected a relationship and portraying herself as the woman wronged was to get me to drown in her vale of tears. As near as I could figure, she'd been a flop as a sexual surrogate and guessed Stoker had plugged the boss to satisfy the wife. Making himself a respectable marriage partner twice removed had led to the fight in the car, and she'd decided to save him by sacrificing herself. But then mares eat oats and does eat oats and little lambs eat ivy. As opposed to big lambs? So it'll scan, the prof would say. And that was my problem.

I called the English Department to get Joanne Ackermann's home phone number. I had a fancy excuse ready if they were loath to give it out. The office was closed. I looked in the phone book. There it was, J. Ackermann. A Belvedere number, had to be. They all live there. She answered. I apologized for bothering her. She'd be on the alert, but she sounded about as bothered as a dry streambed.

"What was it you wanted?"

"There's something I don't understand. What happened to the glasses?"

"Glasses?"

"You said Raskolski was holding wineglasses when he turned from the bar. The police didn't mention any spilled wine or dropped glasses. And you didn't say anything about cleaning up a mess. There must have been one. Unless Raskolski had time to put them back before he was shot."

"Yes. I must have forgotten."

"The glasses or the mess?"

Permafrost crept into her voice.

"Glasses."

"Why would he put them back if he didn't take you seriously? And how could he think of doing that if he did?"

No answer.

"And if full wineglasses were sitting pretty, why didn't your boyfriend flush the contents down the toilet? The police apparently didn't see full glasses. Their presence might have suggested Raskolski decided at the last second to forego a dose of light refreshment with his killer before having his brains blown out. More likely the glasses would indicate whoever shot him politely declined a drink beforehand. In either case the best behaved murder scenario I've ever heard."

"Now that I remember, Mel did throw the wine away. I told him about it."

"You told him but you didn't tell me. You must have been in a far worse state that night than when you were sitting in your office with me."

"I'd forgotten it by then."

"But the rest of your story was in great detail. You're asking me to believe the only thing you didn't remember was what a man did immediately before you shot him. And incidentally, the police told me he was killed by a bullet fired point-blank into his brain. Doesn't tally with an accidental shot fired from a distance, a torn scalp and a lingering death."

"I don't wish to continue with this conversation."

She hung up, and thereby hangs a piece of tail. She could hang a while longer, because I was hungry. Like the penitent I am, I wended my way over to a fast food dump. I got a burger and fries. The fries were all dolled up in a paper box, standing up like wooden matches. They tasted as if the matches had been dipped in grease. The bun, hamburger, sauce and the wilted green lettuce had an imitative taste, as if they were made from scratch-and-sniff rubber moulded into different shapes. I sat in a plastic chair at a tiny plastic table with plastic forks and spoons and surrounded by plastic logos in funhouse colours. It looked like a psychotic chef's hell for those damned for committing culinary sins. The patrons, working class moms and pops and kids, shared the dining area with seedier locals in various stages of mental and physical disintegration. They sucked like vacuum pumps on milkshake straws long after the paper cup was empty of its pink sludge and mashed their cavities and swollen gums on ersatz turnovers with gelatinous apple filling that could be used to set floor tile. I cut my losses and left without sampling any more guess food. For hours afterwards I felt I was walking around with a paperweight in my stomach. It didn't digest, it lodged itself somewhere in my intestines. One day there would be a reckoning. I vowed to quit patronizing fast food dumps. I wondered what Emily ate. Bird seed, probably, and bee pollen, pieces of honeycomb, all washed down with herb tea. Good thing. On what I paid her she couldn't have afforded much else. I could've gotten a secretary with softly rounded perfumed curves. But she would never have taken Emily's wages, even with some sociable persuasion from me, unless she wanted to hogtie me. But I've never wanted the suburban mortgage and what goes with it. I'd rather live among the outcasts. If I could learn to eat right.

At four I left my office and went over to pick up my car. The garage was one of those places run by immigrants who charge twenty-five dollars an hour less to do the same work the born-here do. And they don't pretend it's major surgery. Or give a spiel about high expenses. Rent at the low-price places is probably less, but they don't expect to get wealthy fixing heaps. The body and fender guys are the worst. Plastic surgery comes cheaper. The garage was a throwback. No clipboards, no business cards, no computers, no spotless white coveralls, no auto parts ads cluttering the office walls and counter. A half-naked cutie was trying to look coy on a wall calendar and boxes of parts littered the counter and floor. There was a comfortable dinginess about the place. It smelled of brake linings and old mufflers, bald tires and oxyacetylene cutting torches. Through a side doorway I could see a hydraulic hoist in one of the bays. In the other bay two mechanics were using a portable manual jack, the kind raised by pumping on its long handle. Most of the red enamel had been worn away, exposing the shiny steel underneath. My car was parked outside. There was no one in the office. One of the mechanics, doubling as office staff on Saturday, saw me and came in. Using a towel that had gone grey before my grandmother, he wiped a white cream smelling of lanolin off his hands before he made out the bill. His hands looked covered in broken spider webs engraved in black with auto grime. As a matter of course I pay cash, unless I need a bank draft to cover something big.

"Many of the people pay with a credit card," he said. His English was heavily accented.

"Plastic rots the soul. It's a scientific fact."

He bypassed that and concentrated on a business he knew.

"The clutch will be new. So it may grab for a while. Let up the pedal slowly. You were driving with almost no clutch."

"I've been doing that all my life." It was a passable exit line.

I was tired when I got to my apartment, went to bed and slept through to Sunday. I woke up at noon, fixed myself some eggs and toast and opened a can of peaches. I took inventory. Hadn't had a cigarette in almost fifteen months. Hadn't had a drink since late Friday. Early Saturday morning, but let's not quibble. I'd eaten some decent food. New clutch. Not bankrupt yet.

No major diseases, as far as I knew. No tremors. No delusions, except about finding a willing female. Rent paid for a month on the apartment. Seven months to go yet on the office. Could sleep at the office if I lost the suite. I'd done that. New clutch. I mentioned that. But the case bothered me. Every time I got close I ended up further away. I had Joanne Ackermann thinking but she wasn't in any danger. I didn't even know how Ivan the Gross met his end without meeting hers halfway. Stoker. But he had the prof upsy-daisy over him, and to mangle a metaphor, she was oozing her clear clam sauce from the soft shells. A woman in that state of thermal excitement is not receptive to any offshore breeze of reason. I went to bed early, tired of the whole thing. I dreamt about toast and that's as dull as it gets.

On my way to the office the next morning I stopped at a grocery and picked up a copy of the local rag, the *Herald-Times*. I inflict this punishment on myself a couple of times a week in the good cause of my own masochistic anti-therapy. This fish wrapper's idea of civic responsibility is to put snaps of the mayor's wife on the front page, giving out along with her constipated smile prizes for the best potted petunias at a local flower show, and photos of his onerous honour's wineripe mug dedicating another mall to the cause of his re-election. And there are the endless shots of puppies, kittens, kiddies, babies, grandmas, and features like the halfwit with the world's largest collection of licence plates. A domestic quarrel with blood rates the headline, "Homicidal Maniac Loose in Prairie City." The front page of this edition featured his honour breathing into the cleavage of some visiting prima donna here to give a concert at a mosquito slough. She looked foreign enough to excite the local racists and sexy enough for a few to go somewhere private with her picture and do unmentionably personal things. The rest of the page was a collection of commercials disguised as news items.

I turned to page two. Joanne Ackermann had left her car engine running in a closed garage. The story said there was no suicide note. The one who could have made trouble for Stoker had removed herself. She admits to something the law might be more than mildly interested in, and when I say I don't go for it she takes a quick bow. All I had were photos that proved nothing except she was sharing non-conjugal sweat with two guys, which would rate a listing on the spinsters' honour roll. If I told Grady everything, he'd want to know why I'd taken my time. I'd promised to give him anything I got. But cops don't like messy complications. He wouldn't be expecting anything unusual or odd from a professor. She was more fragile than she looked. She'd put up with a lot. Those sessions with Raskolski must have made her wonder who makes out the punishment duties. By the end of it all she was a jumble of jealousy, self-disgust, bitterness and love. Emotions don't come in separate packages. There was too much to sort out. She gave up rather than try.

I took the stairs two at a time up to my office. Emily was there, freshly laundered and starched. She had replaced the flowers in her vase. I showed her the newspaper and briefed her before going into the inner office. She hadn't replaced the flower in my glass and it looked droopy. I tossed it into the wastebasket. Too early for a drink. I have a rule, no drinking from sunup to noon, and hold off till whenever. It was almost the end of April. The unusually warm weather had gotten warmer. The morning had a hint of June. I hung my jacket over my chair and went back out to see how Emily was reacting. She had taken off her wire-rimmed spectacles and was rubbing her forehead. Looking sad, she handed me the newspaper.

"I thought love was the key to happiness," I said.

She looked at me as if I was a back alley mutt that had sneaked in and done the outrageous on the carpet in her sitting room.

"We're not all poets, like certain people. I'm trying to figure things out. I'm losing time and money. Thanks for the flower. You see, I notice."

She gave me one of her dismissive looks and shook her head.

That morning an English lass with an accent like a chilled breath mint came in and wanted me to trace her lineage. I gave her the once-over. Her lineage looked good enough to trace. Especially the pinker generations. But somebody else would have to do her the honour. I had to be honest. It's the one vice I've always had trouble not committing and it's the most expensive.

"You want a genealogist. He'll trace you back to a duchess of Bedford, a queen of France and Nefertiti or Cleopatra, either one is guaranteed. Put it all on a family monkey tree. Ever wonder who's related to all the executioners and peasants back then?"

Her Devon cream deep pink, she stuffed records and certificates back into her handbag and strutted out. Not a bad keester.

Junk mail vomited through the letter slot and piled up. Credit card outfits, youareaprizewinner crap, survey questionnaires from pollsters wanting you to do their work for them, sports whoopers trying to peddle you season's tickets to their team's mercenary chiropractors, begging letters with a photo of an impoverished dark-skinned girl with seal pup's eyes staring into your soul, chain letters threatening doom if you don't pass them on (I write on the envelope, "Return to sender—do your worst"), and the stuff with the right address and the wrong name or the wrong address and the almost-right name and all from insurance companies or loan sharks that get them off sucker lists. And there's the real mail, the hard core stuff, bills with self-promoting information pamphlets and folded newsletters with in-house news you couldn't care less about, income tax forms on recycled paper (there's government responsibility for you to consider while you're forking over) telling you how many easy ways there are to pay, and trying to get you excited about a quick nickel-and-dime refund of your own money, and bank statements offering financial services that seem to put you even more into their debt-loving hands. It's the old making of the dollar and if you live here you're a part of it. But for once I'd like a letter from somebody who wasn't after my wallet.

I sat in my inner office and thought about the case. It was supposed to be over, and for me it was, financially. This couldn't go on. I phoned Eddy and left a message. On Tuesday he called.

"Sorry, I had other business. I got nothing for you. The guy goes from work to her place. And that's about it."

He said he'd do what he could in his spare time. I told him to forget it. This was costing us too much for something already paid for. Spare time isn't good enough, even for him. A babe, he'd have stayed interested. Trying to catch one with her panties slipping keeps him going. But shadowing a guy, even on full pay, bores him. Bores me. And there was the rent. We weren't making anything. Sometimes though you keep going, even if you figure there's nothing ahead except more questions. Two dead bodies, leaving lots of questions. Joanne Ackermann had proven me right, but I still didn't know how it happened. I had a hunch, but hunches were also-rans on this one. And I had no way of getting close enough to know. The remaining parties weren't going to let me get too near. They would slap an injunction on me to keep my distance. Or I'd be facing an action for invasion of privacy. So I did what most people do when they're up against it. Lie. I took a chance the professor didn't talk to anybody after I phoned her. It wasn't a big chance. She wouldn't bawl into the phone to get her beloved's attention to make him feel guilty before she headed for the garage. Academic martyrs are no different from any other. The ground has been prepared, the moment awaits. She'd most likely been heading for that garage for years and I interrupted her. One more insult to bear.

I got Stoker's business number and phoned. He was out, had to be paged. Who was calling, please? Never mind. A couple of more times. Three hours later he answered. As snotty as usual, even before he heard my voice. I had to be quick, before he could cut me off.

"I talked with your girlfriend the night she killed herself. She told me something the police might be interested in. Been wondering what to do about it. We could decide together."

He wanted to cut me off, and I could almost hear his teeth grinding, but I'd hooked him for another few seconds. As a salesman, he didn't like being sold.

"What do you want?"

"We're going to talk in a secluded place. Don't pack any heat or pull anything, I'm not putting the bite on you."

"Where?"

"Behind the Hotel Fontainebleau. At seven. There's a path leading down to the river. I'll be at the bottom."

I cut him off, looked at my watch. It was after five. I don't like carrying guns. I've got a .38 semi-automatic pistol and know something about using guns but they can be a problem leading to more problems. In Prairie City they're unnecessary except on the rare occasion when you're going to meet a killer.

On the north side of the Prairie River there's a hill, steep as a bluff in places, and at the top is the Hotel Fontainbleau. A plank fence runs along the crest of the hill. The hotel sits between sections of it. The western section begins beside a ramp for underground parking. A footpath there leads down to the river, the entrance almost hidden by a Scotch pine at the side of the ramp. The path zigs and zags, which cuts down on its steepness. The ground is badly eroded and bare except for scrappy weeds. Near the bottom the path widens before disappearing among clumps of grass. The river meanders here, its bank topped by dense brush. No bare slope giving an open view of the river. So the sightseeing crowd doesn't come around, and that's why I picked the spot.

It was almost seven when I got to the entrance. The round tower shape of the hotel rose beside me. The evening sun was glancing off the west windows, making golden mirrors of them, row on indented row, an overstocked honeycomb. The footpath was bumpy. I made my way slowly to the bottom. It had gotten dim, the brush near the bank filling with shadows in that innocent way trees and bushes have of sneaking the night up on you. The river was invisible and as mute as everywhere else along its sluggish course. There's an idiot buzzer in one of the more aware parts of my brain. Wrong time for a meeting there, unless with a woman bringing an inflatable raft. But any woman showing up at that hour would have fangs. What made me run I'll never know. I headed for the brush. Something like a very angry wasp zipped by my ear. I flailed my way through stems and branches and dove head first off the bank, bellyflopping into five feet of gummy water smelling like a public toilet. I buried myself in it. My hardware, getting soaked in a shoulder holster, was useless. I wouldn't have known where to aim, anyway. I opened my eyes. The water was muddy. My dive had stirred up sediment and crap. A sneaker lay on its side, a sunken freighter in the ooze. I'm not much good at holding my breath unless it's an artistic striptease and she's got torpedoes. I swivelled my head sideways and put my lips to the surface and breathed but got mostly water instead of air. I tried again, spitting and inhaling. I ducked. Nothing happened. I did this a few more times before deciding to see how dark it was. It's hard to tell how much time has passed in a situation like that.

It's an endless minute. I peeked. It was deep dusk. I went under and scrambled on my hands and knees over to the bank. I came out turtle speed and touched dry earth, and something else, a jacket sleeve. With most of me still under, I rubbed my eyes. My invited guest, his back against the bank, sat half out of the water, a hole in his forehead clean as if bored by a drill press. A trickle of blood had reached his chin. His eyes looked permanently surprised, his mouth gaped. I waited till dark before climbing the bank and slogging blindly up the hill. Dripping onto the hotel lobby carpet, I pulled a handful of wet coins from a waterlogged pants pocket and phoned Homicide as staring guests passed.

The desk clerk came over, asked if I was waiting for somebody. Frozen grin, attitude on hold until he knew whether I was an outpatient out for a swim or a respectable citizen. When I told him the police were on their way he became politely concerned and offered me a hotel bath towel. Grady took ten minutes. He grinned sourly and shook his head when he saw me, jacket off and rubbing myself dry. I climbed down the hill with him and another detective, who led the way using a flashlight. An ambulance had arrived and the paramedics followed us with a stretcher. The detectives made notes and took measurements. Grady asked me routine questions. I knew he'd save the best for later. The paramedics put the body in a bag, lifted it up the bank and onto the stretcher. "Thanks for letting me know," Grady said. "Change and come by, tonight." A bit heavy on the sarcasm but I suppose I deserved it. We were standing ankle deep in the river. We climbed the bank and stamped our feet. "That's it," Grady said to the other detective, whose flashlight beam found the zigzags in the path on our way back in single file up the hill.

Two hours later, after changing, showering and swallowing a couple of soft-boiled eggs, I was sitting in Grady's office trying to wash off more sewage. Jacket off and leaning back in his padded metal desk chair, he was drinking coffee out of a paper cup and rubbing his forehead. There was a doughnut in a large box on his desk. It was covered in hard pink icing and sprinkled with coloured bits of something shiny. The rest of the squad on duty and the secretaries on the shift had already taken theirs. I figured he wouldn't get to his doughnut. There was too much that was stale in his life. Homicide detectives get used to seeing the worst and they get to not caring, except when somebody plays games with them. It's a matter of respect. That's what they hold onto after being stuck with a lot of unclaimed bodies.

"What is it with you, Quester? You like screwing up? You better have some good reasons for not letting me in on this before it got to shooting, and don't give me any bullshit. I want to hear everything you know."

"I told you before, this one started out as a husband hunter. I do searchforthespouse all the time. It's not something I'm proud of, but the pay is all right. This time the hubby gets a one-way ticket. You sign me up as your bird dog, free of course. I find out hubby is a child molester and couldn't make it with his wife. She has a boyfriend, who has a girlfriend. An English professor at Prairie University, Joanne Ackermann by name, and she commits suicide. Before she does it, she confesses to killing Ivan Raskolski. Her story is crap. But there's a tie-in with the boyfriend. I phone him late this afternoon, arrange a meeting and almost end up dead."

"Why would she tell you she killed Raskolski?"

"To protect her boyfriend, my prime suspect until the mud hole."

"Why would he kill him?"

"There it gets complicated, has to do with a prenup and a wonky heart. Raskolski dead means his wife gets rich quick. Her boyfriend couldn't accomplish it via a heart attack, using the professor as a sexual surrogate for a babe, so had to do it himself. Prof tried to cover for him before taking her own way out."

His phone rang, he picked it up, listened and said, "Five minutes," and put down the phone.

"Ackermann died Sunday afternoon. Why did you hold back?"

"To figure things out."

"You phoned her boyfriend."

"I thought I figured right."

He scowled, shook his head.

"What about the molestation?"

"I promised her I'd leave her out. She's had it bad enough. She's an undergrad at the university now. Doesn't play a part in this."

"That's for us to determine. You're in deep shit already without holding anything else back. You fuck around and three people are dead. You carrying anything?"

"Had a hunch you'd ask. I've got it on me. I didn't get a chance to use it. Raskolski ruined her and you'd be putting more pressure on her, to no good end. She doesn't deserve it, even if I have to take the rap for protecting her."

He stood up and grinned.

"You like her, huh? Must be a real babe. We'll see. I've got to go."

"Want the hardware?"

"Have it checked. For the record. I'll get Marianne. You can make a statement. We'll talk after I get the coroner's report."

Grady left and a stenographer came in took my statement. She wore a wool suit, high heels and had a pile of white hair and was either chewing gum or checking her plates for fit. I was probably among her last customers before retirement and warmer climes. She worked her long fingers at some kind of shorthand machine. I was too tired to tarry over it and stretched and yawned a mite towards the end.

It was after eleven when I got to my apartment. I poured a shot of bourbon and sipped as I stood in the kitchen. I'd feel the aches tomorrow, the strained muscles and tendons from scrambling hither and yon. I had been shot at and my suspect was dead. There was one left. Not the type to tote firearms. Or kill with them. But it was her show, no matter how it happened. The prenup made it that way. The professor protected Stoker, who had bumped off Ivan the Defiler for Wanda Regine. Her Gorgeous had an interest in shutting him up permanently if she thought he was a threat to sell out the firm. She used both of them, probably suggested the phony heart attack angle. She needed a patsy, got her porker to use the professor to pull it off, and be implicated enough so she would stay clammed if it flopped. The salesman had to step in and do the job, and his numbered days depended on how close Wanda Regine thought her keester was to the clink. He told her I phoned. She let him think he was going to make river sewage out of me. That was fatal for him. She'd have to have a hitman on a retainer to do that at such short notice, or have to do it herself. The slug in my direction was to get me to hit dirt. So she or whoever could get away. My bluff had worked. They both thought there was a loose end and I'd found it and so put myself in line for some of the ill-gotten gains.

I had everything neatly wrapped up and it came undone like a drunk's resolve on New Year's. A hitman wouldn't be ready on a couple of hours' notice. And in Prairie City there weren't any I knew of. It's one of the few nice things about the place. And why would the fair one get mud on her shoes when she could have dealt with her porker at her own convenience somewhere dry. To get me at the same time. But I was a waterlogged duck in a shooting gallery. No slugs entered the water. Maybe she panicked and ran. Killing isn't easy, especially the first time. This would be her second, but the first was by proxy. This time she would have ridden with the man she was going to kill, walked down to the bank with him, plugged him in the forehead at close range and positioned the body so it was sitting against the bank. I show up and a slug fans me on my way to the water but she and I don't exchange apologies for bumping into each other's scheme. Too messy for an expert who did her best work in bed. I headed for mine, tired of the whole damn thing.

On Wednesday morning I told Emily what happened. She was duly shocked. Where she comes from, breaking wind in public is a felony. Picking up the wrong fork can get you talked about for years. Not that she's like that. But there's colonial New England in her blood. He posture is Puritan. I asked her what she thought and she knew I was milking her (not the best way to put it) for ideas. She waved me away. I'm not in your class, I said, before realizing I had said something else. She didn't quite gloat, but looked at her nib for a while. I'd have to wait.

An hour later she came to the doorway of the inner office. She comes in when I'm not there. Does a little dusting. I've told her the cleaning woman is supposed to do that, but she frowns. We both know that drunk doesn't even blow her nose. Still, it doesn't look right for your secretary to be doing the maid's work. Emily wrote something about my attitude but I told her I didn't want to hear that one. She sits and reads her stuff to me at her desk most times but occasionally will stand up to read at the inner office doorway. Very formal, and presentation counts, I'm guessing. As usual, she was wearing a dress. This one was of stiff satin, the colour of cold lake water. Way out of date but that wasn't any of my business.

"Stand and deliver," I said.

We shall gather at the river,
At the beautiful, the beautiful river—. . . .

"What?"

She made a curtsey and went back to her desk.

Grady phoned in the afternoon. He sounded tired.

"Coroner's report says he was shot at point-blank range with a .22. Slug fragments match those taken out of Raskolski. Not that we suspected you. Wrong calibre for that size hole, anyway. And yours hasn't been fired recently. Magazine is full. Looks like he was probably shot somewhere else and dumped there. Any ideas, besides it being the same killer?"

"My oracle is on strike. For higher say."

"What?"

"I got water on the brain."

"Same m.o. as the other murder. Head shot. Small calibre handgun. Close up to be lethal. Murderer knew the victim. Like with Raskolski, robbery wasn't the motive. Money in his wallet. He went to the river with the other party or was ambushed."

"No time to plan an ambush. He thought the other party was there to help him get rid of me. A setup. Only he was the pigeon."

"What makes you worth killing?"

"I told him I knew something the prof told me. It was a bluff, he went for it."

His voice got cagey.

"Who do you think the other party was?"

"Raskolski's ghost."

"Cut the crap, Quester."

"There's one other party. You know who she is as well as I do."

"We're going to question her."

"Take your softest kid gloves. She bruises easy."

"You'd know, huh?"

"I saw her take a deep breath once. I'm still recovering."

"I'll bet. All right, that's it. For now. Don't be a stranger."

A getaway line you'd say in a parking lot to people you never want to see again. He thought he was being civil. Etiquette isn't a big thing with his customers. In his business watching your back isn't a figure of speech.

I looked out the window and watched the light fail. As if the sun were slipping, trying to hold on. A way of seeing that ignores the endless rhythms of the universe. Nothing personal. It's the night coming. You're in the dark, floating under the stars. It was after five, I was alone. I thought about the widow. She was alone, too. That wouldn't bother her. She could find company fast. There was a woman with an eye to the main chance. The world is full of salesmen, but to get one to kill somebody, that's a hard trick. She'd found one and then sold him out. She believed I'd found the something there was to find. The prof knew but removed herself. I wasn't killed, so what I knew wasn't damaging unless her salesman stayed alive.

I called Wanda Regine. I'm suicidal when it counts. I disguised my voice, told the maid I was a law officer. I had a writ of habeas corpus. Instead of puzzling over that, she decided to get her mistress. Her Voluptuous came on the line, a bit puffy in the voice. Her "Yes?" sounded like a pout. And nobody could pout like her, even disembodied and at distance. As if ecstasy is on the comedown afterwards.

"Too bad," I said.

"This isn't the time for joking in bad taste, Mr. Quester."

"When is?"

"Why are you calling?"

"I was there, beautiful. Made the appointment. Found the body. After somebody shot at me. I was almost number two."

"You are already." She recovered fast from deep sorrow.

"Didn't know he meant that much to you. Don't lap dogs come cheap?"

"I should cut you off." She did.

She could have meant something more literal than figurative by her tone. But with her it would have been a passing thought. I thought about having a drink but phoned back instead. She came on the line, didn't say anything.

"I'm still recovering from the bullet that missed."

"You're a bastard."

"If it matters."

"Come over here and talk to me."

"I want to stay alive."

"What's that mean?"

"Men don't last around you."

She laughed, catching the double entendre between her tight curls. I'd heard better laughs, but she wasn't made for laughing.

"The police will be around for a chat. If you'd care to tell me anything, I wouldn't mind."

"I don't know anything. I got the news this morning. It was a complete shock. We were going to get married in December. Honeymoon on the Riviera. Off season. Not so many people."

"There'll be one less now."

"So you won't drop in."

"Another word would do it."

"You have a dirty mind."

"And you love it. I'll take a soggy rain check on that. And cry all you want. I hear it's good for the complexion."

"You are a bastard."

"Careful, or I'll bring aromatic oils and rub them in all your impossible places. We'll insinuate sinuously beside the musky glow of a beeswax candle. Burning, maddening, mindless pleasure. You won't come down for a week. You'll curse and adore me in the same breath."

I could hear her squirming. Nothing complicated about Wanda Regine's lower half. The upper, quite different. A woman that yummy can anesthetize your brain while everything else is straining itself in a frenzy on the one chance in your life.

"Till when."

"I'll be waiting."

"No. You'll be too busy being the sexiest babe in Prairie City."

"I'm not a babe."

"The word I was thinking of is too personal for mixed company."

She laughed. If I had told her the word was "liar," that would have spoiled everything.

I sat alone in the dusk and imagined the wonderful things I could do to her body. If I could trust her long enough to do them. How dangerous could she be naked and aroused? How defenceless would I be? I couldn't wear my shoulder holster in bed. She'd never think it could be part of the performance. I couldn't stash it. Pardon me for a second while I tuck this under that pillow. We'll use the other one for what I have in mind. I fast-forwarded a scenario of me gripped between her plush thighs while the maid sneaked up behind us with a weapon of medieval ferocity. Something to deprive me of my manhood. With stuff like that on your mind, tumescence would be a problem. What's wrong, lover, can't do anything with your flabby tubeworm after your sexy talk on the phone? A grown woman not quite your style? My stepdaughter more to your taste, maybe? Too bad she's not twelve any more. Take your drooper and hairy luggage away. This'll be one for my memoirs, tentatively titled, *It's Hard to Keep a Good Man Down,* with a very small chapter. "The Dick Who Wasn't." Get her to my place. You live in this lean-to? Reminds me of my slumhood in Gopher Hole. In the shack by the tracks. Being felt up behind the woodshed by fourteen-year-old pimpleheads who came in their pants. Every man's a rapist. Some take longer, that's all. Hang up a lantern. Fuck me against a dirty wall. I'll feel right at home. And let me walk with damp panties and your cum leaking down my leg back in the dark to that shack. Wake up cold and unwashed the next morning. And see on the dirty mattress where I threw my clothes and my necklace with the red plastic heart your dried cum spots in my panty crotch. Hygienic, mister? For safe sex use a safe, huh? The only safes in my girlhood were blown with nitro. No, lover, I left that shit behind. If you'll excuse the expression. I worked my way up through punks and drunks, bosses and designer silk shirts. Business propositions, slackgrin innuendoes. I'm a woman of my own now. No prick is going to get me so worked up I won't be able to tell him to take it elsewhere when his time comes. I've known enough to know they fart the same the next morning.

The office was dark now. It was very quiet. I thought about what the prof knew that could get a man killed on two hours' notice. If Her Lubricious didn't do it, and I still didn't think she did (her open invitation did not affect my judgement at all), and a hired assassin was unlikely, there had to be another angle to this deal, hidden somewhere. What kind of trouble could stationery get you into except paper cuts or staples in your finger? Brickward's Prairie City branch had been turning a profit, Ivan the Befouler's relatives having seen to that. I closed my eyes and thought of nothing, which is impossible but means not much, but because thinking hard I believe dulls the senses, and in my more relaxed state (this is taking too long to explain) the senses are more alert, I thought I heard something. This always makes you listen harder. A whisper, a door opening like no other. Mine have a little extra personality. I never oil hinges. Makes the thief's job easier. My gun was at the police station. I'm shy about being introduced to strangers in the dark. I eased my feet off the desk, cursed my creaking bones and drifted over to the closet. The inner office door was closed. Behind the sink in the closet is a wall panel that opens onto a passageway. In bygone days people liked to play hide and seek. I found it by accident one cold morning when I was shaving and wiped steam off the mirror above the sink. There was a bit of give. I felt around till I found a button and the whole thing gave way. The passageway is four feet high and narrow. For all I know, it goes to the centre of the earth. The abode of albino gnomes who emerge at night to raid the children's section in clothing departments. And to stock up on vitamin D at health supplement stores. Much of the vitamin D that goes missing in the world can be traced to my office. I waited behind the panel and imagined grotesques of immaculate pedigrees.

Buildings are broken into all the time in that neighbourhood. The addicts need funds, what with the high price of drugs. Welfare won't cover it. Insurance policies are useless except for fire coverage, theft protection entailing lots of fine print and money. I don't have anything worth stealing but whisky. And Emily's writing may be quality stuff but to the wired gang down here they're handy size scraps of toilet paper. They couldn't get high on poetry if they mainlined ink. I don't mean to pick on addicts. Winos, alkies and rummies have been known to do the odd pilfering, and of course everyday thieves looking for something transportable. The cost of living has gone up. The government gets its nice slice from alcohol and tobacco. A jug of red and a pack of menthols spiked with four hundred chemicals on the government's list highlighting the most highly suspected carcinogens (there's irony to inhale) cost ugly dollars now, so what's a crook supposed to do because he doesn't have a job in a corporation and is scraping by on welfare handouts? It's a sad situation. So should taxpayers be complaining because their missing property is helping keep the self-disadvantaged in booze and smokes and drugs and womanflesh and lotto tickets (that's money spent to win their way out of misery and goes back to the government)? They're a part of society, like corporation lawyers, CEOs and PU professors and hookers who put up with guys who carry razors to bed. They all put out at Christmas so the bums down here who aren't enterprising enough can eat turkey at the missions. Not everybody is as lucky as ditchdiggers and farmers, who deal with real dirt.

In a less philosophical frame of mind now, having spent an inordinate and perhaps dangerous amount of time reflecting on the matter, I waited. The inner office door squeaked open. I put my ear to the panel and heard hushed words. Two intruders, unless a psychotic had brought along an imaginary friend.

"Where?"

"Try there."

Girls' voices. I felt relieved, emboldened. Cared not I what they were arméd with. I heard some hackneyed rummaging around in my drawers (there's a joke for some guy who's desperate). I opened the panel slowly on darkness and squeezed between the closet door and sink. I sneaked over to the light switch. Their bustling covered my movements. Nothing like nosy girls. I turned on the ceiling light and saw them bending over in designer jeans. They straightened up but didn't make the usual scared noises, only "Shit." I like playing tough guy with women who won't sneer or laugh, especially if they're not carrying weapons, such as sharp fingernails or large incisors. These were unarmed nailbiters.

"What're are you snotnoses doing in here? I ought to take down your pants and give you both a good spanking."

They looked at each other. One was a busty brunette with bangs, the other a long blonde with milkskin limbs. They caught the excitement in my voice and probably figured my knees were shaking. A dirty old man. A cinch.

"We're Clissie and Sterton from Delta Psi Pi sorority at Prairie University," the blonde said. "We're pledges. It's pledge week. We've got tasks to fulfil before we can be pledged. We had to get into a detective's office and take his holster or licence or badge or whisky bottle or something. We saw your name in the phone book and thought it was kind of cute. C. Quester. Sort of fits what you are. Is that your real name? What's the C stand for?"

"Crap." I had recovered and couldn't resist the obvious.

"Fits the office," the brunette said. The blonde looked at her, then at me, but forgot to change the look.

"We're not lying. We're really pledges."

"Rah rah. You're going to tell me what you're doing here or you don't leave the premises."

"You're keeping us against our will."

"Don't forget, I'm a detective. I'm almost legal. You're guilty of breaking and entering. I caught you in the act of. You're criminals."

"Phone the sorority if you don't believe us."

"Maybe he's after something," the brunette said.

"I'll bet you're Sterton."

"I'm a 40 D cup, want to see?"

She unzipped her windbreaker and unbuttoned her blouse. She wasn't lying. The firm jut of young breasts. She reached inside the low-cut cotton bra and lifted a breast, exposing the nipple. The areola was a fat tan disc around the pudgy nipple. She came over. Nothing in her face changed. Not that I was paying much attention to her face. Her fingers squeezed. This was murder. I managed to notice the blonde moving towards the door. She was holding my whisky bottle upside down by the neck.

"Put the bottle on the desk. And you, cover up."

"We'll say you abducted and raped us," the brunette said.

"With sorority sisters it would be the other way around. You'd have to draw lots."

The brunette backed away and buttoned up. The blonde still held the bottle by the neck but it was on the desk.

"Sit down. We're going to talk."

They hesitated and I moved towards them slightly. They sat, the brunette on the edge of her chair, the blonde against the back of hers. I returned the bottle to its drawer and took the remaining chair for guests, put it between them and the door and sat down. I waited a while, which is usually a good tactic. The blonde got fidgety.

"You two are sorority, all right. With you a proposal is a proposition. Unless I hear what I want, you're going to stay till you pee your pants. And but me no buts about unlawful confinement. I'm making a citizen's arrest, temporarily. I'm a reasonable guy. If I get the truth, you walk out with dry panties. You're no more being pledged than I am. The academic year ends this week. Semester and session finish."

I waited for the birdies to sing but nothing happened. They didn't look at each other. This wasn't their idea. They were being used. What or who could make them stay clammed after being caught after dark by a non-varsity man? At some signal I didn't catch they made for the door. I jumped up, grabbed each by an arm, pulled hard enough to bump them together and they collapsed into a cursing heap. I pointed at the chairs.

"You're going to get bruised unless you're smart. And don't try any sneaky kicks in the groin or that martial arts stuff. I'm a barroom brawler. And neither of you could be as good as Thela Crammond."

I said it without thinking. They sat up and stared at each other. They went back to their chairs and I sat down. All I had to do was wait. If I said anything else, they'd know I was still guessing. I grinned. I look like a gink when I grin. That was beside the point with those two.

"It's all her fault," the blonde said. "She put down sororities in the campus newspaper, especially us. She said we're snobs and prejudiced. We're trying to get her back. Looking into her personal life. You came to the house asking for her and we knew you were a detective. So we came here looking for something. Like letters or photos."

"Getting closer. What did she really do?"

The brunette's tight mouth sneered.

"We don't have to tell you anything. You assaulted us and you're holding us against our will, having used undue force."

"I restrained you in the act of escaping. And I am acting in lieu of the lawful authority. And don't give me any of that grievous bodily harm crap. Wouldn't your parents like to hear about you squeezing your tit in front of me?"

"You're not phoning the police. You're overstepping your authority."

"I'll bet you're pre-law."

She smirked. She was born to smirk.

"I told you the reason," the blonde said. "You've got to let us go now."

"I don't gotta do nuthin'. Let me help you along. Thela Crammond wrote something about Delta Psi etcetera. You say you're mad because of what she thinks of your type. This is more than a personal thing. You'd never come down to the bad end of town and at night unless you had the very best of reasons. You wouldn't put your twats at risk with the freaks around here unless there was no other way, which means you're desperate. Or whoever's behind you is. This is not a prank or grudge. Or you'd have coughed up the truth."

The blonde started laughing.

"We'll get out of this."

"When your pee begins running along the floor, you'll be feeling different. I'm not enjoying this. I've got to be ornery. What you did tells me I'm a target. I don't know what's going on. A guy can get killed that way. Your choice, wet or dry panties."

They looked straight ahead for a while, got bored and glanced around the office. Whenever their eyes met they would look away. An hour of this and they had compressed lips and narrowed eyes, and every so often crossed their arms and uncrossed them. To show how time was dragging I would glance at my watch. I got up and stretched but never took my eyes off them. It was one of those nights the cleaning woman didn't come around. Occasionally there were noises in other parts of the building. Doors slammed, the elevator creaked, and silence again. Another hour wended its way into the past tense, making three since they'd broken in. I realized the situation could be tricky. If the sisters were stubborn, there would be a messy floor. Sometimes easing the pressure helps. From the deep drawer where I stash my whisky I got out a bottle of carbonated mineral water, reserved for customers and guests who like mixed drinks. I took out two glasses, filled them with water and put them on the desk. They stared at them. Thirst versus the bathroom, not a bad tactic, the strain both ways increasing their urge to pee. I sat down and grinned my gink grin.

"Let's try once more. It's getting close to midnight. I don't want to postpone some frat boy's pleasure or keep the junk and fast food manufacturers from making their just profits. You've got lives to lead. Wasting them waiting for your bladders to burst isn't a good idea."

I had left the bottle on the desk. Lime-flavoured mineral water, the label said. Strands of bubbles kept rising in the glasses. The blonde grabbed a glass and drank. The brunette waited another minute before clutching hers. I kept my gink grin. They probably thought it was friendly. They were bonding with me, a jargoneering sociologist or psychologist would say. Rapture instead of rupture. Captives becoming love slaves in some crummy romance. They were tired, that's all. Waves take time polishing pebbles. They were starting to look worn. And a whole ocean was coming.

The blonde broke quietly.

"We were told to get something on you. On your personal life or shady deals or criminals you know. Any kind of dirt. The head of our sorority told us. She said Thela had betrayed us by giving you information that could endanger the sorority. It has to do with a guy some of them knew who's dead now. That's all we know. We were sworn to secrecy and because of you we had to break our oath."

The truth isn't surprising, it's what you expected. Somebody saying it makes it important. That's why hardly anybody tells it. Say it and you have to confront it. Ignore it and you can keep pretending it doesn't exist. You are your own best liar. Makes everything simpler. That's a truth.

"All right, scram. There's a bathroom at the end of the hallway, to your left. Don't worry about your oath. You'll break more important things. Like somebody's heart (can't believe I said that)."

I could hear them running down the hallway and soon a toilet being flushed. I moved my chair behind the desk, put my feet up and leaned back with tie unloosened.

I had a choice. I could take on the sorority myself or tell Grady. On my own I'd face a bunch of angry babes. The lost lambs would blab as soon as they got back. Probably say I threatened to rape them if they didn't squeal. I'd be the talk of the bull sessions. Maybe it's heifer sessions at a sorority. I didn't know much more than before. Merely that a man now dead had once been cosy with some of them. It obviously hadn't been Ivan the Malefactor. When he'd tried to storm the bastion, the sisters called campus security. It had to be Stoker. Was there a connection with the prof? But both were dead, so why would the babes be after me? How could I get them into trouble? Had the salesman been playing the academic field until one of them took exception to his sportiveness? If so, she must have known about our appointment at the river.

I left the doors unlocked and fell asleep. I figured if I was lucky an intruder might know something about the case. Another night at the office. More aches when I woke up Thursday morning at eight. I washed, shaved and ingested more slow-working poison in the coffee shop in the hotel next door. Something that was once bacon now resembled burnt slivers of wood with the smell of crankcase oil. The sandwich these morsels were ensconced in consisted of square slices of white squeezebread toasted to crumbling chunks, a slice of plastic tomato, lettuce that was tired pretending it was and a smear of rancid mayonnaise from a jar with a best-before date worn away long ago. With heroic forbearance I didn't order a cup of coffee grounds or a wedge of imitation pie. My mouth felt waxy enough. The other customers were gobbling their mutant food with an indifferent gusto, forking it down without looking. Undoubtedly a good policy if you're not interested in presentation and have a casual attitude to nutrition. I left with an uneasy stomach doomed again to internecine warfare.

I went to the police station to pick up my gun. The policewoman who passed it to me across the counter at the main office after I signed the receipt said it was full of dirt. I said it was river crud and I was going to clean and oil it. She smiled, I grinned, meaningless and not in an unimportant way that will linger for a moment. I went up to see Grady. He was talking to another detective, the one who'd been with him at the river. The other detective was chunky and looked all routine, keeping an eye on his pension. Everybody said hi and he left. Grady nodded at a chair. I said I'd dropped by to see if he had anything new. He stared at my tie.

"No one is being assigned to the case. The inquest's finding will be death by a person or persons unknown."

"There aren't enough murders in Prairie City to be blasé about them."

"That's the official word." He made a face.

"Could be you're being told to lay off?"

"The department has a budget, there are priorities."

"Parking violations?"

He looked at his hands. His office seemed smaller, a tiny square piece of officialdom that fitted together with all the others. His authority went so far, unless he wanted to risk losing it. Everybody's square included smaller ones and was included in somebody else's. From somewhere among that hierarchy of squares the word had come.

"I guess I'm on my own."

There was no point in telling him about the sorority. He'd call the sisters' raid a prank. And he wouldn't want to hear my ideas about the far-reaching aspects of the case. He saw crime as finding the one answer, not many answers to the same question.

"Off the record, let me know if you find something."

I nodded and stood up. He began looking through some papers in a folder on his desk. On the way out I passed by the main office. The policewoman was talking to somebody else.

When I got back to my office there was still a hint of perfume in the air from the intruder babes. An odour of artificial come-on from an olfactory factory, essence of the rut à la chemistry lab. There wasn't even a look on Emily's face. She was far too well bred, from a society where a gentleman's personal affairs were his own business and no proper concern of a lady. Though on entering my sanctum sanctorum I noticed that the window had been opened. I sat, feet on the desk, and thought about what to do. Somebody had stepped in. I found hanky on the panky, by invitation only, and big shots pay for protection. One nosy private detective had been getting too close to something. Babes who belonged to sororities had well-heeled fathers to protect them, take care of the hit and run on the highway and in bed. Fathers who had enough political influence to squelch a murder investigation. Where to begin to unravel this? I phoned the sorority and asked to speak to their leader. Pim Pritchett was her name, I was told by the snippy babe on the line. Pimmy wouldn't be in till five. I left my name and number. My name got an indeterminable sound between a snort and a sniff and the line went dead. I spent the rest of that windy afternoon dozing and watching the clouds docking at invisible piers. No calls came in. Emily as usual left at five and I waited a few minutes and phoned. This time I got Pim Pritchett, prematurely legal. Early greying at the inner temple of an impoverished politesse. High society hauteur on tap into the bargain. She interrupted before I could finish telling her my name.

"I understand you've already phoned. What exactly is the nature of this call?"

"Not the call of nature. I used that on two of your sisters."

She didn't get it. I live in too many dimensions at once. Thins my audience. But she wasn't the kind to be bothered by ignorance.

"Why are you phoning here? We have nothing to discuss."

"Let's discuss nothing. Two of your sisters broke into my office looking for something. I could prefer charges but I won't if you talk to me. What about it?"

"I have no idea what you're talking about."

"We talk. Or I see the law. Which is it? Do I get an invite to your den of inequity?"

A pause ensued. I checked my fingernails for hangnails. The inevitable is nice when it's nice. When it's not, check my life.

"I can see you at eight," she said in a tone as sincere as a concession speech.

"You can squeeze me in between your appointments."

I forget what she said, it wasn't memorable, merely the kind of incoherent sneering that passes for repartee among the pretentiously post-secondary.

The sorority house was a block from campus and on the boundary with Belvedere. All the fraternity and sorority houses were in this area. Collective snobbery. There were spotlights under the eaves and over the front stairs. From my earlier visit, asking for Thela Crammond, I recognized the two storeys of white stucco, square and roofed with green shingles. Frostbitten brown lawn in a permanent state of shock bordered the sidewalk and sides of the house. Everything was murky now except for the splashes of light. Walking up the concrete steps, I saw the oval of varnished oak beside the door, the Greek letters Delta Psi Pi incised into it. I had parked on campus, far enough away in case the babes had ideas about my car. I had gotten as far as the front door last time. I knocked, and after keeping me waiting for a couple of minutes while they undoubtedly smirked behind the peephole in the door, it opened slightly. I could hear a chain knock against wood. The door swung open slowly. I couldn't see anyone and my idiot buzzer went off, ghost of a cry in the distance. I entered, obliviously deaf.

I stepped into a short hallway. The bulb in the ceiling fixture was dim but I could see that the wall panels and floor were white oak. There was a closet for coats. Whoever had opened the door had gone. Was I being set up? Sorority sisters were too busy being snobs to be clever. They were being incubated to be society matrons and editorial foghorns. I heard a siren. A campus police car pulled up in front, its lights whirling. Two officers jumped out, crouched before scuttling across the lawn. I knew better than to do anything except stand there. They leaped up the stairs, their guns drawn, and flattened themselves against the stucco. I shook my head at the performance.

"Come out, hands high," one of them ordered.

"I'm not armed," I shouted. "I'm a private investigator working on a case."

I stepped outside and the same voice said to put my hands behind me and the steel jaws of handcuffs snapped around my wrists.

"Phone Kerry Grady of city homicide," I said. "He'll vouch for me."

One of them led me to the patrol car and the other went inside. Lights came on and I could hear voices, excited and scared. Not a bad performance. The officer came out and we went to police headquarters, two rooms in the campus shopping mall. They sat me in a chair, didn't take off the handcuffs.

"What were you doing there?" one of the officers asked. He and his partner sat across a desk from me. Sewn onto the jackets of their blue uniforms in silver thread was the Prairie University crest, and on their peak caps was a badge of the crest. They looked too interested in comfort to risk being city law. Protecting sororities was about right for them. The one doing all the talking was looking at my investigator's licence. He had taken it out of my wallet.

"They said you forced an entry. Lock and chain on the door were broken."

"I had an appointment to meet somebody. Who'd break into a sorority except some fraternity halfwit on a panty raid, or are they obsolete? I'm working on a case. Phone Grady. He'll back me up."

"We'll do everything in time. Who you working for?"

"My client wishes to remain anonymous." My client was anonymous now.

"You anxious to go to jail?"

"You don't have a jail. If you prefer charges, you have to turn me over to the city police. Your jurisdiction extends as far as the university. That house is outside. Their call should've been transferred downtown."

"We've got an unofficial understanding with the city. We can respond to nearby emergencies."

"Why didn't they phone 911 if this was life-threatening? They called you once before. A guy was pestering one of them, wanted to get up to her room. They must be convincing."

"You telling us our business?"

"I'm telling you mine, as much of it as I can. All you've got is that I'm supposedly stupid enough and strong enough to smash through the solid oak door of a sorority under spotlights and without a jimmy and carrying nothing but my licence and no motive except the wish to be caught standing around.

I came to talk to them. They conned me."

"You came to talk about what? Why'd they con you?"

"If I told you I'd have to divulge my client's identity. All I can say is that I'm looking for information. I thought they'd cooperate. I was wrong."

My interrogator passed my licence to his silent partner, who looked at it as if it was written in a foreign language. He passed it back and my interrogator tossed it and my wallet across the desk to me.

"Where's your car?"

I told him and the silent one got up and left. I heard the patrol car leave. I couldn't see it because my back was to the window. The talking one came over and took off the handcuffs. I rubbed my wrists, helping circulate the blood. My hands partially numb, I fumbled the licence into its plastic sleeve in the wallet and the wallet into an inside pocket of my jacket. We waited as if there was nothing else in the world. The patrol car returned and the officer came in looking pleased.

"You car is illegally parked. Wrong side of the street and too far from the curb."

He handed me two citations.

"I can go?"

They didn't quite nod, their way of saying yes and putting on the tough at the same time, as if anyone cared. I stood up.

"You didn't check my tires. The left rear leaks."

They glanced at each other. I thought I was going to get another ticket but they stared at me with twin scowls.

"Don't push it," the ticket writer said.

"I won't be able to if it's flat."

I left before they thought about booking me for bad jokes. I checked my watch under a streetlight. I had spent an hour with campus security. I thought about the sorority not phoning the city police. They probably looked on campus officers as faithful servants who'd accept their story without question and give me a hard time. The sisters undoubtedly put on a good show. It made a change from handing out tickets for parking violations. They wouldn't phone Grady. He'd ask why they hadn't transferred the call to 911.

He'd get a laugh out of the idea of me breaking into a sorority. Walking along the dark empty street back to my car I decided to make a second visit. I drove my car several blocks away, outside of the university boundary. As I walked back to the sorority I saw the meter readers looking for me. I had to duck behind a boulevard elm two blocks away from the sisters as the patrol car rolled by slowly. I waited before slipping from tree to tree till directly across from the house. There were a few parked cars, no pedestrian or road traffic. Dense cypress hedges almost hid the houses on either side. There were no fences and few gates on that street. After crossing, I hurried in a crouch within the shadow of a hedge until halfway down the lot and scuttled across to the side of the house. In the yellow disc of a spotlight I peered at my watch. It was half past nine. The cool air had dissipated the day's warmth. I looked the place over. The basement window was dark, the curtains drawn. The first and second floor windows were too high for a look. I drifted in the shadow to the back. The basement entrance was down a short flight of concrete stairs at a right angle to it. A flight of wooden stairs against the rear wall went up to a door on the first floor, likely to the kitchen. A light was on. I'd have chanced an alarm by going through the downstairs entrance, so I elected to eavesdrop upstairs. Hunched over, I crept up the steps. Creaks sounded like the cracking of a whip. The door had an old-fashioned lock with a keyhole, probably not used for decades. The deadbolt was higher up, close to a glass panel. Staying low, I stepped onto the porch and put my eye against the keyhole. At a wooden table two babes were seated in panties and blouses, bare feet up on the edge of their chairs. A bottle of wine cooler was on the table and tumblers half full of the cherry-coloured stuff. One of the sisters, a chubby blonde, scratched her crotch. The other was a redhead with dangerous curves. Her panties were barely there, with at most an inch of clearance. The blonde was nervous after their escapade.

"I can't sleep with that lock broken."

"Don't worry. The alarm is on. I put the chain screws back in. Tomorrow we'll get a locksmith to put in a new deadbolt."

"Think he'll come back?"

"I told the police we don't know him. That way we don't have to get involved. If he comes back we'll call again, say he's harassing us. They'll think he's some kind of pervert, which he probably is."

"Yeah. I'm tired. Going to bed. See you in the morning."

"I'll clean up."

The chubby one rubbed her eyes and gave herself an indifferent pat on the knees and left. The redhead put the bottle into the fridge and washed the tumblers in the sink. A phone on the counter rang and she picked it up. She walked around the kitchen, voice dropping almost to a whisper. I put my ear to the keyhole.

"Where you calling from? Already? Yeah. I took the lock off the door with a crowbar and screwdriver. Took out the screws at one end of the chain. I opened the door a wee bit. Didn't see me. I ran into the common room as Sterton called the police. The campus ones. They took him away. They don't know. I told them he's been phoning about some guy we know nothing about, and tonight he broke in because we wouldn't open the door. He knows I don't want to see him. He won't come back. They don't know. This is better than finding something in his office, because the police will be watching for him. As long as he stays away, right? I mean, he's not going to keep poking around forever. He does have to work. Somebody is going to hire him for something. Why, I couldn't guess. Quite the little prick. Like he knows everything. Sure, take care."

I put my eye to the keyhole in time to see her coming towards me. She pressed herself against the door, looking between the curtains in the glass panel. I couldn't move, an inch away from dark red pubic curls matted behind silky fabric and parting over the indented fold of her lips. If she had looked down, she'd have seen my hunched form under the porch light. She didn't. She turned, swinging away to some hidden song. There are rhythms and rhymes but that is the original. She switched off the kitchen light. I was staring into darkness. I crept down the stairs, revisiting all those creaks again. I hurried back to my car, avoiding the meter readers if they were still about. My lower back muscles were stiffening. I'd have to rub them when I got back to my apartment. I hoped I remembered to buy liniment on my last and long ago trip to a drugstore.

An hour later, rubbing my back with what I could coax out of a forgotten liniment bottle from the recesses of my medicine cabinet, I wondered about creeping up back stairs in the dark and peeping through keyholes at half-naked babes. Eddy did that kind of thing. I was a detective. The difference? He did my spying for me. I was a middleman between client and snoop. Eddy had all the latest technical equipment, the gadgets I never liked, the superminidigitalized stuff I'd rather spend money getting somebody else to use on what I thought was the dirty part of the job, peeking into bedrooms and toilets. He liked catching them in beds and gutters. I liked, or told myself I did, having people in trouble come to me for more personal service instead of going to the police. But that all came down to what they could afford. I was a glorified private cop pretending there was something important about not being on a payroll. But dirt is dirt on anybody's hands. I was a belt notch above welfare and getting tired of presuming to be anything except what I was, a hired spy. Her smell had come through the keyhole as she pressed herself against it, a sweetness far away, the girl I lost somewhere. I put the mouth of the bottle under my nose and sniffed raw sharpness, breathing in stagnant fumes of turpentine and ammonia.

I woke up in the night and knew. The old trout was there. A shadow near the surface. A shade darker than rippling lake water. If the light is right, a fish shape looms up larger than any thought. Still floater. And still in the boat or it's gone, dimpling the surface. The fly on the water a jittery flutter in a breeze. All in a breath. Caught.

The world restricts itself to what someone knows. Each person's reality is marked by different boundaries, things accepted or understood. In my line of business those boundaries reveal a workable truth. A liar never lies about love or hate. Those are the exceptions. And they'll give you away. Because they're so alike, one can be mistaken for the other. Search out the fixed point in someone's life. Person or idea, love or hate. Everything will come from that. It's looking at the sudden stranger. The face in the mirror.

Friday morning was hot for late April. Spring and fall don't exist on the prairies. You're reaching for your overcoat one day and taking off sweaty shirts the next. Time to unplug the engine heater on the car. You can almost sniff the dry heat coming. Months ago snow drifted down like tired confetti from a forgotten parade. It lay around till April, became chewed up brown slush on the roads, and under your boots the white stuff packs down, crunches, shifts like powdered sugar. There's a nowhere quality to these long prairie winters, as if the world is doing better things somewhere else while you're slouching along in minus forty weather feeling the windchill and trying to protect your ears and nose from frostbite. All you've got is the high pale reminder of a blue sky telling you how big a place you've gotten lost in together with runty trees and the patchy grass that never has a chance no matter how hardy it is. Forget the cowboy guff. The West was never tamed. The real West is the weather and parched soil that has a tough time growing anything except hard wheat and red potatoes. The rest is a high-priced dream of government-subsidized beef and pork. On dark nights when the freezing air stings in your lungs it's flatiron miles of freeze-dried fallow and stubble fields rigid as armour plate, and on the frozen pig farms and cattle ranches the breath from dumb animals gives up in steamy silence to the cast seed across the sky.

I didn't bother going to my office. I phoned the registrar's office at the university and said I was a close relative of Pim Pritchett and had to contact her on urgent family business. A secretary read out a list of her classes and times and locations of the final exams. Her last final was that afternoon at one. It was a two-hour exam. I was outside the lecture hall at two. She came out at three wearing jeans and a sweater. But her red hair and figure were unmistakable. I interrupted the flow of students and stepped in front of her. She knew who I was. I grinned.

"You'll have to see me. Sooner or later."

"I do not. You're bothering me."

"It's me or the police. Because I know."

"Know what?"

She knew what I meant. But she wasn't going to make things easy for me. She strutted away, a notebook and some printed papers in her hand. I followed her out of the building to a sidewalk that cut across a patch of lawn. It led to the library, an architectural cliché from the 1920s of a cross between an abbey and a castle. I kept after her, up a flight of broad stone stairs and through swinging oak doors between twin octagonal turrets into a fake Gothic entrance of flagstones and crisscrossed leaded windows, one on each side with the university crest set into them and others with bits of red and gold glass set at random, and a granite staircase rising between stone walls with niches all the way up with trophies and other mementoes dear to yore and lore. Instant tradition, the borrowed and bogus sitting on the windy plains and now surrounded by its own ninety-odd years of academic pretentiousness dressed up as medieval devotion. Vell, um, yes, moan stories, shivery, leg ends riding, stir up the blood of maid ends, through all the middling sages. In the entrance hall she stopped and turned, clenching notebook and papers. Her face was flushed.

"You going to keep following me?"

"Looks like it."

"You're a bastard."

"I'm a detective. Tell me. You know where. That's all I want."

"What are you going to do?"

"I don't know yet."

She stared as people passed, glancing at us. Maybe something in my face told her what she wanted to know. She gave me one of those sighs that are overdone by some women, unless you happen to like looking at women sighing. I do. And she was built for it, breast lift and all. She headed down a hallway to the left of the staircase. It led to a turnstile into the stacks on the main floor and branched left to reading rooms with special collections. She went into the Islington Room, named after a wealthy alumnus or donor or a dean or president or some other member of the long forgotten whose claim to immortality, bought or bestowed, was having a name on a wall. It was a big room with more leaded windows, high up on the west-facing wall, and wooden bookshelves lined the walls. At the far end, below the windows, was the checkout counter, behind which on grey metal shelves was the really important stuff, to be read or perused or photocopied on the spot by those privileged souls who did vital research. After a gander at some books, I realized we were in the headquarters of the prairie history industry. Here for devout scholars would be items such as manuscripts tied with ribbons and in faded inks of devotional and nature poetry from the unsettled minds of pioneer women, journals about surviving frontier life, cures for croup and catarrh, maps with "unexplored territory" and "wilderness" printed on their white expanses, lithographs of trading posts with natives in buckskin standing beside piles of beaver pelts while the factor offers them a metal comb or cast-iron pot, ledgers from those posts recording in detail all the sharp deals made with the heathen, and pencil sketches of Prairie City when it was a muddy village by a swampy river known to local natives as "that place for those which suck blood," and photographs of the early town showing a boardwalk fronting two blocks of hotels, hardware stores, saloons and stables, men standing in front in roughly cut dark coats and pants, calf-length boots, flat-brimmed hats and handlebar mustaches making them all appear the same age and giving the same look of stolid endurance. Men who knew how to move in and take over in the name of, and in return got sadistic winters and dust in their eyes as summer. But whatever interest any of this had now had been killed off by the academese in the tomes gathered religiously there. Nobody read this dead prose embalmed in facts except graduate students, whose inglorious task was to add more of the selfsame to those shelves.

I followed the sorority princess across the pale grey floor tiles to an empty table, the varnished honey oak reflecting the light. There were chairs on the long sides. Half of the tables were occupied by readers and notetakers in the benign silence that usually gathers around lots of books. She dropped her papers and notebook with enough ceremony to announce her presence without distracting the really dedicated bookworms blind to tight curves in cotton. We sat across from each other. She tore a page out of the notebook, scribbled on it and tossed it with an insouciant flick of her wrist. I read it and shook my head.

"This isn't a trick, is it? Be a long way to go for nothing."

"Have to trust me, won't you?"

She gave me what she thought was a seductively provocative smile but it was a schoolgirl simper. She hadn't learned, probably never would, that if you're a woman with a figure and enough looks to get looks, the best performance is not to perform.

"Don't enjoy this too much," I said, "or you might get to hate me."

"I couldn't be bothered."

She was getting her own back as cheaply as she could. I didn't mind. I'd gotten what I wanted. I folded the sheet and tucked it into my inside jacket pocket. I glanced at the soundless academic industry going on around us. It wasn't worth a thought. Something else was.

"You look great in panties. There's a hole you forgot to cover."

She blushed. That's one of the fascinating things about women. You can never know which way they're going to jump, onto your bones or into your bed. Expect one and sometimes you get the other. What disgusts them about guys are the disgusting things that go into making a male. But what they can find to like is a cockeyed mystery except to female hormones. They're in the gift-giving business, with drawstrings attached, and we're in the longest lineup of our lives. Some of us get out of it for a while and then find ourselves at the end of the line again. She was fighting that sorority brain of hers. Her eyes focused on me. Tired grey eyes. Exam prep or wine cooler.

"How old are you?"

"Too old to play doctor."

"You mean with me? Forget it. You must be way over forty. Sorry, gramps."

Her look promised a shared milkshake in the stacks, against the shelves. But the words were as crude as she could say them. Women will never admit they've offered anything, or even thought of offering, after you've gone and nipped it in the bud. She was meant to put some poor bastard through his paces. She stood up, giving her breasts a shake in their thin angora and cotton upholstery. That was in case I had galloping glaucoma. She turned and gave her keester an extra bit of wiggle leaving the room. That was supposed to be filed unforgettably in my memory bank for all the sleepless nights I'd have yearning for her. I laughed. She broke wiggle, stalking off, and a dozen heads turned my way because I had broken their concentration on the archival scrapings of prairie life.

I drove to my office and booked a flight to the coast for Saturday. A store owner who'd been robbed many times came in late in the afternoon. I looked his place over, a corner grocery a couple of blocks from the office. He'd put steel shutters on the windows and bars on the door but they hadn't discouraged thieves. I told him to put a dog with a loud bark inside the store when he locked up and to leave the lights on. Crooks I have known (sounds like a bad title for an autobiography) have told me that light and noise bother them most and barking is the worst. Give them a hard time and they'll move on to something easier.

On Saturday afternoon I was looking down at the Rockies on a sunny day. A gigantic blue wave heaving up and turned to stone, a froth of snow on the crest. The lesser chains followed, and lakes between like trenches flooded with molten silver, scratches of river and a patchwork quilt of green and brown orchards and farmland. Half an hour later I was on the coast at sea level and breathing moist heavier air. I took an airport bus into the city. I saw again the mountains plunging to the shoreline and freighters lined up in a blue harbour waiting to be loaded at grain elevators. But it was simply another city, more crowded than the one I had left, with more cars, people, pollution and mindless expansion. The downtown skyline was nothing but office towers and apartment buildings. The scenery and mild climate had only guaranteed a faster trip down the sewer. I walked to the bus depot and caught one for the trip up the coast highway to the ferry terminal for the five o'clock sailing.

I was headed for the Gulf Islands, one of the larger ones. I'd sailed coastal waters years earlier but never stopped at any of the islands. A friend of mine, a retired newspaper reporter, had moved to one of them with his wife but they weren't where I was going. Pim Pritchett had written four words on that sheet of paper, the name of an island and the name of a commune. Out-of-the-way places have always been popular with communes. Less public attention, whatever their purpose is. End-of-the-world types searching for a handy cave, unemployed psychopaths with axes to grind, deliverers with irons in the fire looking to get extra tail from women who'll put out for a living icon, holy rollings in the hay, cravings as yearnings sanctified by self-anointed messengers from God. Loonies with a touch of the con who need to get away from accepted social practices so they can act out their customized hyperventilated bolt-from-the-blue schemes with those who have to believe in somebody else because they can't believe in themselves. Neurotics led by messiahs. Those who need a world with gaudier trimmings and don't want the facts to contradict their view. And occasionally a small group who leave urban suffocation to make a few clay pots and do some beadwork while they wriggle their toes in the grass.

The trip up the jammed coastal highway skirted beachside and shoreline communities. They burgeoned in a hectic construction that would finally make the area a single elongated constriction squeezed between gulf and mountains. Where there had been old-growth forest and clear streams there were clear-cuts and mudslides. From rising skeletons of housing tracts growled the diesels of dump trucks, bulldozers and backhoes. It was a realtor's dream. In the fifteen years since I'd driven, hiked and sailed along the coast it had been ruined. After a while I closed my eyes and kept them closed until the terminal.

We arrived with five minutes to spare. I bought my ticket, went aboard and up to the passenger deck to watch a declining sun drop a spoke of white sparks along the harbour water. I was well forward, leaning against the railing to avoid diesel exhaust from the funnel. We left a couple of minutes after five. The fat-bellied car ferry rode the light chop like a bathtub. A light breeze swept the warmth of the day away, reminding me this was the Pacific Northwest, where temperate is the usual word for weather. Most of the passengers stayed in their cars, oblivious to the maritime scenery slipping by. A roar from the diesel and the shore and dock drifted away and became blurs. Seagulls followed in our wake, crying as they swerved on sharp-angled wings. This wasn't the open sea. There were distant mountains ahead and scraps of island off our fast-moving sides, all dimming with the first hints of evening.

I concentrated on scenery, keeping myself from thinking about the end of the trip. I didn't know what I was going to do except get there. It was partly a matter of professional pride, of knowing something and finishing it. Beyond that the mathematics of reason didn't go. Something else took over, spoke from the blood. I would have to answer. I looked at the darkening water around me.

One of the lumps on the horizon gradually became a mass. In the early twilight it stood out against a milky blue sky. The breeze had cooled, hit my face like light slaps of a damp towel. A line of pilings became a loading pier. A ramp descended from the end of it. Buildings were clustered behind. The diesel gave a final roar. The ferry made a sweeping curve towards the pier, gliding in silently. A few minutes later I was carrying my suitcase up the side of the wooden ramp as cars thumped past me. At the top I hesitated and glanced back at the ferry, a giant beached dogfish vomiting vehicles from its gaping mouth. I looked away and walked towards the buildings.

They turned out to be a village. There was a hotel with a pub serving a good ale made on the island. I paid for a room for two nights in that overgrown Tudor-style cottage and asked balloonman squeezed behind the reception desk where the commune was. Pursing his puffy lips, he looked like a self-inflating lemon. Bringing up the commune was showing bad taste.

"You want to go to that place?"

"That's why I asked."

"They're unusual. Keep to themselves. Lots of rumours about them. We think it's one of those cults."

"Who's 'we'?"

"Everyone in Frith."

"Ith thith Frith?"

"I beg your pardon?"

"Thith playth. Ith thith Frith?"

"Are you trying to make fun of uth, us, sir?"

"Perith the thought. I wuth juth thinking, if thith ith Frith, then theeth muth be Frithianth I thee thurrounding me. Obtherve the moon thith evening. There ith thur to be thum thkulduggery afoot."

I picked up the room key before bloated and bigoted could take it back. I went upstairs and unpacked. I came down, ordered a ploughman's lunch and a bottle of ale in the pub. It was a tidy room through an archway to the right of the reception desk, varnished maple panelling on the walls and a few small round oak tables with straight-backed chairs, a bar long enough for two serving platters and behind it a door to the kitchen. The bartender, a skinny guy with vague eyes, asked what I ordered.

"Cheese, bread and an onion. It's a traditional English lunch for farmhands."

"It's not lunchtime," he said and brought me a cheese sandwich and the ale. It tasted like good English brown ale but the sandwich was a plastic slice of bilious yellow with a metallic aftertaste between bleached slices of elastic ersatz-bread. I was hungry and used the ale to kill what taste the garbage had. I waved him over and ordered another bottle and asked where the commune was. He chewed on that for a while.

"Commune? Few miles northwest of here, I think. There's a dirt road goes out that way. Might get a lift if you're lucky. I doubt it, though."

"Why?"

"People around here don't have much to do with it." He put the empty on his platter and walked away.

I drank the ale and went up to my room. I lay on the bed, thought about people being strangers in their own country. Being different is breaking the first rule, be like everybody else. It's the big fear, not being accepted or acceptable, that keeps conformists in line. Few make the distinction between the outsider and the psychopath, the outspoken critic and the fanatical subversive. This pontificating kept me from thinking about why I was there. Boring yourself to sleep works as well as most other ways and there's no hangover. Builds up your self-esteem. You can be your own philosopher, take on any subject or question you wish. Nothing is too hard. And there's not a single expert authority academic scholar pundit intellectual deep thinker around to say, a rather simplistic analysis overall, don't you think? I don't think comma I know period oar wood half if eyed bean a loud to bye think curse ur wood ewe cud ewe eve heir image gin a think period holy err thane thou sitz wurst cum ink ass toil et paper a plies to you ill tide turkeyshits damn colon get up po knees.

On Sunday morning I had boiled eggs with toast in the pub. It doubled as a dining room till seven at night. Other patrons included a couple who looked as if everybody should be interested in their dirty weekend. There was another couple, with noisy brats that kept running around the room and hollering. Their mother made an obviously public show of trying to quiet them, more interested in looking like a victim of outraged patience. The beginning of the tourist-trap season, a mustard-stained napkin blown along an empty beach. I was wearing a gink getup for the walk, courtesy of Eddy: windbreaker, checked sports shirt, baggy khaki pants, tan walking shoes. I finished eating and went outside into the sunshine and felt early May in a warm breeze blowing away the last of winter dampness. I ambled through Frith, four gravel-paved blocks of stores, houses and a garage with a gas pump. At the end was a church and there a dirt road went northwest and I started walking. Blackberry vines as thick as woven baskets grew at the sides of the road. Further in were the interarching fronds of giant ferns and behind them stands of spruce and hemlock. In the next half hour two kids on dirt bikes passed and a four-wheel drive and then a creaking pickup truck. The pickup stopped in its dusty wake. When I was level with it I heard the driver's voice.

"You want a lift?"

I glanced into the cab. The driver looked in his late twenties, hair thinning, a touch of red in his tanned face. I thanked him, went around to the passenger side and got in. Bench seat, metal dashboard, AM radio, miles per hour marked on the round speedometer, side vent windows with chromed latches, knob on the steering wheel, two-piece windshield divided by a vertical strip, and floor shift with a crook in it. The old beast had undoubtedly seen a lot of scavenged parts go under the hood.

"Where are you going?" he asked as he shifted into gear and we moved off. The speedometer needle kept guessing within ten miles of the correct speed.

"I'm trying to get to a commune somewhere in this area."

"That's us. Island Earth."

The next question was obvious but he didn't ask it. The old leaf springs and solid axles bounced us around as we passed dense forest. The trees gradually thinned away to hills covered in bush and occasionally some open grassland. The commune was further away than the bartender had told me. It would have taken hours to walk there and get back without a ride. I had imagined a pastoral, comfortable semirural isolation, but the distance and separation were more than I thought they would be. Real time, solid things. The further I got from the village the less I cared about anything except the next stop.

He turned off into grassland. We rode bumpily in two ruts. I rolled down the window, put my arm out and held onto the door. We wobbled down a hill into an area of orchards and tilled land, with eleven buildings in a cluster on one side of the fields. Kids were playing near a cabin. Adults worked in the fields. I saw her among them. I got out before the truck stopped. I crossed weedy grass, stepped onto the tilled earth and between a double row of plants to within several feet of her. It was early in the season and the plants were small. She wore a white T-shirt, bib overalls, straw sunhat and had gathered her hair in long braids. She was barefoot and kneeling, picking weeds. She stopped and frowned before she looked up. He had come up behind me, spoke to her before I could.

"Anything wrong, Thela?"

"It's all right. I know him."

I didn't turn around. He left and she stood up, not bitter, not even angry. But the frown stayed. We took time getting used to the situation. She waited and I spoke.

"This doesn't change anything. No one can touch you. But I couldn't let you think I was that dense. I'd like to know so I can feel better about walking away."

I took off my windbreaker and unbuttoned my shirt to the waist and rolled up the sleeves.

"No recorders or minicameras. I never liked using those damn things, anyway. Nobody knows I'm here. Sooner or later, you're going to have to trust a man."

"I trust the guys here." Tears began welling up and she blinked.

"I'm with you. I had a set-to with the manager of the village inn. Prejudice gratis with your room. He thinks you're all demons in overalls."

"Oh, them." She grinned.

"Frith, for all those who want island life in a cornflakes box. It's a supermarket world. Everything is in our ad. And you thought you left the mainland."

"You believe that?"

"I've always had a hard time believing what I'm told. That's why I'm poor.

Think your own thoughts and you'll never have enough to spend. The world can do without my kind. I'm not a good consumer."

"You love me, don't you?"

A woman will always get to the point when it comes to that subject, philosophizing self-analysis and socio-economic criticism be damned. I stood in the pillory, condemned, had talked too much.

"I love what you are."

"What's the difference?"

"Not much. You can trust one more than the other."

"I'm supposed to trust you?"

"No one will know."

"You want me to trust your love."

"You're a stubborn girl. Yeah."

Her grin widened. But it wasn't a smile. I buttoned my shirt and slung the windbreaker over my shoulder. The windbreaker looked better that way. I left my sleeves rolled up. They looked better, too. I could feel the sun on my back. I glanced at my watch. It was almost eleven. I probably had arrived with the first warm spell of the year and what must have been a rare cloudless spring day on that island.

"I've finished here."

She stood up and began walking towards me. I made way for her between the rows and followed. I watched her bare feet as they patted the cocoa-coloured soil worn smooth by others. Her heels and toes stuck out from the frayed denim. Easy steps, slow from heel to ball and toes, letting naked contact reassure her. Brown soles the earth's footprint on her. She had found a way to grow out of the filth of her past and become her own plant on that collective. Pink-toed beauty in the dirt, the tread of a novice.

She headed across patchy grass towards a windowless squat building, a root cellar or storehouse. She took the hook on the door out of an eyebolt screwed into the frame and pushed the door open, stepping into the dimness inside. She came out in a few seconds holding a jar of dill pickles and refastened the hook. She came over to me.

"Do you want something to eat?"

"No, thanks. I came to talk."

"I'll show you where we eat."

She led the way to another building, of unpainted wood like all the others. This one had windows and a short flight of stairs up to a porch. Inside was a large square room with a cast-iron stove, a sink built into a counter, a pantry and two long tables with benches. The tables and benches were red cedar. The ceiling, walls and floor were unfinished fir.

"This is the kitchen," she said and took off her sunhat and put it on a bench, so I sat there. She put the jar on the table and washed her hands and face at the sink, using a pitcher of water, and went into the pantry and came out with a wooden bowl, a bread knife, a round loaf of wholewheat bread and something wrapped in brown paper. She sat across from me, unscrewed the jar, took out a pickle and unwrapped the brown paper. Inside was a large block of cheese. She cut two slices of the bread, a chunk of cheese, sliced the dill, placed everything in the bowl and made the messiest sandwich I ever saw.

"Where's the onion," I said and explained about the ploughman's lunch.

"I'll have to try it. You should try this cheese. It's made from raw milk from their cows. They don't pasteurize their milk."

"Isn't that against the law? Or is selling it illegal?"

She pouted for a second. She tore the large sandwich in half. A tidy eater, two fingers and slow. A shred of pickle skin clung to her lower lip.

I cut a small piece of the cream-coloured cheese and sampled it. Made all the other cheese I'd ever eaten taste like malleable plastic.

"This is good. How did you find out about this place?"

"The same way you did."

"Don't blame her. I threatened her with the law if she didn't tell. Pestered her. How long have you been here?"

"Three days. Packed up Tuesday night. Gave my laptop and phone to Pim. Got here Thursday and phoned from the village gas station. Was lucky. Hitched a ride with a couple who have a farm nearby. They know Stuart and introduced us."

She finished eating, wrapped up the cheese and took everything away. As she was sitting down again a boy and a girl climbed up the porch stairs on their hands and knees. They edged inside the open doorway, eyeing me suspiciously. She went into the pantry, carried out an enormous earthenware jar and called them over to the sink and washed their hands. She took out two cookies the size of a CD and handed them to pleading fingers. Embracing their cookies, the kids didn't take their eyes off me till they were outside. She came over and sat down, took the elastic bands off her braids and shook the interwoven strands of her hair loose. Two glasses of sparkling champagne flowing together.

"Did you have to do that? I'll forget what I'm here for."

"You're a sensitive man."

"You're the girl who can't be touched."

"Aren't we a crazy combination?"

"There have been crazier ones."

"Was anybody murdered?"

"You tell me."

"It was an accident."

"Which one?"

"Ivan, of course."

She looked at me as if I should have known. She remembered with the obviating certainty of memory.

"He said he wanted to see me once more, to say goodbye. He was going back East soon and was arranging a financial settlement with Wanda. They were going to get a divorce. He wanted to talk about what he was giving me. When I got there he put on this stupid romantic music. He sat beside me on the sofa. He said he wanted to marry me. He couldn't live without me. I laughed. I said that I'd never marry him, didn't love him. Did he think I'd forgotten the past? He got up, said he had to show me something and went into the bedroom. He came out with a gun and said he'd kill himself and me if I didn't agree. He sat down and put the gun against my breast. Is this how you want to die? I wasn't so much afraid to die as I didn't like the idea he of all people was going to kill me. Pretending to think it over, I grabbed the gun and elbowed him in the face. I was off balance. We fell onto the floor. The gun went off. I got up and saw him on the carpet with a hole in his forehead.

I knew he was dead. I didn't know what to do. I kept staring at him lying there with his mouth open. A thin line of blood was trickling down his cheek. I phoned Wanda and told her. She sent Mel, her boyfriend, over. We'll take the gun, so it'll look like a robber broke in and killed him, he said. There wouldn't be any trouble with the police or Ivan's family. I was in shock, couldn't say anything. He wiped things to make sure we didn't leave any fingerprints. He said not to tell anybody and that I'd be getting money from the estate. I said I didn't care. Sure, he said, as if I was lying. He grabbed my ass. I flipped him onto the carpet. He looked surprised but kept his smile on. We've got to stay friends, he said. He said I was a spoiled brat. Touch me again and I'll break your arm, I said. I knew I'd made a mistake, shouldn't have called them, and they'd make me pay."

"You're not the only one. Joanne Ackermann committed suicide."

"Suicide?" I got her biggest stare.

"I went to see her about those photos I showed you. Told me she killed him. I didn't go for that. She acted as if she was covering up for Wanda Regine's porker."

"Porker? Oh, you mean Mel. You saying they were lovers? So that's how she knew Ivan."

"According to her, he convinced her to dress up like a student and play all around the mulberry bush with your stepdaddy because he had a weak heart and sex would kill him, so he'd have no chance of going through with his plan to fire him. She went for it. And professors are said to have functioning brains. He didn't conveniently drop dead, despite her best efforts at playing academic super hooker. Stoker came up with a second plan, bald and bestial supposedly being afraid of guns. He wouldn't cooperate this time either, thought she was playing games. A supposedly unloaded gun with the safety catch still on went off and plinked him. Maybe after I questioned this idiocy the prof decided that stupidity plus debasement eliminated her from any possible consideration other than non compos mentis. She sentenced herself, her crime, being smitten with and double-crossed by a salesman who turned out to be not her true love but somebody else's bed pal. She never did find out what happened in the apartment."

"I told you what happened. Don't you believe me?"

"I know the prof didn't touch any gun. It belonged to heavy-breathing and hairless. He wouldn't, maybe couldn't let go. And you shot him, deliberately."

Her stare wasn't as big this time.

"He must have done something to set you off, get you so that you'd want to kill him instead of step on his bones. Sex or money is usually the motive. But the first is obviously out and the second doesn't fit. You're not the money type. All you did was make your stepmother wealthy. It's something else, isn't it? Took me a while to figure all of it out. Stripping in front of me in Ordway Hall, touching me on the arm in the basement suite. Stomping on Ivan the Oleaginous. Going up to see him when he called, even though you knew his phony moves. Bouncing around Stoker. Undoing your hair now. And you got the reaction you wanted. Making out I overreacted. I'm about as sensitive as a mud turtle. I love gorgeous babes and you know that. But you're not interested in anything happening. You want me to want you and that's the limit. You're damaged goods, courtesy of Ivan the Egregious. You're dead to sex but you get yourself hot by getting a guy hot, then saying sorry. You're a make-work project for any halfwit psychiatrist. I don't think you could be very dangerous out here among the sods and pods. That's only an opinion. Unqualified Quester, the opinionated detective. Between us, why did you kill the bastard?"

She tilted her head to one side and gazed at me, a new perspective in her eyes. She blinked and didn't see me any more. Her gaze went somewhere else. Her voice became distant.

"I waited till he took the barrel away from my nipple. The danger made me crazy. I'd never felt like that before, like I wanted to scream. Before it was teasing, stripping, showing myself. This was exciting, my nerves sizzled. I got up and started to take off my clothes. I knew what was going to happen. I saw it all but it wasn't me. He put the gun on the sofa. I was naked, melting lava oozing down from my belly out of my lips. I was swollen, hollow hot. Itching, heat like a wonderful torture. He was watching, his mouth open. He put his arms out and I went to him. All the hate was like a liberation. I saw myself pick up the gun and squeeze the trigger with both hands. I heard a noise, something fell. I looked down and he was on the floor, his mouth still open and one of his hands caught between sofa cushions. I saw what I was holding and threw it away. I felt wet between my legs. I looked and saw blood. My period had started."

She put her arms on the table, crossed them and laid her head down. Hair fell across her cheek and her mouth. I got up and walked to the doorway. On the porch a cat stopped licking itself and stared at me. Observer and observed, easily changed. I surveyed my surroundings. An almost flat fifty acres, the commune lay at the bottom of a circle of wooded hills. All fallow or planted acreage except for peripheral bush and two orchards. Most likely a creek from up in the hills supplied water for drinking and irrigation. The buildings were within two hundred yards of the fields. There were nine besides the storehouse and kitchen. One was a smaller version of the storehouse, probably a toolshed. The others were cottages, if you're inclined to the picturesque, cabins if you're rustic. All doors were shut. There was no one around now, even in the fields. According to my watch, it was seven minutes after twelve. Lunchtime, and the only one in the kitchen was sleeping cutie. I thought maybe this had something to do with me. She'd had no time to tell them anything. But they could think I meant trouble. She might have said enough already so they'd help in case anyone bothersome came along.

A door opened in one of the cabins and they walked towards me. Leading them was the guy who'd driven me out there. They used a footpath between clumps of dandelions and tufted grass spiny as sea urchins. There were four women and four men, all in their mid or late twenties, and five children, including two babes in arms, both snoozing. West Coast eco-militia, unbeknownst to the beholden the puritanical holding the fort in the rainforest, planting soggy ideals in acidic soil. The leader walked up the stairs and looked in at sleeping bootless. He decided everything was all right and introduced himself as Stuart Dumfries. He said he'd not done so earlier because he didn't know why I'd come. I thought about that. Told me they sometimes held a noon conference to discuss commune affairs. I thought about that, too. He introduced the other adults as they went into the kitchen. They were all paired. His wife, skinny and hair clipped, was born to be a fanatic so she could condemn the rest of the world. She looked at me as if I'd brought the plague. Two of the other guys were save-the-earthworm extremists with slightly mad eyes. Their consorts were obligingly homely. The remaining guy was a gangly Aussie. He wore a knitted woollen cap, had ears made for hanging boomerangs on plus an accent from the outback among the 'roos. His sheila had a pigtail and big eyes and wore jeans fraying into glimpses. Her accent was like her walk, cute.

Dumfries and I stayed outside and talked. We could hear stove lids and grate hinges and somebody making a fire and pots and frying pans being banged around inside. His group looked below strength. I asked him where the rest of his cohorts were. He said four families had decamped that winter, dissatisfied with life in the commune. A rainy spring delayed planting last year and a cool summer produced small crops. Two and a half years of chopping wood and making candles and soap and living on fruits and vegetables proved too much. Buying wheat and rye flour, rice and oats in the village and getting a couple of cows from a local farm hadn't been enough to satisfy them. He said it was better getting rid of the halfhearted than ruining the commune's purpose. Which was? To live with the fewest possible demands on nature and to reject modern technology. What about human nature? It's been perverted, he said, from its true purpose of living harmoniously with the environment. What about the truck and the store clothes? Temporary concessions, he said, until they were self-sufficient. He outlined the commune's background and origin as food smells and assorted voices drifted out to us. His great-grandfather had come from Scotland in the 1870s. He became one of the early timber barons, with a logging company, sawmills and a pulp mill. A clear-cut raper of public land, he gave backhanders to politicians for logging rights on choice tracts. His descendants had bought land along the coast and in the islands for speculation. It was all sold now except for two island properties, one used as the family's summer resort on another island and fifty acres here. They were slated for sale, but Dumfries convinced his father to let him have them. In return, he had gladly given up any further claim on the family estate. For the sins of Angus, the old Scot, there would be an overdue atonement. And through that an organic social revivification, a moral renaissance hearkening back to native ways.

"Sounds drastic," I said.

"It'll come in time."

"Even if nobody wants it except you?"

"People have to be shown the right way."

"Must be quite an honour."

"Do you like the way things are going?"

"Nobody ever likes the way things are going. But they seem to go that way."

"You're a fatalist."

"I'm a believer in humanity because I have to be. There's nothing else. It's a long trip, so hang on. But nobody tells me what to think, least of all reformers who say they know what no one else can figure out."

"We don't preach. We're an example that more and more are going to follow. They're going to because society is nothing but selfishness and nobody is getting anywhere. Things do change. Because of income and property taxes and servants' wages, my family's mansion in our fair capital city is now a restaurant."

"It must be murder putting on a tux by yourself."

"Why did you come here?"

Nice sense of logical progression, this guy. An infant woke up and began to cry. A mother's soothing words followed. Somebody dropped a pot.

"That's for her to say."

"Have you finished your business?"

I shook my head. He looked into the kitchen.

"Thela came to us a few days ago, fitted right in. She's a good worker. I've talked with her and she believes in our ideas. You're welcome to stay tonight. There's plenty of empty cabins."

He allowed himself a grin, a small one. I accepted the invitation, not knowing how long it would take to get all of the truth. Getting to and from the village would have been brutal.

Dumfries' wife came out and told us lunch was ready. I accepted another invitation. Insubordinate stomach. We went in and I took my seat, figuratively speaking, next to Thela Crammond. She was smiling, looked rested and didn't have the demeanour of someone who'd admitted an hour ago that she'd committed murder. But I expected now what I saw. On the other side of the table and directly across from her sat the Aussie, still wearing the cap, earflaps up. He also sported fingerless woollen gloves of the same pale blue. Narrow face to a pointed chin, dirty complexion (or was it dirt?), diluted eyes, pinprick pupils, smirk of a permanent adolescent, brain on hold forever. Specimen of agro-worker, ecology style.

On the menu that afternoon was a salad of dandelion greens with mushrooms and beans and rice in a sauce using their own sun-dried tomatoes. There were chunks of butter heaped onto butter dishes and round loaves of sourdough bread. The cutlery and plate were Harbour Mission, with a few heirloom pieces. The adults sat at one table and kids and nursing mothers at the other. They turned out to be the wives of the earthworms. Nobody said much, probably because I was there. Everybody pretended the food tasted yummy, as if a parental hand was ready to slap if they didn't eat it all. Wilted greens, mushrooms smelling like mouldy sponges, runny sauce reminiscent of watery ketchup, and beans and rice tasting the way they always do, pasty. The butter was fresh. But the bread was stale. They seemed to be mortifying themselves with bad cooking, ruining good ingredients. Self-flagellation with forks, immolation in frying pans, impalement on a serrated edge. They wanted to be culinary martyrs and endure the punishment. But I was hungry and my act was almost as good, butter my lips.

The Aussie didn't take off his gloves. He kept looking Thela Crammond's way with a feral fix. He ate without ever quite closing his mouth. In what conversation there was, his sheila mentioned taking an agricultural degree down under. She must have picked him out of a holding pen for the incurably arboreal. He was friendly, the friendliness of somebody who thinks no one can see what he's trying to pull off, which were Thela Crammond's panties. He obviously didn't know anything about her and she ignored him. His mate was the best looking of the consorts but sometimes that doesn't mean much.

Lunch broke up after one. The kids left, began playing outside, and the infants were burped and carried away. The rest discussed chores for a while but I suspected it was for my sake. I was an intruder, and like a lot of self-isolating reformist groups they had the collective consciousness of an ant colony. I kept an eye on Thela Crammond. She was cleaning the tables, the zealous convert trying to please. I needed to get her alone. The offer of a night's rest in that asylum for the purely pure, while not to be belittled, didn't give me much more time. Not for what I'd come to find out. The others drifted away and we were alone. During lunch she hadn't said much. She hadn't been in on any chore discussions. She wasn't one of the blessed yet. They let her do odd jobs, like tidying up the kitchen. I couldn't decide if she liked it there or it was a temporary refuge. She came out of the pantry, classic stray hair down one side of her face. She flicked it away with a shake of her head. Most women would have managed to look awkward. Her move was for connoisseurs. It had me staring. No matter where or what, she would always have that.

"Let's go for a walk," I said.

I picked up my windbreaker and slung it over my shoulder. She led the way down the stairs and around the back of the fields. The door of the toolshed was open and somebody inside was hammering. Two women were hoeing out in a field. A grassy incline on the far side of the fields led down to an orchard. She headed for it. On the way I saw what looked like a wooden garage with double doors. It was at the bottom of the incline. I hadn't seen it from the truck or the kitchen porch. I asked about it.

"It's the cow barn, and there they are."

A couple of Holsteins grazing further down the slope didn't pay any attention to us till we were fairly close, then casually lifted and swung their boxy heads our way and gave us an unhurried look with dark glossy eyes the size of boiled eggs. They winched their heads away, lowered them and went back to mowing the meadow. A calf was close by each cow. Where was the bull?

"Stuart told me they reached an agreement with a farmer on the other side of the island. The farmer has a herd of cows and a bull and they bought these cows from him and had them serviced. They plan to have a herd of four. They'll sell the extras."

The orchard was a double row of pear and apple trees among tufted grass and wild flowers. She touched some budding leaves on a pear tree and sat under its arching fountain of branches, her back against the scaly grey trunk splotched with lichens. An occasional breeze made the leaves quiver. I sat down a few feet away. The ground was warm under the early afternoon sun, the broadleaved grass a comfortable cushion. I looked at her. Her eyes were closed. A streak of sunlight through the branches brought out a candy floss red fluorescence in the spun gold on the crown and right side of her hair, lit up fuzz on the question mark of her ear and made a halo of it along a soft cheek.

"I know you love me," she said.

"I thought we'd covered that."

She opened her eyes and gazed at me.

"I phoned Wanda afterwards. Mel came and said and did everything I told you. He put your card in Ivan's wallet, said that was Wanda's idea. The police would find it. If you said anything bad about Wanda, she'd say you had gone to see Ivan on your own and probably tried to make some deal with him. Sell him the photographs, or something like that. Mel grabbed me and I flipped him and he said I'd better get friendly or else he'd tell the police everything. You're an accessory now, I said. There aren't any witnesses, he said. Then it's my word against yours, I said. Don't forget, you phoned your stepmother. It's our word against yours. She won't want to hear about you going after me, I said. You think she'd believe you? Think it over, honey. It's me or prison. After that slob it'll be a pleasure for you to go to bed with a real man. Touch me again and I'll kill you, I told him. He didn't do anything and we left. Later he started phoning the basement suite. Meet me or it's the police. I hung up every time.

"After a while I didn't hear from him. Until he phoned and said you called. Said you knew what happened and he had to meet you at the bottom of the path that goes from the hotel to the river. He said he'd tell you about me if I didn't see him that afternoon. I thought he'd force you to go to the police, threaten you with withholding evidence from them. He sounded scared, as if you were going to get him. I thought that meant Professor Ackermann was involved. But I didn't know how and hadn't heard she committed suicide. I said all right and we agreed to meet at five at the sorority house. I went there right away and told Pim. Not everything, but almost. Pim said they would hide me once I got rid of him. When he got there I was alone, she was in the kitchen, there wasn't anybody else around. But he said we had to talk privately, so I took him up to my old room. As I shut the door he grabbed me and started tearing my clothes off. I tried to knee him in the crotch but I was way off balance. I yelled and Pim came running in. She had a .22 everybody knew about that had been her brother's. She was holding it. Said she would shoot him if he didn't let me go. I was half-naked, he'd torn my blouse off and scratched my breasts. I felt blood dripping from my nose. He must have hit it. I felt a corner of the bed in my back. She kept hollering but he was crazy. I finally got a hand loose and kept punching him. He fell off me and I stood up. Pim was swearing and shaking. The .22 was bobbing up and down. I went over and took it off her. He got up and his face was swollen from being hit. You fucking bitch, he yelled. He came at me. I shot, didn't bother to aim, and he fell down. Pim was still shaking. I wanted to cut his head off and throw it out of the window. But that passed and I went over to her and we hugged. She wasn't trembling any more. We looked at the body and could see he was dead. You know how two people can get the same idea at once? We agreed the best thing to do was take it to the river, where you'd find it and tell the police. We carried him in a sleeping bag to her car. Drove to the south side of the river. There's nothing there but bushes. We're both pretty strong, so it wasn't hard carrying him down the hill there. The river isn't more than chest high, so we towed the sleeping bag across and pulled him out and propped him against the bank. We took longer than we planned because through the bushes I saw you coming down the path. We hurried across the river and I shot so you'd have to duck and wouldn't see us climbing back up the hill. I saw you dive into the water. I tried to shoot high."

"You didn't shoot that high."

"I'm not a good shot."

"Two bullseyes isn't bad."

"What are you going to do?"

"You killed under duress and provocation. Strictly speaking, there should be charges, court appearances and a psychiatric examination. There should be lots of things, strictly speaking. But there won't be. The shrinks and case workers wouldn't do you any good. Prison would destroy you, in the unlikely event you went there. You've had enough punishment. Hope you can work things out."

"You going back today?"

"I'm spending the night here."

"You're not such a bad guy, you know." She smiled.

"They treat you well?"

She nodded.

"Stuart is Pim's cousin. She told me to tell him I'd dropped out of university, wanted to get away from society. Said his family doesn't have much to do with him. Said he's got some weird ideas but he's a good guy. She got to know him when her family went on vacation years ago to his family's resort in one of these islands. She knew about the commune. She phoned his father and found out where it was. Told his father she was doing research."

"She managed to squelch the investigation."

"Pim's family is rich. Her father is on the board of directors of several corporations. He's involved in politics. She said he'd fix everything."

The breeze picked up and the light played across her face. Strands of hair blew over her eyes and fell away, a broken blonde cobweb. She closed her eyes. Her smell came to me. I'd seen her naked, sat next to her. But scrubbed, soapy clean to the cavities. Soap takes away something besides dirt and oil. The natural odour of flesh, chemistry and hormones. It's the sexiest perfume and the most delicate. The tiniest excess of dirt or body oil ruins it. Sour sweat, a rancid gaminess. Any woman like any man can stink, and some women when they're clean smell domestic or don't have an odour, but some exude a fragrance. And she was one. She'd know at that moment I smelled her. Not easy to think, especially about a woman whose armoury includes her knees and her forearms and guns left lying around. Nobody tells all the truth. But there are better versions of it. Like mine. Her version wasn't as good. I'd considered that along with those inevitable mitigating or exculpatory or somehow extenuating circumstances. But one thing had to be cleared up before I left.

"There's something I don't understand."

"What?" Her eyes were still closed.

"Why he didn't desist when you had company. No man can go through with a rape when there's an enraged woman standing by with a gun and threatening to blow his balls off."

"He went crazy, I guess."

"He'd made a good career out of looking after himself. He wouldn't risk becoming a soprano."

She smiled and raised her head towards the sky but kept her eyes closed.

"I smell like popcorn."

"Hold the salt."

"You really do smell me."

"Up in the balcony, among the darkened seats. But that's my lost youth. We're going to finish this. I want all the truth."

Nice scene. Detective in gink clothes under the swaying boughs. Ass on the grass. Trying to pin down a flirt fatale who'd had enough of the tight fantastic and written her own escape clause twice.

"A salesman's dream, finally making the big commission. But you were the one who suggested going up to the room. And he fell for it. The .22 was already there, the one you shot your stepfather with. The police didn't find it because you took it with you. You're a lovely liar. You tease with the truth, like your body."

"I have it with me." She opened her eyes.

Present. Tense. My eyes watching her face. Quick calculation of distance.

"Don't forget, I love you."

"I know. Mel didn't. He was like Ivan. Worse, because he wasn't sick. He wanted to make me. I hated him for using what happened. When he phoned I thought it's got to be finished. I went to the sorority, talked to Pim. There was no one else in the house. I hid it under a bed cushion in my old room. She kept out of sight. When he got there I mentioned going upstairs. He knew right away. Fat grin. Don't touch me until I'm ready, I said. As I stripped I felt the excitement again. I reached under the cushion. Pulled out the gun. That took the bulge out of his pants. Never thought it would happen to him. I gave him a chance. Write a note about coming to the apartment that night and what you did, sign it and I'll let you go, I told him. I had put a pad and pen on the desk. He shoved the chair back and sat down and wrote really fast. He threw the pen down. I bent over to look at the pad and he tried to grab me. I shot, pure reflex."

She focused on me. My gaze must have slipped.

"You thought I had it on me? It's in my bag in my cabin. I was going to throw it overboard when I came across. I forgot."

"You'll have to get rid of it."

"Maybe you?"

"Maybe I? I'd be an accessory. Sounds familiar. I'm already aiding and abetting."

She stood up, springy young. Topics were like potato chips to her.

"I've got to get back to weeding. They expect me to work."

I hauled myself stiffly to my feet. We didn't say anything as we walked. The cows were still mowing the meadow. Near the barn she groaned, went down on her knees and fell over onto her left side. She bit her lower lip and moaned. The toes of her right foot were flexing. Everyone says the obvious.

"You step on something?"

"Yeah, what is it?"

I squatted and looked at her foot. Sticking out of her instep was the nubby head of a carpenter's finishing nail. A blob of dark blood had oozed out. It had gathered behind some stuck grass like water behind a logjam.

"It's a nail. I'll pull it. All right? Hold on."

I put my fingers between her toes till we gripped each other. With two fingers of my other hand I eased out the shaft. It came out like a skewer from a roast, the blood on it slickly red. I threw the nail aside and put my mouth to the puncture and sucked. I tasted sweet grass and salty blood, dark loam and underneath them her skin. I squeezed her toes with my fingers and she wriggled tighter. Fingers pressing into her heel, I sucked harder. She curved her foot to my mouth. I spat out blood. I did this several times before licking the area around the puncture with my tongue. I spat out blood and spit and wiped my lips dry with the back of my hand. I looked at her.

"You can't walk. It has to be bandaged. You'll have to lean on my shoulder. Unless you want to wait for a woman to come along."

She shook her head, lips against her teeth. I pulled her up slowly. She was heavier than I'd figured, that is from her figure. I put her right arm over my left shoulder and we began. I tried not to think of certain things. But the soft weight of her kept rubbing against me. I thought of Emily. Of New England. Of bundling and frottage. What she'd think of this damsel in distress I could guess. Rhyming. Emily again.

It took us a good (as opposed to a bad) fifteen minutes to get near the cabins. Dumfries was the first to see us. He helped get her into the kitchen and put a blanket on a bench. We laid her down and I told him what happened. He played leader.

"She needs an anti-tetanus shot to prevent lockjaw. I'll drive her in."

"I had a shot less than a year ago for a cut on my foot," she said. "The nurse told me it was good for five years."

"You have any peroxide or antiseptic cream here so we can start fixing her up?" I said.

Dumfries didn't enjoy being told anything. He went to fetch his wife, whose name was Brun. She brought over a pitcher of water and a towel and got some cream and a bandage from a first aid kit in the pantry. She mentioned the wound was clean.

"I sucked the hole and used my tongue, and lots of spit," I said.

She cleaned and dressed the puncture without saying another word.

"Did you have to say that?" Thela Crammond said later.

We were alone, sitting across the table from each other.

"I didn't go to college. You'll have to make allowances."

"You talk as if you did."

"An auricular illusion. Brun is a name? Of course, you're sorority. They specialize in names."

"Hope they won't think I'm useless."

"I was told by your august, self-directed leader he's impressed with you.

He thinks you're one of them already."

"This is important."

"I'm telling you, you're in. You're a wormer, junior grade. Great things in your future. Member of the tally-hoe brigade, digger corps."

"You going tomorrow?"

"I'm going tomorrow. Don't worry. I won't step on any dirty toes. How is it?"

"Hurts. I'll survive. Thanks for helping. You going to take it with you?"

"Let's see. Aiding and abetting. Accessory after the fact. Carrying a concealed murder weapon. No permit. Getting rid of evidence. Withholding information on two homicides. Eating dandelions."

"They're good for you."

"Why are they at the top of every gardener's most wanted list?"

"Because they're stupid."

"You belong out here with these ecoids."

"Where else could I go?"

"Nowhere, I guess."

She stared at me with one of those enigmatic female expressions that mean they're sizing you up. For what they haven't quite decided themselves yet, or maybe knew before they met you.

"I'll give it to you tonight. Come to my cabin when they're sleeping."

"They'll be going to bed with the chickens, I suppose."

"They don't have any chickens. They're sort of vegetarians, don't eat meat, fish, but cheese and milk are OK."

"What's for supper, more weeds and tomato water?"

"I made the sauce."

"Next time put a little more of your personality into it."

She smiled and we looked at each other for no reason. You can only do that for a moment before there's a reason.

"I'd better get some rest before I help with dinner."

"You don't have to be beholden to these salad greens. Hopping around like a lame sparrow. Let somebody else do it. I'll take a quick turn, whet my appetite."

"There's water in the pail outside."

She put her arms on the table and rested her head on them and her hair fell over her closed eyes. I grinned and went outside and looked over the fields. Almost everybody was out there planting or weeding. Dumfries and another man were working on the truck, parked beside the toolshed and up on blocks. Its wheels were off. I stepped off the porch and walked over. The other man was underneath the truck. He was using a small wrench on the left front drum. Dumfries went into the toolshed and came out with a can of brake fluid. I'd become an audience.

"We changed the shoes. We're bleeding the brakes."

He got into the cab and they bled the line to each drum and he helped put the wheels back on and tighten the nuts. He rolled a floor jack underneath and hoisted each end in turn and they removed the blocks. He wiped his hands on a piece of shirt, using that well-done motion guys save for when they've done something that's not their usual job. He sauntered over to me.

"Have to keep the old beast going." He looked in the direction of the meadow, expecting an extra moo. He stuffed the rag into a back pocket of his jeans. "I should show you around." Not a word about the injured girl. Wifie might not approve. I was trapped.

"Too bad you won't see our tomatoes."

"I've seen them."

Oblivious.

"Only the sun-dried."

I was tempted. He pulled a folded page from a magazine out of his shirt pocket and showed me a picture of a tomato. It looked huge and was the colour of dark blood. It had swollen lobes, as if four tomatoes had been jammed together.

"It's an old variety. That's what we grow, heritage varieties. Nothing gene-spliced, everything organic. We do composting for fertilizer, green manure. Rotate crops to replenish depleted soil. We plant close for cover whenever possible. Keeps out weeds. It takes a lot of manual labour. Much of our work out in the fields is weeding. We can't use drip hoses for irrigation because there's no water line, but we've built sluices to carry water out there. Helps cut down on labour."

It all made a kind of sense but I still wondered about the commune.

"Other farmers grow organic produce and sell it to supermarkets."

He folded the page and put it back into his shirt pocket.

"They're helping to prop up a rotten system. Putting some organic apples on a supermarket shelf won't change anything. Real change comes from the way people relate to each other. It has to begin with social reorganization at the grass-roots level. People have got to learn to think for themselves so they can see the treadmill that they're on and get off. They'll have to opt out, stop this suicidal depletion of the planet's resources that goes to support an unchecked global network of multinational corporations."

He lost me on his rapid descent into cliché land. I wondered how long the latest convert would put up with diatribes of puredirt philosophy. Some had thrown away their haloes and decamped. And she was more intelligent than any of them, gone or yet in residence.

I was finished with Dumfries but he wasn't finished with me. I got the tour, up and down row after row and field after field. The sheila was among the pole beans, weeding what she assured me proudly would be a bumper crop. Romano, she told me, with long wide pods, pale and mottled with what looked like wine stains. They made good stews. Not here, I thought. She asked my guide if he'd be buying anything in the village that week. Maybe, he told her, and looked at me. He said they sold produce from the truck at the edge of the village to pay for wheat and rye flour, rice, oats and gas. I thought beans gave you gas, I said. She laughed, he didn't. He got the point of my bad joke. She went back to weeding. The tour had finished.

Finally it was time to eat and we washed up with creek water in a plastic pail on planks across a couple of sawhorses beside the kitchen. There was a ladle, so you didn't have to share your bacteria with anybody else. Dinner turned out to be stew and yogurt and those dandelions again. The yogurt was in a big mixing bowl. A curd of deep cream colour lay on top and tasted like soft cheese. Dumfries told me it was made daily from full-fat raw milk. Made me think of udder things. The stew was mushy and tasteless. Everything tasted like everything else, someone's idea of culinary political correctness. Wilted greens and stale bread again. I probably missed the tin cup for donations outside the door. Thela Crammond had a look of martyred splendour, her eyes raised slightly towards the ceiling. Everyone's concern had gone her way. One of the Aussie's fingerless knits crawled along the edge of the table and slipped underneath to cop a feel but she moved the injured foot away. She never looked at him. She couldn't quite hide her dislike but he was too busy being ewe-man to notice. He was the patient type, and he had the sheila.

The talk was as sparse as before. I decided this had nothing to do with me sitting there. Farm talk ain't much, nohow. It's whether the weather and a sick cow. Calluses, sore backs, sweating under July heat, watching a downpour wash a crop away. Dumfries' ideas were so much manure for their collective psyche. That psyche tolerated me because I would be leaving the next morning.

After dinner Brun told me I was being put up in the furthest cabin. The one next to Thela Crammond's. I couldn't argue with the arrangement. It made everything easy. After the others left, Thela Crammond cleared the tables and washed dishes. I asked who made her the skivvy and she said Brun did. That didn't bother her. She wanted to show Dumfries she was serious about the commune. About our business she said everybody was in bed by nine. I should come around ten.

Outside I stood on the porch and looked at my watch. Almost seven. The light was going. On the east side of the fields a low line of leafing alders and maples fronted tall groves of red cedar and fir turning from lemon or inky green to a burnished gold mass with staccato points, like the fortified wall of a medieval town at sunset. A couple of seagulls drifted overhead, reminding me the gulf was a few miles away. A low flight of mallards quacked by in that hectic duck way of flying. Higher against a faded blue sky a lopsided vee formation of geese headed north. The spring air, getting damp now, smelled of leaf resin.

The door was open in the furthest cabin. I surmised mine host's better half had taken a look-see at my temporary abode to be sure there was nothing I could make off with. There were two steps made of scrap lumber, a four-pane window to the left of the door and an unstable-looking stovepipe wired onto a cedar shake roof. One room inside and flea market furniture, a scarred end table with a kerosene lantern on it beside a metal-frame bed minus a box spring. The mattress was thin and too small. Three chairs from an ancient maple set were around a card table and a battered waterfall dresser with four drawers was missing two handles. A cast-iron potbellied stove took up the middle of the room. In a far corner a toy dump truck lay upside down and on the card table part of a jigsaw puzzle showed a farm with mountain backdrop.

I hung my windbreaker on a chair and sat down and put my feet on the table. It was better than trying to get comfortable on a meagre mattress. I decided to take a nap and dropped off right away. When I woke up it was dark and I saw stars through the open doorway. I got up slowly, stiff and chilled. I put on the windbreaker, got out a pocket flashlight I'd brought with me. I looked at my watch and saw it was after ten o'clock. I almost tripped on a table leg getting to the doorway. There was no moon, so I used the flashlight going to the next cabin. Through the window I could see a kerosene lantern burning. Thela Crammond sat naked on the edge of a bed. A guy stood looking down at her. I recognized the cap and gloves and the simian stance. It was the Aussie. His pants were down and his staff at half mast. Thela Crammond's hand reached under a pillow and I knew why. He wasn't in a waiting mood and shoved her over and onto her belly. Her hand wasn't fast enough. He was on top and trying a forced rear entry. I twisted the doorknob and barged in. He glared at me and his hand left his boomerang on its droop into disappointment. He took his other hand from between her cheeks as I advanced but he had some mouth.

"Oy, mate. Git the fuck ahta here. Nosy buggah. Oim busy, 'less you're bloind. Aht."

"You go through me to get to the door or you go through a wall."

I took off the windbreaker and rolled up my sleeves.

"Oy, aldtoimer. Dahn't bust a blood vissil."

He got up, pulled his pants after him and buckled his belt. Shook his head, a friendly dog. I saw she had the .22, was aiming it at him. In the second I'd glanced away he swung and hit me on the side of the head. I didn't catch all of it and he didn't know how to throw a punch. I returned the favour, slammed a left hook against the side of his jaw. He staggered. I shot a straight right into the other half of his stupefied apeface stare. He went down to stay. I hurried over to her. She held the .22 slackly on her knees and tried to focus on me.

"I thought it was you. I let him in and he wouldn't go. I thought, all right, you too. I got excited and stripped. I wanted to kill him."

"You can't stay here now."

"Where can I go?"

"You're coming with me."

"You want me?"

"I want you."

"As I am?"

"As you are."

"You really love me."

"Get your clothes on, we're leaving tonight."

"What's going on?"

A voice behind me. Dumfries stood in the open doorway. He was wearing jeans and a pyjama top. Behind him, faces in the dark. Groggy, the Aussie still lay on the floor.

"He tried to rape her," I said.

"She invited me in. Oy was coming back from taking a piss. She's standing there in a bra and knickers. Oy says hoi to her. She says her lantern won't loight. Can oy fix it? All right, oy will, oy said."

"He's lying. I saw him."

"Why is she naked?" Dumfries managed to ask, and saw the gun. "Is that hers?"

"It's mine, I'm a detective. I forgot it and came to get it."

"Oy think he's a blood loyer. Nah worries on that."

"Why did you come here?" Dumfries said.

"I told you, I had business with her. It's private."

"I trusted you," he said to her.

She didn't bother answering him. It was too late for explanations he wouldn't understand, anyway.

"I think you both should leave right away."

"It's dark. I don't know the area."

"You take the same road out I brought you in."

"You think she can walk miles on a dirt road in the dark on an injured foot?"

"I can't help that."

"You goddam well can. You've got a truck."

"It's old. It's used when necessary."

"I'll pay you. How much?"

"Fifty dollars."

It was Brun. She'd been standing behind him. At the mention of money she'd come into the room. She was wearing a grey terrycloth bathrobe with the nap gone and strings dangling from the cuffs. It was wound tightly around her skinny frame. She looked like a Russian wolfhound.

"I'll give you twenty-five. Fifty if you have any trouble."

"What if something goes wrong after I drop you off?"

"Get the truck. Or I'll hotwire it and drive it myself."

"That's illegal."

"Lots of things are. But they happen."

"Get it," Brun said. He turned to go.

"It's nice dealing with commune folks," I said. "What's theirs is theirs."

Dumfries left. Brun looked. Thela Crammond's outrageous curves on display brought an anemic sneergrin. Brun turned, walked out, her keester the size of grapefruit halves jostling her bathrobe. The creature on the floor got up and wobbled to the door frame, grabbed with uncertain hands before taking the steps carefully. His sheila was waiting. She was in a commiserative mood, blind to what she married. Assorted voices before the sound of a cranky engine covered them.

I took the .22 out of her hand. She didn't react. I snapped my fingers. Waved my hand.

"Get your clothes on. We're leaving."

She saw me finally and yawned.

"Get dressed. Get your things."

She sprang up, hopped into jeans and sneakers and slung on a sweatshirt and jacket and limped around and threw stuff into an overnight bag. Included were panties and bra. Why observe the niceties of dress when you look nice already? There wasn't much to pack. Two sweaters and T-shirts, a blouse, an extra bra, one extra pair of socks, panties and jeans, hairbrush, wallet, toothbrush. I didn't see the bib overalls anywhere. They must have been on loan.

I picked up the windbreaker, put the .22 into a pocket, blew out the lantern and we stepped down into cool darkness. The air felt damp, like fog. Dumfries was ready to go. A layer of fog like white smoke had begun drifting in, twisting and curling over the fields. It flowed to the slope, obliterating the orchard there, but the densely wooded hills surrounding the commune were clear under starlight. I thought of a fortified medieval town again but now the walls were blackened and the smoky vapour hung over gutted remains. Thela Crammond was leaving her dream of sanctuary among the zealots. Island Earth was a feudal fantasy. Instead of divine order, faith was in a few farmers sharing poverty and isolation and their assumption everybody else was blind instead of not interested. Pass the spiritual beans and beware of gas. Or wait, not very long, and have a burger and a side of fries, after some real estate developer has planted townhouses and a strip mall there, part of a resort complex that promises more noise and beach sewage and home security systems and barbecues and dog shit.

The headlights glowed, throwing yellow shafts marbled by swirls of fog. I was carrying Thela Crammond's overnight bag so she would be able to walk easier. She barely limped and I didn't have to slow down much. Dumfries was in the cab. I opened the door. She climbed in, wincing when her right foot hit the edge of the running board. I waited till she got comfortable before I joined them. Dumfries shifted into first. The truck groaned forward and tilted in bumpy ruts, headlights gauzy beams piercing the fog. It rose up out of the sunken land like a plane, the ground seeming to drop away beneath us into mist. At the road we were clear of it and the truck lurched to the right and did a good twenty over those long miles to the village. No one spoke as the chassis bounced and banged in and out of potholes. A solid mass of trees flanked us on both sides, the narrow channel ahead barely visible, and high above us the stars. Finally a light, and more ahead, and the tires found gravel.

We coasted to the front of the inn and those new brakes grabbed and pitched us forward. I got out with the bag, waited for her to climb down before I went around and handed over the twenty-five. He took the money without saying a word and drove away.

We went inside to the reception desk. I said I had my daughter with me and she was going to sleep in my room.

"It's a single, sir."

"Give me a double."

"We don't have any available." He knew I knew he was lying.

"You telling me there's no room for her? Look at her foot."

He didn't look down.

"You arrived not more than two minutes ago. Everybody in Frith knows the commune truck."

"So? You can't deny her rest."

"Does the young lady have any identification?"

"What are you, the morality squad? I'm taking her up."

I looked at her.

"You can waste your life talking to clowns."

"I heard that, sir."

"Good. Do something about it."

"I'm going to notify the police."

"I'm sure they'll be interested in why you're interested in what interests a man and a woman."

"You used defamatory language."

"I made a general statement that could be applied to many in the population. I've paid for my rathole till noon tomorrow and if you bother us before then I'll ram your teeth down your throat."

"Are you threatening me?"

"I'm notifying you in colourful language that we need rest before we clear out and that any disturbance would exasperate my normally placid disposition."

Didn't like it I could talk so good. Pale and sweating, Thela Crammond was leaning against the counter.

"Lean on me," I said. "I'll take you up."

We took the stairs slowly. I half-carried her to the bed. I put her down and turned on the bedside lamp and unwrapped the dressing around her foot. The puncture was slightly swollen. There was no pus. She was tired, that's all. I rewound the bandage and looked at her. She was already asleep. I took off her jacket, sweatshirt and sneakers and jeans before putting covers on her. She shifted in her sleep when I did so, clearing her throat. I went downstairs to get the overnight bag, felt hungry and went down again.

The restaurant and bar were closed. I made do with a package of peanuts from a vending machine in the lobby. There was no one around. I sat in a leather armchair and ate the peanuts and went back upstairs. She was still sleeping. I took off the windbreaker and put it over the back of an armchair. I dragged the armchair over to a bureau. I pulled out a drawer before turning off the bedside lamp. I came back, sat down, took off my shoes and put my feet up on the drawer. I fell asleep right away.

I felt cold when I woke up. But that's not what woke me up. Her voice whispered hoarsely across the darkness, sounding as if it belonged to somebody else. Nobody I'd want to meet.

"Charleeee. Do you love me, Charleeee?"

I reached for the windbreaker. The .22 was not in the pocket.

"Charleeee. Do you really love me?"

Pretend to be sleeping. Any movement, the slightest. Get legs down slowly. Chair creaks, drawer creaks. Bones creak. Every goddam thing in the world. Crawl to the door. Hallway light. Small calibre. Have to be a good shot. She was. Practice makes—a goddam cliché. Of all the mistakes. Stepping over dead bodies and I still didn't see it. Homicidal maniac with great rack seeks position with dumb detective as ersatz lover girl. Excellent references. Prairie City coroner's office. Stepmother. Cloud cuckoo land. Any two-bit psychiatrist who fondles close personal articles of female patients. American Association of Pedophiles, Prairie City branch, currently lobbying to lower the age of consent to fourteen (that's months, not years). Of trusting disposition and trustworthy if it's daylight and you're agile. Crack(ed) shot. Knock off at forty paces an eyelash belonging to any male hankering after the lusciously reminiscent, recently post-pubescent curvatures of female anatomy (i.e., tight pudendum, firm dugs, broad cup, fundament enclosed by cheeks not less than four handwidths wide, lisp optional, if not an incipient sign of mental declivity). Hours to be negotiated. No nightwork. Interests and hobbies include stripteasing, markedmanship, not coming across the great divide, travelling to hidden places, and weeding out organic males.

Down another inch. Under a live wire. Hands on the floor. Cold wood. Crawl. Strip of light under the door. Enough for a good shot? In the ass. What would that feel like? Fatty tissue. Maybe she—. Not in the dark. Couldn't be that good. Have to reach up to the knob. Deadbolt higher up. Shot in the back. Spinal surgery. Wheelchair. What happened to you? Played hide and seek with a babe who favours guys with overeager erector sets for target practice. A few more inches. Hard on my knees. Up slow. The knob. Deadbolt. Slow so no click. There's always a click. Louder in the dark. Salty mouth. Peanuts. Salty blood squirting out the holes. Hey. .22s wouldn't do much damage. At this range. Has to be point-blank. Sure. Stand up and wave. She didn't hear anything. Down to the knob. Cold knob. Cold hands. Everything cold. Shivering. Turn slow. Slippery. Dammit, slow. Get ready. Head first.

I flung the door open and threw myself out, banging a shoulder against the moulding. I crawled behind the wall. Nothing happened. I waited. She was waiting for me to poke my head around so she could blow my brains out. What brains? She would've shot by then. She was crazy, though. No, wounded, like her foot. I got up and rubbed my shoulder and peeked into the room. Light from the hallway shone in. She was lying on her stomach, the covers half on the floor. I turned on the ceiling light. The .22 was under my chair. It had fallen out of the windbreaker when I was sleeping. That's probably what woke me up. Right on time to hear her talk in her sleep. I picked up the pistol and put it into the pocket of the windbreaker, shut the door and turned out the light. I slumped onto the chair and put my feet up. When you're that big a fool you don't think about it. You get some sleep.

Light was peeping under closed window curtains when I woke up. I yawned and stretched. My knees and shoulder reminded me of my night crawl. I stood up, groaned, went over and drew aside the curtains. It was eight forty-five by my watch. I looked at my charge. She was still sleeping. I washed and shaved. When I came out of the bathroom her half-awake eyes were taking in the room. I took my suitcase down from the closet shelf and put it on the bed. She was still foggy.

"What time is it?"

"Ten after nine."

"I slept a long time. Where did you sleep?"

"In the chair."

"That fat slob. He do anything?"

"No. You talked in your sleep."

"What did I say?"

"Your subconscious was very friendly."

"The friendliest part of me. I feel dirty." She laughed. "I'd better take a shower."

She raised her arms to stretch and the covers slipped down, exposing her breasts.

"Have some pity for the depraved and deprived. Harness those."

"Think of me as your daughter."

She put her bare feet on the floor and tested the injured one and made a face, as if to say, not too bad. She limped into the bathroom and I packed. After a while, "Throw in my bag, please." Twenty minutes later she came out in jeans and blouse, wearing a bra and I assumed panties. Her face was pink and her hair was tied back with a blue ribbon. She twirled gamely on her good foot. She lost her balance and grabbed the armchair.

"I'm hungry."

"Then let us partake of the sumptuous repast at this hostelry for nefarious wayfarers."

"Sure you didn't go to university?"

I carried our luggage down to the pub. It was almost eleven and I wanted to make the noon sailing. The bartender-waiter said it was too late for breakfast and too early for lunch. Everything was too late or too early on that island. We had cheese sandwiches and the local ale for me and milk for her.

More slices of white elastic hiding individually wrapped desecrations that could pass for window caulking. But the ale was still good and she guzzled the milk. The place was empty except for us. We finished quickly and left. As we passed the reception desk I tossed the room key onto the counter. The clerk didn't look up. We made the noon sailing and ten minutes out I drifted aft on the passenger deck, as close to the stern as I could get. I went back to the lounge and sat down and she glanced at me. At the ferry terminal on the mainland we took a bus to the city and caught another one to the airport. Cancellations made two seats available on the five o'clock flight. It was quarter after four and she wanted a hamburger. There was a restaurant in a nearby hotel. Watching her eat, I felt like a lawman returning with a prisoner and a pervert taking advantage of a sick woman. The situation was different. What was the situation? I had broken the law to save her from the professionals. The institutionals who would throw her into the system and forget her except as she could be used to justify and advance their careers. They never cured anybody. They drugged them silly or shut them up with other broken people. There was a room waiting for her and she'd die in it. I wouldn't let that happen. More than that I didn't know.

She wiped her chin with a napkin and looked at me as if she read my mind.

"What are you going to do with me?"

"For the nonce, hire you as assistant to my secretary. Later on, when you're ready, you can go back to university."

"Your secretary won't like sharing. Especially if she likes you."

"Emily is different. She writes stuff and keeps it in her desk drawer. She gets so quiet sometimes I think she's not there. I'll tell her you're a student who'll be returning to university."

"I planned to. Now I don't know. I thought going to the commune would help. After last night—."

My stomach flip-flopped. I must have given myself away because she stared at me.

"Oh, don't worry, I didn't invite him in. He lied about that. He'd been after me since I got there. He's one of those guys who thinks he's got to make every woman he can. As if it's a contest. I didn't know what to do. I knew they'd kick me out, take his word against mine if he tried anything. Want to know the truth? I hated that place. I didn't want to let on to you or them. Stuart talked with me and I pretended. Trying to change the world. While they're changing diapers. Everybody attends those boring meetings. Stuart talks about being the vanguard of society. I hate that political shit. Had to go back to my cabin and freeze at night. He won't even bring in generators for lights or oil stoves to heat the cabins. We had to use those smelly lanterns and start a fire in an old stove. I noticed you didn't like their shitty food. I couldn't stand it. Dandelions, yogurt, beans every day. I was acting. You believed me. Dennis—that's his name, his wife pronounces it 'Dinnis'—caught on I was faking. His wife's the believer. He's so shit-useless he'd be nothing without her. He made jokes when there was nobody around. 'How'd you loike the grub? Miserable, oint it? Let's get some burgers, all roight, Thalie? Oy'll git the truck and we'll roide in. Moom's the woord.' What a retard. Tried to ignore him. He's like a sore throat. I thought it was you last night. I opened the door and thought, he's making his move. Told him I was tired. 'Loy down, then.' Breathing garlic on me. I started getting that way again. Hating so much it excites me. I forget everything else, like it's not me. I can see myself doing everything. I backed towards the bed, stripping. It was under the pillow. He grabbed me and I pushed him away. He had those gloves on, with his fingers sticking out. I've never seen him wash. It was like being touched by slugs. Told him to wait and he took his hands off me. I was by the bed, naked, but I had to sit down to get it. He dropped his pants as I leaned towards the pillow. He pushed me over and I could feel him trying to get into me. I was reaching for the gun when you came in. I was glad but wanted to kill him. And I imagined blood being on the sheets and they'd need washing."

She frowned, giving herself time to look puzzled.

"You believe God, or whoever's running the universe, thinks about us?"

"Such questions are beyond my scrutiny. Other minds can delve."

"Why is everything so tough for some people, for instance, me?"

"Religio-philosophical discussions are best held in surroundings conducive to ratiocination. Hotel restaurants hardly rate."

"I get these thoughts anywhere."

"Better get the next one running for the plane or we won't get out of here tonight."

We almost missed it, raced through the departure lounge and boarding gate. Then the plane was delayed for some reason. We finally took off and an hour later were in Prairie City. I picked up my car at the airport and drove directly to my apartment. I didn't want to sit in another restaurant. At the apartment I made toast and she made a big omelette for us. It tasted better than anything I'd ever done with eggs. After talking about how good a cook she was, we retired for the night. She slept in the bed and I slept on the couch. I told her this was going to be the permanent arrangement. She offered to exchange.

"You'll get stiff on the couch."

"I'll get stiff anywhere. Where's my hair shirt?"

On Tuesday morning I took her to the office to meet Emily. The outer office door was locked. Emily had never been late before. I unlocked it and we went in. Emily's desk was bare, the drawer pulled out part way, her chair against the wall. No slips of paper. I knew she had gone. Probably had a hunch I would be bringing in somebody new one day and figured her small salary wouldn't go far if split up. I would've found more money, taken jobs I had turned down before. But it was too late. Thela went over and looked at the desk. She touched the chair and blew dust off her fingers.

"Nobody's sat here for ages."

From the Sigurdsen Papers
Archives, Prairie University Library
Undated fragment

I, Sigurdsen, have burdened the world with one more book. Pleasing myself, I leave the distress of the unleavened to them. What do they care, bereft of words, beleaguered. They can read traffic signs. They take directions well on the commute to greater things. To believe this yet? There was once a place in the heart where the spirit ranged. Look to the grey whelming seas, dark forests of the north. Sagas of heroes, monsters and thundering gods. Wind screeching over a frozen land. Stone is hardest to forget, and simple words. Icy fingers chiselled bladed farewells. Emblazoned with serpent, acanthus and cross, weathered granite vaguely tilts, time on its shoulders, hard-bitten letters tribute to hewn and whittled lives. On them the snows have melted for a thousand years.

I, wordy and for no reason but my own, have carved this monolith of academe. Useless lives, useless purpose. And the few who look for truth. The runes tell my tale. Hammering them into stone, blows ringing out defiance, each stroke fainter until there's silence. Echoes lost in the galaxies. Stone will speak for me now. I put aside mallet and chisel, seek a path through the forest. The moon hovers in the high branches. Shafts of radiance dart between, pointing the way.

www.ingramcontent.com/pod-product-compliance
Lightning Source LLC
Chambersburg PA
CBHW030133060726
47499CB00014B/127